They a.

But the silent are waking.

THE SILENT

Kyra has lived her life in the shadow of a powerful Grigori brother. She's ignored her own desires for the good of her family. But an unexpected request from Thailand sends her on a mission that could change her life and alter the fate of free Grigori all over the world.

A simple diplomatic mission sends Leo to Bangkok, but he doesn't expect to see a familiar face in surveillance photographs. Why was Kyra halfway across the globe, living with Grigori who might or might not be Irin allies?

Leo has bided his time. He's given Kyra her space. But this scribe is ready to hear a *kareshta* sing.

THE SINGER is the fifth book in the Irin Chronicles, a romantic fantasy by Elizabeth Hunter, author of the Elemental Mysteries.

October 2017 "TOP PICK" RT Magazine

PRAISE FOR ELIZABETH HUNTER

October 2017 "TOP PICK" Developing compelling and unforgettable characters is a real Hunter strength as she proves yet again with Kyra and Leo. Another amazing novel by a master storyteller!

— RT MAGAZINE

The love story is perfect. The characters are flawed, yet relatable. The alliances are brilliant, and the world Hunter has created becomes more complex and exciting. Add in a good dose of wanderlust and you have yet another winner to add to the Irin Chronicles.

— TYPICAL DISTRACTIONS

The pace is brisk, the world-building is excellent and the characters both main and secondary are very charismatic and memorable. As usual, pure magic.

— NOCTURNAL BOOK REVIEWS

THE SILENT

IRIN CHRONICLES
BOOK FIVE

ELIZABETH HUNTER

THE SILENT
Copyright © 2017
Elizabeth Hunter
ISBN: 978-1-959590-26-2
Paperback edition.

Cover art: Elizabeth Hunter
Illustrations: Chikovnaya
Edited: Anne Victory
Proofread: Linda at Victory Editing

Recurve Press, LLC
PO Box 4034
Visalia, CA 93278
USA

For first loves
and old loves
And everything in between

PROLOGUE

The Black Sea Coast
Bulgaria

K yra sat cross-legged in front of the fire, breathing in the incense and focusing on the door in her mind. It was a small door, growing smaller every day. Behind it lay the soul voices of humanity.

Her gift. Her torment.

The voices had once battered her mind, rendering her incapable of normal human interaction.

> Emetsam tarrea.
> Ya emetsam tarrea.
> Emetsam tarrea me.

The whispers grew quiet.

> Emetsam tarrea.

Kyra reached out in her mind and closed the door, imagined pressing her palm against it and holding it until the pressure in her mind eased. Then she took a deep breath and released it slowly, grateful for the silence that followed.

Kareshta. The silent ones. Daughters of Fallen angels and human women. They were her sisters, her friends, and her burden.

Kyra breathed in and out, tasting the damp sea air on her tongue along with the spice of the incense and the scent of orange blossoms coming from the orchard outside the farmhouse above the sea. Her eyes were closed as she focused on keeping her breath steady and her body still. She wore the loose sundress she always wore to meditate and prayed the beam of morning light she felt across her back wasn't burning her pale skin. Her thick hair was piled on top of her head, and dark tendrils brushed across her neck, moved by the warm breeze rolling down the hills.

She, her brother, and their charges lived a nomadic existence. This retreat was in the mountains near the Bulgarian coast. It was isolated and remote. The neighbors either had no curiosity or her brothers had dissuaded them from inquiring, but no strangers had ever come to visit.

In the months and years that had followed the Battle of Vienna—the great struggle among the Fallen where her father had finally sacrificed his life—many of Kyra's sisters had sat with her, practicing the mental discipline that would allow them to mingle among humans. One by one, they had left.

The *kareshta* who had longed for the world had learned the necessary spells and fled. Some to Irin scribe houses in the major cities, eager to find among the sons of the Forgiven mates who could protect them in their strange new reality. Others took human lovers or struck out on their own, longing for a taste of the life that had been so long denied them by the angels who had sired them or the Grigori brothers who had guarded them.

And then Kyra was alone.

Some of the *kareshta* who remained had tried to learn from her, but most were unmotivated. They didn't desire community

2

with humans, felt too exposed by silencing their minds, or had psyches too damaged to practice magic. Many were old, far too old to learn new magic, they said. They only wanted peace in their final years.

Then there were the children. The children were the most damaged of all.

While her brother, Kostas, remained in the city hunting minor angels and Grigori who threatened the human population, Kyra resided in the mountains outside Burgas with her half brother Sirius, caring for the weakest and oldest of their family.

She heard raised voices coming from outside her cottage. Sirius and Kostas were fighting again.

"Then you tell her!" Sirius shouted. "*You* tell her she's to remain here, locked away from the world while her sisters—"

"Her sisters are not *my* sister. Not *my* twin. You know why she needs to remain close to me. I have to find a way—"

"She deserves her own life, Kostas. She deserves far more than we can give her, but while she still has time…" Sirius's voice trailed off as Kostas dragged him back inside. She heard a door slam.

And then silence.

While she still has time…

Kyra closed her eyes, and her lips tingled at the memory of a dark corridor and a tall scribe's stubble against her mouth. His scent was in her nose, and her fingers clutched his shirt. His arms were strong around her, holding her as she pressed her ear to the wall of his chest, searching for the sound of his heartbeat. She'd been afraid, *so* afraid for him.

"Come away with me. Or stay here. Just don't leave again. Give this a chance, Kyra."

"I can't."

"Your brother—"

"My brother is not the reason."

3

"Then what?"

The farmhouse door slammed again, and she heard foot-steps on the path to her cottage. Sirius. After one hundred years, she recognized his step. She'd watched him grow from a baby to a boy to a man. Now the tall warrior was the protector of the weakest ones. The ones who remained.

And Kyra.

Sirius knocked quickly and opened the door, only to pause and fall silent when he saw her sitting before her fire.

"Give me a moment," she said quietly.

"I can come back."

"Or you can wait. Patience."

She breathed in and out for five more breaths, trying to ignore the frustration bouncing around the room. Sirius was usually the calm and quiet one, but something her sullen and serious twin had said must have riled him, and Kyra suspected it had to do with her. Sirius was constantly pushing her to be more independent. He'd trained her to fight with daggers when Kostas had refused. She'd learned how to fire a gun properly and even participate in hand-to-hand combat under his instruction.

The baby she'd raised after his mother's death had become her teacher. He pushed, always gently, for her to go into the village more often despite Kostas's objections. He regularly gave her tasks that would put her in the path of a variety of humans, from the local priest to the clerk at the village store. At his urging, she'd even learned to drive a car and taken a drawing class in Burgas.

She turned and motioned to the spot on the carpet next to her. "Come. It'll do you good to meditate a little."

Sirius rolled his eyes a bit, but he came and sat beside her.

"What are you two shouting about, *bata?*"

He couldn't stop the grin. "Should you still be calling me little boy when I'm taller than you?"

"I wiped your nose when you were a baby. I can call you what I want."

Sirius laughed and kicked his feet out, laying his head in Kyra's lap as he had when he was a child. Kyra put her head on his forehead and let some of the nervous energy that had built up in her mind release against her brother's skin. He'd been working in the sun, and his usually fair complexion had turned a pleasing light brown.

Sirius grabbed Kyra's hand and pressed it to his cheek. "You're upset."

"No, just feeling anxious today."

His forehead wrinkled. "The voices?"

"Not that." She took a deep breath and imagined herself walking among the orange groves, smelling the heady fragrance of the pale cream blossoms. "I was thinking about a visit to Ava in Istanbul."

Ava Matheson was a *kareshta* who had lived as a human for most of her life. She'd had no idea she was the granddaughter of a Fallen archangel; she just thought the voices she heard were the result of mental illness. When she met Malachi, an Irin warrior, she discovered a shadow world where angelic and human blood mingled. Now Ava and Malachi were "mated" in the Irin tradition, and Ava and Kyra spoke frequently by phone or video call.

Kyra suspected a visit to Ava might not be too objectionable as long as "that damn scribe" wasn't there. Ava understood Kyra better than any other person she'd met. She'd lived with mental chaos and didn't take silence for granted.

"It'd be good to see Ava," Kyra said softly. "I haven't seen… anyone outside our family. Not in months."

"What if I had an idea other than Istanbul?" Sirius asked quietly, his eyes closed, and Kyra stroked his cheek.

Her touch, and the contact with his sisters, was one of the reasons Sirius was nearly faultless in his interactions with humans. Offspring of the angels all hungered for soul energy.

Irin males got it from their Irina, but Grigori who were starved of soul energy turned to taking it from humans since most weren't raised with sisters. They were slaves to their angelic fathers and would stalk humans like a lion hunting his next meal. Kyra had no illusions about the Grigori. Most were evil. Only a few managed to live an honorable life.

But Sirius had been raised in Kyra's arms. Never had the boy been hungry for love or affection. Instead of a predator, he'd grown into a protector.

"What kind of idea?" Kyra asked. "You know Kostas won't let me travel far without him."

"You could go back to the compound in Sofia."

Kyra shook her head. Two of her half brothers had found mates among the archangel Jaron's daughters. Kostas's men had once protected the women by hiding the *kareshta* for Jaron, but since the angel's death, the women were free and happy to find husbands among Kostas's men. It wasn't mating like the Irin had, but it was something, and the Grigori couples who found each other were happy.

While Kyra was delighted for her brothers, she felt out of place at the compound in Sofia where they lived. Added to that, seeing his men content with wives seemed to have an adverse effect on Kostas, whose simmering anger bled into Kyra's mind, sending her anxiety through the roof.

No, Sofia was not an option.

"If you don't want to visit Sofia"—Sirius sat up and crossed his legs, grabbing Kyra's hands and holding them between his own—"then I want you to listen to me."

She could feel his excitement. "I always listen to you, *bata*."

"And you have to keep an open mind."

"What are you talking about?"

"There is a theory among some of the free Grigori. Others like us. About how to better control our magic."

Kyra frowned. "What kind of theory?"

"Have you heard of Yantra tattooing?" Sirius asked. "*Sak Yant,* to be precise?"

LEO PUT HIS HANDS ON HIS HIPS AND SQUARED OFF AGAINST HIS opponent. She was small, but Leo knew not to underestimate her.

"No."

"Yes!"

Two-year-old Matti mirrored Leo's stance, tiny fists on her hips and her rosy-pink cheeks covered in chocolate. They stared at each other. The tall, blond warrior had faced off against his small rival on many occasions when babysitting for Ava and Malachi. This wasn't the first time. It wouldn't be the last.

"You've already had two cupcakes. You were only supposed to have one." Leo lifted the plate from the counter and set it in the bread cupboard. "Your mother will be angry with me if I give you more, Matti."

"Mad?" she asked.

"Yes, mad. Angry."

"I'm not mad," Matti said. "Hungry. Need mo' cake."

Leo narrowed his eyes at the tiny terror. Her dark curls and sweet face were only a front for a master manipulator. "If you were hungry, you would have eaten your apples."

Matti's twin brother Geron sighed deeply and put his chin on his hands. His face was also covered in chocolate. His liquid grey eyes were pools of pleading, but Leo refused to be moved.

"No cake," Leo said more firmly.

This did not suit Matti well. She raised her voice and shouted, "Baba! I want mo' cake."

Leo pointed at her. "That won't work this time. Your father is in Vienna."

Leo's Irin brother Rhys walked into the kitchen and scooped

Matti up in his arms. "What are you doing to the child, Leo? She's hungry."

"She doesn't need more cupcakes. She barely touched her lunch."

Rhys kissed the top of Matti's head. "Poor darling. Why would she eat lunch when there are cupcakes? I wholly agree with you on this, Matti. Hold out for the sweets."

Sensing an ally, Matti giggled. "Reez, more cake. Peez."

Rhys turned to Leo. "She said please."

Leo grimaced. "You're not helping. Aren't you supposed to be working on a new translation of the Hokman Abat?"

The pale British scribe walked to the bread cupboard and reached inside. "Well, I thought I'd take a break and have..."

"Don't do it!" Leo yelled.

"Cake!" Matti squealed. "Want mo' cake, Reez."

Geron lifted his arms. "Lo!" he shouted at Leo. "More cake."

"This is the problem," Leo said, lifting Geron into his arms. "They gang up on you. And they have... chubby cheeks. And they're very, very cute."

"Relax," Rhys said. "You take minding them too seriously. What's the fun of being uncles if we can't make them sick to their stomachs on sweets?"

Matti giggled, which made Geron chuckle. Soon the kitchen was filled with laughter, and Rhys was stuffing more cupcakes in both children.

Leo licked chocolate frosting from his thumb. "If they get sick, I'm blaming you."

"I only gave them one cupcake, you gave them two."

"Three cakes!" Matti yelled, her tiny fist raised in triumph.

"They're frighteningly intelligent," Rhys said. "Developmentally, they're very advanced. Did you see Geron copying Malachi last week?"

Leo nodded. "He's so quiet, but he can already write both old script and the Roman alphabet."

"I wouldn't think a child would have that much small-muscle coordination."

"And Matti…" Leo trailed off as the little girl started to sing and dance around the kitchen table.

It was a childish song she'd learned from one of the Irina, a song intended to teach young girls control over their magic, but Matti had already mastered it. As she lifted her voice, the flowers in the vase on the center of the table bobbed along to the tune, dancing and nodding their heads when she called their colors in turn.

Rhys stared with wide eyes. "I haven't seen children in so long, I don't know what's normal and what's not. But that seems very advanced for her age."

"I'm fairly sure it is."

Leo had no experience with children other than Matti and Geron. His mother had been killed during the Rending, the attempted annihilation of the Irin race, when he was no older than the twins. His father had been lost for years and was never really the same after the loss of his mate. He and his cousin, Maxim, had been lost for a year until they'd shown up at a scribe house in Vilnius. He had little memory of his life before his grandfather had taken him and Maxim in. Leo liked children, but he'd never spent time with any.

But now there was a baby boom in the Irin world. Leo would give anything to join in the numbers of scribes and singers starting their families, but he wouldn't be satisfied with any mate. He wanted his *reshon*. His soul mate. The woman chosen by heaven to be his partner in life. He hadn't practiced patience for two hundred years to settle for anything less.

"What about your own family?"

"I don't know if that is possible for me."

"How do you know it's not possible if you won't give us a chance?"

"Leo, you don't know me."

"Are you sure about that?"

9

A loud crash broke through his reverie, and Leo spotted the source of the racket in the doorway to the living room. Matti was sitting on a rug that Geron was pulling across the wooden floor. It was unfortunate that a side table was in their way. The glass lamp sitting on it had not survived.

"Oops!" Both children turned wide eyes to Leo before they raced out of the room and up the stairs.

"Come back here!" Leo ran after them just as his phone began to buzz. "Hello?"

"Are you on patrol?" It was his cousin, Maxim. "Are the Grigori hunting in daylight now?"

"I'm on twin patrol," Leo said, pounding up the stairs. The two culprits would scatter, of that he was sure. They had excellent evasion tactics. But where would they hide? And did they have any glass shards in their little bare feet?

"I need you to go to Bangkok," Max said.

"What?"

"Bangkok," Max repeated. "Thailand."

"I know where Bangkok is." Leo pushed open his own bedroom door and walked to the closet. "I'm just not sure why I need to go there."

"I've cleared it with both Malachi and Damien. The scribe house is expecting you."

Leo pulled open his closet door. The first thing he checked was his weapons cabinet. Locked, as expected. One couldn't be too careful. "Matti?" He bent down but didn't see anything under his clothes.

"What are you doing?"

"They broke a lamp. There are probably shards. I haven't seen any blood, but you can't be too certain."

"What are you talking about?"

"The children, of course. What's in Bangkok?"

"What do you think? The usual. You'll meet your contact at the airport."

"I still don't understand—" Leo walked backed to the hall.

"Geron? Matti?" He heard giggling from Ava and Malachi's room. "I know it was an accident, but I need to check your feet. I don't understand why I need to go to Bangkok, Max. There's an active scribe house there, and as far as I know they have an excellent reputation. Why is Damien involved?"

"Just get there. I have to go." Max chuckled a little. "And good luck with the little ones."

Another crash came from downstairs.

Leo shoved his phone in his pocket. "You have got to be kidding me."

MATTI GIGGLED AS SHE WATCHED LEO'S FEET WALK AWAY FROM her. She loved her uncles, especially Leo. He was like a giant bear with yellow hair and beautiful drawings all over his skin. His drawings were different than her baba's. When she looked closely, she could see little animals playing in Leo's writing, which made his *talesm* much more fun.

Her uncles played with her every day, even when they were very tired from hunting. Leo never got impatient like her mama or baba, but sometimes he didn't understand her games. She crouched in the closet and turned to the black cat who watched her with gold eyes as brilliant as her own.

Matti pointed at him. "You're not a kitty."

The cat opened its mouth and spoke clearly. "You are very perceptive, small singer. And very magical to have seen me. Your parents and your uncles do not."

"My name is Matti."

"I know your name. You should be careful not to offer it so freely."

Matti narrowed her eyes. This creature didn't sound like it wanted to play with her. How rude.

"Do you want to know my name?" the cat asked.

"We can play."

"Yes, I've seen your play." The cat hissed words that Matti had never heard before. Special words like Mama and Baba warned her about. At his words, the shoes in the closet began to tap their toes, dancing in the low light from her parents' bedroom.

Matti clapped for the dancing shoes. This was a fun game! It was much better than making the flowers dance when she sang their colors. She imagined making all the shoes in the house dance. Her mama's and her baba's. All her uncles' big boots. She could make them dance down the stairs and into the street. Or up onto the roof where Baba grew his vegetables!

Matti opened her mouth to say the cat's words but felt Baba's magic holding her back. She growled in frustration.

"Soon, small singer," the cat said. "You are still growing into your power. One day I think you will make all of them dance."

Matti played with her toes and watched the cat that was not a cat. "I like to sing."

"I know you do. And I think I should like to hear your song," Vasu said. "One day."

CHAPTER
ONE

Chiang Mai, Thailand

K yra stepped off the airplane, the loaded carry-on bag heavy on her shoulder. Sirius had told her what to expect, but she'd been wary to leave Europe without bringing most of her belongings. She didn't own much, but what she'd kept over the years was precious to her. A lock of her mother's hair and a book she'd found in her meager belongings. A picture of her and Kostas. Another picture Ava had sent her from Istanbul with all the scribes and singers there. A locket. None of these were things she was willing to risk to the vagaries of checked baggage.

It was her first time out of Europe. Her first time on a long international flight.

Her first time traveling alone. Anywhere.

She'd already muddled through the visa lines in Bangkok where her flight from Istanbul had landed. Now she headed toward the baggage claim and hoped her bag would show up. And her ride. And someone who spoke English, Bulgarian, Serbian, Turkish, or French.

Kyra wasn't used to being alone. From the time she'd been

born, her brother had been with her. Now Kostas thought she was visiting Istanbul where she was familiar with the streets and the language and the customs. Sirius hadn't told their brother he was driving Kyra to the airport.

She put her hand in the pocket of her loose pants and touched the phone Sirius had given her. It was prepaid and loaded with the names and numbers of his contacts for the small city in Northern Thailand.

Kostas would be furious.

Kyra took a slow breath and tried not to panic. She was a grown woman, far older than even the oldest humans on her flight. She was powerful and trained in self-defense against both human and supernatural opponents. She was well versed in Thai history after the crash course she'd taken in the previous two weeks, and well shielded thanks to multiple meditation sessions and a last-minute call to Ava for advice.

She was terrified.

Catching sight of her bag, Kyra nearly ran over an elderly man in her rush to grab it.

"*Khor toht krab*," she said awkwardly. "Sorry. So sorry." She was relieved when the old man smiled and patted her arm. After grabbing her bag, she pulled away from the crowd and leaned against a wall a small distance from the rush of people leaving the airport. She took a deep breath and bolstered her shields. She closed her eyes and pressed a mental hand to the door in her mind, feeling the burgeoning pressure of so many people and so many voices. They had been muffled and silent on the plane with many humans sleeping, but in the airport, where worries and anticipation filled their minds, the voices shouted, tumbling over each other in a rush that would quickly overwhelm her unless she took a moment to steel herself.

Calm.

Breathe.

Emetsam tarrea.

The door stayed closed, but the pressure remained.

She needed to get out of the airport. She glanced around, hoping no one had noticed the odd European woman and double-checked that she had her bags before she walked with purpose toward the exit.

If you don't know where you're going, just act like you do. Ava's advice came back to her. If all else fails and you get lost, stand out of the way and look at your phone until you figure things out. Cell phones are the best for pretending that you're busy and important.

She walked out of the airport and into the surprisingly crisp air of the city. Chiang Mai was in the mountains. In the early evening, the air was cool and dry, though she could hear the hum of mosquitoes as she stood under the artificial lights of the walkway.

Kyra pulled out her phone to see if she'd received any messages. She texted Sirius that she'd landed just as another message came through.

Your picture doesn't do you justice.

She looked up, her eyes scanning the crowd, but no one was staring at her.

Walk to the right and look for a silver Toyota pickup truck.

Who are you? she typed back. Something about his initial flattery rubbed her the wrong way.

I'm the man your brother sent to pick you up. Why else would I have your phone number?

She couldn't find any fault in his logic, but she was grateful Sirius chose that moment to text back.

Glad you landed safely, her brother typed. *Did Niran find you?*

Did you send him my picture?

Sirius typed, *A bad one, but yes.*

Kyra smiled. *I think he just texted me. He's here at the airport.*

I've only met him once, but I trust him. I know you'll be cautious. If there are any problems, call me. We have other resources in Chiang Mai.

Kyra was unsure what that meant, but she didn't want to keep her host waiting longer.

I'll walk toward you, she texted to her first contact. *Who is this?*

"My name is Niran," a voice said.

Kyra looked up. The Grigori was like all of her race. Perfectly symmetrical and pleasing features with an unmistakable aura of power. He was taller than she'd expected—just slightly taller than she was—but angelic blood usually produced larger-than-average offspring. His eyes were golden brown and his skin a warm bronze.

He was beautiful.

"I'm Kyra."

The Grigori offered her a polite nod, his hands held in front of his chest. "And I am Niran. Welcome to Chiang Mai."

* * * * * *

"You're staring," Niran said, glancing at Kyra from the corner of his eye. "Don't they have Asian people where you're from?"

"I'm not from anywhere," Kyra said, averting her gaze. "I've spent a lot of time in Istanbul. There are many Chinese tourists there."

"This isn't China."

"I know that." Kyra forced herself to restrain the temper that wanted to break through. "I'm not stupid."

"I didn't say you were." Niran sounded amused.

They had driven out of the city quickly. Large buildings gave way to smaller ones. Neat hotels and shops grew farther and farther apart as they drove away from the bustle and traffic of Chiang Mai and into the countryside. The press of voices had eased as they sped away, and Niran's own soul voice was unusually pleasant and calm when she cracked open the door in her mind.

"Is this your first time in Asia?"

"Technically, Istanbul bridges Europe and Asia. So this is

not my first visit to Asia." She glanced at Niran, who looked skeptical. "This is my first visit to *Eastern* Asia," she admitted.

"Thailand is a very welcoming country for most visitors."

"Most?"

Niran shrugged. "My mother was Burmese. It's a complicated history."

"I understand." If there was anything Kyra *did* understand, it was complicated history.

She picked at the seam of her jeans. She was already chafing at the constricting travel clothes. From the look of the tourists she saw in the city, she would be able to wear her dresses and skirts without attracting undue attention. That was good. She'd never liked the feeling of trousers, but she wore them to fit in with modern human women.

"I met Sirius fifteen years ago," Niran said. "We've only spoken over the telephone since then. He is well?"

"He is." Kyra smiled. "He is as he has always been."

"An honorable man and a formidable warrior then."

"Yes."

"He seemed quite certain that you would be able to help us."

Kyra opened her mouth but paused. "Tell me what it is you need help with. Sirius told me of your agreement, but I would like to hear it from you."

"Understandable." Niran turned off the main road and into a stand of trees. "The road is rougher from here to the monastery. I hope motion sickness isn't a problem."

"Not usually." They went over a pothole that caused Kyra's jaw to snap shut. "But we'll see."

They drove farther into the forest before Niran spoke again. "The deal is this: if you can help our sisters to protect their minds, we will help your brothers control their magic."

Kyra looked at the dark markings that peeked from Niran's collar. "You tattoo yourself like the Irin?"

"*Not* like the Irin," he said. "We learned this discipline from humans. But we think it may accomplish something similar to Irin tattooing."

"And it works?"

Niran narrowed his eyes. "Do you feel unsafe with me?"

"No, but you wouldn't attack one of our kind, would you?"

"Wouldn't I?" Niran said quietly. He held out a hand. "Touch me. Feel my energy. See for yourself."

Kyra was surprised to find herself hesitating. It was just a hand. He was just another angelic bastard like herself. She reached out and took it. Immediately, Niran's fingers closed around her palm. Her first impulse was to pull away from the presumptuous hand, but she relaxed into his touch when she felt the nervous energy built up over hours of travel leave her body and flow into Niran like water releasing from a dam.

Kyra let out a breath she didn't realize she'd been holding.

"Better?" Niran asked quietly.

"Yes."

"How do I feel?"

She poked at the emotions she sensed from him. "You feel… steady. Calm."

He released her hand to grab the wheel and steer the car across a shallow stream. "You feel powerful."

She watched him, but his eyes remained on the road.

"I'm not a warrior like Sirius."

"There are many kinds of power," Niran said. "It is a foolish man who thinks physical strength is a substitute for mental discipline." He smiled a little. "I am not a foolish man."

"That's good."

"Can you truly teach my sisters how to make their minds safe from humans?"

"I think so," Kyra said. "Their father is dead? You're sure of it?"

"I am."

"How are you sure?" Kyra had thought her own father was dead for decades, only to find out he'd been in hiding with help from his allies. The knowledge that she'd been living in false freedom had been devastating.

"I know my father is dead because my brothers and I killed him," Niran said quietly. "We killed him with our sisters' help."

THE TEMPLE WHERE NIRAN TOOK HER WAS HIDDEN IN THE HILLS northeast of Chiang Mai, surrounded by lush green forests of bamboo and fat-bottomed trees covered in moss. Sunlight filtered in where the road and courtyard had been cleared. Ferns and orchids covered the leaf-strewn forest floor, competing with sprawling roots for space.

The grey steps of the temple were the first human structure to meet her eyes. They were ancient, but neat and in good repair. Though this place didn't have the lustrous gold-covered statues and brilliant painted columns of the wats she'd seen in her research, it hummed with power.

She could feel the energy contained within the humble structure as she stepped out of the car. Stone dragons flowed down either side of the stairs, and potted palms dotted the courtyard in front of bungalows surrounding the central structure. The houses were simple stilted buildings. Dark, varnished railings lined the front of each one with flowers flowing from window boxes and hanging baskets. Orchids clung to tree trunks, and the air was filled with the scent of fragrant flowers and the chirp of birds.

"Welcome," Niran said, walking to the back of the truck to grab her suitcase. "I'm sure you'll want time to wash and rest. A house has been prepared for you. It's not modern—"

"I'm not modern," Kyra said. She couldn't stop turning to take in the forest around her. It was so quiet, yet so full of life. "Are there animals here?"

"Birds. A few deer. Pigs sometimes. Nothing dangerous."

"Snakes?"

Niran smiled. "There are always snakes. And bugs. I hope you're not afraid of them."

"No more than is sensible." She walked toward a fountain in the center of the courtyard and trailed her finger in the water, watching the shy goldfish dart away. "Plumbing?"

"We have a very nice bathhouse—men on one side, women on the other. We share that, but your room will have a pitcher and sink. You can refill at any of the fountains. The water is from a spring here, and it's very good. We eat together in the evenings unless…"

Kyra said, "Unless there is conflict. Then some of your sisters will want to be alone."

"Yes." Niran appeared relieved. "You *do* understand."

"I'm no different than they are."

Niran stepped closer. "But you are. When I first saw you at the airport, I didn't really believe that you were one of us even though Sirius had sent your picture. You didn't appear to be in pain or cringing from people. When the cab drivers shouted at you, you simply walked away."

"I couldn't always do that. I used to hide from the world just like they do."

Niran's eyes shone. "My youngest sister, she reads books on mathematics that are beyond my comprehension. Her mind is beautiful and brilliant. She could do so much, but even going into the nearest village gives her seizures. Another sister is an artist so gifted she should study with masters. She has a gentle spirit and weaves the most intricate tapestries, but she cannot be around people without wanting to hurt them. We have a sister as fierce as any warrior in battle. She has tried to fight but cannot concentrate on her opponent. Anytime she is touched by a human—"

"The voices only get worse," Kyra said. "I know all this. And you have to realize, this life I have"—she motioned to her suitcase—"this ability to travel, to be part of the world around me, it is very recent. Two years ago I was as sheltered as they are. My hearing is so acute that my own twin would have to leave me at times because when we're together, my hearing amplifies."

"Some would find a use for that." Niran frowned. "I'm sorry. It's none of my business."

"I'm not offended." She wasn't. Exactly. But there was some uncomfortable emotion that pushed at the back of her throat and caused her heart to race.

"But this new magic the Irin taught you—"

"It's not new. It is ancient." Kyra's voice rose. "It is what we should have been taught for generations. What we should have learned from our fathers if they had any care for us."

Niran stepped closer. "Did your father harm you?"

Had he harmed her?

Kyra's throat tightened. She wanted to scream. Wanted to rage. She didn't allow herself.

"It doesn't matter. What matters is that I'm over two hundred years old," she said carefully. "Far older than most of our kind. Now that my brother has severed his ties to the Fallen, he and I will die. They have no reason to give us the magic that could keep us alive. I live on borrowed time, Niran. I lived two hundred years as a prisoner, and just as I am tasting freedom, my life begins to wane."

Niran's eyes flashed, but he did not speak.

"I want to do something important before I die." Kyra looked into the trees and saw the shadow of simple houses hidden in the brush. Windows, like dark eyes, looked back through the forest. She could feel their eyes. Sense their curiosity. She was being watched. "I don't need to rest. Give me a moment to wash, and then I want to meet your sisters. I can help them." She'd never felt so sure of herself. "I know I can."

THE GIRL WAS NO MORE THAN THIRTEEN. HER HAIR WAS straight, black, and chopped short to frame a round, pale face. She didn't spend much time in the sun. Her full, round lips pursed for a moment before she let out a long sigh and relaxed into Kyra's arms. Her eyes were closed and her cheek rested on Kyra's leg as she sang along quietly with the song the *kareshta* was teaching her.

"*Emetsam tarrea me. Kul-me shayen ya-ohme.*" Kyra sang the spell to a playful tune, exactly the way Ava had taught her.

Shut the door in my mind. Give me peace this day.

It was the simplest of tunes, and the spell only lasted for a few hours, but it was enough to get some rest. Enough to silence the worst of the voices. Plus it worked quickly. It was the first spell Ava had taught her, and the one Kyra started all *kareshta* with. More complex shield spells could come later.

To begin? Peace.

The girl named Intira breathed out in one long exhale and fell into a deep sleep. Kyra sang over her for a few more minutes, then she eased the girl's head onto the pillow near her leg and moved away. This was the youngest of Niran's sisters. The one whose birth, Niran told her, had given them the final push to break free from their angelic sire no matter what the cost.

As Kyra rose and looked around the room, she felt profound wonder. Complex equations, the likes of which Kyra had never understood, covered the walls of the room. White plaster covered by black charcoal pencil marks, as complex and beautiful as the intricate tattoos that covered Niran's arms. She looked at the neat stacks of books sitting by the girl's pallet and the rolls of paper she used to write even more equations. A star map covered one wall, and a telescope perched delicately in the corner. Constellations were drawn around the windows.

Niran watched the girl as she slept, disbelief battling with wonder in his expression.

"How long will it last?" he asked, staring at his sister.

Kyra nodded toward the door and walked out, slipping on her shoes before she walked down the wooden stairs to the gravel path linking the forest houses.

"That spell lasts only few hours," she said softly when Niran joined her.

"A few *hours?*"

"I can teach her more complex spells once she clears her mind, and I can guide her meditation. Those spells will last longer. It's obvious she's extremely bright, so—" Kyra nearly fell over when Niran grabbed her hands in both of his and bent over, pressing his forehead to her fingers in a deep bow.

"Forgive me," he whispered. "Forgive me. I cannot…" His voice was hoarse. Thick with emotion. "Forgive my rudeness, but you have given her hours. She has never had *hours* before. You are a miracle. This is a miracle from the gods."

"It's not a miracle." She didn't know what to do. She wasn't accustomed to physical contact from men. Not unless they were related to her. Niran's previous reservation was comfortable and safe.

"Anytime you need me, Kyra. All you have to do is ask."

The memory of Leo's voice threatened to break her. Leo was the opposite of comfortable and safe.

She was worn out. Exhausted. And Niran's gratitude overwhelmed her. It was the only reason, she told herself, that her thoughts turned to "that damn scribe" again.

"I wrote you letters. Do you want to know what I wrote? I can tell you. I remember every word."

"Everything isn't *possible… Not for me."*

"Forgive me," Niran said again, releasing her hands and pulling back. Two spots of red colored his dark bronze cheeks. "I apologize. I don't usually…"

"You are grateful for your sister," Kyra said diplomatically. "I understand. I was also grateful when my Irina friends taught me. Shielding your mind is like finding a medicine that you never imagined existed."

Niran nodded.

"I know you have more sisters," Kyra said. "But for tonight, I think I need to rest."

"Of course." Niran motioned toward a house farther along the path that led to the temple. It was already glowing with warm lamplight, and the smell of woodsmoke and spices scented the air. "Please rest, Kyra. We are so grateful you are here."

CHAPTER
TWO

Bangkok, Thailand

L eo wasn't even out the door when he felt the oppressive wall of humidity bearing down on him. He groaned inwardly. Though he'd been born in the far north, his chosen home for decades was Istanbul. He stuck out like a sore thumb in the warm Mediterranean city with his height, blue eyes, and sandy-blond hair, but Leo didn't care. He loved the sunshine and the warmth. Loved the vibrancy and the energy of the city.

He didn't love humidity.

"A desert," he muttered, slipping on black sunglasses to protect his eyes from the glare. "One assignment in a desert would be welcome."

As the youngest scribe in the house, Leo was frequently loaned out for missions. His cousin, Maxim, gathered intelligence for their watcher, but Leo was a foot soldier and an experienced one. In the previous year, he'd been called on to consult with various scribe houses around the world on how to develop relationships with the growing groups of free Grigori, sons of the Fallen who were trying to live more peaceful lives.

He walked out of the airport and paused on the covered sidewalk. He needed a haircut. His thick mane was hanging over his neck, and the weight of it had already gathered perspiration. His senses tuned to the crowd around him. Lots of Westerners mixed with local Thai and a crowd of Chinese tourists. Two hundred years of instinct could not be denied. He scanned the crowd for Grigori, who often gathered in areas where tourists dwelled, though they more often hunted at night.

Yes, there were free Grigori who tried to live peacefully, but there were still far more Grigori in thrall to their Fallen fathers. And even free Grigori had a tenuous relationship with the Irin.

Many had no other skills than hunting humans, so when they tried to reform, they turned their attention to hunting angels instead. It was a goal that aligned well with the Irin mandate of protecting humanity, but the process of turning former enemies into wary allies was far from smooth. The Istanbul house had taken the lead in their relationships with the free Grigori of the Eastern Mediterranean and had formed successful alliances. Other scribe houses around the world wanted to know how to do the same thing. Tel Aviv, Shanghai, New Orleans.

Now Bangkok.

Humid. Every single one of them.

A cacophony of languages swirled around him, slowly settling into streams of understandable conversations he could sort through.

The gentle cadence of Thai. The sharper tones of Mandarin. Threads of English and a little French.

"Leontios! Brother Leontios?"

Leo turned toward the unfamiliar female voice. "Leo." He smiled and put his hands together in greeting toward the Irina who approached him. "Only Leo, please."

She met his polite greeting with pressed hands and a polite nod. "It is very nice to have you in Bangkok, brother. May I help you with your luggage?"

"Not necessary. I only have this." He kicked the duffel bag at his feet. "What may I call you, sister?"

She was small, but most women were compared to Leo, even Irina who tended to be taller than average. Her body moved with quick, efficient energy, and her black hair was cut in short layers around her face. Both things made Leo suspect the woman was a warrior. Her skin was a smooth, sun-kissed gold, but her eyes were hidden behind dark sunglasses like Leo's, and he could see her scanning the crowd for threats.

"My name is Alyah. Were you waiting long?"

"What a beautiful name," Leo said. "Alyah. I've never heard it before."

She was impatient, but too polite to show it. "It's not Thai. My mother was Malay. She named me after her mother."

"It's very beautiful." Leo couldn't stop his smile. He liked meeting people, particularly new Irina, who—he was forced to admit—still left him a bit tongue-tied. He'd spent the majority of his life believing most of the Irina were gone. Women of his own kind were still a novelty. "It's nice to meet you, Alyah."

Impatience gave way to amusement, and the corner of her mouth lifted. "It's very nice to meet you too. Leo…?"

"Just Leo." He lifted his duffel bag to his shoulder. "Should we go? Please tell me you're driving. I've never grown comfortable driving on the wrong side of the road."

"You mean the correct side?"

"You remind me of my sister Ava," Leo said. "I suspect that the Bangkok house will feel very much like home."

"I hope it will," Alyah said. She maneuvered through the crowd, walking toward the packed parking lot in the distance. "We're very grateful you were able to come so quickly. Thailand has not had a focused Grigori threat in years. There were still random predators preying on tourists, but Anurak's reputation —along with Dara's leadership—kept the population from growing."

"I know that Anurak is on the Elder Council," Leo said. "Is

he also the watcher here?" It would be unusual for an elder to head a scribe house as well as serve on the council in Vienna. They reached a small silver Honda that Leo prayed he wouldn't have to bend himself in half to enter.

"Officially? Yes." Alyah clicked the remote on her keys, and the car chirped in response. "Unofficially, his mate, Dara, has led the scribes and singers in Bangkok for decades. She and her brother share duties, but she's a brilliant strategist even though she no longer fights. The warriors follow her gladly."

"An *Irina* watcher in a scribe house?" Leo's smile grew. "Perhaps I can learn as much from the Bangkok scribe house as you can learn from me."

"I hope you can." Alyah got behind the wheel, and Leo opened the passenger door.

He didn't have to fold in half, but it was close.

"As I said," Alyah continued, "we have not had a focused Grigori threat in years, much less a Fallen flexing his power. And yet in the span of a year, it appears we have both."

"Grigori presence *and* one of the Fallen?" Leo asked. "It's likely the two are related. If there's some shift in Fallen territory, the angel could be increasing his offspring in order to fight off a challenger."

"That would be the most logical conclusion. The problem is these Grigori are the sons of an angel we know to be dead. The Fallen is pressing east from Myanmar. We're not sure if these Grigori are acting in collusion with him or not. They could be looking for protection and power since their own father is gone—"

"Or free Grigori just trying to live their lives," Leo said.

"The lack of attacks in their city lead us to hope," Alyah said. "But until we know more, Dara and Rith need to know more about free Grigori and how to approach them. Some in the house are willing to give them a chance, but there is no agreement."

Alyah maneuvered the car through the traffic of the parking

lot, pausing to let pedestrians and scooters shoot across the lanes.

"One thing you'll need to consider," Leo said, "is whether or not they are protecting *kareshta*."

"*Kareshta*?"

"Female Grigori," Leo said. "In my experience, free Grigori are as protective of their sisters as the Irin. How long has the Fallen who sired them been dead? Do they have children in their group?"

Alyah had stopped to let a group of tourists cross the road, but she didn't move forward again until a waiting driver honked behind her.

"Alyah?"

"I've heard the rumors," she said. "We received the mandate after the Battle of Vienna like everyone else. 'Scribe houses are charged to find and protect any female offspring of the Fallen who seek shelter or succor from their sires.' I read it, but…"

"You don't really believe it?"

Her chin went up. "I've never seen one. I've been a warrior for over one hundred years, and I've never seen a female Grigori."

Leo said quietly, "Probably because most of them are killed."

Alyah's jaw tightened as she left the parking lot and maneuvered through traffic. "Why?"

"They call themselves *kareshta*," Leo said. "The silent ones. Only the ones who learn to be silent survive to adulthood." It was a sad litany he'd repeated many times in the previous two years. "And they are killed for three primary reasons. First, they serve no purpose for the Fallen because the Fallen will not use them as fighters. Second, they are considered a threat because their magic is uncontrolled. And third, they don't instinctively hunt humans as Grigori do. So they are killed."

Alyah steered the car onto the highway, joining the late-afternoon rush of commuters filling the roads. "I have more questions."

"We all do."

Řekaves, Czech Republic
One year earlier

LEO WATCHED HER GLIDE ACROSS THE COURTYARD OF THE castle, nodding at the solemn guard before she climbed the staircase to the walkway along the eastern wall. She spoke to no one, and no one seemed to bother her. There was an air of aloofness that surrounded her. It wasn't anything she intentionally projected, but it was as clear to others as her dark hair, luminous skin, and crystalline gold eyes.

Kyra was *other.*

Leo's heart ached for her.

His body ached too, but he was ignoring that for the moment. She was so alone. He'd hoped, after the Battle of Vienna, that she would find her freedom. Hoped that she'd break free of the shell she'd been forced into for survival as his watcher's mate, Ava, had done. He wanted her to explore the heart of who she was and who she wanted to be, but all evidence pointed to her still residing in a self-imposed prison.

His feet followed her steps, up the stairs and along the top of the wall.

It was none of his business.

He'd told himself that for months.

She was none of his concern.

He'd written letters to her, in the care of her brother, which was the only address he had. They'd all been returned unopened. After the third one, Kostas had called Leo's watcher and told him to desist.

Kyra was none of his business. Which didn't stop Leo from desperately wishing she was.

When he came upon her, the blue dawn light was fading into grey. Kyra was standing at the wall, looking out over the hills where the sun would break free. Leo didn't try to remain quiet. He didn't want to startle her, but he'd seen no other opportunity to talk to her alone. She went still for a moment, cocked her head slightly in his direction, then turned her head back to the horizon.

Knowing she'd heard his inner voice and accepted his presence twisted something in Leo's chest.

"You make the voices go away."

She'd said it to him the first time they touched, and he wanted more. How? Why? What did it mean? He itched to reach out and embrace her, wrap his arms around her shoulders and bend to inhale the skin at her neck. He wanted to slide his hands down her sides so his arms could encircle her waist. He wanted to enfold her in his warmth, because she looked so cold. So alone.

He didn't. The only contact she'd ever allowed was when she'd been in true mental distress. He wondered if his presence brought back those memories. He hoped not.

"I like the sunrise," she said. It was nearly a whisper, as if she was sharing a secret.

He kept his distance. "Why?"

"Before… it was when most people were asleep. It was quiet then. Or mostly quiet. It was the most peaceful I could feel. Dream voices have a different flavor than waking ones."

"And now?"

She turned her head so he could see the curve of her cheek as she smiled. "I still like the quiet. And the possibility. Everything is possible at dawn, isn't it?"

"I think so." He stood beside her and looked at the hills. "I missed you, Kyra. I wrote you letters. Did your brother tell you that?"

She didn't speak for a long time. When Leo risked a glance at her, he thought her eyes were shining, but it was hard to tell in the light. Her eyes always shone to him. In the grey predawn light, they glowed.

"Kostas told me," she said. "Thank you for thinking of me, Leo. I didn't expect you to remember me after that day."

"I could never forget you." He inched closer. "Do you want to know what I wrote?"

She blinked and shook her head.

Leo ignored the stab of disappointment and turned to face her. "Why not? I can tell you. I remember every word."

She turned and looked him full in the face. "Because I lied."

"What did you lie about?"

The rising sun touched her face. Her ebony eyelashes. The threads of copper in her hair.

"Because everything isn't possible," she said. "Not even at sunrise. Not for me."

"Why not?" He wanted to grab her shoulders and shake her. He folded his arms across his chest instead.

"You wouldn't understand."

"I wouldn't?" he asked. "Or you don't want me to?"

She reached out and tentatively touched the back of his hand. Her fingertips were cold.

Sparks. Electricity. Leo closed his eyes and let the sensation flow through him. Touching Kyra was like tasting sunlight.

Leo unfolded his arms and reached for her other hand, pressing them together between his own. He drew Kyra's hands to his mouth and blew air between his palms, warming her cold fingers with his breath. He knew he didn't imagine the shiver that ran along her skin.

"Let me tell you what my letters said," he whispered against her fingertips. "Please, Kyra. Let me tell you."

"Don't." She swallowed hard. "Just give me this, Leo. We're going into battle tonight; I don't know what will happen."

"So let me tell you."

"It will only make it worse when I leave again."

"So don't leave. Stay here."

"I can't."

"Why not?" He locked his eyes with hers as the sun rose over the battlement. "Why not, Kyra? When Ava came to us—"

"I'm not Ava." Kyra closed her eyes. "In so many ways, I am not Ava."

"Then tell me why? I want to know."

"Don't ask me today," she whispered. "Just give me this. Please, Leo."

Leo closed his eyes and bowed his head over her hands, pressing kisses to her fingertips.

And he didn't ask for more.

CHAPTER

THREE

K yra repeated the spell for the third time, and the *kareshta* in front of her echoed it. She felt a surge of raw power in the room. Intira—the young *kareshta* she met first—was present, as were three others. Bun Ma and Kanchana were repeating the words along with Intira, and the other sister was staring out the window. The woman, nearly forty according to Niran, had suffered much abuse at the hands of their father. Prija appeared to be in her late teens, but her eyes were far older.

Niran had told her there might not be much hope for Prija. She rarely spoke and was prone to rages. But Kyra could feel the barely contained magic within Prija. If she was ever able to break out of her shell, she would be formidable. So Kyra encouraged the sisters to bring Prija to lessons even though most were skeptical.

"Breathe in," Kyra said softly. "And out. Now that you have the spell, try saying it in your mind." Intira translated Kyra's words. "Imagine a door at the end of a long hallway. The voices you hear are coming from the rooms off the hallway."

It had been a challenge to convince Niran to cooperate. He was accustomed to keeping himself and his brothers away from their sisters. To purposely expose them to the soul voices of the Grigori at the temple took some convincing.

"Keep backing away," Kyra said. "Back and back until the voices aren't all around you anymore. They're only coming from the one open door at the end of the hall."

She forced herself to remain open and walk through the steps with her students, though much of this meditation was automatic for her. The voices of the Grigori outside were muted and far more gentle than she was accustomed to. Niran had still not shared their secret to self-control with Kyra, but she would not stop teaching his sisters even though Sirius was becoming impatient.

She'd been in Thailand for nearly three weeks, and Sirius had been bearing the brunt of Kostas's anger.

"All the voices are coming from the door now," Kyra said. "So many voices. But you're pushing them farther and farther away. They're crowded together now."

She heard Bun Ma suck in a sharp breath.

"Repeat your mantra," Kyra said. "*Emetsam tarrea. Ya emetsam tarrea.* Don't worry about the longer spell. Focus on this one."

The breathing in the room evened out again.

"See the door at the end of the hall. Reach out and close it. Hold it with your hand if you need to. Close the door and say, '*Domem.*'"

"*Domem,*" they said together.

Still.

Still.

"*Domem livah,*" Kyra said, and her sisters repeated. "*Domem livah.*"

"*Domem manah.*"

"*Domem manah.*"

Still the mind.

Still the soul.

Still the heart.

Livah was a word in the Old Language that encompassed all

three. It was the center of oneself in a spiritual sense, as *manah* was the holistic body. Kyra was slowly learning much of the language that had shaped her thoughts, though she hadn't understood it for most of her life. The Old Language was the angelic tongue. The voices of the soul in humanity. There were accents and variations, but beyond superficial differences, every human and angelic soul spoke the same language. It was universal. A spell spoken by *kareshta* or Irina worked the same, though Irina were stingy with the knowledge of more powerful magic.

It was fine, Kyra told herself over and over. Shielding would allow her sisters to live. To exist as more than shadows.

Finding true power was for others who would come after her, those who had more years left. Those like Intira and Bun Ma.

The magic in the room pressed close and settled in each woman like a warm flame. Kyra felt her *livah* shining bright and whole in her mind's eye. She opened her physical eyes and saw Prija staring at her. Her gold eyes flickered as if there were a fire burning behind them.

"Prija," Kyra said calmly. "*Domem.*"

The fire flickered brighter.

"*Domem*, Prija."

The other women were aware now, watching Kyra with wary eyes.

Kyra felt the mental punch a second before she shouted, "*Zi yada!*"

Prija fell over unconscious as Kyra's nose gushed with blood. Intira held a hand towel out to Kyra as Kanchana and Bun Ma rushed to their unconscious sister.

Bun Ma spoke quietly as Kanchana rolled Prija to her side and put a blanket under her head. If the previous three weeks were any indication, the woman would sleep for several hours, then wake and continue on as if nothing had happened. Kyra didn't know if she was getting through at all. She just hoped.

"Bun Ma said that our sister lasted much longer this time," Intira said.

"She did." Kyra pressed the cloth to her nose and pinched the bridge. "Progress."

"Why do you let Prija come every day when she makes you bleed?" Intira asked.

"Does she want to be here?"

"Kanchana says she does," Intira said.

"Then she may come," Kyra said. "As long as she wants to attend, she is welcome. I can defend myself."

"Her rages are getting better."

"Then something is getting through." Kyra patted Intira's hand even though the girl flinched. "We will keep working."

Intira rubbed her hand where Kyra had touched her. She wasn't offended, just startled.

Like Kyra and her sisters, Intira was unaccustomed to any human or Grigori touch. Soul voices were usually stronger with contact, so *kareshta* learned very early to avoid touching any other being unless absolutely necessary. It was why few of them ever took lovers or mates until some had learned to shield themselves. Kyra used to think she didn't like to be touched, until one day a tall scribe took her hand and made the voices go away.

Was it Irin magic? Or was it simply Leo?

No one else had ever given her true silence. Then again, Leo was the only scribe she'd ever touched. She'd craved it after a single moment. It was part of the reason she couldn't allow her fascination with him to grow.

"Let me tell you."

"It will only make it worse when I leave again."

"So don't leave. Stay here."

"I can't."

Intira crouched in front of her. "Kyra, are you feeling well?" Kyra nodded and took the towel from her face. The

39

bleeding had stopped and Kanchana had drawn a blanket over Prija. They left her in the meditation room they used for instruction. At some point during the day, Prija would wake and slip back to her room or escape into the forest. It was hard to keep track of her, but Niran was adamant. The compound was not a prison. As long as Prija wasn't hurting anyone, she could come and go as she pleased.

"Come," Intira said. "Kanchana says the brothers have prepared a meal for us."

And it was a good thing they had. Kyra's stomach was rumbling when she rose. Practicing controlled magic burned energy. Fighting off mental attacks from out-of-control *kareshta* burned even more.

PRIJA 1

She woke alone in the empty cottage.

It was Prija's preferred way of waking. Alone.

She sat up and looked around at the meditation cottage.

A place of peace and learning, the pale woman had said.

Peace and learning.

Learning was useful. Peace was an illusion. She'd had no peace since Kanok had died.

A playful song danced at the back of her mind. Kanok's voice. It was the only sound she heard in her mind anymore. The other voices had been snuffed out. The stars were dim. She'd never told her brothers or sisters that fact. But then, Prija didn't like to speak. She'd avoided it for years.

The only power she had left was like a stone. Once, she'd woven delicate, secret magic. Magic that had frightened her own father. Now she could only throw her power at others, hoping to wound them enough that they'd leave her alone. She kept trying to wound the foreigner, but so far the woman had proven surprisingly resilient.

Moonfaced girl. The first time Prija had seen her, that was what the woman reminded her of. Her skin had a luminous quality that seemed to reflect light like the moon. She had soft edges and a gentle voice.

Prija was not soft. Her fingers were callused from playing her *saw sam sai*; the three-stringed bowed instrument was her only voice since her father's death. Her feet were broad and padded from running and climbing through the forest. Her hair was perpetually tangled. She was thin and hard.

She was not like Bun Ma, whose soft face and body reminded Prija of her dead mother. Kanchana wanted to be a warrior. She pretended to be hard, but she was soft inside. Prija sometimes heard her crying at night. And as for Intira, the girl was soft as boiled rice, and Prija would kill to keep her that way. Intira's mind was like one of the crystal vases Prija had seen once in the village. Cut finely and reflecting a thousand facets, the young girl's mind was as beautiful as it was complex.

The moonfaced girl was interesting. She was hard but appeared soft. And she was stronger than the others realized. Stronger than any of them thought. If she weren't, Prija would have knocked her unconscious by now.

Silently, Prija picked herself up off the bamboo floor and walked into the forest. She liked the lessons because they allowed her to spend quiet time with her sisters, but they weren't useful. Prija already knew how to control her thoughts. It had been an accident, but she knew.

All you had to do to mute the voices around you was to kill your father and destroy most of your mind.

CHAPTER

FOUR

L eo woke to the smell of lemongrass and coconut drifting through the Bangkok scribe house as the setting sun backlit the bamboo shades that covered his windows. He could hear the bustle of the city below where the vendors at the night markets were setting up stands and preparing food for the crowds that Friday night.

He'd indulged in a short nap before dinner after greeting Dara and her brother Rith when he'd arrived. Alyah showed him to his borrowed room and told him to rest and refresh himself before dinner.

The Bangkok scribe house was a narrow wooden house that stretched five stories up from the street. The painted gates concealed a peaceful garden decorated with lily ponds and a myriad of ladders and stairs leading to rooms surrounding the central courtyard. It was the most immaculate scribe house Leo had ever seen. His room was small and the bed was short, but both were more than adequate. He stayed in far less comfortable lodgings for most of his assignments.

His room was also close to the kitchen. He suspected someone in the Istanbul house had warned them of his appetite.

On cue, his stomach grumbled.

He stretched up and forward, reaching for his toes as he flexed his feet. The *talesm* on his arms appeared to move as his muscles did. The black ink had been patiently scribed over hundreds of years. His longevity spells, halting his age in what humans would guess was his late twenties. Spells for patience and self-control. Spells for clear vision. For empathy—he'd long suspected Chamuel's blood flowed in his veins. For swiftness in battle and wisdom in strategy. His *talesm* were as much a part of him as his hands or feet.

Bent over, he breathed out a prayer for clarity and perception. Though he had been called to this scribe house to advise, he also needed to learn. If he was to advise his brothers and sisters here, he must hear their needs first.

Leo was young, and any request for instruction still humbled and surprised him. For decades, he'd been the lowest-ranked warrior at the Istanbul house. The fact that he'd acquired a reputation for being a good teacher still surprised him.

He rose from the bed and dressed in the loose pants and cotton shirt he'd seen the other scribes wearing. He was glad his last visit to Shanghai had been in the summer. He had plenty of clothes for warm weather even though he'd had to have most of his tailored. He stood out like a blond Goliath in Southeast Asia. Fortunately, Thailand had enough international tourists and residents that locals rarely gave him notice.

He walked down the old wooden staircase and into the courtyard to see dinner preparations taking place. The long table stood under a covered patio with benches and chairs surrounding it. Scribes and singers hurried to place steaming dishes and plates of fruit to share. This scribe house, like most, took their meals communally. Leo was glad. Eating with strangers was the best way to make new friends.

He saw Alyah walking toward him and raised a hand. "Hello, sister!"

"Did you rest well?" she asked.

"I did, thank you."

She nodded. "The cook was informed that you love Thai food, so she's prepared quite a feast. She was very excited about a new visitor with a large appetite. I hope you are hungry."

Leo grinned. "Starving. Always."

Alyah smiled. "Do you really eat six times a day?"

"Did they warn you about me?"

"There may have been a note at the bottom of the introduction e-mail."

Alyah and Leo walked to the table, which had attracted most of the Irin from the surrounding rooms. Leo counted four Irin and two Irina who appeared to be warriors along with two Irina in the kitchen and another Irin who stood watch at the gate. A surprisingly balanced table for a scribe house. Across the globe, scribe houses favored males. It was a near-universal tradition.

Dara sat at the head of the table with her brother on her left. She was a short, round singer with hair twisted into an elaborate bun at the back of her neck. Her features were sweet and pleasing, though her dark eyes revealed the sharp mind of a keen strategist. Leo suspected that Dara saw *everything*. Rith, her brother, could have been her twin. His hair was clipped short and he wore a neat beard, but his features were the same. His stocky build, the same. His gaze was just as arresting.

"Leo." Dara rose and motioned to the seat on her right. "Please come and sit with us. Alyah, if you would take his other side."

"Thank you, Watcher," Leo said.

"You are very welcome." She sat and lifted a glass of beer. The others at the table joined her. "Leo of Istanbul, find rest at our table."

"Well met and well greeted, Dara of Bangkok." Leo lifted his glass and looked down the table. "I find joy and rest with my brothers and sisters."

The words had not changed in hundreds of years, but the fact that Leo was actually eating with both his brothers *and* his

Irina sisters delighted him. The scribe houses of Europe could learn much from this model, and Leo was eager to question how Dara had integrated Irina warriors so quickly into her house. They sat and plates of fruit were passed around the table.

"May I ask, Watcher—"

Dara held up a hand and Leo paused.

"Technically," she said, "I am not the watcher of this house. I am only standing in place for my mate, who is in council in Vienna at the present time. I apologize for interrupting. You have questions."

The servers went around the table, piling heaps of fragrant rice and curries on plates. A whole fish appeared in front of him, and Leo's mouth watered.

"I do have questions," he said, trying to ignore the food for a moment. "I count three Irina warriors at your table. May I ask if they are recent additions to the house?"

Leo noticed that Alyah paused, as did Rith. He wondered if they considered the question impertinent.

"I ask this sincerely," Leo said. "And with all respect. Integration of Irina warriors into scribe houses has proceeded very slowly in Europe and the Middle East. Many on the singers' council in Vienna have been hesitant to press for it, so it has been left up to individual watchers. Unfortunately, not all of them are utilizing the resources available to them. I know of a dozen singers of Mikael's line in Rěkaves alone who are ready and waiting for assignments to scribe houses."

Dara nodded. "Please eat. I will answer your question, but do not let your stomach continue bellowing, brother."

A scatter of laughter around the table, and Leo eagerly dug into his food. It was, as he'd suspected, delicious and very spicy. He was glad the beer came in large bottles.

Dara picked up her spoon as she spoke. "I believe your explanation answers your question, Leo. I have overseen this house with Anurak for over fifty years. Because of this, singers have always been welcome here, though prior to the Battle of Vienna, there were only a few who ever fought openly with us."

"But they did fight on their own?"

Dara's expression revealed little. "Irina have always fought. In their own way."

"And now they fight with you." Leo used his spoon to taste the curry. *Heaven.*

"Some do," Dara said carefully. "Some prefer their independence. This house is unique. The majority of scribe houses are still overseen by Irin watchers. When they are given the chance to recruit warriors, they recruit from their own training houses, which are full of other scribes."

Though a few murmured conversations were taking place at the other end of the table, most of the attention focused on Dara.

"What advice would you give me to share with our leaders?" Leo asked. "Many want more Irina participation but do not know what steps to take."

"If you want more singers in your scribe houses, you must have more Irina in leadership," Dara said. "Not watchers, for they are appointed by the Watchers' Council. But trainers. Weapons masters. Most of our intelligence is gathered by Irina assets."

"And watchers' mates, obviously," Leo said, smiling. "A mated Irin couple at the head of the house is always more powerful."

"Clearly," Rith said quietly. "But many of us are still wanting for mates. Of the five singers in our house, only one is unmated."

"And she will likely remain so," quipped Alyah.

Rith smiled, but his eyes were tired. "We have four unmated warriors," he said. "Including myself. Our people are still working out of balance. It is contrary to the Creator's wish."

"I agree," Leo said. "But in your house I see hope, brother. Scribes and singers together. It is balanced."

"Thank you."

"Now," Dara said. "To the present problem. These so-called 'free' Grigori. I do not like to admit that I didn't know of them prior to your watcher's revelation in Vienna. To know that there have been Grigori among us who might have been trying to change their fate and live a more honorable life is… unsettling. At the same time, I am not sure I am confident of their motives. They could easily be a threat."

"We cannot ignore that most Grigori still hunt humans," Leo said. "Even those with no living sire often hunt. While I do hope to build a point of connection between your house and the free Grigori here, Irin protection is very necessary, particularly in a country like Thailand that sees so many visitors."

Dara nodded. "Travelers have always been Grigori's favorite prey because they are vulnerable. That is why the house here and the house in Phuket are quite large for the size of the city. But we may have a population of these free Grigori as well. Particularly in the city of Chiang Mai in the north. Local scribes have reported that the city has not seen a tourist attack in over two years. Could you tell me why that might be? We are optimistic. But… cautious."

Leo said, "I cannot know for certain. It's possible that the free Grigori there have cleared the city of threats to their control. I don't know Chiang Mai. Is it very large?"

"No. A medium-sized city, though one with many foreign residents. Very international. It's situated in the mountains in the north."

"But you've seen these Grigori?"

"We've had reports from local scribes," Rith said, "but we don't have a clear number. It could be a few Grigori. It could be a large group."

"If a Grigori community wanted to hide there, would it be difficult?"

"In the city?" Rith asked. "There are Irin and Irina who train in Chiang Mai and keep an eye on things. They would have noticed a large group in the city. But in the surrounding hills? It would be possible to conceal a large group there."

"If there is a large group outside the city, it's possible they are concealing sisters."

Rith asked, "Sisters?"

Leo felt all the attention in the courtyard zero in on him as he explained the existence of the *kareshta*, as he had to Alyah in the car. Questions came quickly.

"You have seen them with your own eyes?"

"They have magic?"

"How many are there?"

"Voices? They hear the voices as we do?"

"Your own watcher's mate?"

"Are they violent?"

"Are they mad?"

Leo patiently explained the history as well as he knew it and the mandate given by the Irin and Irina councils to find and help the *kareshta*.

Just as he had in other cities, Leo perceived the same sense of combined dread and pity for these women who were so powerless to control their magic. Also, the same veiled anticipation from the males in the room that, just possibly, there were more women of a related race. The wish for more potential mates was rarely stated openly, but when Leo explained that some *kareshta* in Europe had taken Irin mates, he knew the Bangkok scribes would see the possibilities as well.

"There may only be a few," Leo explained. "There are far fewer *kareshta* than there are Grigori. But I suspect if your free Grigori are creating a safe haven, it is in part to protect their women and girls."

Dara asked, "And these women are now under the official protection of the scribe houses?"

"As per the mandate of the Elder Council, yes."

Dara nodded and fell silent.

Rith asked, "And these women would be Grigori *sisters*, correct?"

"They would likely have the same father," Leo said. "Most free Grigori communities we know of were formed by Grigori trying to protect the female offspring of their sires. They live communally in family groups. The women need to be protected as most can't function well in the human world."

"Why not?"

Alyah said, "We shield our minds from the humans, Rith. Constantly. Have you forgotten this? If these *kareshta* cannot do that, they are mentally handicapped."

Her tone made Leo's hackles rise. "Handicapped implies that they are incapable. If they are taught to control their magic—"

"But they are not," Dara said.

Leo didn't try to explain Ava. His watcher's mate had Grigori blood and more than a little skill with magic. With training, Leo knew *kareshta* were as capable of performing magic as Irina were. However, it wasn't his place to instruct a singer of Dara's status unless he was asked a question.

Dara said, "If these women are *sisters* to the free Grigori, it does not explain where this woman came from."

"What woman?" Leo asked.

Rith said, "Angels can sire children from many women."

"It still doesn't explain where she came from," the Irina said. "Nothing about her appearance says sister to me."

Leo frowned. "Who are you talking about?"

"Our surveillance," Rith said, motioning toward a singer at the end of the table, who pulled out a manila envelope.

Leo said, "You've been watching them? *Spying* on them?"

"As I stated," Dara said, "we are curious about these '*free*' Grigori. We will not be caught unaware."

Leo had been called to broker contact between the two groups, but it was clear the Irin of Bangkok were far from trusting. He would have to tread carefully. It wasn't in anyone's interests to push a relationship if both sides were too suspicious to work together. He'd have to see if their known Grigori contacts in Europe had any relationship with this group.

Rith said, "The Grigori we identified kept to themselves. We didn't approach them because they didn't hunt women. We were suspicious. A few did have some human contact, but there were no deaths. No assaults. Mostly they were solitary. Then a few weeks ago, an unfamiliar woman showed up. She's been seen many times in the company of the one we think is the leader."

"European," Alyah said. "Definitely not local."

The envelope was set down in front of Leo. He opened it and slid the pictures out.

And his heart seized.

"She's not his sister," Rith said. "I'm fairly certain of that. But she's not human either."

Leo's heart was pounding out of his chest. "These were taken in Chiang Mai?"

"Yes," Rith said. "A few days ago."

"How long has she been here?"

"A few weeks," Alyah said.

Leo couldn't believe it. She'd disappeared. She was in hiding.

Except that she wasn't.

Kyra walked with the Grigori at her side, smiling as they passed through what looked like a night market. Her hair was piled on top of her head, and she looked tan. She wore colorful, loose pants and a tank top. She was as carefree as he'd ever seen her.

Leo stood up, his food forgotten. "I need to go to Chiang Mai."

CHAPTER

FIVE

T hough the food at the temple was simple, it was filling
and delicious. One afternoon after lessons, Niran
joined Kyra, Intira, Bun Ma, and Kanchana for lunch.
Since both Niran and Intira spoke English and could translate,
conversation flowed freely. Kyra envied the gift of the Irin and
the Grigori, who could learn language with hardly more than a
look at the writing and a little bit of conversation. Females of
angelic blood did not have such gifts, though the Irina had spells
that could spur language acquisition.

Kyra listened to the flow of Thai with receptive ears, hoping
to hear anything that might sound familiar. Every now and then
she caught a word, but she was mostly clueless.

"Intira," Niran asked. "Would you like to join Kyra and me
at the market tonight?"

The girl's eyes lit up. "Are you sure?" She turned to Kyra.
"There are so many people."

Kyra said, "I think you're ready for it. You're the most
advanced of your sisters, but you won't be able to progress until
we test your shields around someone other than your brothers.
Their minds are too calm to challenge you anymore."

"We will take two cars," Niran told her. "If you become

overwhelmed, one of the brothers can drive you home while we finish patrol."

Niran had explained to Kyra that there were few Grigori attacks in the city because he and his brothers had put the word out that they were not welcome. In the previous two years, Chiang Mai had become a haven for free Grigori who wanted to live a quiet life. As long as they kept the peace and kept to themselves, Niran allowed them to live peacefully. Patrolling the night markets and busy areas of the city was crucial to maintaining that control. It was a familiar pattern to Kyra. Kostas and her brothers did much the same in Sofia.

Of course, many free Grigori were coming to Chiang Mai to obtain the tattoos that Niran and his brothers wore. As far as Kyra could tell, only a few outside their family were granted the privilege. She hadn't even seen the monk who performed the ritual. In the three weeks she'd been at the temple, only one Grigori had come to get tattooed, and that man already wore extensive marks.

Niran touched the back of her hand. Like Intira, Grigori were hesitant to touch, even with casual contact.

"Kanchana said Prija attacked you a few days ago."

"It's nothing I can't defend myself from."

Niran frowned. "I do not approve of this risk."

"Intira said her rages are improving."

"But at the cost of your safety?"

Kyra smiled. "I've defended myself against worse."

"I gave my word to your brother that you'd come to no harm here."

"Sirius understands the reality of dealing with our sisters," Kyra said. "We have our own damaged ones. We care for them even if they are dangerous."

He nodded. "You are very patient."

Kyra laughed a little. "I try to be. I'm not always successful."

Niran smiled and cocked his head, watching her.

"What is it?" Kyra asked. "Do I have something in my teeth?"

"Not a thing," he said. "I am enjoying how you shine."

She lost her breath for a second. "Oh."

"You do, you know. Since you've come here, you shine more each day."

Kyra ran a hand over her hair. "I think it's getting lighter with all the sun."

"That's not what I'm talking about." Niran leaned forward. "When you first came here, you were like a bird just pushed from the nest. Now you are flying. You are a good teacher, Kyra."

"Thank you." Her chin lifted. "I've only taught my sisters and one other group—mostly children—but the majority of them are leading successful lives now."

"As you are."

Her life was slipping away a little more every day, but she forced a smile. "I like to think so."

"Are you comfortable here?"

"Very comfortable. Thank you."

"Not too bored?"

This time, her smile came freely. "Not bored at all."

It was exhilarating to experience so many new things. Every night that Kyra went to the market with Niran and his brothers, she learned a little more. How to bargain. How to cook new foods from the street vendors. New music. New ways of walking and talking and living.

Kyra had never felt more alive.

"Good." He folded his hands. "Would you like to see a tattoo this afternoon?"

Her mouth dropped open. "Yes! Sirius would be grateful. He might even stop texting me every morning."

Niran's smile was devastating. His teeth were straight and white. He had a dimple in his left cheek. "Your brother has been far more patient than I would be. You are both to be commended. But I don't think it's Sirius's texts that make you scowl."

"No, those would be from Kostas."

"He's still calling?"

"It's every other day rather than every day now. I texted him daily at first. He seems to be relenting."

"We brothers are protective," Niran said. "It is our nature to protect our sisters. As for the tattooing, I'd planned to let you observe a ritual last week, but the Grigori requesting the tattoo was not comfortable with an audience."

"But this one is?"

Niran nodded. "He is an older Grigori who has sisters of his own. He is comfortable around women and not tempted."

"I would be grateful to witness the ritual. I hope you'll explain it to me."

"I'd be happy to." Niran rose. "Let us leave the table so our brothers can clean up. Intira, why don't you go back to your studies while Kyra and I go to the temple?"

Intira nodded. "Yes, brother."

"Be ready for the market at five o'clock."

She smiled. "I will be!"

Intira, Bun Ma, and Kanchana pressed their hands together and nodded their goodbyes as Niran and Kyra rose and walked toward the temple.

"The thing you must understand is that this practice is very old," Niran said. "Far older than Buddhism. Far older than Hinduism even. It is possible this is something that was once practiced by early Grigori, though it was lost to us and only survived in the human world."

Kyra said, "The Irin have tattoos, but I don't really know what they're for. Other than controlling their magic. I don't know the specifics."

"As far as I can tell, what you do with your singing—the words, the spells you say—they do with their writing. The

55

tattoos just capture the magic more permanently. It is the same history with the *Sak Yant*."

"But you said you learned it from humans."

"We did," Niran said. "My brother, Sura, was dissatisfied with his life even before our sire was dead. He used to say he felt as if he were rotting from the inside. He became friends with a very old holy man who lived not far from here."

"A monk?"

Niran shook his head. "No. I don't know what gods he believed in, but his life was honorable, his body was healthy, and he claimed to be over one hundred and ten years old."

Kyra said, "Humans don't live that long."

"Sura believed him. And this man, he had many markings. All over his arms..." Niran rolled up his sleeves to show Kyra a stylized tiger on his forearm surrounded by unfamiliar writing. "His legs. His chest. The old man had tattooed himself the same way his father tattooed himself. The same way he taught his sons before they left him."

"But what did the tattoos mean? They were human? Or did he learn them from the Irin?"

"He was human. And the tattoos were very old mantras written in Pali, the language of the Buddha. He called them *Sak Yant* and told my brother Sura that he would teach him if Sura was willing to learn and to take care of the old man until he died. The old man also told Sura that in order to teach him, he would have to live according to five laws."

"What kind of laws?"

"Simple things for a human." Niran paused and pulled a ripe mango from a tree near the temple. "Don't kill. Don't steal. Don't lie. Don't lust. Don't live a hedonistic life of pleasure." Niran pulled out a knife and sliced the mango neatly, carving petals from the flesh of the golden fruit. He handed them to Kyra as they walked. "These laws are all things humans endeavor to do anyway. Most human laws relate to this."

Kyra understood immediately. "But not Grigori laws."

"We have no laws," Niran said. "And to Sura—for a Grigori raised by a Fallen angel—these ideas were revolutionary. We and all our brothers were taught from birth to kill and lie and steal and lust. That was our identity. It was also what was rotting my brother from the inside. He took advantage of our father's absence and fled into the forest to learn from the old man. Over the years, he went back again and again. He discovered that the meditation he practiced and the words the old man tattooed on his body—later the words he tattooed himself—cleared his mind."

"It did what the Irin tattoos do for their warriors."

Niran shook his head. "I'm sure their systems are more extensive. Their spells are far more complex. They have thousands of years of scholarship behind their traditions. But for us —for those who don't have anyone to teach us—these human tattoos do help." He motioned to the temple where saffron-clad Grigori walked in prayer or meditation.

Some were cleaning. Some tended plants. Some sat in quiet conversation. All of them bore the same intricate tattoos Niran did.

"You've seen the Grigori here," he continued. "We still train to protect the city, but all of us live according to those five rules. All of us wear the tattoos that Sura taught us. All of us live more normal, more controlled lives. We're not special, Kyra. We were as violent as any in our race. If we can do this, so can others."

Kyra didn't need more convincing. She'd listened to the soul voices of Niran and his brothers. It wasn't an illusion. They were more calm. More controlled. More peaceful. "This could help my brothers," she said. "This practice could help them too."

She imagined Kostas with tattoos that could help him control his cravings for human energy. She imagined Sirius being stronger and more focused. They patrolled every night, plunging into temptation over and over again, battling the worst parts of their nature to defend humans against Grigori in thrall to other Fallen angels and themselves against Irin who were trained to stab first and ask questions later.

Niran stopped at the steps of the temple. "There's another side effect of this," he said. "We're also better fighters. Because we're more focused and present, we are far more deadly to our enemies. That is why I am so cautious with this knowledge. I am not being greedy or controlling, but this practice in the wrong hands could undo everything free Grigori like me and your brothers have been trying to prove to the Irin world. We are capable of living peaceful and protective lives. But we have to make sure that those who hold this knowledge are willing to live as we do."

"I understand."

Kyra toed off her shoes with Niran and ascended the steps to the temple. She could smell the fragrant incense and the flowers filling the front of the space. A large golden Buddha sat peacefully at the front while a line of monks sat along the side of the room, chanting a mantra. Kyra followed Niran to the opposite side of the temple where a young monk, no more than twenty, bent over the back of a shirtless man. The man looked up, nodded at Niran and Kyra, and closed his eyes. It was the Grigori who had come to receive *Sak Yant*.

"Sit with me," Niran said. "Make sure the soles of your feet are not exposed."

Kyra sat cross-legged, her palms resting on her knees as she watched the young monk and the Grigori.

The monk's lips moved in prayer, then he opened his eyes and began to write on the man's back in a quick, curving script. His pen didn't stop until he'd written multiple lines across the man's shoulders. He set the pen aside and took a long bamboo rod with a metal tip and dipped it in ink.

As the monks on the far side of the temple chanted, the young monk set a quick rhythm, piercing the man's skin with the metal point over and over again as he tattooed the words into the man's back. Kyra watched in amazement as the Grigori sat motionless, not even flinching. He kept his eyes closed, his lips moving in his own prayer as he sat in the lotus position on the ground of the temple, a string of marigolds in one hand, a small gold coin in the other.

The tattoo must have taken an hour or more to complete, but the wind passed through the open windows of the temple, carrying the smell of frangipani to her nose. The incense and the chanting lulled her into a meditative state, and in what seemed like only moments, the bamboo rod ceased moving. The monk sat up straight. He prayed over the Grigori in words Kyra didn't understand. Then the Grigori turned and bowed to the ground, offering the flowers and the gold coin the monk took and put on the altar beside him.

He said a few more words over the man, then the Grigori rose, nodded to Niran and Kyra, and walked silently out the door.

Kyra sat silently until she felt a movement on her hand. Looking down, she realized she'd taken Niran's hand at some point, and their palms were lying pressed together. She looked at him, blinking as if just waking up. His voice was a quiet murmur in the background of her mind, like the soft chanting of the monks in the temple.

Niran smiled. "Hello."

Kyra pulled her hand away and felt the heat on her cheeks. "Hi. I apologize."

"There is no need."

"That was…" Extraordinary. Unearthly. "Magical."

"Yes." Niran pulled his knees up and rose, holding his hand out to her. "It is very magical."

She took it and rose to her feet as the young monk who had performed the tattoo rose with them.

"Kyra," Niran said, motioning to the monk. "I'd like you to meet my older brother, Sura."

Sura walked with Kyra through the night market, nibbling on noodles and crispy tofu as the sounds of pop music and bargaining surrounded them. There was a band at the end of the street, and the rhythm filled the air, along with honking horns and the sizzle of frying food. Niran had walked ahead with two of his Grigori, and Intira walked beside them.

"I'm so glad you like our city," Sura said. He'd abandoned his robes and was wearing a pair of jeans and a traditional cotton shirt. "It's a very cool place. Niran worries so much, sometimes I don't think he enjoys it at all."

Kyra was delighted by Sura. He looked like a college kid, had the aura of an old man, and a wicked sense of humor. He'd jumped at the chance to visit the market when he learned his sister was coming. Then he'd hung back with Kyra and Intira, offering a running commentary on the best shopping, the most delicious noodles, and the coldest beer while Niran and the other Grigori kept watch on the market where locals and tourists mingled.

"How are you doing?" Kyra asked Intira.

The girl's dimples told the story. "Good. This is fun."

Intira was wandering the market with the wide, innocent eyes of a child. She'd visited the city before but hadn't ever been exposed to crowds like those at the night market.

Kyra said, "You must tell me if you have trouble with your shields. There is no shame in asking for help. You're doing so well, but everything is still new to you."

"I understand," Intira said. "When we passed the music I had trouble. Then once it quieted down, I remembered to sing."

"Loud noises distract me too. I'm glad you recovered. If you get in trouble, grab my hand."

"Thanks."

Sura grinned at the girl and gently touched her shoulder.

"I'm so happy for you, sister."

"You're the youngest and the oldest," Kyra said. "I just realized. Niran said you were the oldest brother. And Intira is the youngest sister."

"Yes," Sura said. "There are more stories to tell, but maybe not at the market tonight."

"No." Kyra watched Intira take everything in. She was like a sponge. A delighted sponge. "This night is too beautiful to share those stories."

"You speak the truth."

Kyra remembered the first time she'd experienced the public market in Thessaloniki, near where she'd been born. It was the first time Kostas had taken her into public with him after they thought they were free of their father.

Kyra had ended the day shaking and in tears. The voices in the market had nearly rendered her unconscious. She'd been told from birth she was weaker than her brothers. Told she was fragile and breakable and incapable. No matter how valued her twin brother was, Kyra was useless and always would be because her mind was weak.

Her first foray out of her father's compound confirmed every fear she'd harbored.

Kostas had told her she was strong, but she'd never believed him. And his protection over the years and decades since—no matter how well-meant—hadn't helped her confidence. She still struggled with malicious voices in her mind. Once, they'd come from the outside. Now they whispered from within.

"Sura, look! Is that the ice cream?" The young girl pointed in the direction of a stall selling elaborate treats with candied fruit.

Intira didn't wear Kyra's shadows. According to Niran and Sura, she'd been sheltered nearly from birth. Her mother had died, not from the strain of an angelic pregnancy, but from trying to escape from their father. It was the woman's death that had spurred Niran, Sura, and Kanok to action. Sura had gathered allies from his travels who helped them, other Grigori who bore the tattoos he'd learned to ink.

"The Grigori you tattooed today," Kyra said. "Is he still around?"

Sura paused. "I believe he's staying at a temple closer to Chiang Rai. Many of our free brothers choose a monastic life if they can handle it. It lessens temptation."

"You're a monk."

"For now. My vows were not for life. I try to be open to possibilities in all things. Right now my sisters' well-being is at the front of my mind. That's why I'm so grateful that you've come to teach them what I can't."

"Kyra is a great teacher." Intira looked up at her brother. "But you're still my favorite big brother."

"Fine. You can have the rest of my noodles," Sura said, handing his bowl to Intira. "But that doesn't mean I'm sharing my ice cream with you."

"You said you would!"

"I'll buy you your own." Sura slung his arm around Intira's shoulder and steered her toward the ice cream vendor who was spreading fruit and other sweets over the ice-cold slab where he mixed the treat.

Kyra watched them walk away and wondered if she should try to catch up with Niran. She eased past a crowd watching a street performer with puppets and started when someone grabbed her hand.

She stopped with a gasp when everything went quiet.

Everything.

The crowds.

The band.

The background hum of the souls surrounding her.

Kyra didn't need to turn around to know who held her hand in his warm grasp.

She turned anyway.

"Leo."

S he was here. In front of him. Real and tangible, not one of the dreams that tormented him. Her gold eyes were wide with shock. Her fair skin had grown tan, and her dark hair had streaks of amber through it.

"Leo."

She said his name, but he couldn't speak.

"What are you doing here?"

Leo's heart was beating out of his chest. His mind was a jumble, and no coherent thought would form. A singular instinct took hold of him.

Away.

He tugged Kyra's hand and turned, ducking under a hanging rack of lanterns and pulling her down a narrow alley between two market stands. She went with him for a few meters, then pulled on his hand.

"Stop!" she cried. "You don't understand. I'm with friends. It's not what you think."

He turned and Kyra's momentum pushed her into his chest.

She looked up, her expression still baffled. "Leo, I don't understand what you're doing here."

He swallowed and opened his mouth, but again no words came out. How could he explain? How could he explain anything? His appearance. His actions. The reaction he had toward her.

Reshon.

The longing thought leapt to his mind. Was it the voice of his soul or a mad wish? He'd vowed to wait for his *reshon*—his soul mate chosen by heaven—when he was a young scribe, hopeful and romantic. A vow he'd wondered about since the first time he saw Kyra and she told him, *"You make the voices go away."*

"Leo, tell me—"

Leo bent down and wrapped his arm around her waist, drew Kyra's mouth to his, and kissed her.

Her taste exploded on his lips. It was everything new and everything familiar at once.

Yes.

There you are.

Her kiss tasted like ginger and oranges. Her lips were as unpracticed as his own. Kyra's arms came around his neck, and he felt the contact move through him like an electric current. Her kiss was the rain. Her touch, the lightning. He gripped her waist harder. Would he bruise her? She kissed him back, one hand gripping his hair at his nape as her mouth moved eagerly against his own.

He'd only kissed her in his dreams. He'd imagined it in real life a hundred times. A thousand perhaps.

The heady taste of Kyra was far better than dreams.

She pulled back, gasping. "What are you doing?"

"Kissing you." His voice was rough. "I'm kissing you."

Leo kissed her again, ravenous for another taste. Her head fell back and he kissed her neck. Behind her ear. He set her down so his hands could slide over the delicate wings of her shoulder blades where her skin was bare. Was his skin too rough? He had many calluses from training. Would they scratch her? Did she like to be scratched?

"I've wanted to kiss you for so long," he said against her mouth.

"I don't understand." Her teeth scraped across his lower lip, and Leo shuddered. "What are you doing here?"

"I told you." Heaven above! Did every woman's skin taste so delectable? How did their mates keep their mouths away from them? Leo kissed along Kyra's jawline. And her scent! "So good," he muttered.

He'd been aroused before; after all, he was hundreds of years old and scribes were never meant to be monks. But nothing compared to the pounding urgency in his body to take her, devour her, consume her passion to feed his own.

A mate chosen by heaven.

"We need…" She let out a short gasp when Leo nibbled on the muscle at the side of her neck. "Leo, stop."

What? No! Why?

He frowned and lifted his head. "Am I doing something wrong?"

Kyra blinked. "I don't… know. No?"

His eyes fell to her swollen lips. "I like kissing you."

She let out a small groan.

"So much."

Her chest heaved. Which caused her delicate breasts to rise and fall. Which was so, so good. They drew his gaze like magnets.

"Did you like it too?" he asked.

She nodded. "Yes, but——"

"Good." Leo bent his head, but she put a hand over his mouth and pushed.

"What are you doing in Chiang Mai?"

He opened his mouth. "I'm——"

"*Other* than kissing me," Kyra said. "I think I understand that part."

Oh. Hmm. How to explain? "I was called to Bangkok by the watcher there."

"The Irin watcher?" Her eyes went blank. "But why are you in Chiang Mai?"

Leo hated the blank expression. He automatically knew she was hiding something. "There were pictures of you."

"What? Where?"

"In Bangkok. Surveillance pictures."

"They've been watching the Grigori here," she said quietly.

He smoothed a hand over her mussed hair. "That's what we do."

"They are not your enemies," she said. "No one here—"

A slight sound caused Leo to turn a second before the knife would have sunk into his shoulder. He batted it away and pushed Kyra behind him, putting himself in the path of his assailant.

"Leo, no!"

"Stay back." He drew a silver dagger in one hand and a silenced 9mm in the other. In a place like the market, he didn't want to have to use the gun, but he would if necessary. His aim was steady.

Leo's attacker didn't hide. He walked out of the alleyway with his own gun pointed in Leo's direction. Leo brushed a thumb over his *talesm prim* and felt his spells come alive. With that brush, he was effectively wearing a suit of living armor. His hearing sharpened. His vision became hyperaware. His skin would be hotter if Kyra touched him.

"Who are you?" the Grigori asked. "Let her go."

Kyra said, "Niran, he's a friend."

Ah yes, it was the Grigori from the picture, Leo realized. The one walking with her and making her laugh. He had a gun pointed at Leo's head.

"Please," Kyra said. "Both of you, put the weapons down."

"Him first," Leo muttered, unwilling to leave Kyra unprotected.

"You have no purpose here, scribe," Niran said, still walking slowly toward Leo. "Go back where you came from and tell your watcher you're not needed."

"I'm not here because of my watcher," Leo said.

"Will both of you put the weapons down?" Kyra said. "Someone is going to get hurt. Niran, where is Intira?"

"With Sura. Step away from the scribe, Kyra."

"I don't take orders from you. Both of you put your weapons away!"

"No." The answer came in unison.

"For heaven's sake." Kyra shoved her way from behind Leo and stepped between the raised guns, which were immediately lowered as soon as she came in their sights.

"Kyra, what are you doing?"

Leo dropped his gun. "Are you insane?" He tried to push her back, but she twisted away.

"Both of you, listen!" She was angry. "Just *stop*. Niran, Leo is a friend. He's from the Istanbul house, which has an alliance with my brother. Leo, I am here as Niran's guest. Please, do not attack the man who has welcomed me and taken care of me in this country."

Leo narrowed his eyes at Niran, who was looking equally hostile. Reluctantly he put his arm down as Niran did the same. He slid the 9mm in his holster… as Niran did. Then Leo's knife was put away. He glared at the Grigori whom Kyra had defended.

"If it weren't for her, you'd be on the ground," Leo said.

"Keep telling yourself that if it makes you feel good." Niran whistled and three more Grigori stepped from the shadows. "Myat, go tell Sura and Intira to walk back to the truck."

"Niran, don't," Kyra said. "Don't spoil her night because of this. Everyone needs to stop and think. There is no fight here. No one wants to hurt anyone."

Leo was fairly sure he wanted to hurt Niran.

"I'm not leaving her in the market with an Irin scribe

around," the Grigori said. "We've all heard the stories of them taking our sisters. Where there is one, there will be more."

Leo said, "I'm not here to take anyone who is not in danger." He glanced at Kyra. That might not be strictly true, but it was none of this Niran's business.

Kyra seemed to sense his thoughts. "Don't. We need to talk. Just talk."

"As long as you're not running away from a real conversation, I can agree to that."

"How many scribes are in my city?" Niran asked.

"I'm the only scribe who came from Bangkok," Leo said. They didn't need to know that Alyah was with him. "And I came for Kyra, not to attack you."

"Yes, I've heard that before. Right before two scribes tried to grab a sister of mine from a local temple."

Leo frowned. "I know nothing about that."

"Watchers know best, do they not?" Niran said. "We don't want anything from the Irin. Leave us alone."

Leo examined the Grigori with new eyes. The man was of medium height and carried a commanding presence. The men who flanked him took orders effortlessly. Clearly these Grigori were disciplined and well organized. Looking again, Leo saw dark lines of tattoos at each of their necks. He glanced at their arms. Tattoos there too.

What was going on here?

Kyra put a hand on his forearm. Her touch nearly caused him to moan in pleasure. She felt so good. He controlled himself.

"You have questions," Kyra said. "I have answers, but I need to confer with Niran first. Allow me to talk with him in private."

She wanted to leave him and go off with the Grigori? Leo's lip curled.

"Or we can take her now and you'll never find her," Niran said. "What will it be, scribe?"

Kyra's chin lifted. "No one takes me against my will. You don't speak for me."

"I speak for your brother," he said. "I promised no harm would come to you in my territory."

Leo said, "I've got her brother's number on speed dial. Shall we call him now?"

"No!" Kyra shouted. "Leo, don't you dare."

What the hell was going on here? Kyra looked panicked. Niran was hard to read, but Leo would swear there was some confusion in his eyes.

"Fine," Leo said. He drew a hotel card from his shirt pocket and handed it to Kyra. "I'm here when you're finished talking to him."

Kyra relaxed. "After we talk, I'll find you."

"I want your phone number before you go." Leo didn't take his eyes off Niran.

Kyra was reluctant, but she nodded and put a hand out. "Your phone?"

Leo unlocked his phone and handed it to her.

Kyra quickly entered a number and hit Send, then she held up her own phone for him to see the number flashing. "Satisfied?"

His eyes raked down her body. "Far from it."

She turned bright red. "I'll call you later."

"I'll wait for you."

She walked toward Niran, and everything in Leo screamed at him to grab her and run.

He didn't. She wasn't his to steal. Plus he had a few questions for Alyah before he and Kyra talked.

"Kyra," he called to her back.

She turned.

"If you don't come to me, I'll find you."

The smile she gave him was sad. Amused. Skeptical. Far too complicated for a single emotion.

"You could try."

Leo opened the heavy gate to the hotel garden on the other side of the river. He'd ignored the hails of the tuk-tuk drivers and walked the distance from the night bazaar, needing time to gather his thoughts. The hotel where Alyah had brought them was close to the old city and the bazaar, just on the other side of the river and downstream. High walls protected it from prying eyes, and lush gardens greeted him when he entered the compound. His suite faced a narrow pool where lilies floated and fish swam. Across a small bridge, Alyah had taken her own room, but all her lights were off.

The garden was silent. The staff was gone. But Leo's thoughts were in a riot.

Their kiss.

The sheer pleasure of it kept leaping to his mind, scattering every other conscious thought.

He unlocked his room and walked inside, tossing his keys on the small table by the door and falling back on the bed to stare at the ceiling.

"*I like kissing you.*" He closed his eyes at the memory of her lips. "*So much.*" Her hands gripping his hair. "*Did you like it too?*" Her breasts. Heaven above…

Leo had dreamed of kissing Kyra for no less than two years. From the time he'd met her, he'd been aware of the desire, but Kyra had been a tentative bird in the beginning. She could barely manage to walk down a street without cringing from the rampant human thoughts that invaded her mind. The last thing Leo wanted was for her to feel that a large, clumsy giant of a scribe was preying on her vulnerabilities.

But then he'd seen her in Rěkaves, standing up to the scribes and singers of Mikael's line, holding her own with Sari, one of the most dominant and warlike singers Leo had ever known. She'd grown. She'd come into her power.

Then…

Then he'd wanted her. He'd craved her. He'd sought her company but always felt a wall hanging between them. He longed for her. Wondered where she had gone when she left with her brother. Sari had tried to convince Kyra to stay at Rěkaves with her, but Kyra had refused. Leo suspected her brother had been the reason why.

Then Kyra had reacted with panic when he'd offered to call Kostas tonight.

What was going on?

Had she been cast out? Impossible. Was she hiding? Niran's words indicated otherwise.

How long did she want to talk to Niran? Would she come tonight? He glanced at his phone and noticed it was after midnight. Then he tapped the number she'd entered earlier, adding it to his contacts along with a picture he'd snapped of her in Rěkaves. She'd been laughing with one of the children Damien and Sari had rescued, holding the little boy as he tried to squirm away.

Happy. She'd been so happy.

"What about your own family?"

"I don't know if that is possible for me."

Though the *kareshta* were daughters of the Fallen, they were still angelic. They could have children. There were several *kareshta* who were pregnant from Irin scribes. Some they'd identified even had children with human mates, though it was unusual. What was the sorrow that shadowed her eyes?

A tapping came at the door.

Leo sprang up and rushed toward it, flinging it open only to see Alyah on the other side.

"Oh," he said. "It's you."

Her eyebrows rose. "Clearly not who you were hoping for."

71

No, but he did have a few questions. "Why don't you come in?" He held the door open and Alyah walked inside.

"Did you find her?"

"Yes."

"Was she safe?"

"Apparently." How to broach the topic without having Alyah clam up? She was highly loyal to her watcher. She practically worshipped Dara, and Leo understood why. "I spoke briefly to the Grigori you've been watching. There are some interesting things about him."

"Oh?" She sat on the bench in the small living area. "We have been watching for some time. It's apparent he's not feeding on humans."

"When we first spoke, you were skeptical about the existence of the *kareshta*. You didn't know if this group of Grigori were protecting any sisters or not."

"Are they?"

"It would seem so," Leo said. "It would also seem that two or more scribes—I wasn't able to get specifics—attempted to abduct one of their sisters recently."

Alyah wasn't prone to strong reactions, but that got her attention. "What?"

"Two scribes. He said they tried to grab one of his sisters from a temple."

"I know nothing about this."

"Then this Grigori said: 'Watchers know best, do they not?' Alyah, are you sure that Dara has no knowledge of the *kareshta* this Grigori is protecting?"

She frowned and leaned forward. "I told you we were skeptical they truly existed. Why would Dara lie about them if she knew they were there?"

"Why would scribes try to abduct a woman praying at a temple?"

"Maybe they thought she was human," Alyah said. "Maybe they thought they were protecting her from Grigori."

"We're not supposed to touch humans," Leo said. "It can be harmful to them."

Alyah gave him another skeptical look. "Do you truly think all scribes are as honorable as that? Besides, Dara doesn't command every scribe in Thailand. Perhaps they were independent and believed this woman was *kareshta*. Maybe they believed they were saving her from an angel."

"Or perhaps they were eager to find an available female," Leo said quietly.

Alyah's lip curled. "They wouldn't—"

"They would," Leo said. "They have. It's happened in Europe."

"Scribes have kidnapped these *kareshta*? Abducted them?"

"They dress it up," Leo said. "Say they're rescuing them from the Grigori. Or the Fallen."

"Maybe they are."

"And maybe they want a grateful female who looks to them for protection," Leo said. "A *kareshta* in debt to them for their freedom. If that's happening in Thailand, you must put a stop to it. The mandate from the council is clear: the protection of the *kareshta*, not their exploitation. Sometimes protecting them might mean protecting the brothers they depend on."

"Grigori?" Alyah said. "Leaving them alone is one thing, but protecting them?"

"Some of these men have given everything—given their own lives—to keep their sisters safe. Many love their families just as much as Irin love theirs. Taking a *kareshta* away from brothers who have been her caretakers and protectors only traumatizes them again."

"Unless they want to go." Alyah stood. "Who says these Grigori aren't keeping their sisters under their thumbs just as much as the Fallen did? Irina have options. We have power. We have independence. We have *magic*."

"You have independence because you have magic. You want the *kareshta* to have that too?"

Alyah fell silent.

It was one thing to rail at the Grigori. It was another thing to offer magic to a race that had very recently been the enemy. Alyah's reaction was not unexpected.

"We wait for Kyra to call me," he said. "At this point, it's all we can do."

T he ride back to the temple was completely and utterly silent. At least on the outside. Two Grigori sat in the back of the pickup truck, watching for any hint of a tail as Kyra sat in the front seat next to Niran and Intira sat in the back with Sura.

Niran was furious. His soul voice raged, and Kyra had a difficult time blocking him. Most of his anger felt like it was projected outward, but some sounded like it went within.

Kyra glanced over her shoulder and saw Intira's jaw clench. If Kyra was having trouble blocking Niran, she could only imagine what Intira was feeling.

Very calmly, she said, "Just because you're silent doesn't mean we can't hear you."

Sura said something Kyra couldn't understand, but whatever it was ratcheted down the tension in the truck. The atmosphere still wasn't pleasant, but it was better.

Once they arrived at the temple, Intira fled to her cottage, and Kyra waited by the vehicle. Niran barked orders at his men, then turned to Kyra.

His eyes flashed, and Kyra saw the predator he was bred to

be. A frisson of fear worked its way down her spine, but she stood straight.

"We need to talk," he said.

She shook her head. "Not when you're like this." She started back toward her cottage, and Niran grabbed her elbow. Kyra twisted under his arm and brought her fist down hard on the inside of his elbow as Sirius had taught her. Niran hissed and dropped his hand.

"Do not make the mistake of thinking," Kyra said in a low voice, "that because I am quiet, I am defenseless. I will talk to you in the morning, Niran. You attacked a friend of mine, provoked a powerful scribe, and turned this night into a bad memory for a sister you love. Think about that." She turned to Sura, who was watching quietly. "Would you walk me to my cottage, please?"

Sura inclined his head and lifted an eyebrow in Niran's direction before he walked off with Kyra, his hands clasped behind his back.

Kyra walked into the trees where faint lights lit the path back to the *kareshta* cottages. She had controlled her emotions all night, but in the quiet rustle of the wind in the bamboo, her walls began to crumble.

Her skin felt brittle. Her belly was liquid. Her emotions were everywhere, and she couldn't stop thinking about Leo's kiss. She'd never imagined anything feeling as good as his lips pressing against hers as he lifted her in his powerful arms and held her tight. Why had that act—which seemed so inherently messy and awkward—felt so good? Her skin felt like she'd touched a live wire. Her lips were numb. She desperately wanted to try it again, and yet she knew it wasn't a good idea.

Kyra felt as she imagined the humans did when they'd had too much wine.

Drunk. She was drunk on Leo.

"I'm sorry I did not get a chance to meet your friend," Sura said into the heavy silence.

Kyra barked out a laugh.

Sura smiled. "If you call him a friend, you must trust him."

"I do."

"Then I imagine he is a person worth knowing."

"That is probably a matter of opinion. Niran didn't seem to think so."

Sura cocked his head to the side and looked up at the moon. He walked in silence for a few steps before he said, "Niran has organized his world in very strict ways. Black-and-white. Family and other. He trusts very few, and he keeps a narrow focus. He has done this in order to control himself and provide for our sisters. He was once the most feared and powerful of our father's sons, so this order in his life is hard-won, and anything that disturbs it is avoided."

"I understand."

"I suspect you do," Sura said. "From reputation, your brother is much the same."

"Sirius?" Kyra said. "Not really. He's always been—"

"Not Sirius." Sura's lips twitched. "Kostas. The one who is not supposed to know where you are."

Kyra sighed. "Do you know everything, Sura?"

"Hardly. But I know brothers and sisters." He met Kyra's eyes. "And I also know that Niran has come to care greatly for you. Not only because of your work with Intira and the others. His reaction tonight does not surprise me."

Was Sura saying Niran was… jealous? The idea of Niran caring for her pained Kyra. Not because he was an unworthy man, but because he *was* worthy. If she was free—and if she didn't have such complex feelings for Leo—Niran was the kind of man she would admire.

But that wasn't reality.

"He knows…" Kyra blinked hard. "Niran knows my life will not last much longer, Sura. I know things for free Grigori are different now, but he must know a future with me is not possible."

Sura shrugged. "What we know in our minds and what we feel in our hearts are often quite contrary, aren't they?"

Kyra said, "I don't know why I've lived as long as I have. Any time—"

"None of us are guaranteed time." Sura stopped and Kyra realized they'd reached her cottage. "You have to live while you can, Kyra. Not a single one of us is guaranteed tomorrow. We cannot predict the future. Trying to do so only leads to arrogance and selfishness. Exist in the present. *Live* in the present. If your heart is leading you to someone, it is a gift, not a burden."

Kyra blushed. "Sura, I know he's your brother, but I don't think my feelings for Niran—"

"I wasn't talking about Niran." Sura smiled. "I think I would like to meet this scribe friend of yours. Tomorrow night, maybe?"

Kyra narrowed her eyes. "Are you trying to cause trouble?"

"Trouble is life made interesting, isn't it?" Sura said, backing up the path. "So yes. Maybe I'm trying to cause trouble. Sleep well, sister. I'll calm Niran down by morning."

KYRA STOPPED A BLOCK AWAY FROM THE HOTEL.

"What are you doing?" Sura asked. He frowned, his hands in his pockets. This night, he wore loose linen pants and a white dress shirt. With his head shaved, he still looked monk-like. "This is the way to the hotel. I've walked past it before."

"I'm..." Nervous. Excited. Confused. Eager. Unsure. Kyra cleared her throat and tried to stop her heart from pounding out of her chest. "Are you sure this is a good idea?"

"You trust this scribe?"

"Yes." Of that she was certain. Never had Leo given her any reason to distrust him.

Sura paused. "I think you are hesitating because of feelings you may have for him as a man. However, we also need to ask him what interest the Bangkok scribe house has in us. I've wondered for some time if they would be suspicious of our practice of *Sak Yant* on Grigori because it helps us control our magic."

"But it makes you less violent. Controls your instincts."

"Exactly," Sura said. "Which is good for our city, but also could make us a greater threat in their eyes."

That hadn't even occurred to Kyra. Would the Irin scribe houses actually sabotage free Grigori to keep them from harnessing their magic for good?

Kyra started walking again. "Sirius has complained that the Irin will not teach free Grigori their magic, but I cannot imagine they would keep the Grigori completely at the mercy of their basest instincts."

"I'm sure the most honorable of them—like your Leo—would not." Sura sidestepped a large family exiting a restaurant. It was nighttime again, and the lanterns strung across the street glowed with cheerful red light. "But not all Irin are honorable."

"You're talking about the ones who tried to take Prija?"

Sura had told Kyra about the attempted abduction that morning at breakfast. Prija often wandered, but she usually stayed in the forest. This particular time, she'd walked toward the human village and the small temple where the locals worshipped. No one was certain whether the Irin scribes had been looking for Grigori or if it was purely a coincidence, but two men with heavy tattoos on their arms had tried to grab Prija and take her toward a car. She had screamed, causing both the men to bleed from their ears and run back into the forest. It took four days to find her. Some of the humans in the village had told Niran about the episode when they heard a girl had gone missing.

Sura said, "There are good and bad people everywhere. The Irin have a culture that promotes honor. We can learn from that.

But that doesn't make them perfect, just as our birth doesn't condemn us to being demons."

Kyra saw the sign for the hotel. Having a list of questions helped Kyra conquer her nerves, but the butterflies in her stomach didn't settle completely. "So we need to ask about why the Bangkok house is watching you."

"And also find answers for Prija if possible."

"That happened over a year ago," Kyra said. "He might not know anything about it."

"But whoever is with him would."

"Leo said he was alone."

"No." Sura smiled a little. "Niran said he claimed to have no other *scribes* with him."

"You mean…"

"The Bangkok house is well known for their female warriors," Sura said. "I'm surprised it escaped Niran's attention. There." Sura pointed at a high, nondescript gate across the road. "This is where we must knock."

"But the hotel sign is here."

"That is only for show. This hotel is very discreet." Sura knocked at the wooden gate. "This is where he will be staying."

Within moments, the garden gate cracked open and a short woman with neat silver hair offered Sura a polite wai in greeting. They exchanged a few words of Thai, and the woman shook her head. Sura spoke again, this time in a longer string of words. He motioned to Kyra and said something else. Seeing Kyra turned the woman's face from polite reluctance to cheerful welcome. She opened the gate and waved them inside, offering another wai before she escorted them across a small bridge and toward two low houses that sat on the other end of a garden.

More lanterns burned there, along with candles and the distinct tang of mosquito coils and lemongrass. Sura spoke to the hostess, who nodded and walked away, leaving them in the candlelit garden where a bubbling fountain was the only background music.

"She says our friends are the quiet sort, but they told her they might have visitors, though they only mentioned you."

"I'm glad she didn't kick you out." Kyra rubbed her palms on the long flowing skirt she wore. She'd told herself not to take extra time with her appearance, then utterly failed and checked her reflection at least a dozen times.

She'd lost weight since she saw him in Řekaves. The past year had been stressful, and she often forgot to eat. Her face was thin and tan, and her hair was bleached from the sun. She looked like one of the girls on the beaches of the Black Sea who came and stayed on the sand for too long, though her skin was still soft and didn't resemble leather like theirs.

"You look lovely," Sura said quietly.

"It's not important." Kyra shook her head. "It's never been important."

Sura looked at her.

"What?"

"It bothers you," he said. "Being beautiful."

Kyra had known from a young age that she was far more beautiful than most women. It was an accident of angelic blood, yet she was given respect and privileges for no other reason than her looks. After living with her own beauty for so long—being the object of lust for so many while constantly sensing their true thoughts—superficial beauty felt like a burden she would happily lay down given the chance.

"It's nothing I've done," she said. "I'm like a pretty, useless vase bought to decorate a shelf. An object."

"I think you are unfair to both yourself and to the vase."

She scoffed. "I'm being unfair to the vase?"

Sura looked up. "Look at these lanterns. These flowers. Creating more beauty in the world is never a bad thing if it is offered freely and accepted with grace. There something beautiful about desiring to please another when it is not an obligation. It can be a gift we give those we love."

His perspective humbled Kyra. "I've never thought about it that way."

"I'm sure Leo sees what I see," Sura said. "A gifted woman with a generous heart. That is the most beautiful thing of all."

"I'm sure he sees—"

"You." A voice came from the other end of the garden. Leo stepped out from the shadows. His face was glowing. "I see you."

Her heart seized again, just like it had at the market the previous night. Would he ever stop having this effect on her? It was very disconcerting.

"Sura," Kyra said, "this is Leo. Leo, please meet Sura, Niran's brother."

Leo blinked and tore his eyes from Kyra. "Sura," he said, walking toward them with an outstretched hand. "It is a pleasure to meet any friend of Kyra's."

"I feel exactly the same way," Sura said. "Join us for a beer?"

"You must be the calm one." Leo grinned. "I'd love to."

"THAT'S THE REASON I CAME," LEO SAID, TALKING LOUDLY TO shout over the band playing at the end of the street. "They knew you were here and they knew you were patrolling the city regularly. They want to open a dialogue. See if you're open to cooperation."

Sura nodded. "And this is something you have practice in?"

"Leo and his cousin Maxim have coordinated with my brothers for years now," Kyra said, leaning over the table. "They seem to work well together."

"Not that Kostas can stand me," Leo said. "He doesn't like anyone who is too interested in Kyra."

She blushed, but Sura answered as if Leo had said nothing

extraordinary. "Kyra's brothers reached out to us asking for information. We wanted something in return."

"Which was?"

Kyra said, "They have sisters of their own. Four of them. The youngest is only thirteen. They'd heard that I could teach them to shield their minds."

Leo said, "An exchange?"

"It seemed like the fairest way," Sura said. "Our sisters needed help that Kyra could give. We have practices that could help Kostas and his brothers control their magic more. She would come here first. If she proved trustworthy, her brothers could be sent."

Leo raised an eyebrow. "Kostas didn't approve this, did he?"

"Sirius did," Kyra said. "Kostas is furious with both of us right now, but I text him regularly. He knows I'm safe and that I'm doing something important."

Leo smiled. "Guts. Ava would say you have them."

Kyra shook her head. "That phrase has never made sense to me. Everyone has intestines."

Sura raised his hand for another beer. "I'd like to know who you've brought with you, scribe."

"Excuse me?" Leo finished off his bottle. "Who I've brought?"

"I see two women watching us from the noodle stand," Sura said, waving. "Can I assume they are both Irina?"

"What?" Kyra blinked. She thought she had good instincts, but she hadn't spotted either woman. One appeared Thai and the other European. They disappeared by the time she'd looked twice.

Leo shook his head. "You've got good eyes. Yes, they're Irina. One from Bangkok and one local."

"I thought I recognized the taller girl," Sura said. "She's come up to the village before. She trains in one of the gyms here in Chiang Mai."

"Trains for what?" Kyra asked.

"Muay thai," a cheerful voice called in an American accent. "I'm Ginny. What's your name?" She stuck out her hand.

"Kyra." She took the woman's hand, somewhat cowed by her energy. "I'm Kyra."

"Nice to meet you." Ginny sat down next to Kyra and raised her hand to get the waiter's attention. She held up two fingers and motioned to the table.

"And I'm Alyah," the other woman said, sitting next to Leo. "From Bangkok."

"From the scribe house," Sura said.

"Yes, but don't hold that against her," Ginny said. "She's still okay."

Superficially, the two women couldn't have looked more different. Ginny looked more human than any Irina Kyra had met. She didn't have the reserve or formality and reminded Kyra more of Ava's easy manner. Maybe it was an American thing. Her skin was suntanned, and she had gold streaks in her long brown hair. Her smile was easy and bright. The Thai woman was shorter, her body compact and strong. Kyra could see defined muscles in her arms and shoulders. Her hair was cut in short layers around her face, and she didn't smile easily.

But both women moved with the innate confidence Kyra associated with the Irina. They were warriors. Survivors. Women with centuries of history and an extensive command of magic. Kyra could feel it surrounding them. Feel the warmth and energy they projected. Without even trying, Irina always made Kyra feel small.

Sura nodded at Ginny. "I know you."

Ginny smiled. "And I know you. Nice tattoos."

"Thank you. I did most of them myself."

"I thought so."

Leo clapped his hands together once. "That's what it is. The tattoos. I've been trying to figure out what Kostas and Sirius want. It's the tattoos. They're human, but you've found a way for them to help you with your natural magic. That's why Kyra is here."

Sura nodded. "You are correct."

Ginny said, "Oh, that is way cool."

"It *is* way cool," Sura said cautiously, eyeing Alyah. "And what does the Bangkok scribe house think of Grigori using *Sak Yant*?"

"The Bangkok scribe house doesn't have an opinion about it," Alyah said. "My task—with Leo's help—is to start a dialogue with you. I'm not here to talk about tattooing. Sounds like scribe business to me."

Sura still looked skeptical. "A dialogue about what?"

"You have options," Leo said. "The Bangkok house considers Chiang Mai part of its territory."

"There is no scribe house here," Sura said.

"But there are humans," Leo said. "And protecting humans from Grigori is the mandate of every scribe house and every individual scribe, warrior or not."

Kyra sat up straighter. "The Grigori here don't hunt humans."

"So they say," Leo said. "Kyra, I cannot simply take their word for it. We have to ask questions."

Before Kyra could respond, Ginny spoke up. "So ask questions," she said. "I live here. I train here. I keep an eye on things. I don't answer to any overbearing scribe house, but I'm Irina. Ask me if you want to know."

Leo said, "Fair enough. Have you witnessed or heard reports of any attack on humans by Grigori in Chiang Mai in the past two years?"

"Yes," Ginny said immediately. "And those Grigori were killed by Sura and the Grigori I assume are his brothers."

"How do you know it was them?" Leo asked.

"Dude, the tattoos are pretty distinctive. The Thai scribes use a similar style, but the letters are Old Language, one hundred percent. The tattoos these guys were flashing were all *Sak Yant*. Hard to miss."

Alyah turned to Ginny. "Why must you use 'dude' so often?"

"It's a great word. Don't hate on 'dude.'"

Kyra asked, "Are you from California?"

"Yes, I am."

Kyra smiled at Leo. "Like Ava," she said. "Ava says that word too."

Leo was staring at her. Alyah nudged him.

"Hmm? What?"

"You're staring," Alyah said. "Don't stare."

"I'm… concentrating." Leo cleared his throat. "So there have been Grigori attacks, but Sura and his brother Niran have defended the city. Sounds very much like Kostas and his brothers."

"I agree," Kyra said. "I've been with them for three weeks. And if my opinion means anything in this—"

"It does," Leo said quickly.

"—then I would say that though their methods differ, their objective is the same as my brothers'," Kyra continued. "Sura and Niran obtained their freedom at great cost; now they are trying to live their lives and protect their community from other Fallen and the Grigori who might try to exploit the humans here."

"And protect our sisters," Sura said. "And try to engender discipline within our kind for those who choose to pursue it."

Ginny's eyes shone. "So you do have *kareshta* up there."

Sura said, "We do."

Ginny and Alyah exchanged a look that made Kyra want to question them alone. Before she could suggest the three go for a stroll through the market, Leo spoke again.

"So now we know," Leo said to Alyah. "They have *kareshta*." He turned to Sura. "The mandate of the Irin council is that *kareshta* are to be protected. So what do you need? And how can we help you get it?"

CHAPTER
EIGHT

L eo tried to keep his eyes on the road as Ginny drove over the twisting mountain paths that led to the temple where Sura and his Grigori lived. He had no problem letting Ginny drive, but the blank space before him where the steering wheel should be was disorienting. He kept his eyes on the road as she swerved around potholes and dodged motorbikes and scooters.

Sura and Kyra had left the night before, but not before giving Ginny directions to their compound.

She'd left. And Leo had not a single minute alone with her.

"I know what you're thinking," Ginny said.

Alyah was sitting in the back seat. "That you're a terrible driver?"

"No, I'm an excellent driver, and I wasn't talking to you." She elbowed Leo. "He's thinking, 'How do I get some of that fine Kyra of my very own?'"

Leo raised an eyebrow. "How old did you say you were?"

"Old enough to know what a lonely, lonely scribe is thinking when he goes all quiet."

"Who said I was lonely?" Leo said.

"Your puppy dog eyes," Ginny said. "Alyah, am I right?"

Leo looked over his shoulder. Alyah looked like she was very deliberately keeping her mouth shut.

"What do you two know about being lonely?" Leo said. "Irina have never been prohibited from socializing with human men. It's not the same."

"True," Ginny said. "But we're crap at relationships with them. Ask Alyah."

"Don't bring me into this," Alyah muttered from the back seat. "If you want to torment the scribe, do it on your own."

Leo was leaving that one alone. Alyah had made it very clear from the beginning that she was a warrior uninterested in a mate. They were colleagues, not friends.

"So…" Ginny wasn't letting up. "Give us the details, man. When did you meet her? What's her favorite color? Dogs or cats? Are you planning on marking her and making tiny, adorable babies?" She glanced at Leo. "Come to think of it, between the two of you, they'd probably be Amazonian babies. There are some very good genes happening with both of you."

"I don't…" How did one respond to an Irina with these wild ideas? She couldn't be serious. And yet, Leo sensed she was genuinely curious. "I don't know Kyra… intimately." *I've simply obsessed over her for three years and hope she is my soul mate.*

"Really?" Alyah spoke up from the back. "I didn't get that sense."

"Me either," Ginny said.

"We met in Vienna before the battle. Her brother has known my cousin for many years, but none of us knew about the Grigori sisters. Kostas, Kyra's brother, brought her to Vienna to stay with my watcher's mate, Ava. They became friends, and that is how I met Kyra."

Not that it was the whole story. He didn't tell them how Kyra's eyes had glowed the first time he touched her hand. How his body went electric at a single brush of her finger. He didn't tell them how he'd held her during the battle, felt her body jerk and wilt when her father died. He didn't tell them about their whispered conversations and long embraces in Řekaves or the kiss in the night market.

Just the memory of that kiss was enough to wake his body from its centuries-long fast. Leo had quashed sensual hunger for over a century with a strict regime of discipline and resignation to a mateless life. *But if she was his* reshon…

Kyra had changed everything. His soul and his body were hungry now. They'd tasted her delicacy and wanted to feast.

"So you've only met her once?"

"I saw her again last year when I went to the Czech Republic to fight one of the Fallen and she was there with her brother." *I held her before the battle, and she embraced me on the return.*

"Wow," Ginny said. "Sounds epic."

Leo stared at the road. "I'm not here to entertain you."

Alyah said, "It sounds like the two of you only meet when there are problems. It doesn't sound like you've had any time alone."

"We definitely have not," he said under his breath.

"Aha!" Ginny said. "So we have our mission, Alyah."

Alyah leaned forward between the two front seats. "I am here to assist in the instruction of these women and make sure they are protected. I'm here to gather information for my watcher on the workings of the free Grigori. I am not here to play matchmaker."

"Fine," Ginny said. "I don't answer to a watcher, and I think we need to hook the brother up. I think Leo needs to get laid."

Leo thought he needed to disappear. Flinging himself out of the car sounded like a not-horrible-at-all possibility. If this was what it was like to have sisters, he preferred the scribe house.

"Isn't that the turn?" he said, trying to ignore Ginny and Alyah.

"Oh yeah." Ginny swerved and flung the car into a U-turn. "So Leo, how do we get you and Kyra alone? Kidnapping seems the obvious choice."

"Seriously?" he asked. "That seems like the 'obvious choice' to you? I don't see that going over well."

"But the direct approach might work better with her protection detail. Sura was awfully possessive of her."

"It's not Sura he needs to worry about," Alyah said. "It's the aggressive one at the market I told you about. He also is attracted to Kyra."

"*Niran?*" Leo asked.

"I like it." Ginny grinned. "A little competition always makes a girl feel good."

Leo said, "What did I do to deserve this?"

THE AIR AROUND THE TEMPLE SMELLED OF GREEN BAMBOO AND incense. There was a tinge of sandalwood in the scent that set Leo's instincts on edge. It was the sign of Grigori. All around the world, Grigori smelled of sandalwood. His reaction was automatic. He'd been trained to seek it out and kill Grigori from the time he was thirteen. Learning to *not* go into a killing frame of mind took focused concentration.

Floating over the sandalwood was the lush, heady aroma of jasmine and frangipani. It calmed him. He got out of the car and straightened, waiting for some signal from the quiet buildings surrounding the temple. None of them were fancy. They weren't layered with gold and paint like those in the cities. This structure was moss-covered stone. Flowing dragons guarded the stairs, and the ivory eyes of a dark wooden Buddha winked from the doorway where natural light and candles were the only illumination.

Alyah and Ginny stood next to him. Alyah, a tiny powerhouse, and Ginny, tall and lithe. They waited with the patience of Irina, knowing the free Grigori would want to meet them in a neutral place. Though they were only three, Irin and Irina warriors were powerful. Their discipline and magic were unmatched. Irina could take an enemy to the ground with their voice alone.

On the far side of the courtyard, Leo heard a door open. It was Niran, and he was alone. He walked to the center of the courtyard and waited.

Alyah stepped forward. As the only official warrior of the Bangkok house, it was her duty. Leo and Ginny fell in behind her, but not too close.

"May the light shine on your house," she said.

Niran put his hands together and nodded. "I do not know the proper Irin words, but you and your people are welcome."

His words said one thing, but his body language said another. Leo was reading Niran, and the Grigori was not pleased.

"We appreciate the welcome," Alyah said. "You've already met Leo, I know. He is of the Istanbul house. And this is Ginny, an Irina who resides locally."

"The American Sura met?" Niran greeted her as well. "You are also welcome."

Shockingly, he ignored Leo.

"Come," Niran said. "My brothers are serving tea in the garden. Join us so we can talk."

"It would be my pleasure," Alyah said.

Leo walked at the back as Niran guided them around the monastery walls and toward an open teahouse set in the middle of the garden. A long, low table surrounded by cushions sat under the shaded structure. Grigori in monks' robes walked to and from it, carrying trays and setting out dishes. The teahouse was surrounded by a massive garden. Vegetables grew along the edges with flowering plants surrounding the dining table.

"You have a beautiful home," he told Niran.

Niran said nothing, but he nodded.

They passed a gate to the left. Leo peered past it to see a path nearly concealed by thick bamboo. Moss-lined cobblestones disappeared into the hedge, which fronted a dense forest. Instinct told him that path led him to the guarded homes of the *kareshta* sisters. Perhaps they met in the evenings at the outdoor table, joining their brothers to partake of the evening meal, but none were there when Niran, Alyah, Ginny, and Leo arrived at the garden house.

They sat down on thick silk cushions and watched the Grigori pour tea.

Everything about their hosts' outward appearance told Leo they were Grigori. They had the perfectly symmetrical faces and bodies of angelic offspring. They were handsome and fit. They exuded a near intoxicating magnetism. He could see that both Alyah and Ginny noticed it.

But nothing in their manner said Grigori. They all wore the orange robes of a Buddhist monk. Their heads were shaved, and their bodies were covered to varying degrees by the intricate *Sak Yant* tattoos Leo had seen on Sura the night before. Lines of text down their shoulders and backs. Words and animal figures inked on their forearms. Many bore the tiger that Niran wore, but he also saw birds and lizards. A crocodile and a dragon. A mythical figure with four arms carrying swords. Each man seemed to have slightly different markings, much like Irin scribes.

"You have questions," Niran said.

"I do," Leo said. "If you are willing to answer them. Is Sura joining us?"

"He'll be here soon," Niran said. "Perhaps you might save your questions about *Sak Yant* for Sura." He turned to Alyah. "Any other questions the Bangkok scribe house has, I can answer."

"Would you share with us how you obtained freedom from the Fallen who sired you?" she asked.

"I can. My brother Sura planned our father's murder without my knowledge. He had been away from our father for many years, and our father had forgotten him as he was not considered a particularly adept warrior. He was too passive."

"Who was he?" Alyah asked. "My watcher would like his name for our records."

Niran hesitated, but only for a moment. "His name was Tenasserim."

The name wasn't familiar to Leo, but both Alyah and Ginny fell silent.

"Your brother's plan must have been very good," Alyah said, "to kill such a powerful Fallen."

"It was."

"We heard rumors that Tenasserim was dead, but we had no confirmation."

"It happened nearly thirteen years ago." Sura spoke from the edge of the garden.

Leo was surprised by the strength of Sura's hearing and wondered where Tenasserim's power had manifested. Every angel had particular gifts. Barak, Kyra's father, had been a listener. He'd been created to roam the heavens and the earth, acting as the ears of the Creator. Some of that preternatural hearing was passed to his offspring. It was possible Tenasserim's power was similar. Or it was possible Sura had excellent natural hearing.

Sura approached the table and bowed to them. "Forgive me. I was in the middle of performing a ritual on a brother."

"The *Sak Yant*?" Ginny asked.

"Indeed." He sat and folded his legs beneath him. "And we are complete. Five is better than four."

Alyah and Niran nodded.

"You were asking about our father," Sura continued. "He was very powerful. He also had very powerful enemies. I used those enemies to our advantage, informing my brothers Niran and Kanok of the plan only when it was already in progress." Sura smiled at the brother who poured him a steaming cup of tea. "Kanok died in the fight. Tenasserim was killed. That is all you need to know."

Niran said, "Sura wears his modesty like a robe. It was he who killed our father. Not rival Grigori. His hand was the only one with the strength of will."

"And yet our brother was killed," Sura said. "Let us not forget that."

Leo could see Sura blamed himself. "You freed your sisters," he said. "Your brother's sacrifice was a worthy one."

"I hope so."

Niran said, "There were six of them when our father died. One fell ill immediately after. She was already quite old, and Tenasserim never fed his daughters. She died shortly after he did."

Leo said, "What do you mean he didn't 'feed' his daughters? They weren't given any food?"

Sura and Niran exchanged a look.

"Our magic is not the same as yours," Niran said.

Sura said, "Five of our sisters were left. That was thirteen years ago. Now there are only four."

"There were almost three," Niran said.

Ginny asked, "What do you mean?"

"It was something I wanted to ask about last night," Sura said, "but we didn't have time. There were two Irin scribes some months ago who drove through the village on the road to Chiang Rai. They saw our sister Prija and tried to abduct her."

Ginny said, "Oh, hell no."

Sura quickly raised a hand. "I do not want to be ungenerous," he said. "It is possible they thought Prija was lost. She is not often lucid, and she can be quite dangerous if provoked."

Niran turned to Alyah. "She hurt them during the escape. She screamed and ran away, and the men appeared injured. They drove away, and we have not seen them again. But I need to know if the Bangkok house thinks it has the right to take our sisters."

"You will not have them," Sura said quietly. He looked around the garden. "All this, it is temporary. If there is any threat against them, we will be gone, and you will never find us. I eluded a Fallen angel for a hundred years. A company of Irin is nothing to me."

Alyah said, "Leo informed me of this incident two nights ago, and I will inquire about any scribes who came through this area when I return to Bangkok. Please know, we have no desire to take your sisters if they are safe. Our mandate regarding them is broad, but we respect family. If you are keeping them safe and they want to stay with you, then that is their right."

Leo glanced at Ginny and suspected she had something to share, but the Irina remained silent, sipping her tea and letting Alyah talk.

"If there is any training we can give them, we would be happy to do so," Alyah said. "That is why my watcher sent me and not one of my brothers."

Niran looked at Leo.

"He is here for his own reasons," Alyah said.

"I can guess what they are," Sura said. "She is leading meditation with Intira this morning. That is why Kyra isn't with us."

Niran's eyes were sharp; Leo felt them like blades.

"I would like the opportunity to speak with her when she finishes teaching," he said.

"What would an Irin scribe have to say to a *kareshta*?" Niran asked.

"That is for Kyra to hear," Leo said. "Not you."

Alyah was right. Niran wanted Kyra, but that was too damn bad in Leo's opinion.

He'd fallen for her first.

Sura walked with Leo through the bamboo forest, deeper into the trees where deep shadows sheltered them from the sweltering heat of the afternoon sun. The houses in the forest were raised on bamboo platforms, simple structures open to the trees around them. He saw one set of eyes in a window he passed. They looked young and curious. Leo smiled.

"Our sisters have been practicing with Kyra," Sura said, "but they are still new. I hope you are keeping your thoughts as peaceful as possible."

"I'm trying," Leo said. "I do have some practice with it. My watcher's mate is Grigori, and she has also struggled. I have a tune I hum when she's stressed." Leo smiled. "It's a Latvian lullaby. She claims it drives her crazy, but I know she likes it because she sings it to her babies."

Sura smiled. "I sing 'When You Wish upon a Star' in my head."

"That could get annoying too."

"It does." The voice spoke in English from the steps of the house they'd just passed.

Leo turned. Ah, there were the young eyes that'd been watching. He smiled at the cocky jut of the girl's chin.

"I'm Leo."

"I'm Intira."

The young *kareshta* girl Kyra said was so gifted. "I hear you are an excellent student."

"I am." She kicked her foot idly against the steps. "Only so I don't have to listen to Sura's bad singing though."

Leo burst into laughter and heard a door open in the distance. He turned in the direction of the sound.

Kyra.

"Intira, who…?" She fell silent when she saw Leo.

Kyra stood on the porch of her small cottage, her hair falling around her, wearing a flowing dress in a deep blue that matched the ocean. She looked like she'd just bathed. Her hair was damp and her face glowed.

Leo walked toward her, forgetting about Sura and Intira. Forgetting about Niran, Alyah, and Ginny. He forgot about his responsibilities, Max's warnings, and Kyra's many vicious brothers.

He saw Kyra and a door. And beyond that door, he saw privacy.

Leo strode up the steps and grabbed her hand. "We need to talk."

CHAPTER
NINE

B efore Kyra could object, Leo had spun her around, tugged her into the dim interior of her cottage, and slammed the door. She stood still, her mouth gaping, wondering what exactly had happened.

"I... Hello," she stammered. "I didn't know you were—"

"I have feelings for you," Leo said without preamble. "Strong feelings."

Her mouth fell open, but no words came out.

"I would like to talk about this," Leo continued. "Can we do that?"

Kyra had been raised in secrecy. Truth was suppressed and hidden. Thoughts were kept to oneself. If feelings existed, they were expressed in furtive glances and whispers. The goal of her life had been to remain as small as possible, as insignificant as she could be. Invisible.

Silent.

Leo's desire to speak openly about his feelings was both thrilling and terrifying. Everything about Leo was both thrilling and terrifying.

He put his hands on her shoulders and lowered his voice. "Kyra, please."

"I don't know how…," she started—cleared her throat—continued in a firmer voice. "I don't know—"

"We have known each other for several years," he said. "Every time I see you, this attraction—which is not merely physical—grows. I *want*, Kyra. I want to know you. I want to see you. I want more every time we're together, and yet you—"

"You need to let me speak," Kyra said quietly.

Leo opened his mouth again. Then closed it. He nodded, then led her to the low cushions in the corner of the cottage where a small table sat. There were bolstered wedges and pillows for sitting and eating. He arranged the cushions carefully, side by side, then paused. He looked at her, then at the room. She saw him evaluating it with the eyes of a soldier, noting the layout, the doors and windows. Then he bent over and rearranged the cushions, putting them at an angle so both their backs were against the wall.

Kyra realized Leo had rearranged the pillows so that both of them had equal access to the door.

To make her feel safe.

"I've never felt unsafe with you." She had to force the words through her mouth. Every word felt like stripping off skin.

He paused. "Even at the beginning?"

"No. Just… cautious. You were something new."

He led her to the cushions and waited for her to sit. Then he sat on the other side, folding his long legs under him.

"I'm very large," he said. "Damien says if I'm not thinking about it, I mow through a room like an enthusiastic tank."

Kyra smiled. "I've never felt mowed down."

"I'm glad."

Kyra felt like her heart must be audible. They were alone. Utterly alone. She heard nothing from the outside, could hear only faint signatures from deeper in the forest. *Be brave.* It had been her mantra for the past three years. If she could survive among the Grigori and the Fallen, she could survive anything.

Be brave.

"When I was young," she started, "scribes were things to fear. Our brothers would go out and not come back. We knew the scribes had killed them."

"Who is we?"

"My other sisters." She pushed past the feeling of exposure. These weren't secrets anymore. Telling these stories wasn't a betrayal. They were her past, not her present. "There were never many of us. The daughters. I wasn't close to the others, not as I am with Kostas."

"But you were afraid of scribes?"

"I was. Kostas wasn't. He knew what his brothers were—what he was. If he hadn't had me, I imagine he would have let your brothers kill him long ago. But... he did have me. And the others."

"He stays alive for them?"

"I think so." Kyra stared at the swaying palms outside her window. They caught the breeze, waving at her in encouragement. "When Kostas and I thought we were free, he worked so hard. He tied himself in knots just to be..." She looked at Leo. "Like you, I suppose."

"How?"

"Controlled. Not an animal."

"I don't think Grigori are animals." Leo caught himself. "I don't think that *anymore*. Now that I know the truth."

"But some of them are." She said it quietly. A truth none of them wanted to face. "Even Kostas did things he hated himself for. He stopped long ago, because he could see how his behavior affected me."

"You felt it?" Leo's eyes turned sharp.

"I felt his hunger. The demand of his need." How could she explain honestly without condemning those she loved? "Imagine your brothers with no mothers. No fathers who cared. Raising themselves with little or no guidance. Would they fight?"

Leo smiled. "Constantly."

"As my brothers did. As some still do. They take what they

want because the Fallen tell them the human world is their plunder. Their birthright. Grigori hunt humans because they can. And because we—all of us—are so desperately hungry." She felt her cheeks warm. "Not for food. You understand?"

"I understand." Two spots of red rode his cheeks. "Scribes also feel this hunger, even with the control our *talesm* give us. It's why we are stronger when we are mated."

"So you understand."

He reached for her hand and took it, enclosing it between his two large palms. Kyra let out a breath. The effect of Leo's touch was instant.

A torrent of images fell in her mind. Leo with his arms around her during the Battle of Vienna, his presence and touch the only armor against the violence surrounding them. His embrace in Rěkaves and the solid wall of his chest at her back. The kiss in the night market. The thrill and the peace of it. When Leo touched her, the voices stopped. She could hear him, clear and resonant, but his voice sang to her. It was like nothing else she'd heard. She'd hungered after peace for two hundred years. With Leo, she felt it. And she *craved* it.

"You're not afraid of me," Leo said, his lips flushed red. "But you avoid me."

"I'm not good for you," she said.

"I don't believe you." He pressed her hand to his chest. "I see your heart every time we meet. And your soul is beautiful, Kyra. Why—"

"It's not about my soul." The futility of her life enraged her. "I may be able to touch you, Leo, but I am not Irina. I don't have the magic they do. I don't have the spells. Don't you understand?"

"No!" His blue eyes were wide. "I *don't* understand. I don't care about how much magic you have. I try to get close to you, but every time we meet you leave. The minute the crisis passes, I look for you, but you—"

"I'm going to die." She pulled her hand away. "I may not look like it yet, Leo, but I am old."

He frowned. "You're no older than I am."

"You have no idea." She shook her head.

"So explain it to me," Leo said, his voice growing harder. "As far as I know, we are the same age. So explain why that is the reason you keep me at arm's length when I want to know you more."

She reached out and ran a finger along one of his tattoos, ignoring the subtle glow her touch created on his skin. It was so beautiful. Everything about him was beautiful. Every dark line was a mark he'd given himself. Each piece of magic on his skin grew from an ancient tradition she had no part in. The Irina may have said they wanted to help her, but not a single one trusted her enough to teach her the spell that would save her life.

"Which one does it?" she asked quietly. She traced a twisting line that led from his right wrist up to the tender skin at the crook of his elbow.

Leo's voice was rough. "What?"

"Which one prolongs your life?" she asked. She forced her eyes to meet his. "Which one makes you immortal? Which spell makes time stop?"

The dawning realization in his eyes gave her no satisfaction.

"No," he said.

"I've already lived far longer than any other *kareshta* I've known. I should have died decades ago, but Jaron was feeding Kostas and me his energy. Now he's gone, and—"

"No!" Leo shouted. "I don't know the Irina spell, but I know the Irin spell. I can draw it on you. If we mated—"

"For life?" She shook her head. "The Irin mate for life, Leo. That's not fair to you. And I won't—"

"Why not? I'm the one suggesting it."

She refused to let the tears come to her eyes. "How would we ever know? How could *you* ever know if I tied myself to you because of *you* or because you saved my life? What kind of mate would I be, never knowing if my feelings for you were because—"

"Bullshit." His lips firmed into a line. "Stop it, Kyra."

"You think I'm saying… *bullshit?*"

"I think you've had feelings for me from the beginning. Just like I've had feelings for you. When we were in Vienna, were you thinking about dying? When I held you and protected you, were you thinking about me giving you my magic so you could live longer?"

"Yes." She could hardly hear her own voice.

Leo's eyes widened. "What?"

"Of course I was," she said. "If you were dying and you wanted to live, what would you be thinking of? If mating with another would save your life, what would you be focused on, Leo?"

He didn't say a word.

"The *kareshta* have no power in this world," she said. "We walk around with a bleeding wound in our mind, at the mercy of the humans and Grigori around us. The Irin spells are a bandage a few of us have been given, but we don't own it. We don't own that magic. We don't have any *real* power. Do you think every one of the *kareshta* finding their way to scribe houses and mating with the Irin is looking for true love? They want to *live*, Leo. They want to be safe. The Irin can make them safe."

"So it was all about protecting yourself." His eyes were blank, staring at the cut frangipani on the table. "You let me touch you—hold you—because you wanted me to protect you?"

"Of course I did. Anyone would. I was vulnerable to every-thing then."

His eyes narrowed, looked up, and met hers. "And now?"

"What about now?"

"Now, Kyra." He shifted into her space. "Now, when you're not as vulnerable. Now, when I touch you. Are you thinking about me giving you my magic?"

Yes. No. "That's not all, but—"

"When I kissed you at the night market"—his head dipped and his lips hovered over hers—"you were thinking about my longevity spells?"

"No."

"Were you thinking about finding a protector?"

"No!" She could feel the heat of his lips on her own, but he did not touch her.

"I kissed you because I wanted you more than I've ever wanted a woman in my life. Because the thought of tasting you has haunted me for three years." His breath brushed her when he spoke, but Leo didn't move the inch forward that would have brought their lips together.

Kyra was frozen in place. "I wanted your kiss."

"Why?"

"Because I want you."

His hand reached up, and Leo wove his fingers in Kyra's hair, letting his wrist sit warmly on the nape of her neck. His lips still hovered over hers.

"How much did you want me?"

Every hair on her body stood at attention. "It was all I could think about. You're all I can think about. Even when I try to forget you, you come to my thoughts."

"That's how I know." Leo pressed his hand forward, bringing Kyra's lips to his own.

Madness and peace.

She sank into his kiss. It was gentler than the last time. Their mouths more familiar with their partner's. Leo's lips moved on her with hunger, but also with exquisite control. He drew away. Paused. Changed the angle of his mouth and took hers again. Everything was slow, deliberate, and maddening. She reached up, gripped his shoulders, and kissed him harder.

With a low growl, the dam broke. Leo reached over and hauled Kyra from her cushion onto his lap. He spread her legs and gripped her thighs, settling Kyra over his lap so his hand pressed to the small of her back, welding their bodies together. Her head swam from the searing kisses he pressed along her neck, the scrape of his teeth along her jaw.

Both her hands were on his cheeks. She could feel them, hot and flushed beneath her palms.

And in his touch…

Silence.

There was a low, resonant singing in the back of her mind, but all she could think about—all she could register—was Leo.

His arms hard around her. His lips meeting her own over and over and over. His hand twisted in the thick length of her hair. His massive body, rippling with muscle, between her thighs. She pressed her knees into his sides and he bit her lip.

Leo pulled away from their kiss, but his hands kept Kyra plastered to his chest. "We are going to try this. And it has nothing to do with you needing my magic."

"What?" She couldn't pull her eyes from his lips. They were flushed and full. She wanted to bite them and leave a mark.

"I understand everything you told me," Leo said, "and I'm making the decision to see what we might be together. Do you agree?"

"Yes."

He nipped her chin. "Don't try to make decisions for me again, Kyra. I may be inexperienced in some areas, but I'm not a boy."

She froze. "I didn't think you were a boy."

"When you decided that we couldn't be together because I would never know your true intentions regarding my magic, you treated me like a boy."

"That's not what I meant to do, Leo." She brushed a hand along his temple. "That's not what I wanted."

"I know when a woman wants me." His lips trailed down to her collarbone. "I see her lips flush. I see her eyes get hazy. Your heart"—he tasted the rapid pulse in her neck—"pounds when I'm nearby. It has nothing to do with my magic."

That depends on what magic you're talking about. Kyra's eyes rolled back when she felt him lick the delicate indent between her collarbones. Leo lapped at it, nuzzling kisses into the curve of her neck.

"What are you thinking of right now?" he whispered.

"You." Her hands twisted in his hair. "Just… you."

"Do you want me?"

She wanted him like it was a madness. Kyra had never experienced this kind of pleasure before. She couldn't even speak. She nodded, and Leo pressed his cheek against hers; she loved the rough texture of his stubble against her skin. Every nerve was on fire.

"I want you so much," he whispered. "But I don't want to rush."

"Okay."

"Have you ever…?"

She felt her cheeks flame. "No. Any kind of contact was too overwhelming."

"Mine?" His voice was sharp with concern.

She closed her eyes, dipped her head, and ran her lips along the column of muscle in his neck. "Your touch brings me nothing but pleasure."

"Good." Leo's shoulders relaxed. His hands drifted from the small of her back down to the top of her buttocks, caressing her over her thin dress.

Kyra shivered. The sensation was thrilling, but his iron-clad control soothed any nerves that threatened to riot. She felt utterly safe with Leo.

And nearly out of her skin with excitement.

"Do you want to try, Kyra?" Leo kept one hand caressing her bottom and the other reached up to cup her cheek. "I need to hear you, because the minute your brothers hear about this, they're probably going to try to assassinate me."

Kyra's eyes went wide. She tried to pull back, but Leo wouldn't let her.

"Which is fine," he added. "I'm not worried about them as long as you are willing."

She nodded.

"Speak." He smiled a little. "I need to hear the words."

"Yes." She leaned forward and pressed a kiss to his lips. "I want to try."

"And you're not going to run away without talking to me?"

She smiled. "No."

"And you're going to give me your phone number? The correct one, not a burner? Maybe even share your e-mail address?"

Her face was flaming. She ducked and pressed her face into his neck as he laughed.

"Yes?" he asked.

"Yes."

"Good." He continued caressing her over her dress. His hands were large and warm. His fingers were teasing. He trailed them over her shoulders where her sundress bared her skin. "This is all new to me too."

"Oh?" Kyra kept her eyes closed and her head on Leo's shoulder, luxuriating in his touch. When she sat on his lap, his height wasn't quite so intimidating. "You seem… far more comfortable doing all this."

"I've been thinking about it"—he leaned back, taking her with him so Kyra was draped over his chest—"for a long time."

"Waiting for the right Irina?" Kyra asked.

He said nothing, but his mind whispered to her, words so jumbled she couldn't discern where his thoughts ended and hers began.

Kyra sat up so she could see his expression. His gaze was tender. Painfully open.

"I think I was waiting for you," he said. His words, like so much of that day, were both thrilling and terrifying. But his smile was sweet and crooked. "I think you're going to need some time to get used to that idea."

"Leo—"

"That's fine," he said. "I have time." He kissed the tip of her nose. "And you will too. I promise."

Kyra's doubt must have shown in her eyes, because Leo continued.

"So many thoughts going on behind those beautiful eyes. Why won't you tell me?"

"I don't want to hurt you. Or dismiss your feelings."

"But?"

"You don't know me," she said. "Not really."

He paused before he spoke. "You're partly right. I don't know many things about you. But I know your heart for your sisters. Your dedication to your family. You intelligence and your talent." He drew her to his side and settled her in the crook of his arm. "I know that you're fierce even when you're afraid. That you protect those who are weaker than you even if it means sacrificing your own desires."

"You make me sound like a warrior."

"If there's one major failing of Irin men," Leo said, "it's that we don't recognize a truth our women have been trying to teach us for centuries: there are many different kinds of war. And many different kinds of warriors."

"But you're smarter than the average Irin man, I assume?"

"Oh, far smarter." He kissed the top of her head. "Which I will be happy to demonstrate in the future."

She tried to hide her smile but couldn't. "So generous."

"Another of my many fine qualities."

Kyra enjoyed the feeling of Leo's rumbling laughter in his chest. She also liked feeling tucked under his arm, but she didn't know what to do with her arms. Leo solved the problem by grabbing her hand and draping her arm across his hard abdomen. She could feel the layer of muscle under his shirt and wondered if Leo would allow her to touch it. She wanted to press her fingers into that muscle to see if it was as hard as it felt. She wanted her mouth on it too. Wanted her lips to feel the line of hair that ran below his belly button. She'd seen him with his shirt off, but now she had the driving urge to feel, to taste, to touch *everything*.

Then Kyra saw the rather large bulge in Leo's pants just below his waistband and decided to ask to touch his abdominal muscles at a later time. Secretly, she was excited to see his arousal. For the first time in her life, a man's desire didn't feel threatening or impersonal. Leo had said he liked *her*. Not just her appearance. His soul voice gave her no indication he was lying. If Leo was an honest person, Kyra needed to believe him.

Leo had picked up a book that was sitting in the corner. It was a bird-watching book, though she hadn't seen many birds in Thailand so far.

"Do you like books?" she asked.

"I do. I like audiobooks especially. When I'm training or driving, I often listen to them." He craned his neck and saw the stack of books by her bed. "I see you are a reader."

"Yes." He hadn't asked, but she decided to offer some information anyway. "For most of my life—before I learned to block my mind—books were my best friends. I could listen to them and only hear what they wanted to tell me, not another voice behind it."

Leo's arm around her tightened, and she wondered if there was something he didn't like about the story. Perhaps she shouldn't have offered so much information when he hadn't asked.

"Yes, I like books," she said quietly.

"I'm glad you had them," Leo said. "Tell me something else."

"Like what?"

"Like everything."

PRIJA 11

"He went right into her cottage!" Intira was almost jumping up and down. "He is so bold. Are all foreigners so bold?"

Prija raised an eyebrow and examined the loom where Bun Ma was teaching Intira to weave.

"I like him. He's funny."

He wasn't funny. Or that wasn't why she liked him. Intira was bright and curious. She hungered for new sights, new experiences, new people. She'd been bubbling over with news of the night market for days. She'd been talking about the people and the music. She couldn't believe how many different-colored dresses there were and how many foreigners. She'd be talking about the Irin scribe for a year if he stayed a day.

Intira stared out the window. "What do you think they're doing? Should we go over and say hello? He looked mad. But not mad."

Prija knocked on the floor to grab Intira's attention. The little girl didn't need to be thinking about what was going on between the two foreigners. It was none of their business, even though Prija had seen Niran's eyes. He'd *like* the moonfaced girl to be his business.

But Prija was wary of foreigners. One of the scribes who'd tried to take her had been foreign. His accent told her he was Chinese, but from far, far away. She had no idea why they'd tried to take her. She couldn't be useful to them. Why would they take her if she wasn't useful?

Having a scribe in the compound put Prija's nerves on edge. She didn't like their hard black tattoos, which were so much uglier than the delicate *Sak Yant* of her brothers. Sura's tattoos had animals and beautiful patterns. Scribe tattoos were like ugly black scribbles. Like a child would make. She didn't trust them. Didn't like them. She had no idea how the moonfaced girl could let one touch her with his ink-stained hands. For Prija's whole life, scribes had been the ones trying to kill her.

Niran and Sura told her that the Irin weren't their enemies now. That the scribes knew all Grigori weren't the same as the bad ones. Prija didn't have as much faith as her brothers, but she knew where to run and where to hide Intira if things became ugly. Prija could defend herself. Of that she had no doubt.

"Bun Ma says it's ugly." Intira sat in front of her loom.

Prija gave her a reproachful look.

"No, not ugly. She is too kind to say that. But she doesn't like it."

Bun Ma was a traditional girl. She didn't like any weaving patterns that weren't like those she'd been taught. She was an excellent weaver and a good sister, but she lacked imagination. Prija looked at the scattered pattern. They were stars. Or knives, perhaps. The pointed stars sat at angles to each other, riding the lines of red and gold Intira had woven with the cotton thread. It was an odd geometry. A pattern, no question, but not one that Prija could read.

"Do you see it?" Intira asked, her face glowing with excitement. "Bun Ma doesn't see it."

Prija doubted that anyone other than Intira saw meaning in the pattern. There was something… She frowned. It did remind her of something. There was a low humming in her mind, a vibration that tickled the base of her skull, but it teased her only a moment before it shot like needles to her temples.

She closed her eyes and put her hands over her face.

"Prija?"

She didn't like to worry her little sister, but she could barely stand the pain. It felt like claws ripping into her mind.

Kanok, where are you?

He'd been the only one who could heal her when the voices became too much. He'd been the only one whose touch pulled her back to sanity.

But Kanok was gone.

Small hands shoved a long wooden bow into her hand.

"Play," Intira said. "It will make you feel better if you can. Play something, Prija."

Prija kept her eyes closed, but she held the delicate neck of the *saw sam sai* on instinct. She put the bow to the strings and pulled a tentative note. It was scratching and flat. She pulled again.

"Keep going," Intira said.

She kept playing until the worst of the pain had passed. The music pulled it from her like string tugged from a deep pocket. The pain unfurled in the air and drifted out the window, escaping into the night sky.

CHAPTER

TEN

L eo's elation lasted until dinner that night. As soon as they walked into the garden holding hands, he saw it. He noticed the glances between Sura and Niran. Saw Ginny's unveiled curiosity and Alyah's blank expression.

"They will not like it," Kyra said. "Neither my people nor yours. *Kareshta* who decide to go with Irin men…"

"What?"

"People make assumptions." She kept her voice low. "That the *kareshta* are after something. That the Irin men are taking advantage."

"That has nothing to do with us," he said.

Kyra shrugged, but he could see her turning inward. "People will think what they think."

"Exactly." He wrapped his arm around her shoulders, leaned down, and kissed her full on the lips. "People will think what they want. And we will ignore them."

She offered him a smile, but it didn't reach her eyes. He saw the trepidation, and it made him want to rage. He decided that, for the night, he would ignore the pointed looks and unspoken curiosity of the people around them. But if it persisted past natural curiosity, he'd be breaking a few heads. Irin or Grigori, he didn't much care. Their stares had turned Kyra's earlier happiness to caution.

Damn them.

They sat next to each other at the low table where they had taken lunch earlier in the day.

Niran was the first to speak. "We didn't see you this afternoon, Kyra."

"No." She folded her hands on her lap. "I took the afternoon off to spend time with Leo."

Leo couldn't have been more proud of her if she'd stood on the table and shouted that she was his. Her voice never rose, but it never wavered either. He saw Sura smile in his direction and suspected they had at least one ally at the table.

"So!" Ginny was smiling. "How is this going to work?" She waved a finger between them. "I'm going to be nosy. I'll just warn you in advance."

Leo raised his eyebrows. "Didn't your parents have that conversation with you, Ginny?" Kyra squeaked beside him. Actually squeaked. "I'm sorry," Leo pretended he hadn't heard Kyra. "Maybe after dinner, Alyah and I can find a website for you. I'm pretty sure there are a few that might explain things, probably in more detail than you want."

Ginny laughed, but Alyah broke in with a serious voice. "You're different. It's not very sensible to ignore it. Your magic is different. Your lives—"

"Our lives are our business," Leo said. "But thank you for your concern, sister. I'm sure it comes from a sincere place."

Alyah lifted her hands and looked away, clearly not sharing Leo's opinion but unwilling to offer offense.

Kyra was a silent statue beside him. He took her hand and put it in his lap, playing with her fingers as the monks poured tea for the table and Niran and Sura's brothers served the food. There was fragrant rice and delicate curry. A whole fish coated in a thick layer of salt sat on a platter. Noodles with fresh vegetables were passed around the table, but the tension remained.

"Niran," Leo began. "I'd like—"

"I am not her brother." Niran stopped Leo before he could finish. "It is not my place to grant permission for you and Kyra to form any kind of attachment."

"Permission?" Kyra said quietly.

Leo didn't say a word.

"We are not seeking *permission* from anyone." She looked at Leo. "We're *not* seeking permission."

"I wasn't going to ask for it." Leo didn't smile, but he wanted to. His little warrior was angry.

"Good." Kyra turned to Niran. "Leo and I met over three years ago. While we may come from different places, our experiences have bonded us. I do not expect anyone to question the decisions we make for ourselves."

A muscle jumped in Niran's jaw and he looked away. Disapproval had nothing to do with Niran's attitude. He admired Kyra as well. He wanted her.

Too bad.

Kyra had chosen him.

"Am I still welcome as your guest?" Kyra asked. "Or should I find other accommodations while I am here?"

Niran's expression said he was not expecting the question.

Part of Leo wanted them to kick her out. He was imagining the large bed at his hotel in Chiang Mai, which would offer far more comfort than Kyra's simple cottage at the monastery.

It was a small part of him; he tried to ignore it.

"Of course you are our guest," Sura said into Niran's silence. "Nothing will change your welcome here when you have done so much for our sisters." Sura's eyes were pointed at Niran. "No matter what our personal feelings may be, your generosity is a debt we can never repay." He turned back to Leo and Kyra. "And I believe it is a beautiful thing when two souls meet and find connection. No matter where they come from."

Leo said, "Thank you, Sura."

"You are welcome." Sura raised his hands. "And now we eat."

Everyone dug into the food, even mischievous Intira, who joined them halfway through the meal. She sat next to Kyra, watching Kyra and Leo intently.

"I have heard from the Bangkok house," Alyah said later when the food had been taken away and fruit was laid on the table.

Intira was shooed off to play in the forest with two of the monks to guard her so the grown-ups could talk.

"They have questioned the brothers there extensively," Alyah continued, "and can find none who were in the area at the time of Prija's attempted abduction. So we may be dealing with travelers who misunderstood the situation."

Sura frowned. "Ginny, do you know of any scribes in Chiang Mai that the watcher in Bangkok might not know about?"

"Lots," Ginny said. "There are so many training gyms there. It's very popular, especially for younger scribes from America or Canada who were never placed in a proper academy. There is only one in the United States, for instance. It's on the East Coast, and it's very costly."

"You have to pay for the scribe academy there?" Leo asked.

"Yes."

He'd never heard of that before. "So scribes wanting further training in martial arts come all the way here?"

"Sometimes." Ginny shrugged. "It's not just the money. In the States, they'd be different. Odd. Their tattoos would be noticeable and asked about. Here, they're different and odd, but humans will usually dismiss it as foreign mannerisms and most people wouldn't ask about tattoos. Also, Thai people tend to be more conservative about casual touch." She pointedly looked at Kyra's hand where Leo was playing with it. "So scribes can avoid contact more easily."

"Our culture is more suited to Irin customs than American culture," Alyah said.

Ginny said, "You're just saying that because you hate it when I hug you."

Alyah allowed a small smile.

"Interesting," Leo said. "So regarding Prija, it could easily have been foreign scribes traveling through who didn't know or understand that Prija wasn't being exploited. That she was safe here. They must have known she had angelic blood, and they might have thought they were doing the right thing in trying to take her."

"Possibly."

Leo could tell from Sura and Niran's faces they were skeptical. Perhaps Leo was being too forgiving, but he could understand how the mix-up could happen. There wasn't enough guidance from the Elder Council on such things. The rules of this new world weren't clear.

"Either way," Alyah said. "What they did was not sanctioned by the Bangkok scribe house. I have explained the situation here, what you have been doing in Chiang Mai to secure the city, and our watcher is interested in further conversations to coordinate our activities."

Niran nodded. "Thank you. I'll talk to Sura privately and let you know what we decide is the best course for our family."

"Of course." Alyah nodded but didn't press for more.

Leo suspected the free Grigori of Chiang Mai and the Irin in Bangkok would be able to form an alliance to benefit them both. While Niran wasn't the easiest person to deal with, Alyah was more than diplomatic, and Sura's personality tended toward cooperation. The fact that the emissary from the scribe house was female instead of male probably helped, given past tensions between Grigori and scribes. Either way, it appeared that Leo's mission to Thailand was nearing completion.

But how long did Kyra expect to remain? And how would

Leo build her trust in him when he was thousands of miles away?

Leo, Alyah, and Ginny departed the temple that night with an invitation to return the next afternoon. They spent a quiet morning in Chiang Mai, drinking coffee by the river and talking about everything they'd learned, while Ginny gently teased him about Kyra and Alyah tried to change the subject. By the time they arrived back at the temple, Leo was jumping through his skin, he was so eager to see Kyra.

To his disappointment, she was teaching her meditation classes with the other *kareshta*. Alyah and Ginny went to find the class while Leo tamped down his impatience and accepted Niran's invitation to watch Sura perform a *Sak Yant* tattoo for one of his brothers.

Despite Niran's subtle antagonism, the process was utterly fascinating.

"What do you use for ink?" Leo asked Niran quietly as Sura inked the tattoo with a long bamboo stick with a metal point. The process was similar to Irin tattoos, though Leo used an ivory needle rather than a metal one.

"Normal human ink." Niran frowned and looked at Leo's *talesm*. "Why? What do you use?"

"We make our ink from ash." Leo didn't know if he was supposed to share the information with Grigori, but Sura had been open about their tattooing practice with him, so Leo didn't feel right being secretive.

"Interesting."

"I don't know if it's only tradition or if there is a magical element to it," Leo said. "But our sacred fires do hold power. I was healed from a heaven-forged blade by the sacred fire." He lifted his shirt to show Niran the scar where he'd been stabbed in Istanbul. "It still stings sometimes, but it doesn't make me weak." The scar itself was an ink-black jagged line that Leo had tattooed around to help the wound heal. It had been two years before he felt back to full strength after the injury.

"We don't tattoo around injuries."

"You might try. This tattooing is powerful," Leo said. "I can feel it."

"Day-to-day practice is where the power comes from," Niran said. "The tattoo is only a symbol of that."

"Don't discount the power of the tattoo," Leo said. "Your natural magic lies with the written word. It's the same magic that allows us to learn languages so quickly. Any written system speaks to us, even if it's human in origin. The fact that this practice is so old means it holds power. The words are in Sanskrit?"

"No, Pali. Older than Sanskrit, but I believe they are related."

"I believe you are correct."

The origins of *Sak Yant* were *very* interesting, in Leo's opinion. He'd spoken with Ava about the spells she'd learned from the Fallen, primarily from the trickster Vasu, and Azril, the angel of death, who was neither Fallen nor Forgiven. The spells she'd learned from both of them reminded Leo far more of Sanskrit than the Old Language of the Irin. Leo made a mental note to find a Pali scholar among the scribes in Thailand or India as soon as possible. It could be the Pali language was more closely related to the Old Language than any scribe had realized before.

"How many brothers do you have now?" Leo asked.

"Around fifty altogether," Niran said. "But not all of them live here."

"Your father was prolific."

"He was a bastard. And he *was* prolific. I'm only counting the sons who follow our path. There are more who have fled north. They're not allowed in our territory unless they're willing to follow Sura's and my rules."

"Similar to how Kostas operates then."

Niran nodded. "That's what Kyra said. I think Kostas and I would agree on many things."

Oh, I bet you would.

Leo ignored the jab at his relationship with Kyra. Niran had been a good host, and he was hardly to blame for being attracted to a woman like Kyra.

"When will Kyra be done teaching?" Leo asked.

A muscle jumped in Niran's jaw. "She usually teaches until dinnertime."

Leo smiled. "I'm so glad Sura invited us."

"Yes," Niran said. "I'm sure you are."

BUT SOMEHOW, DESPITE LEO'S BEST INTENTIONS, THEY NEVER seemed to find a minute alone. Kyra waved at Leo from a distance as Intira dragged her away to show her a new game before dinner. They sat beside each other during the meal, but both of them were peppered with questions on one topic or another.

As the hours passed, Leo's frustration grew.

"Come with me for walk," he said. "After the meal is finished. We'll walk in the forest."

Kyra smiled. "I would love to. But before we do that—"

"Kyra, do you have a moment?" Sura asked.

Leo squeezed her hand, then released her to talk with Sura.

Niran and Alyah remained at the table with two other free Grigori warriors, chatting about training regimens and discussing logistics for merging activities and improving communication between the houses.

Leo stood and wandered through the garden between the temple and the forest. It was clear night, and the moon was nearly full. The wind soughed through the bamboo, and Leo let

THE SILENT

his imagination run wild. He wanted to kiss Kyra in the shadows. Watch the silver moonlight touch her skin. He felt greedy with desire for her.

Ginny was sitting in the garden, smoking a thin cigarette and staring at the moon.

Leo walked out to her. "Those are bad for you."

She raised an eyebrow. "I know. Good thing I'm magic."

"True." He sat next to her on the bench. "Tell me your story."

She eyed him. "Are you always so cheerful and up-front?"

"I try to be. My cousin is the secretive one. There's only so much stealth allowed in one family, so I'm the optimist."

Ginny smiled. "I can see that."

"So?"

"My story?"

He nodded.

"Not very interesting." Her eyes told him different. "I live here. I'd like to say quietly, but it doesn't suit my personality. I didn't feel comfortable in America. The few Irina there tend to be very…"

"Conventional?"

"Yes." She took another drag on her cigarette. "So I came here. I keep to myself and avoid Bangkok. Chiang Mai is much more relaxed, and I can train with good fighters."

"Were you always a warrior?"

A flicker in her eyes. "No."

And that was that. There was clearly more to the story, but Leo wasn't going to get it out of her no matter how cheerful and up-front she found him.

But the conversation about convention gave him an idea. "I want to ask you a question. Please know that, despite having three new sisters in my house with whom I talk frequently, I am ignorant of most Irina magic."

She smiled at the corner of her mouth. "What makes you think we'd answer your questions if you asked, scribe?"

"Nothing." He raised his hands. "Obviously it's none of my concern." He glanced at Kyra. "Except when it is."

Ginny's eyes narrowed. "What's wrong?"

The reminder of Kyra's mortality felt like a punch to his solar plexus. "How old are you, sister?"

"Ah," Ginny said. "I think the more important question is, how old is she?"

"Too old. And she fears... She doesn't know how long she has. I know it frightens her."

"With good reason," Ginny said. "If *kareshta* are anything like Grigori, they don't have that much longer than humans without help from the Fallen. They don't age like humans do, but one day they'll just snuff out. Like they've got an expiration date or something. I've seen it happen. A Grigori fell to dust in front of my eyes without me lifting a finger. Weirdest thing I ever saw."

He stood—wanting to rage, to hit something—but then he sat again. There was nothing he could do to prevent it. Kyra was clearly not open to mating with him solely to save her life, even though Leo was willing. For some reason, he'd thought they'd have some warning. To hear Ginny say Kyra's life could be extinguished like a candle flame filled him with fear and anger.

"Will she know?" Leo asked.

"I don't have any idea. Maybe ask Sura or Niran? If you love her, why don't you just—?"

"She's not willing," he said. "Not right now. She's probably right. It's too early. She knows we mate for life, and she's not willing... I mean, we've known each other for three years, but we've only just—"

"She's not sure of her feelings," Ginny said. "Or yours." She nodded. "I can respect that."

"Can you?"

"Yes." Ginny tapped an ash off her cigarette into a small

brass ashtray. "It's better than rushing into something to save her life and then being miserable for eternity."

"I don't want her miserable. I don't want her trapped," Leo said. "But I do want her alive."

She tapped her finger on her knee. "I don't think your feelings are in question, are they?"

No. The rage-inducing thought of losing Kyra was enough to make Leo near-certain Kyra was his *reshon*. He didn't care that she wasn't Irina. Ava wasn't technically Irina either. The Creator wouldn't continue to set them in each other's path if they weren't. His touch wouldn't give her so much comfort and his voice wouldn't be so clear.

His heart wouldn't feel raw at the thought of her death if she wasn't meant to be his life.

"I don't want her coming to me out of obligation or fear," he said, his voice rough. "Is there anything you can do?"

Ginny pursed her lips. "I could sing some magic for her. It wouldn't be anything long term, but it would give her a boost. Give you two some time."

"Can you teach her the spells to use herself?"

Her eyes went wide. "What?"

"She's powerless, Ginny. The Irina teach the *kareshta* to shield their minds, but everything else? They're on their own. They have nothing."

"Leo, you're asking me to give Irina magic to Grigori sisters."

"I'm asking you to trust *Kyra*," he said through gritted teeth. "Are they our allies or not?"

"You tell me." Ginny's voice was brittle. "You tell me if they're our allies, Leo."

"I can't believe you're asking that. You know—"

"I know what?" Ginny stubbed out her cigarette in the grass. "I know… They say the right things. They have sympathetic stories. I'm open to listening. I'm open to believing they could be more."

"But you don't trust them?"

"You think I don't have reason to doubt?" Ginny asked. "Did you see your sisters slaughtered by Grigori? Have you seen whole families wiped out from their savagery? I've felt their blood spill hot on my hands after they raped and killed my sister, so *you tell me*. Should I give them magic that could make them even more powerful? I'm glad it's so easy for you to know."

Leo heard movement at the edge of the garden. Sura and Kyra stood near the pond, clearly having overheard Ginny's devastating words. Sura's eyes were wet with grief. Kyra's face was stricken.

Ginny stared at them, then she stood and walked toward the temple without a word.

"Kyra." Leo stood.

She was shaking her head. "It's not going to work. It's not fair for anyone, Leo. We can't ask them to accept—"

"We can!"

"No." She turned and walked toward the forest path.

Leo started after her, but Sura grabbed his arm. Leo was surprised at the iron grip of the smaller man.

"Wait," Sura said. "Think about what she's saying before you go to her."

Leo wrenched his arm away. "Do you think she's right?"

"No. I think union between Irin and Grigori brings healing. But healing can be painful."

Leo could still hear Ginny's footsteps on the gravel. He could hear Kyra walking through the bamboo.

"I'll try to talk to Ginny if you think it will help," Sura said quietly. "I don't want to cause her more grief."

"I don't know her well enough to know what is right. Perhaps you should talk to Alyah."

Sura nodded and walked toward the dining room.

Leo took a deep breath and headed toward the cottages. He wasn't willing to give up. Not when she was finally giving him a chance.

HE MARCHED TO HER COTTAGE AND PAUSED BEFORE HE KNOCKED. He didn't want to barge in like the tank his brothers joked about, but he wanted to take some action to make everything better. Fight something. Break something. Get everyone laughing. He was good at those things.

Leo knew this wasn't a problem that could be fixed that way. *Think about what she's saying before you go to her.*

Kyra had lived in secrecy, watching her brothers killed by those of Leo's kind, often after they had already turned away from preying on humans. By all rights, she should be terrified of him. Irin law had been black-and-white. Irin good. Grigori bad. There had never been any nuance allowed.

With good reason, from the Irin perspective. Grigori had slaughtered their families, wiping out eighty percent of their women and children in the Rending. Irin society had been torn apart for hundreds of years and was changing now only by increments. Layer upon layer of trust had to be rebuilt. Between Irin and Irina. Between free Grigori and wary scribes. And trust between free Grigori and Irina?

Did you see your sisters slaughtered by Grigori? Should I give them magic that could make them even more powerful?

Perhaps they were asking the impossible.

Frustrated, Leo turned and sat on the top step of Kyra's porch. He sat there, looking at the moon and feeling the weight of Kyra's sorrow in the back of his mind. He didn't know how he felt it, but he did. He could feel her pain. Feel her hopelessness.

He tangled his hands in his hair and gripped hard, wishing he could take her pain into his own body and knowing that every moment that ticked by could be her last.

The thought of it pushed him toward madness.

Her door opened, and Kyra came and sat beside him, being

careful not to touch. "You aren't shielding your thoughts very well."

"I have nothing to hide from you."

She drew in a long breath. "Leo, what were you asking Ginny?"

"To give you the spells you need to save your life." He paused, kept himself from looking at her. If he looked at her, he'd want to hold her, and he didn't think she wanted to be touched. "It seemed like a reasonable request at the time."

"Irina were targeted for centuries," Kyra said. "Hunted down. Forced into hiding. They have reasons for their secrets."

He let out a rueful laugh. "Trust you to be understanding about someone withholding magic that could save your life."

"It's not about me."

"It should be!" He couldn't help himself. Leo turned toward Kyra and cupped her cheeks in his big hands. She was so small. So delicate.

Like a fairy princess, Ava had once said.

"It should be about you," Leo whispered. "Because you're kind and wise and beautiful, inside and out. You deserve more than to have your life taken away just as you're beginning to really live."

Tears fell down her cheeks, and Leo's heart went to his throat as he brushed them away with his thumbs.

"It should be about you," he whispered. "Hasn't anyone told you that before? You deserve that. You deserve everything."

"Leo." She closed her eyes.

"Please don't stop looking at me," he said. He kissed her cheeks, felt her tears hot on his lips. "Please stay with me." He pressed his forehead to hers. "Be my mate, Kyra. Let me give you my magic. Let me give you everything."

"I can't," she said. "Not yet."

"Because you might be taking advantage of me?" He curled his fingers around her shoulders. "*Please* take advantage of me. I'm begging you."

Kyra let out a watery laugh and sniffed. She lifted a hand to Leo's cheek and let it rest there.

Leo let out a long breath, grateful that she hadn't pulled away but still frustrated at her stubborn sense of honor.

Even though it was one of the things he loved about her.

He loved her. Everything about her. It wasn't just about her being his *reshon*, even though he was nearly certain of it. He loved *her*. Her goodness and her loyalty. Her quiet determination and pride.

The words were on the tip of his tongue when he heard a child running toward them.

Leo let Kyra go and stood, sweeping his eyes through the trees. There was something about the panicked breath of a child that put every instinct on alert. He brushed a thumb over his *talesm prim* and activated his magic between one breath and the next. His heartbeat slowed and steadied. His eyes became sharper. His hearing keener. Power rippled over his skin like armor.

"There." Kyra stood next to him, pointing into the forest. "It's Intira. She's terrified. The others are already coming this way."

Leo bounded down the stairs and toward the sound of the frightened child crashing through the forest. He saw her stumble over a rock and caught her as she fell. "What's wrong?" he said, going to his knees. "Intira, what has happened?"

"It's Prija." Her face was dirty and tearstained. "They took Prija."

T error tore through Kyra at the girl's words.
They took Prija.
Anselm is gone.
Gina took some poison.
We don't know where Sana is.
Barak killed Lazlo.
Diman.
Jarrod.
The mothers. Gone.
The brothers. Gone.
Her sisters. Gone.
Gone gone gone.

Kyra fell back into the nightmare. Someone caught her arms, and there was shouting. Voices pounded against her mind. Scraping pain along her arms. The careful shields she'd built around her mind closed in on her and she was left with chaos. Intira's panic. Niran's spike of anger. An inky black flood of power rippling from Sura. The bright flash of Alyah and Ginny's magic like a flame in the darkness. Thoughts from every direction attacked her, and she felt herself falling inward.

And then…

Slemaa.

Two hands gripping her arms.

Slemaa, reshon.

A single voice, like a deep bell tolling in her mind.

Slemaa.

He enclosed her, lifted her. Kyra reached for him and pressed her face into his chest. She tightened her arm around his neck as he surrounded her. The silence gave way to white noise, which gave way to Leo's voice.

"Breathe, Kyra."

She took a deep breath and opened her eyes. Leo was carrying her toward the porch.

"Intira," she said.

"The others are with her."

"I collapsed?"

"I think her panic must have unraveled your shields. Everyone came running, and you collapsed when they got close. I can't imagine what all our thoughts were, but they must have overwhelmed you."

She nodded. "Someone needs to check on the other *kareshta.* They could be having similar reactions because of Intira's fear."

"Ginny is checking on them while Niran and Alyah try to find out what happened to Prija."

"Set me down, Leo."

"No. You're white as a sheet. I thought you'd hit your head when you—"

"Set me down." She wasn't panicked anymore.

He stopped. "Are you sure?"

She nodded. His touch had wiped her mind of the sudden rush of voices, and she knew she needed to try something. "Set me down and step away. Just for a minute."

Kyra could tell he didn't want to do it, but he slowly set her on her feet. She held on to his hand as she calmed her mind and opened her senses. She focused on the memory of Prija's voice. Not the silence of the woman, but the voice of her angry soul.

She closed her eyes, dropped Leo's hand, and listened.

In her mind's eye, Kyra soared into the night sky and over the forest, leaving the immediate voices in the background, white noise among the rustle of bamboo. She welcomed and sifted through the friendly cacophony of voices from the human village, veering away from it and searching for Prija's voice when she found nothing familiar close by. She ranged over the mountains and through the trees, the wind guiding and whispering to her as she searched.

This was why Barak had kept Kyra and Kostas together. Her father had been a Guardian of Heaven, the bearer of a Guardian's blade, and Kyra and Kostas were the strongest of his children, the most gifted when they listened for danger. When the twins held hands, Kyra's range was nearly as powerful as their father's had been. Alone, she could still hear for miles.

"What are you doing?" Leo's voice came to her as if he were talking from beneath the sea.

Kyra ignored him.

Voices of humanity. Voices she'd never understood. The same, everywhere in the world. Over hills. Through forests.

There.

Kyra focused on the familiar voice and tracked it.

Prija's soul was spiked with anger. She was headed north. Directly north. Her thoughts were blood-red and wavering on the edge of violence. Kyra tried to listen to the voices closest to her. One Irin. Two… Grigori?

What did it mean?

She opened her eyes and grabbed Leo's hand. The weight of silence made her head swim, and she took a deep breath. "Prija is with an Irin scribe and two Grigori. She's headed north. Fast enough that I think she must be in a car. She'll hurt them if we don't find her soon, and I doubt she'll stop with her attackers."

Leo's eyes went wide. "How can you hear that far?"

"My father was a cardinal angel," she said. "I am not without power of my own."

"I'm going to have more questions about that later, but for right now, we need to get back and let Niran and Sura know. Are you steady enough?"

She squeezed his hand and began reciting the spells Ava had taught her. Her battered walls clicked into place. The door she'd flung open in her mind eased shut. After a few moments, she nodded. "I'm fine."

His brilliant blue eyes were wide. "That is amazing."

"I'm sorry I collapsed before." She swallowed, trying to rid herself of the tightness in her throat. "Intira's voice was so panicked, and the memories…"

"Do you want to talk about it?"

"No." She could tell by the set of his mouth that the answer didn't please him. "Maybe… not now."

He nodded, and the tight set of his mouth eased. He was so open. So expressive. But he hid deep feelings behind that happy facade. She was beginning to see him now.

As they walked, Leo kept her hand in his, and Kyra remembered the words she'd heard from him when he held her, the voice of his mind that sang like a crystal bowl.

"Leo?"

"Hmm?"

"What does *slemaa* mean?"

He frowned. "*Slemaa*? It means peace."

"Peace." She smiled. "You were thinking that when you were carrying me."

He smiled. "That's not what I remember thinking, but I'm glad that's what you heard."

"And what does *reshon* mean?"

He stopped in his tracks. "What?"

"*Reshon*. Your voice was very, very clear, and you were thinking that too."

Leo's jaw dropped.

Kyra was adept at reading expressions, but she couldn't read his. The closest she could come was picturing a paper lantern glowing from the inside. She'd seen people lifting them into the air at the lantern festival in the city. That's what Leo's face reminded her of.

"What does it mean?" she whispered, her stomach in knots.

She didn't know what she was expecting, but it wasn't for the giant man to drop to his knees before her, kneeling on the forest floor. He took both her hands in his and pressed them to his forehead, whispering words in the Irin language she didn't understand. He pressed her palms to his face, and she felt tears on his cheeks.

"Leo, I don't understand."

He lifted his face, and she had no trouble interpreting his expression then.

Pure, incandescent joy. His smile lit the night.

"What does *reshon* mean, Leo?"

He rose before her, pressed her hands over his heart, and took her mouth in a fierce, radiant kiss. "We don't have time right now, but I'll explain later. I promise." He started jogging through the trees, Kyra forced to follow.

"That's not fair." She tried to keep up with him. "Leo, you need to tell me now."

He lifted her in his arms, picking up the pace as if she weighed nothing. "After we get your sister. I promise you."

LEO'S ELATION HAD BEEN TAMPED DOWN BY THE TIME THEY reached the others. Someone had cleared the dining table and a map spread across it. Alyah was talking on the phone in rapid Thai while Sura, Ginny, and Niran examined the map.

"Kyra found Prija," Leo said. "She listened for her and heard her."

"How?" Sura didn't look anything like a laid-back college kid anymore. His expression was blank, but Kyra could feel the slow-burning anger in him. She could even see his tattoos lighting up like Irin tattoos sometimes did. They had a silver tinge she'd never seen before.

"When I focus my mind, I can hear very far," Kyra said. "When I heard Prija, she was heading north. I'm almost sure she's in a car because she was going too fast to be walking."

Ginny looked at the map spread out on the table. "This road, maybe?"

Niran nodded. "If she's heading directly north, that would be the only path. It's a good road. Very clear. Winds through some small villages, but it's all paved."

"It'll take them straight into Burma," Ginny said. "How long?"

"Two, two and a half hours perhaps?" Sura said.

Niran asked, "Any reason why Irin would take Prija into Burma? You don't have any scribe houses there."

Ginny shook her head. "That whole area is controlled by Arindam."

Sura looked up. "You know of Arindam?"

Ginny said, "The Fallen who controls most of Myanmar? Of course we know about him. He's been making attacks into Irin-controlled areas of northern India. It's a huge problem."

Niran was staring at the map. "We don't have fast cars. They're taking the most direct route. There's no way to cut them off. I'll take the motorbikes with two others and see if I can catch up with them." He nodded to Sura. "Keep your phone on. I'll call if I find them."

"Wait!" Kyra said. "There were three of them. One Irin and two Grigori."

Every eye turned toward her.

"What?" Niran said.

"Only one Irin has her. There are two Grigori with him."

Sura said, "One Irin and two Grigori?"

Everyone was silent for a moment.

"It doesn't matter," Niran said. "We have to go after her. We won't go into Burma, but until they reach Arindam's territory, they're fair game." He nodded at two of his men. "Let's go."

"I'll go with you," Leo said.

"You don't know the roads and you'll slow us down." Niran was nearly out the door. "Stay with Sura and protect the temple."

Leo looked like he wanted to argue, but he nodded.

Ginny asked, "Leo, do you know of any other Irin who are looking to cooperate with Grigori?"

"No," he said. "Or not in this area. There are smaller-scale alliances being made in Europe. One that I know of in South America and two that already exist in sub-Saharan Africa. But in Asia, our meeting is the first I've heard of." He pulled out his phone. "This warrants a call to Damien and Sari. If there are any other rumored alliances among the council, they'll know."

Kyra noticed Ginny staring at the map. "What are you thinking?"

"We knew." Ginny looked up. "We've always known. There are Irin who work with Grigori. There has to be. It never made sense otherwise."

Sura asked, "What didn't make sense?"

Alyah walked back to the table. "How we were so thoroughly betrayed. How our retreats were compromised. How our hiding places were found. It wasn't just the Rending, you know. It's been happening for years." Her face was bleak. "Anytime we found a safe place, it would be compromised. Who were *we* telling? Not the Grigori."

"But word got out to our brothers," Ginny said. "To the scribe houses. To the council."

"And then word got to the Fallen and the Grigori eventually," Alyah said. "And we'd be hunted and killed."

Ginny placed a hand on Alyah's shoulder.

Sura said, "I am sorry that happened. No one should have to live in fear."

"One Irin, two Grigori," Ginny muttered. "Arindam's children?"

"Most likely," Sura said. "They are the only ones who would dare come this close to us. Most of the Grigori we find in Chiang Mai—"

"Are wanderers," Ginny said. "I know. That's what I've observed too."

"We need to find out who tried to grab Prija the last time," Alyah said. "If they're not working with Grigori themselves, then they told someone who is."

Kyra said, "Can you call your watcher in Bangkok? Is there any way of knowing?"

"Yeah, there is." Ginny walked to the door. "Tell Leo I'm taking his car."

"But he'll have no way of getting back to the city," Kyra said.

Ginny offered a droll look. "You really think he was going back to the city with you here?" She slipped out the door, leaving Alyah, Sura, and Kyra in the dining room, a giant map on the table and Sura's quiet rage permeating the room.

Kyra walked to him and put her hands on his shoulders. "*Slemaa.*"

At once, his shoulders relaxed.

Alyah's eyes went wide. "Where did you learn that?"

"I heard it in Leo's mind when he carried me," Kyra said. "He said it means peace. I was just trying to comfort Sura."

Sura squeezed her hand. "It worked. Thank you, sister."

Alyah fell quiet, and Kyra knew the Irina probably didn't approve of Kyra using the Irin language. She hadn't thought about it. It had been instinctual. She had felt Sura's anger overwhelming the quiet man, and she'd wanted to help.

In a blink, a dark man appeared before her, leaning his elbows on the dining room table, staring at Kyra.

"Such familiar energy I feel on the wind," the dark one said. "Hello, Barak's daughter."

The Fallen smiled, and Kyra screamed.

"HE IS NOT ALLOWED TO BE HERE!" ALYAH SAID, HER SILVER blades drawn on the Fallen angel sitting at the dining table.

Leo stood between the Fallen and the rest of them, his hands up. "He's not an enemy! Not... precisely."

"I don't need you to defend me," the angel said. He was picking at the fruit on the table. "Do you have any sticky rice? I love sticky rice."

Kyra stared at him. "Who are you?"

"I'm Vasu. I felt you when you went looking for the other one," he said. "You're Barak's daughter."

"How do you know that?"

"His power was distinctive," Vasu said. "Can anyone find out about the sticky rice?" His eyes darted up to Sura. "You're not what you seem. You're interesting."

"I don't consider that a compliment coming from a Fallen," Sura said quietly.

Vasu cocked his head, reminding Kyra of a curious bird. The Fallen had taken the form of a tall, handsome man with Northern Indian features. His skin was the color of cinnamon and his eyes were a vivid gold rimmed with black lashes. His lips were full and sensuous, and his hair was streaked black and amber. The angel exuded an erotic allure that was alien to Kyra, but there was something innately familiar about him at the same time.

Vasu's eyes turned toward her. "You remember me."

"I don't think so."

"I am a friend of your father's. I was with him often when you were young, but I was likely in a different form."

"My father is dead."

"No." Vasu shook his head. "We don't die, you see. Barak is merely... returned."

"Is that supposed to comfort me?"

Vasu frowned. "Why would I want to comfort you?"

Leo said, "Put your daggers away, Alyah. You won't be able to kill him anyway."

"That's true," Vasu said.

Leo spun and faced the angel. "You're not helping."

"Again, why would I want to help?"

"Why are you here, Vasu?" Leo asked.

Vasu nodded at Kyra. "Because of her."

"What?" Kyra asked. "Why?"

"You're surprisingly powerful. I no longer wonder why he had such patience with you and your brother."

Fear stabbed Kyra's heart. "What do you know of my brother?"

Vasu waved a hand and continued picking at the fruit. "I don't care about your brother. But why are you here?"

"Why are you?"

Vasu rolled his eyes. "We're going in circles. This is boring. Maybe I will go."

"Wait," Leo said. "What do you know about Arindam?"

The flare of anger was fast and frightening. In the blink of an eye, the lazy man with hooded eyes vanished, and in his place, a giant of seven feet appeared. Every trace of humanity was gone from Vasu's visage. His eyes flashed, and the air around the table heated.

This, Kyra realized, was a hint of the angel's true power.

Alyah drew her blades again, but Vasu flicked his wrist and they flew from her hands, sinking into a palm tree bordering the garden.

"Why do you ask about Arindam?" Vasu said, his voice low and lethal.

Sura stepped forward. "Because he has taken one of my sisters."

Vasu looked at Kyra. "Is this true, Barak's daughter?"

"We think so. That was the *kareshta* I was looking for when you... heard me."

"I felt you." Vasu's form became more stable, but he didn't shrink. "Why would Arindam take your sister? Is she powerful?"

"Yes," Sura said. "But very uncontrolled. She can be quite violent."

"He admires that," Vasu said. "Did he take her himself?"

"No. His sons did."

Vasu shrank back to his tall but still human-sized form. "Then she is probably an offering. Once he has her, he won't give her back. But you might be able to trade her for another sister if there is one you like less."

Kyra gaped at Vasu. "She's the daughter of an angel."

Vasu shrugged. "I'm not saying I'd want her. But these Grigori slew their father, did they not?"

Sura said, "Yes."

"Then he's not violating anyone's territory. If his sons want to collect *kareshta* from other angels, then I doubt Arindam would stop them."

Leo was fuming. "Jaron said there were prohibitions against things like this. That the Fallen wouldn't take other angels' daughters."

"Not to *mate* with her." Vasu shuddered. "Most of us considered Volund quite aberrant in that regard."

"So why—"

"You said she was powerful. He probably wants some talent she has."

Niran and Sura were both deadly quiet.

Sura finally spoke. "Prija is too uncontrolled for anything but rage."

"Liar."

"It's true," Niran said. "She takes after our father in that way."

"Does she?" Vasu's eyes gleamed. "It all becomes clear."

Leo said, "Explain."

Vasu sat back at the table. "If you want me to explain, get me sticky rice."

Kyra said, "Are you a child?"

Another blink, and a beautiful child sat on the bench, swinging his legs. "When I want to be."

Kyra shook her head and turned away. "Come on." She put a hand on Sura's arm. "Let's get him some sticky rice so he'll stop speaking in riddles."

Sura said, "Why do I get the feeling that will probably never happen?"

CHAPTER

TWELVE

L eo watched the child eating the mango sticky rice. As
     Vasu ate, he grew. And grew. Until the man who had
     first appeared sat before them again, licking sweet
coconut milk from his fingers.

"That was delicious."

"Talk," Leo said.

"You used to be more amusing," Vasu said. "Though I see a
slight glow around you, scribe." His eyes darted to Kyra. "Does
she know yet?"

Kyra said, "Know what?"

"I'll tell you later," Leo said. "Tell us why Arindam would
want an uncontrollable *kareshta.*"

Vasu turned to Sura. "Was she young?"

"One of the younger ones, yes. Around forty years, but she
looks much younger."

"And she's powerful?"

"Yes."

"How? Her voice?"

Sura said nothing.

"But she doesn't speak, does she?" Vasu asked. "She can
wound the mind in other ways."

"If she's angry enough," Kyra said.

Alyah sucked in a breath. "What? She doesn't need to speak to use magic? That's unheard of."

"Well, you've heard of it now," Kyra said. "Half our blood comes directly from the angels. Did you think we had no power of our own? It's not having the power, it's controlling it."

Vasu turned to Kyra. "She hurt you."

"Yes."

"Then why do you care about helping her?"

Kyra said, "Because I was her once."

Vasu shook his head. "You were never her."

Kyra paused. "No, I suppose not. Because I had my brother Kostas. But Prija has brothers too. Sisters who care about her. It's not always about a person's usefulness or threat level, Vasu. Sometimes you just care."

"You and your brother were very powerful. Barak spoke of it often."

"He despised us."

"No," Vasu said. "You're wrong. Also, you should know your father would be very pleased with you and this scribe. He was... fond. I think that is the closest word."

Leo asked, "What are you talking about?"

Alyah's phone rang. She picked it up and walked away from the table.

Vasu turned back to Sura. "Your father was skilled in mental combat, even from a distance. It's why he retained power for so long, even though he wasn't as old as many of his enemies. Including *me*. It's why you and your brothers can exist as peacefully as you do. It's why your sisters are such bright stars. This sister who has been taken is powerful, and Arindam wants to use her as a weapon. He is trying to expand his territory now that Tenasserim is gone. Thank you, by the way. I found your father very annoying."

"You're... welcome?" Sura looked confused. A common problem with Vasu in Leo's experience.

"So now that Tenasserim is gone," Leo asked, "Arindam is looking to expand into Thailand?"

Vasu said, "No, the Irin are too powerful here. Anurak and his mate rule in Bangkok, and now they've made an alliance with these Grigori. He's not interested in going east. He's looking west."

"Is Arindam expanding into *your* territory?"

Vasu's eyes cut to Leo, but Leo did his best to appear innocent.

"That doesn't work with me," Vasu said.

"I don't know what you're talking about."

Leo knew exactly what he was talking about. He also knew —or he suspected—why the mention of Arindam's name had provoked such a reaction in Vasu earlier. Ginny had said Arindam was making attacks in northern India. According to Ava, who knew Vasu as well as any of them did, Vasu made his home in an ancient city in Rajasthan, which was northwestern India. It was likely that Vasu, who didn't have many sons after years in hiding, was feeling the pressure of an enemy near his territory.

"That was Niran." Alyah walked back to the dining table. "They rode up to the border, but they couldn't find any trace of them."

Kyra shook her head. "They should have taken me with them."

"No, they shouldn't have," Leo said.

"Don't be overprotective," she said. "You're not my brother."

"No, I'm your..." He shut his mouth. It wasn't the time. Not with a Fallen angel and an audience. "They wanted to ride as fast as possible. I'm sure that's all they were thinking."

Sura said, "They won't go into Burma without more people. Once you go that far north, Arindam's Grigori are everywhere."

"So what are we going to do?" Kyra said. "We need to get Prija back."

"We will," Sura said, "but it's better to be prepared than fast. Don't forget, Prija can defend herself. Like the Fallen said, they want to use her as a weapon. They won't harm her."

Vasu pointed at Sura. "He has a plan. They both do."

Leo asked, "What is he talking about?"

Sura sat at the table and folded his hands. "We'll wait for Niran."

Vasu rested his chin on his hand. "Boring."

"I don't care."

Vasu disappeared.

Everyone froze, but the Fallen didn't reappear. Not even when Kyra reached over and took the bowl of sticky rice.

"Vasu?"

Nothing.

"Huh," she said. "I guess he'll come back when it gets interesting again?"

Leo said, "With Vasu, you never know."

Alyah said, "My country was boring until you came to it, Leo. Tell me why I shouldn't put you on a plane and send you far, far away."

"Because I think I know what Vasu was talking about." Leo looked at Sura. "And so does he."

"When we killed our father, we didn't do it alone," Niran said. "There was no way we could have managed it. We had help."

The two Grigori brothers, Alyah, Leo, and Kyra were sitting at the dining table again, the map still spread in front of them. Niran looked exhausted and angry. He'd ridden for two and a half hours, up to the Burmese border, trolling through the villages and side roads for an hour in the middle of the night before he returned. There was no sign of Prija or her captors. Niran was certain they'd crossed into Arindam's territory.

Leo said, "Sura said he used his father's enemies in the plan to kill him. Were they Arindam's sons?"

Niran hesitated, then nodded.

"I am the one who made the connection," Sura said. "I'd performed *Sak Yant* on several of them. I was living away from our father in the mountains along the border. There were like-minded Grigori there, trying to live quietly. After some time, trust built between us. We knew we would never be free if our fathers lived. As long as they ignored us, we could live as we wanted. But the minute our fathers called us, we would come." Sura's face was bleak at the memory. "We would answer their call and do whatever they asked."

"We had no choice then," Niran said.

Sura lifted his eyes. "We made a plan to free ourselves. First we would kill Tenasserim. Then we would kill Arindam.

"But it didn't work out that way."

"No. Our brother Kanok had become close to Intira's mother when she was pregnant. Though she was human, he developed strong feelings for her. Intira's mother survived her birth, but Tenasserim called for her too quickly after the baby was born. She did not survive more than a month." Sura's face filled with sorrow. "She was a bright woman. A student at the university in Chiang Mai, but she was enamored of our father, as all the human women were. Kanok was devastated when she died. He could speak of nothing but killing our father. Prija helped him. She spoke then. They plotted to kill Tenasserim and only told us a few hours before they moved. We were able to call a few of Arindam's sons who were close, but we didn't have many. Prija engaged our father while the three of us attacked him."

"Arindam's sons held off our brothers as well as they could, but two of them were killed," Niran said. "Sura and I survived, but Kanok did not. Prija was in a coma for a year. When she woke, she didn't speak anymore."

Leo said, "And Arindam's sons lost the taste for rebellion."

Niran nodded. "They decided that they could not bear the losses to their number, even if it meant staying under their father's rule."

"You cannot discount that Arindam has always been more generous with his offspring than Tenasserim was," Sura said. "Many of their number are hundreds of years old because their father feeds them power."

Alyah said, "So they'd rather live longer, even though they serve a Fallen master?"

"It's easy to judge them," Kyra said, "if you don't fear sudden death."

Leo heard the brittle pain in her words. He reached for her hand and brought it to his lap. He wanted to steal Kyra away and perform the mating ritual immediately, but that would mean explaining how he knew they were *reshon*.

It wasn't a conversation he wanted to rush, but fear for her life tormented him. He also didn't want to raid a Fallen compound weak from the mating ritual, but he'd do what he needed to keep Kyra alive.

"Arindam's sons returned to him, and because of my tattoos on their bodies, they are more powerful," Sura said. "We knew it was a risk, but we trusted them. That trust was misplaced."

Leo nodded. "Do you know where their compound is?"

"There are several where they could keep Prija among their own sisters." Niran marked three locations on the map. "There are very few *kareshta* among Arindam's children, but here is where he keeps them. I would guess they would take Prija to one of these places."

"How far are they from the border?" Kyra asked.

"The first is around one hundred kilometers into the country. The others are deeper in."

"I'll be able to read the first one before we cross," Kyra said. "I should be able to give you an idea of what you'll be facing."

Sura nodded. "Then you'll come with us. Leo, can I assume that means you will too?"

"Of course," Leo said. "Keeping the *kareshta* safe is within the mandate of every scribe. I am happy to help in the search for Prija. Plus we need to find out the identity of the Irin who is working with them."

"Agreed," Alyah said. "I have just spoken to Dara. With your permission, she would like to assist. She can have five warriors here in the morning if you wish."

"I think stealth is our friend," Niran said. "With Sura and me, two of my men, Leo, Kyra, and you, that is already seven. Any more than that and I think we risk attracting too much attention."

"Agreed," Leo said. "But perhaps some Irin scribes and singers would be able to help keep watch over the temple while you are gone? That would allow you and Sura to focus on finding Prija without worrying about your sisters' safety."

It would also be a startling act of trust, and Leo doubted Niran would agree to it. He was surprised when the suspicious Grigori spoke directly to Alyah.

Niran said, "Do you guarantee that my sisters will be safe with these men? That they will do nothing to expose them or take them from their home here?"

Alyah said, "I give you my word. I will choose the scribes myself. Dara will listen to my suggestions. If you want only trained singers here, that is also possible."

"And Ginny would help," Sura said. "I'll call her once we have a plan."

Niran stared at Alyah for a long minute before he nodded. "Then I accept your help in guarding our sisters. My men will remain in authority here, but we will take your offer."

"Understood," Alyah said. "Thank you for your trust."

Niran said nothing else, but his eyes returned to the map. "The longer we wait, the farther they can take her."

"Where is Arindam himself?" Leo asked.

"He moves." Sura gestured over the map. "I can think of half a dozen secluded places he might hide."

Leo shook his head. "I know nothing about Myanmar, so I don't know how much help I'll be."

"We'll plan everything." Niran glanced at Kyra. "You take care of our radar system."

SHE LOOKED EXHAUSTED. HER EYELIDS WERE DROOPING, AND there were dark circles under her eyes. Leo picked her up halfway through the forest and carried her to the cottage.

"I can walk," she protested even as she laid her head on his shoulder.

"But why would you when I can carry you so easily?"

"Leo…"

"Hmm?"

She yawned. "I don't remember what I was going to say."

"I'm going to stay with you tonight," he said. "I can sleep on the floor. Or if you don't want me in the cottage, I can sleep on the porch."

"That doesn't sound comfortable."

Leo smiled. "I've slept in worse places. Trust me."

She paused, and Leo thought she might have fallen asleep.

"My bed is big enough for both of us," she said quietly. "But… just for sleep."

"Whatever you want, *ana sepora.*" His heart sang. He'd be able to hold her as she slept.

"That's Irin language. I recognized the sounds. What does it mean?"

"My bird." He kissed the top of her head. "Because I want to watch you fly."

"Leo..."

"Hmm?"

Kyra had fallen asleep.

Leo sang a low song as he walked through the forest. It was a song of thanksgiving, the same song he'd sung kneeling before her when he realized that Kyra was truly his *reshon*.

"And what does reshon *mean?"*

"What?"

"Reshon. Your voice was very, very clear..."

Kyra was his *reshon*. A soul created to match his own. A gift of heaven and the truest mate in every sense. Her soul would feed his own. His touch would soothe her, and his voice would resonate the most clearly in her mind. Always—for the rest of his life—she would be his other half.

Profound gratitude filled his heart, and a prayer fell from his lips in the Old Language:

"I give thanks to the Creator
For in my heart I have found
The other half of my being
My search is over
My soul is complete."

Leo walked through the silent forest, nodding at each of the Grigori who stood watch among the *kareshta* cottages. Clad in deep saffron robes, Niran's men looked like monks and bore the intricate *Sak Yant* tattoo marks Sura had given them. But every face, no matter how calm, had the determined look of a warrior.

He climbed Kyra's steps and opened her door, toeing off his shoes before he entered. A lamp was burning in the corner of the room, and Kyra's eyes flickered open when he closed the door behind them.

She murmured, "We're back."

"And you're exhausted," he said. "But do you want to clean up before you get in bed? I can get water."

"My feet…" She wrinkled her nose. "There's water in the corner."

Leo set her down on the bed and took off her sandals. Her feet were dusty from the dirt and gravel paths through the temple and the forest, so he walked to the corner and poured some water into the large bowl on the nightstand. He took it to her, then placed her feet in the cool water.

"What are you doing?"

"Washing your feet."

Her cheeks turned delightfully red. "You don't have to do that."

"I want to."

Leo brought the pitcher to the side of her bed along with a lump of fragrant soap and a towel he found hanging in the corner.

"Pull up your dress," he said, kneeling at her feet. "Just a little."

Kyra slowly pulled the sundress up to her knees, baring her ankles and calves to his gaze. Leo's pulse picked up and he hardened, but he ignored his reaction and poured the water over her legs, following the path of the clear liquid as it ran over her shapely calves, caressed her ankles, and fell quietly into the ceramic basin. He picked up the soap and dipped it in the water, lifting his eyes to hers as he ran his hands up and down her legs, washing the dust and grime of the day from her skin.

Kyra said nothing, but her lips were flushed. Her breasts rose and fell with each breath as she watched him. Leo took his time, running the soap over every inch of her skin, slipping his fingers behind her knees to ease her foot up before he traced the lines of her legs down her shins and around her ankles. He stroked the arch of her foot, and her toes curled in his palm before he washed them too. He massaged her ankles and her calves, easing the tension from the muscle there with long strokes.

Her skin was soft and smelled of jasmine. The oil in the soap shimmered on the surface of the water as he tipped the water pitcher over her legs again, rinsing the suds from her skin before he lifted each foot and dried it with the soft towel. He pushed the basin to the side and placed her clean feet on his thighs before he closed his eyes. He put his forehead to her knees and kissed her skin, hugging her legs to his chest.

"Leo, you—"

"Shh." His breath warmed her knees. "This is enough."

"I want to wash you too," she said quietly.

Erotic images bombarded his mind. He wanted to bite her knees and kiss the soft skin of her inner thighs. He wanted to spread her legs and search for the lush scent that tormented him. He wanted to cover her with his body, invade her heat, and find release. He imagined Kyra wet and naked, pouring water over him in the bath. He would circle her waist with his hands, lick at her belly, dip his tongue…

His erection was so hard it was painful.

"Not tonight," he said, his voice grating in the silence.

Leo stood and lifted Kyra's legs over and onto the bed. "Do you need to change?"

She nodded. "My nightgown is hanging on the peg by the washstand."

He walked over and retrieved it for her, trying not to envy the cool cotton fabric that would touch her skin. He handed her the gown, then went behind the screen in the corner, facing the wall as he heard her change from her dress to her nightclothes.

"I'm changed."

He walked back toward the bed and sat on the edge, forcing his thoughts to remain on the mundane. He took off his socks and placed them at the end of the bed. He removed his shirt; he would need to borrow one in the morning if anything could be found big enough for him. His pants... were definitely staying on.

Kyra was lying on her side with the bedspread pulled over her, watching him as he undressed. Leo blew out the lamp and decided sleeping on top of the bedspread was probably a good idea. In the darkness, her eyes fell to his chest and the dark tattoos that covered his arms and shoulders.

"So many," she said.

"Call me an overachiever," he said. He scooted up next to her and put his head on the pillow. "You're certain you're comfortable with me sleeping on the bed?"

"Yes." She lifted a hand, then let it drop. "You make me feel safe, Leo. You always have."

Leo took her hand in his. "Did you want to touch?"

Kyra's cheeks went red again, but she nodded.

Leo placed her palm over his heart. "Touch anywhere."

Her eyes went wide. "Anywhere?"

Oh, heaven give him self-control. He folded his hands behind his head and breathed deeply, the muscles of his chest hard under Kyra's hand. "Anywhere you want," he said. "Anything you want. Touch me, Kyra. I'm yours."

CHAPTER

THIRTEEN

He'd presented her with a banquet and commanded her to feast.

Kyra was wide awake now. It had started when he knelt before her and washed her feet. Who knew washing feet could be so seductive? Every moment of self-control, every evidence of restraint only teased her further. Ratcheted up her own need.

Kyra felt the tension in Leo's muscles rippling under her palm and knew he was practicing the most ardent discipline. His eyes were closed, but his lips were deep red and swollen. She remembered how they kissed her skin when he was washing her. Shifting a little, she leaned over and pressed her lips to his shoulder. His skin came alive under her hand and her lips. He drew her energy into his body, drinking it like a parched desert soaked up rain.

He breathed out her name. "Kyra."

"Leo." Her mouth moved from his shoulder to his collarbone as her hand traveled south to the defined abdominal muscles she'd been thinking about. She traced each one individually, and he didn't try to muffle his groan.

"Is it too much?" she asked.

"More." He turned his face to hers, and his self-restraint slipped. He reached a hand behind her head and pulled her into a hard kiss, devouring her mouth with his own, biting at her lower lip, sucking her tongue into his mouth, shifting so that her hand was pressed between their bodies on the bed. The gold hair trailing down his belly called her, and the black tattoos covering his body began to glow with a silver light. She ran her fingers up and down his belly as she swallowed the moans Leo poured into her mouth.

"Kyra, Kyra, Kyra," he panted.

"Too much?"

"More."

"Are you sure?"

His laugh was tortured. "You can do anything you want to me."

His kisses made her bold. She slipped one arm under his neck and pulled him harder into their kiss while her other hand searched for the hard rock of the erection she felt pressing against her thigh. He was so tall. So powerful. To know she commanded his body like this made her head swim.

"I want to touch you," she said, tracing his erection over his pants. "May I?"

Leo was in the throes of pain. Or pleasure. It looked very similar to her.

"Leo—"

"This was not what I intended when I offered to sleep with you," he whispered, his eyes pressed closed.

Kyra began to pull her hand away, but he grabbed it and kept it over his pants.

"That's not a complaint or an objection. But that's not why I got in bed with you. You need to know that."

"I want to… explore," she whispered. "May I?"

"Heaven above, yes." He let go of her hand and curled his arm over her shoulders, pressing his face into her neck. "Just be prepared for the reaction you're going to get."

"I am familiar with biology, Leo."

"When you say things like that, it only makes me harder."

"Really?"

"Yes."

How curious. She scooted down so she could reach better. Leo didn't want to release her but he did, stroking her hair away from her face and bending down to press kisses to her lips.

"You're so tall," she whispered.

"Hmm." More kisses. A low rumbling sound in his chest that sounded a little like a cat purring. His *talesm* were definitely shimmering now. They filled the room with a cool glow like moonlight.

She slipped her hand under his waistband and felt the muscles there tense. "Is my hand cold?"

"No," he forced out.

She heard him swallow hard. Kyra didn't wait any longer. She slid her hand down, past his hip, and over his hard erection.

Leo's whole body shuddered.

So did she. Why was his pleasure making her so needy? Every sensation made her more curious. His skin was hot and smooth, but the flesh was impossibly hard and swollen. She ran her palm up and down the length of his penis. "Knowing where this is meant to go, the mechanics of it seem… improbable."

"I promise you they're not." He kissed her over and over. "I promise. Promise, Kyra."

His forehead smoothed out and his eyes closed again.

"Am I doing this right?" she whispered.

"Heaven above, yes." He pressed his cheek to hers and groaned when she closed her fingers around him. "Kyra!"

The warmth of his release pulsed over her hand. "Oh!"

Leo let out a shuddering breath. "I did warn you."

"Let me—"

"No, stay there." Leo gently pulled her hand from his trousers and rolled out of bed, walking to the basin in the corner again and wringing out the washcloth. He walked back to the bed and cleaned her hand, then unzipped his pants and washed his belly. The casual intimacy of it made her need spike again.

Leo's eyes landed on her, hot with intent. "Your turn."

She rolled over and hid her face. "Not yet."

Leo tossed the washcloth in the basin and crawled over her, bracing himself on his arms and caging her with his massive body.

"Are you joking?" he said. "Kyra, the things I want to do to you—"

"Not yet," she whispered. "Later."

He paused, rolled to the other side of the bed, and gathered her into his arms. "Tell me why?"

Kyra's heart began to race, and Leo caressed her back with long, soothing strokes. She buried her face in his chest and breathed in his scent. Kyra knew, for the rest of her life—however long it was—the scent of Leo's skin would be the most comforting thing in the world. Touching Leo's skin, there was peace. Breathing him in, there was happiness. His arms made her safe. His kisses made her brave.

Kyra took a deep breath and tried to explain. "Just watching you is overwhelming."

"Are you scared?"

"Not of you," she said. "Just… the unknown."

He bent down and whispered in her ear. "Have you ever touched yourself?"

She shook her head.

"Never, Kyra?"

"I never felt alone," she said. "There was never any privacy. And all the women who came to my father… What they did felt obscene. Dirty."

"Is what you did to me dirty?"

"No," she choked out. "It was beautiful." She looked into his eyes. "You're beautiful."

"So are you," he said, smoothing a hand from her neck,

down her back, and lightly over her bottom. "And everything we do together will be beautiful too."

She nodded and tried to regain her boldness.

"Later." Leo pressed her cheek to his chest. "Sleep, *ana sepora*. We've had a long day. Right now is the time to rest."

SHE WOKE TO THE SOUND OF BIRDS IN THE FOREST AND A MAN snoring in her ear.

Kyra's eyes went wide.

Oh yes. Leo was in her bed.

Leo was... *in her bed.*

And she'd done rather wonderful and brazen things to him in the middle of the night.

She'd blame exhaustion, but that would be dishonest. She'd been wanting to touch him like that for... possibly years. Yes, years.

And now... *he was in her bed.*

He drew in a giant breath and shifted, turning toward her and snaking an ink-covered arm over her waist. He pulled her back and spread his hand over her belly, tucking her body into his. His chest pressed to her back. Her head rested on his arm. His hips snugged against her bottom as he arched and pressed...

Good morning! It was back.

Kyra's eyes went wide, but Leo didn't wake up. Apparently he could sleep that way with no problems. She wondered what happened if he rolled over. It was very hard and stiff. Would it break? That seemed painful.

But the sleeping man wasn't inclined to move. He rested with his face in her hair, breathing in and out with a happy rumble in his chest. His warm skin pressed against her back, and his hand rested on the soft skin of her belly.

It was all rather wonderful.

Kyra smiled and snuggled closer, enjoying the feel of Leo's skin against hers. She was happy. Despite everything, she didn't think she'd ever been happier.

He took another deep breath and cleared his throat a little.

"Good morning," she whispered.

A quiet grunt was the only response she received. Leo wasn't a morning person. That knowledge made her smile too. What else would she learn about him that would be only for her?

Leo lifted his arm from around her waist and put a heavy palm on her hip.

Kyra sighed and closed her eyes. His hands always felt wonderful. He rubbed her hip up and down in long strokes, following the line from her knee up her thigh, over her hip, and dipping down to her waist. His fingers teased her ribs and then started the journey down again. He did it over and over until she felt liquid in his arms.

Then he slid his hand up the inside of her leg, stopping at the juncture of her thighs.

Kyra sucked in a breath. "Wait."

"Over your clothes." His voice rumbled behind her. "That's all. Just touching over your clothes."

Oh. That sounded nice. Leo always made her feel good. She relaxed.

"Is that something you would like?" he asked.

"Yes," Kyra whispered.

His fingers danced delicately over her inner thigh, nudging her legs wider as he explored her body like she'd explored his. His erection felt heavy at her back, but Leo didn't move or press against her. He seemed solely focused on exploring the delicate and sensitive mound between her legs. She felt wetness pool, felt her body become heated and liquid. Leo kissed the back of her neck. Her ear. Her jaw.

"So beautiful," he whispered.

His fingers ran over an excruciatingly sensitive point. Kyra's breath caught, and Leo paused his movements.

"There?" he asked softly.

Kyra nodded.

Leo used his legs to spread hers, nudging her onto her back as he kissed her. His hand dipped down to that aching point, then retreated. Dipped again. Retreated.

"Leo?" Her breath was coming faster. Tension captured her spine and her breasts throbbed.

"This is right," he whispered. "Does it feel good?"

"Yes. I don't know. It aches."

He bent down and closed his mouth over the peaks of her breasts, over the thin cotton nightgown she wore to sleep. *It felt so good.* Kyra's hand came to the back of Leo's head and pressed him to her breast. "Keep doing that. Leo, *please.*"

His hand didn't stop stroking her as he teased her nipple. The pressure built. Her breath came faster.

"So beautiful," he whispered again, lifting his head to catch her eyes.

She locked onto his gaze as her body started to tremble. Kyra felt utterly out of control. She held on to the edge, clutching for something familiar, something sane, some balance to grab.

Leo smiled. "Let go, Kyra."

With a firmer touch, he pressed up and held her on the edge of a precipice… then her body broke. Kyra split open, shuddering with the most extreme pleasure she'd ever known. She cried out, and Leo captured her mouth, muffling the sounds of her climax with his kiss. He held her at the edge again, stroking her body into another jolting wave of pleasure. He covered her, his right arm lifting her as her legs drew up and her hand reached down, holding his left hand over that exquisite place. Pressing him closer, unwilling to let it end.

He eased his movements but kept his hand between her legs. Her skin was damp when he pressed his lips to her forehead. Her cheeks. Her lips.

"So sweet," he whispered. "Kyra, it was beautiful."

She felt beautiful. She felt like she was glowing from the inside. Her *livah* and her *manah* radiated, mingling together as her heart and her mind, her soul and her body, leapt toward Leo. He held her close, warm and safe and exactly where she wanted to be.

"What was that?" she finally managed to say.

"That was an orgasm."

"*That* was an orgasm?"

"Yes." He nibbled her ear. "Did you like it?"

"When can we do it again?"

Leo laughed, and it was a very satisfied, very male, laugh. It bordered on smug. "We can do it every night if you want. And during the day when we have the time." He leaned down and whispered, "It will be even better with your clothes off."

Her heart went galloping. "We may have to work up to that."

THE SWEET INTERLUDE IN THE MORNING CARRIED KYRA through another day of worry and dread. Scribes from Bangkok arrived around ten in the morning, driven up to the temple by Alyah. Tension blanketed the courtyard as two scribes and two singers greeted Niran. Dara had sent her brother, Rith, to lead the group. Grigori monks ringed the courtyard, watching their leaders welcome the ones who had spent a lifetime learning how to kill them.

No one looked pleased.

Alyah stepped forward and bowed to Sura. "My friend."

"Your people are welcome here," Sura said. "Our sisters have requested that only the Irina singers venture into the forest near the cottages. They would prefer the scribes stay in the more public areas of the temple compound."

Rith asked, "How are we supposed to guard them effectively if we can't be near them?"

Leo stepped forward. "The Irina are more than capable of assisting the guards Niran has already set in place, Rith. The scribes can help covering the temple and the village. There are already numerous fail-safes built in."

Rith grunted, but he didn't say more.

Niran watched the Irin survey the compound. Unlike Sura, he had not greeted anyone but Alyah. He caught the singer's eye and strode back to the dining table in the garden where they had continued to plan their trip to retrieve Prija. They were hoping to leave that night and make it to the border town directly north of Chiang Mai where Kyra could do her first reading into the dense forests and remote valleys of Myanmar.

Like the human government, passage through the remote country had been strictly limited for decades. There was little the Bangkok scribes knew about Myanmar. Most of the Grigori still called it Burma, and they knew more, but not as much as they'd like. Sura had the most knowledge regarding Arindam's people, but even his knowledge was a decade old.

They would take a small bus the Irin had rented in Chiang Mai, which should get them north of the border with little problem. The scribes in Bangkok had also assisted with papers for both Leo and Kyra, who would be scrutinized as Westerners. They were fortunate that the professional fight scene in Myanmar was popular and more and more foreigners were going there to train. Leo would be posing as a fighter traveling with a group of Thai professionals and their promoter. Kyra's papers labeled her as Leo's wife, which would mean they'd be sharing hotel rooms wherever they traveled.

After that morning, Kyra found the idea extremely appealing.

She nodded politely at the Bangkok scribes before she walked to the back garden, trying not to notice their stares. Leo came next to her, draping his arm over her shoulders.

"They're staring," she said.

"Because you're so beautiful."

"Because you're with me."

"Because they haven't seen *kareshta* before." He kissed the top of her head. "But truly, you are stunning this morning."

She felt heat touch her cheeks. "I think you're biased."

"Wholly and completely," he said. "But I'm not wrong."

"We're going to be posing as husband and wife," Kyra said. "Is that a problem?"

"I'm hoping I can talk to Kostas and Sirius before someone tells them. Or sends them pictures." Leo tensed, and Kyra paused, putting a hand on his chest. "I just want to tell my brothers first. Tell them we're together so they know I'm okay. That I'm not being coerced. It's not Sirius I'm concerned about; it's Kostas of course."

"Does he think so little of me?" Leo asked. "After everything we have been through?"

"I'm his sister." She stood on her tiptoes and kissed his cheek. "He has watched over me always. He would be worried no matter who I am with."

"Me," Leo returned the kiss. "Let him know. It will always be me."

She smiled. "Is that so?"

"Yes."

"Hmm." She started walking again.

Kyra saw Alyah waving at Leo, a duffel bag in her hand. It probably contained the spare clothes he'd requested from his hotel room.

"I should go talk to her," Leo said. "There are a few details to sort before we go."

"You still haven't told me what *reshon* means."

"Haven't I?" Leo took her hand and kissed her palm. "Later."

"I'm going to say goodbye to my students."

Kyra walked back to her cottage to double-check the bag

she'd packed. She wasn't taking everything, but on the off chance she had to fly directly back to Europe from Myanmar, she didn't want to leave anything essential. Halfway down the forest path, Intira, Bun Ma, and Kanchana stopped her. The little girl ran to Kyra's open arms.

"You'll find her," she said.

"I will. I promise. Prija is so strong. They won't be able to hurt her. She can defend herself."

Bun Ma said, "Sura said your hearing is very powerful. That you can hear over hundreds of kilometers."

"When I focus, I can. It wasn't always a good thing, but after years of practice, I can use it better. And I'm going with Niran, Sura, Alyah, and Leo. Between all of us, we will find Prija and bring her back."

Bun Ma and Intira smiled, but Kanchana still looked skeptical.

"I promise, Kanchana."

"I'm not worried you'll find her," Kanchana said. "Sura said this Fallen wanted to use her. Use Prija like a weapon."

Kyra nodded.

"She might not want to come back. That's what I am worried about. There's so much darkness in her. If they let it out, she may not want to put it back."

"I know."

It was the single true fear Kyra shared about Prija, and she hadn't spoken it aloud to the others, though she suspected Sura guessed her thoughts.

Prija was dangerous and angry. Prija was powerful. Not all *kareshta* were good, even if parts of them wanted to be. Sometimes the voices didn't whisper; they shouted. Kyra had lost more than one sister to the seduction of evil. Kostas had killed his own blood when they became a danger to others. Would Sura and Niran be capable of that? Would they be able to kill Prija if she fell too far into darkness?

"Find her," Intira said. "Save her. Prija wants to live more than any of us. I told her all about the night market and she wants to go there. She told me."

"Did she?" Kyra brushed a hand over Intira's hair. "I will do everything in my power to bring her back. I promise you."

"Wait here!" Intira rushed off to her cottage and Kyra waited with Bun Ma and Kanchana.

"There are two Irina singers here from Bangkok," she told them. "They will be able to teach you things that I can't. Ask questions." She looked pointedly at Kanchana. "Make them answer you. They may be reluctant, but I know how persistent you are. Tell Intira to ask questions too. It's hard to withhold answers from the young."

"I will, and I'll tell her," Kanchana said.

Bun Ma had a shyer disposition, but there was nothing retiring about Kanchana. If anyone could bully the Irina into giving up some of their magic, it would be Kanchana's persistence and Intira's charm. Kyra felt for Bun Ma. She saw so much of her younger self in the woman who wanted to live a quiet, domestic life. Kyra had been forced into one crisis after another, but she hoped Bun Ma would get her wish. She would make a wonderful mate and mother if she ever found the right partner.

"The scribes from Bangkok are also here," Kyra said. "They may seem reserved, but Leo says they are good men. Alyah would not have chosen them otherwise. It would be good for them to meet you so they understand us more."

"And what about the foreign scribe, eh?" Kanchana lifted her eyebrows. "I think you are understanding each other better every night."

Bun Ma failed to hide her smile behind her hand, and Kyra's face turned bright red.

"He is very kind."

"He is very *eager*." Kanchana pursed her lips. "If you like him, I like him. Make sure he treats you well. If he doesn't, tell Sura."

"Not Niran?"

"Sura," Bun Ma said. "Always tell Sura."

Intira ran up, a length of fabric folded in her hands. "Give this to Prija to bring her home."

Kyra took the fabric. It was a handwoven length of cloth, designed to be hung on a wall or pieced into a jacket. "Intira, this is beautiful. Did you make this?" Kyra knew Bun Ma had been teaching the girl how to weave as part of her meditation practice, but she had no idea her weaving was so advanced.

"Yes." Intira jumped up and down. "Give it to Prija and she'll come home."

Kyra looked at the fabric. Clusters of knots were worked into colored lines that ran the length of the fabric. At first she thought they were stars, but then she realized it was far more regular than stars. This was a system or code of some kind.

"Intira, what is this?" Kyra looked at Bun Ma and Kanchana, but both of them looked as mystified as she was.

The girl was still jumping up and down. "Prija will know. She'll know, Kyra. Just show it to her. Tell her I figured it out, but she has to come back so I can finish."

Only half the fabric was knotted. While the bottom half of the piece was beautifully woven, it lacked the knots on the top half. Kyra had so many questions, but she knew Intira loved her surprises, and she'd never tell before she was ready.

"She'll know what this is?" Kyra asked, holding out the weaving.

"Mm-hmm!" Intira nodded. "She'll know."

"Okay." She carefully folded the woven panel. "I'll give it to her."

"And tell her I'm *only* going to finish if she comes back."

"I'll tell her," Kyra said. She opened her arms, and Intira ran to her, giving her a swift hug before she ran back to the forest, her ever-present brothers jogging behind her.

"That girl is spoiled," Kanchana said.

"That girl is precious." Bun Ma held out her hands. "Let me see it?"

Kyra handed Bun Ma the weaving.

"This is very good," Bun Ma said. "But so different from anything I make. She'll progress past me within a few years."

"She's too bright to keep here," Kanchana said. "But where would she go?"

"If she had more magic," Kyra said, "she could go anywhere. Anywhere at all."

PRIJA TITI

S he sat in the back of a windowless van. Her captors were not intelligent, but they were stronger than her. They tried to torment her by forcing skin contact—no doubt thinking it would have a detrimental effect on her psyche—but Prija didn't react. She stared straight ahead and tried to give every appearance of being unaware.

Silent.

She was good at being silent.

But of course she was aware. She was aware of everything.

They were in Myanmar now. She could hear the language change when they stopped for petrol. Feel the roads grow rougher. They spent one night at a Grigori outpost, but the men there wanted nothing to do with these combative sons of Arindam and the Irin scribe who skulked in the background.

"We don't traffic in our own," one said. "They are untouchable."

Prija smiled when she heard that. *Untouchable.* She liked the label.

"That's not what we want her for," her captor said. "That's not why our father wants her. She's something different."

"Then we really don't want her."

"She's powerful."

"All the more reason she's not welcome here."

So her captors knew her lethargy and blank stares were an act. Not surprising. What was surprising was the case in the corner. They'd stolen her instrument from her cottage and taken it with them, even though they didn't let her play. Did they know? Perhaps what had happened to Tenasserim wasn't as much of a secret as she and her brothers had thought.

What do you want with me?

"She's an offering," they told another outpost, "for our father. She will please him."

Why would she please Arindam? She had nothing but contempt for the Fallen angel. She had even more contempt for Arindam's sons, who had dishonored Kanok's memory with their cowardice. He'd sacrificed his life only to have them back out of their bargain. He'd sacrificed his life, and now Prija was alone.

On the third day of traveling, Prija decided to kill the scribe.

He'd sat in the back of the van with her. He sat on the opposite bench and looked at her with greedy eyes. He'd taken out her *saw sam sai* and run his filthy tattooed hands all over the wood.

"Beautiful," he'd said. He looked and sounded Indian, but she didn't know enough about India to identify his accent. She knew it was a big country with many languages, but the man spoke English. "Your violin is beautiful."

It isn't a violin.

He tapped the blue jewel attached to the skin of the instrument. "This is valuable, isn't it? It's not a fake."

Of course it wasn't. Kanok had stolen the jewel for her. It was the last gift he'd given Prija. The scribe had no idea how valuable it was.

"Why do you hold your instrument in such high esteem?" he asked. "Is it your voice?"

She met his eyes and knew that the scribe understood.

167

"It is, isn't it? I kept wondering why they called you danger-ous. I kept wondering what it was that made you the one we needed to take. I voted for the little one. She's a genius, isn't she? A prize like that one could be very valuable if one could make her compliant. The right angel would have to—"

She knocked him to the ground with a lob of power aimed at his forehead. The scribe started bleeding from the corners of his eyes.

He blinked and droplets of blood scattered across his face. "How—?"

Prija punched her power out again, catching her instrument as the scribe slumped to the floor of the van. She set her *saw sam sai* delicately in the case and closed it before she moved back to the scribe.

He was dazed and bleeding. It was the only reason she had been able to break past the tattooed armor he covered himself with. His magic was far superior to hers, but he'd looked at Prija's slight body and seen weakness. He'd believed her silence was defeat.

A foolish mistake. The surprise was hers, and he would die.

She saw him reaching for the intricate spiral of ink on his left wrist, and she slammed her foot down on his hand, blocking him from activating more magic as she thrust more power at his frontal lobe.

"Can't... do this."

I can do anything I want. She smiled. *I am untouchable.*

She felt a twisting black power grow around her. Prija ground her foot into the scribe's wrist. He was bleeding from the ears now. She had no subtlety in her attack. Prija's power had been fine and fierce once. Now it was the equivalent of a brick to the skull. She kept battering his mind over and over and over. Eventually his eyes rolled back in his head. He went limp. Then she knelt over him and put one hand to his windpipe and the other over his nose and mouth.

As the car wound farther into the mountains of Myanmar,

she smothered the Irin scribe who had taken her. She took his own dagger from his waist—a small curved saber—and stabbed him in the back of the neck as she'd been shown. Irin and Grigori called themselves different, but they died the same way.

She opened a window to let the scribe's dust swirl out of the van. The black shadow that settled in her mind didn't dissipate. Killing the scribe had felt good. Satisfying. She wondered if she'd be able to kill the other men who had captured her.

She secured her *saw sam sai* in its case, sat back on the bench, and waited for the next stop, the silver dagger tied into a corner of her dress.

FOURTEEN

L eo and Alyah sat at the table, checking off things from a
list Sura had put together. They had all packed their
bags in the bus to take them north, along with some
training equipment Ginny had given them in Chiang Mai.

"Is she coming?" Leo asked.

Alyah shook her head. "Ginny said she was following up on
the scribe with the two Grigori."

"She thinks she knows who it is?"

"She suspects." Alyah looked up from her notebook. "Ginny
is… different. But she knows people, and she means well. I'm
sure she regrets your fight the other night, but she may never
apologize."

"I didn't mean to cause her pain, and I'm sorry I did. I was
asking about longevity spells for Kyra."

"For Kyra?" Alyah frowned. "How old is she?"

"Far older than she looks, and much longer than her natural
life would have granted. Her brother had been given extra
power from a Fallen ally before the Battle of Vienna, but since
then there has been nothing."

"That is unexpected," Alyah said. "And unfortunate. We

need to do something. I assume you're planning to mate with her. Can you—"

"It's premature," Leo said. "She doesn't want to rush into anything, and even if we did, performing the ritual now is not ideal."

Alyah nodded. "A very good point. You don't need to be depleted before an action like this, and she won't know her half of the ritual to make you stronger." Alyah paused. "Her tracking skills are unparalleled. We need to shore up her energy to make sure nothing happens to her before we find Prija."

Leo bristled. "And to make sure she's safe?"

"Of course." Alyah's expression revealed little. "Leo, I have to think strategically. That's my job. Even if Kyra meant nothing to you, I'd still want her as an ally because of her skills. That doesn't mean I don't value her as a person too."

"Can you do it?"

"Not as well as Ginny could." Alyah pulled out her phone. "Let me talk to her and see what she says. For now, track down whoever makes the food around here and ask them to pack some for us. Niran wants to be on the road within an hour, and I don't disagree. The sooner we get up to the border, the faster we find Prija and the less likely she's drawn into Arindam's orbit. Angels can be seductive for more than sex."

Sura walked into the dining room as Alyah walked away.

"The food is already being prepared," he said. "I'll make sure it's packed. We should be on the road within the hour."

"Good." Leo put his hand on the map. "Tell me about Myanmar. Tell me about Arindam."

"If I tell you about Arindam, it will explain more about Myanmar, I think." Sura sat at the table. He was dressed in his Western clothes, but he still looked like a young monk with his shaved head and wise countenance. "For many years, my father and Arindam were enemies. But my father was the clear superior."

"Spoken with prejudice because he was your sire or objective fact?"

"Objective fact," Sura said. "I had no love for Tenasserim. He was a monster, but a powerful one. He controlled far more territory than Arindam ever did. Few people know this, but his hold extended into southern China. Arindam was jealous of him, coveted his territory, but was never able to unseat him from power."

"But you and your brothers did?"

"Using our father's own gifts against him," Sura said.

"Prija?"

Sura nodded. "That is why I am not more concerned about her. I do not fear for her personal safety. I fear more for her soul."

"An interesting way to put it."

"Don't you think we have souls, Leo?"

"I do," he said. "I guess I didn't know if you did. Is that Buddhist teaching?"

"What do our sisters hear if not the voice of the divine in all humanity?" Sura said. "But speaking of the soul does offer perspective into Arindam's people. I think that was the main difference between my brothers and Arindam's sons."

"They don't believe in the soul?"

"They don't believe the soul can change," Sura said. "They are born to evil, but they are given more power and gifts than humans. It is an imbalance they have no control over, so they do not strive. They will sacrifice their lives for their father. They will die and hopefully be reborn as something less unbalanced."

"They're fatalists," Leo said.

"To the extreme. When my brother was killed defeating Tenasserim, they believed it was a sign that they were destined to remain under the Fallen's power."

Leo paused. "So we shouldn't expect any help from Arindam's sons."

"I do not believe so. Even if some are sympathetic personally, they will see Prija's abduction as her fate. They would be interfering with fate to help her."

"I see."

"This attitude is why Arindam propped up the human government in Burma for so long. Their isolation suited him and kept those under his influence quiet. His compounds in the hills remain hidden."

"But you know where they are?"

"I know the rough locations. I believe Kyra will be able to be more precise."

Leo hated that Kyra was even going on this mission, but now that she'd revealed her power, there was little chance the strategic Irin of Bangkok would allow her to stay behind. Plus, Leo knew his reluctance was based on his heart and not his common sense. She was a huge asset. The mission would be impossible without her.

Without Kyra's gifts, Prija would remain under Arindam's power. And if the Fallen managed to feed her anger, who knew what could happen? A *kareshta* powerful enough to tip the scales against her own angelic sire was a force to be feared.

THEY TRAVELED DIRECTLY NORTH FOR TWO HOURS, TAKING rooms at a small hotel in the hills south of the border. They were the only visitors at the country inn; their bungalows sat sheltered from prying eyes by dense bamboo hedges that blended into the trees. Leo pushed open the door to farthest bungalow where he and Kyra had been assigned.

She walked in behind him. "This is very nice."

"I was expecting something more basic, but you're right."

The log bungalow was set on decorative stone pilings with a covered porch that extended the traditional grass roof. The railings and furniture were made of bamboo, and white drapes fluttered behind plantation shades. Inside, mosquito netting hung over a wide bed also covered in white. The wood floor was parqueted with dark and light wood, and grass rugs lay on the floor.

"This is heaven," Kyra said, peeking around a corner where Leo suspected the bathroom was. "There's a *bathtub*, Leo."

Leo looked over her shoulder and saw a luxurious claw-foot tub with various glass containers sitting next to it. Herbs, pink salts, and flower petals turned the bathroom into something far closer to one of the fancy spas that he'd seen in Chiang Mai.

"This is wonderful." Leo kissed her shoulder. "After we train, you'll be able to soak."

Kyra turned. "After I what?"

"Train." Leo grinned. "I recognize the need for you to go into this battle, and I'm not going to leave you unprepared. You need to know how to defend yourself."

"But Leo—"

"I will be there every moment to protect you." He put his hands on her shoulders. "But I'm not complacent. Should something happen to me, you need to know the basics."

A wrinkle formed between her brows. "But I think you'd be surprised—"

"No buts." He kissed her nose. "Now, let's get changed and go find a clear spot we can practice. Don't forget the bug spray."

Leo walked out of the bungalow feeling very virtuous. No mate of his would face battle unprotected. He had every confidence of his ability to protect Kyra, but he also believed in being prepared. There was nothing better than a woman who could hold her own in battle. That's what his watcher, Damien, had taught him. Damien's mate, Sari, was a warrior equal to any Irin scribe. And even pacifists like Ava learned the basics of hand-to-hand combat once they entered the Irin world.

It was only an hour later, once Kyra had managed to give him two slices across his back with her daggers, that the virtuous glow wore off.

"Who taught you dagger fighting?" he said with a scowl.

"Sirius." She flipped one knife in her hand—the knife with his blood on it. "He was also of the opinion that a woman should know how to defend herself. So he taught me—how did you put it? *The basics.*"

Leo's nostrils flared. "He did well."

"Thank you."

He found her smugness adorable. He found her skills more than tempting. Who knew his mild-mannered *kareshta* would be nimble and ruthless too? She hadn't hesitated to give him a taste of her skills.

"You didn't feel like telling me?" He circled her, enjoying the sight of her in workout leggings. Kyra rarely wore pants, much less anything figure-hugging.

"After the second time you interrupted me, I thought a demonstration would be more effective."

He leapt on her without warning, one arm going around her waist and another reaching for her right wrist, even as he felt the dagger point pressed to his neck. She held the knife in her left hand, and the point was at his artery.

He hissed but didn't let go. Her bottom was pressed against his groin, and it felt too good. He pulled her closer and ignored the bite of the blade against his skin.

"Leo." She pulled the knife away. "What are you doing?"

Mortal peril avoided, he bent down and pressed a kiss to her neck. "How is it possible for you to be even more attractive than you were an hour ago?" He continued kissing along her neck. Her collar. He tasted the pulse pounding in her neck.

"You scribes find the strangest things attractive."

"Any man who doesn't see the allure of a lethal woman is a fool." He nipped the soft skin at her neck. "I am not a fool."

He heard the daggers drop to the forest floor. She reached one arm up and hooked it around his neck. With the right force and angle, she might be able to flip him over her shoulder with that hold.

He groaned at the thought.

Instead of flipping him, she pressed her bottom back into his hips, making his erection leap with joy.

Sadly, the forest make-out session was not to last.

"There's someone coming," Kyra whispered.

He sighed and pulled away. Kyra was too private to endure many public displays of affection, much less public displays of ardent groping.

"Later," he said, pressing one last kiss to her neck.

"After this morning, I will never be able to hear that word again without blushing."

Was that a self-satisfied chuckle on his part? Yes. Yes, it was.

THEY ATE TOGETHER, SURA, NIRAN, ALYAH, KYRA, AND LEO. Niran's other two men were ghosts, patrolling the hotel in utter silence. Leo wondered if the owners even knew they had seven guests instead of five.

"Your men," Leo asked Niran, "have they eaten?"

"They have." Niran was scooping chicken *panang* over a bowl of rice. "They take very simple meals."

Kyra said, "There is more than enough here to share with them."

Niran lifted his gaze, and his usually steely expression softened. "Like many of my men, they choose to focus on discipline in all things, and they believe food that appeals to the senses could weaken their resolve."

"So they are monks as well as warriors?" Alyah said.

"In a sense," Sura said. "Though both of them have taken the *Sak Yant*, they have also sacrificed inner peace for a life of protection for those weaker than themselves. If their violence is confined to the protection of others, they do not feel they have violated the precepts of *Sak Yant*."

"Do you feel the same way?" Kyra asked Niran. "Is violence in the protection of others acceptable violence?"

"I have to believe it," Niran said. "Who else will protect my sisters in a world that hates their existence?"

"But you also eat delicious food," Kyra said with a smile. "Not very monk-like of you."

Niran's expression turned to something very far from monk-like. "My resolve is tested by far more tempting things than food."

Leo would have to be blind to miss the way Niran looked at Kyra. The whole table was aware of the Grigori's double meaning. Kyra looked down at her plate. Alyah watched with amused curiosity. Sura wore a thoughtful frown.

The rest of the meal passed in awkward silence. After the dishes had been cleared and others were taking their leave, Leo grabbed Niran by the arm.

"You and I need to talk."

Niran wrenched his arm away. "And you need to learn manners."

Leo spun on him. "So do you."

Their interchange had come to the attention of Sura, Alyah, and Kyra. Kyra's eyes were wide and pleading.

Don't, they said.

Leo shook his head. Niran's comments were putting Kyra in an awkward place, and it wasn't acceptable.

"Fine," Niran said, nodding toward a side door. "Let's talk, scribe."

They marched out the side door and into the darkened forest. The full moon had waned, and the forest was grey and black with shadows.

"Do not desire another man's lover or spouse," Leo said, turning on Niran. "Isn't that one of your precious precepts?"

The blow to the side of the head came as a surprise. It was a sucker punch. He hadn't expected that from Niran.

Leo snarled and came up swinging. He might not have had the light feet of the Grigori, but he had speed and size. He plowed into Niran, bringing the smaller man to the ground.

They rolled in the dry leaves, Niran wrestling away from Leo and jumping to his feet.

"She does not belong to you," he spat out, blood at his lip.

"She does," Leo said. "And I belong to her."

"Just because she's known you longer does not mean you can understand her, *scribe*."

Leo rolled up. "She is my *reshon*. I don't expect a Grigori to understand that."

"*Reshon*." Niran sneered. "Ah yes. The precious Irin soul mates. Did she hear it? Did she hear it coming *from your own mind*? That's not heaven's will, scribe. That's wishful thinking."

Leo struck out, only to have Niran parry his blows. Fists and feet flew. The Grigori was clearly a master of muay thai fighting. His speed was more than a match for Leo's own. But punching Leo was akin to punching a wall. Leo knew it, and Niran knew it too.

As they fought, Niran aimed for Leo's knees and elbows, trying to attack the scribe's weakest points to gain the upper hand. Leo brought his fist down on Niran's jaw, jolting the Grigori and rattling his brain. It was the only thing that seemed to slow Niran down.

Leo had taken another jolting kick to the knee when he heard a quiet voice say, "Enough."

A blur of movement, then a punch to the chest that felt like a gunshot.

Leo flew back into the brush. When he opened his eyes, he saw Niran on the other side of the clearing. Sura stood between them, his arms extended and his palms facing the two fighters.

"We are facing a common enemy," Sura said quietly. "This fighting is unacceptable and useless."

When Leo could breathe again, he rasped out, "Was that one punch?"

Niran groaned a little. "I hate it when he does that."

"You need to teach me," Leo said.

"You both need to calm down." Sura reached out to Niran

and helped his brother up. "She loves him. She has loved him for years. This has nothing to do with besting you. Don't let your resentment ruin a partnership with Leo and a friendship with Kyra."

Niran's face was unreadable. He nodded once at Sura and disappeared into the shadows.

Sura walked to Leo. "I'd offer to help you up, but you don't need it."

"That is a hell of a powerful punch for a small man," Leo said. "I hope you don't mind my saying that."

"Compared to you, I am small. Why would I mind your telling the truth?"

"Good point." Leo climbed to his feet. "For the record, I didn't start this."

"I didn't think you had." Sura began walking, and Leo fell in beside him. "I'm not going to try to explain my brother. That's not my job. As I'm sure you can imagine, your relationship with Kyra will cause some to disapprove. I hope you don't think that all my brothers or I feel the same way as Niran. His feelings are his own."

"I don't." Leo stopped. "I didn't think I had the right to love her. Not for years. I didn't think she would even want me in that way when she'd been through so much. But I think she does love me, and I'm not going to be noble for anyone except her."

Sura frowned. "She chose you. It has nothing to do with rights or being noble. You love her and she chose you. You honor her by respecting that."

"She is my *reshon*."

Sura smiled a little and began walking again. "In my hopeful moments, I like to think the Creator has such a blessing for the children of the Fallen as well as the children of the Forgiven. If we prove worthy of it."

"Ava has Fallen blood. Kyra has Fallen blood. Why should the daughters of the Fallen be capable of soul mates but not their sons?"

"An excellent question," Sura said. "Logically, I think you are correct. But when we have no experience of something, it is often hard to imagine it."

"True."

"For many of us, hope like that feels greedy." Sura turned and looked up at Leo. "All of us live knowing that our births probably killed our human mothers. Most of us feed on human energy, often stolen from those who die giving it to us. We are not optimists, and we don't come by virtue naturally."

"If virtue was natural, it would have no value," Leo said. "The Irin aren't perfect either."

"Perhaps not," Sura said. "But you start from a culture where you are valued for being good. We start from the opposite."

"If I were the Creator," Leo said, "that would make the sacrifices and the life you and your brothers lead even more worthy of reward."

Sura laughed. "Then I only hope our Creator is as generous as you."

CHAPTER

FIFTEEN

K yra had avoided spending time with Alyah as much as possible. Unlike Ginny, the Thai Irina didn't have the easy American temperament that made casual conversation simple. Alyah reminded Kyra of her brother. She was focused and serious. Smart and frighteningly efficient. Though she was patient with the *kareshta* at the temple in Chiang Mai, she had never been warm like Ginny.

So when Alyah knocked on Kyra's door the next afternoon while Leo and Niran were scouting the border, Kyra was surprised.

"Leo said you have no longevity spells," Alyah said, "which puts your life in danger."

"I…" How did one respond to something so intensely personal? "He's correct," Kyra said quietly. "*Kareshta* have no longevity spells."

Not that it was any of Alyah's business. Kyra didn't like talking about her impending death with anyone, much less someone who didn't seem to like her. She was having a hard time not being angry with Leo for mentioning it, even though Kyra was sure he had a purpose. Just like he'd had a purpose talking to Ginny about it. Then Ginny had become angry and hadn't spoken to Kyra again.

"You are necessary for this mission," Alyah said. "I don't want to insert myself into your and Leo's... relationship. But your health is a priority if this mission is going to succeed. I hope you would find it acceptable if I sang a longevity spell for you. I can't guarantee it will last for long, but it should give us some breathing room. A few days at least. I can always repeat it if necessary."

So Alyah was willing to give Kyra this magic, but only because she was "necessary?"

It made Kyra feel small, like she had when she was younger and Barak called her "useful." Her father wanted her around to strengthen Kostas, but he occasionally acknowledged Kyra's gifts as well. The recognition made her feel less, not more. Perhaps because it was given so reluctantly.

It didn't matter what Kyra's feelings were. She was getting tired more quickly, which she'd initially put down to jet lag, but she'd been in Thailand for weeks. It wasn't jet lag.

"Well?" Alyah asked. "Will you allow me to sing over you?"

Kyra nodded and opened the door to allow Alyah in the bungalow. Alyah scanned the room quickly, taking in the luxuriously appointed bed, flowers, and candles.

"They gave you the best room," she said. "That's nice."

"Perhaps because they thought we were newly married."

"Aren't you?" Alyah said. "In a way."

Again, Kyra found it difficult to read her. "You dislike our relationship."

Alyah turned. "I find it confusing."

"Why?"

"You are not equals."

Her words stung. "No? I thought the Irin valued their women, even if they were not warriors. I may not be as accomplished as you are, but I do have some skill."

Alyah cocked her head. "That is not why you are unequal."

"Then how?"

"You have no magic. He is a scribe trained in the academy in Riga. He grew in a world without the tempering influence of the Irina council. He was born in blood, raised among nothing but warriors."

"And yet he is more gentle than many who boast more," Kyra said. "It is true I do not have the same magic he does." She stepped closer to Alyah. "But I do have magic."

"Not enough."

Kyra's temper snapped. "And how am I to learn more when that knowledge is withheld from me? Did you spring from your mother's womb versed in the magic you wield now? Or did you learn from countless generations who came before you? I had no such luxury. The fact I am *alive* is a miracle. Ginny spoke of watching her sisters die. Do you Irina think you were the only ones?"

"Do *you* think you know the loss we suffered at the hands of your brothers?"

"Most of us are killed at birth," Kyra said. "Those of us who live are usually abandoned to the humans, who call us crazy. We are locked up. Drug-addicted. Hunted because of these faces." Kyra slapped her own cheek. "Do you think I like looking like this? Do you think I love the attention it brings? Do you think I like hearing the lust of the humans and the revulsion of my brothers?"

Alyah took a step back.

"We are driven mad by what we hear," Kyra continued, walking toward Alyah. "Those Grigori you hate so much are sometimes the only thing standing between us and insanity or death. The *luckiest* of us end up in padded rooms. The weakest —the ones with the *most* magic—are preyed on by the Fallen who want to use us or by humans who see us as easy targets."

"Magic doesn't make us weak," Alyah spit out. "Do you deride your own gifts?"

"What has your *precious magic* ever done for me but bring torment?"

Alyah's eyes went wide. "Is that why you are with Leo? To gain control over it?"

Kyra raised her hand to strike, but stopped before Alyah could react. She clenched her fist, pushing back the rage that threatened her. She took a physical step back. Then another.

"You don't know me," Kyra said quietly. "You don't know me at all."

Most assumed the rage belonged only to Kostas. Most saw Kyra's calm demeanor and quiet life as evidence of peace or some internal fortitude. What they did not see was the well of rage she swallowed daily, just to live a normal life.

She didn't want to feel it. She often wondered if her repression hurt Kostas by shoving her emotions into him.

Kyra took five breaths.

In. Out.

Slemaa.

In. Out.

"*Domem,*" she whispered. Kyra walked to the corner of the room where she had set out a pillow for meditation. She sat and closed her eyes.

Domem livah.

Domem manah.

Breathe in. Breathe out.

Give thanks for each breath. Give thanks for each moment of peace.
She swallowed her anger again.

And again.

She was silent.

Seven breaths later, she felt Alyah sit next to her. The angry part of Kyra wanted to kick her out of the room. The pragmatic survivor needed her to stay and give her magic. Alyah took Kyra's hand and began to sing in a low voice. It was a tonal chant, dipping and weaving over words Kyra didn't recognize. As she sang, Kyra felt the energy touch her and spread like oil over water. It rippled over her and sank beneath her skin. She felt luminous and strong.

Her soul wept at the beauty of it. She longed to weave power like this, as Bun Ma wove thread in her loom. As Alyah sang, Kyra listened to the notes climb up and down, measured steps in a heavenly dance.

She fell asleep.

VASU CROUCHED BEFORE HER. "DO YOU SEE IT YET?"

"See what?" Kyra opened her eyes.

She was in her bungalow, but everything was hazy. The vibrant colors had leached from the room. Vasu sat back on his heels and peered at her like a curious bird.

She blinked. He was a raven.

She blinked again. A cat.

"Will you stop?" she said. "One form is confusing enough."

He shifted back to the beautiful man with the heavy-lidded eyes. "Do you see it yet?"

"See what?"

Vasu sighed. "Children are so much wiser than adults."

"Not usually."

"Yes, they are. The little one saw it immediately. Like stars, she said. A perfect geometry."

The little one... "Are you talking about Intira? Have you been talking to her?"

"Her mind is a very interesting place."

Kyra spoke in a firm voice. "Stay away from Intira."

Vasu frowned. "No."

The petulant expression reminded Kyra that she wasn't dealing with a typical angel. There was something intensely childlike about Vasu, a brightness and curiosity her father had never exhibited. Vasu was like the naughty child who dropped a rock on another child's finger. It wasn't cruelty. It felt more like curiosity. Of course, it was curiosity without moral restraint.

Kyra understood amoral creatures. She had been raised among the Fallen.

"Vasu, you must stay away from Intira. Her mind is young and impressionable."

"I know."

"But think," she said carefully. "If you visit her too often, she may soon mirror your thoughts and not her own. Then what makes her interesting and unique will be spoiled. Her mind should remain her own. That is what makes her wise."

Vasu crossed his legs and sat in front of her. "You may have some insight."

"Is that why you visited me?" It wasn't the first time she'd been visited by a Fallen. Her father had sat in her dreams when she was young. Sometimes he felt benevolent. Mostly he felt cold.

"I visited you…" Vasu cocked his head again. "Why did I visit you?"

"I don't know, Vasu."

He closed his eyes. "Oh!" They popped open. "Do you see it yet?"

"That question still makes no sense to me."

"The music." He leaned forward and exhaled a hot breath over her lips. "You have to see the music."

"You're not making sense. You don't see music, you hear it."

"I do make sense; you just don't see. But you will."

His presence was so heated she felt her body react. She didn't like it but knew the reaction had little to do with Vasu's intention. Angels were seductive by nature.

"What do you want, Vasu? What do you hope to gain by this meddling?"

He sat up straight but said nothing.

Vasu had been allied with both Jaron and Barak. Jaron and Barak had both returned to heaven.

"Do you think it worked?" Kyra asked quietly. *Were they redeemed?*

Vasu saw inside her mind. "I have no way of knowing."

There was a note of longing in his voice. She felt it more than she heard it.

"Are you lonely?" she asked.

"If I was, daughter of Barak, what would you do to remedy me?" Vasu leaned forward and captured her lips.

Vasu's kiss was heated and lush. Honey and saffron. Sweet milk and raisins. Kyra opened her mouth and pulled away, taking the angel's breath into her lungs. Vasu captured her chin and held her, forcing her eyes to his. His gaze was not cruel, but the power in it filled her heart with dread.

"You have nothing to fear from me," Vasu whispered. "You do not carry the thing I need, Barak's daughter, but you may take this gift anyway."

Kyra blinked and he was gone.

She woke in the bungalow, still sitting in the corner where she meditated, tears rolling down her cheeks and the taste of honey in her mouth.

LEO FOUND HER HOURS LATER, STILL SITTING IN THE CORNER. He carried a tray into the bungalow and set it beside her.

"Alyah said she sang to you. She said you might be tired. She apologized as well. Did she offend you?" He sat beside her and stroked her hair back from her forehead. "I didn't want to disturb you when you didn't come to dinner, but I thought you might be hungry."

Kyra glanced down at the tray. Fruit and rice. A bowl of vegetables and chicken bathed in fragrant coconut curry. A pot of tea and a single cup.

She looked up at Leo. "I love you. Or I think I love you. I'm not sure I know what that is, but I feel something for you that is so huge. Sometimes it frightens me, but I cannot seem to stop feeling it."

Leo didn't say anything, but his face... She couldn't read his face.

He sat beside her and tucked a strand of hair behind her ear. "Why wouldn't you know what love is?"

"The only people I have loved are my brothers and sisters. And this is not the same."

"No." He leaned over and delicately kissed along her ear. "No, it's not."

"Do you love me like this? I think you do, because you are so kind to me. You take care of me. I think... you must think about me as much as I think about you. I try not to listen to your thoughts, but your voice is so clear. Even when I hear you, I can't know if you have this feeling inside you. Is that what *reshon* means? Does it mean you love me?"

He placed a warm hand on her neck and tilted her head to the side, laying kisses along skin that hadn't known sensation until he touched it.

"*Reshon,*" he whispered, "means that you are mine and I am yours. That we were created for each other. This is love—because I love you *so much*—but it's more than love."

"What can be more than love?" Her heart felt like it might burst. *Leo loved her too.* He had been raised with love, so he must know the feeling she was talking about. He didn't have her fractured past.

He loved her.

Leo pressed his cheek to hers. "When we have time, when we are safe, I will show you what it means to be *reshon*. What I can tell you now is that it is a connection ordained by the Creator. It means my voice will always be the clearest for you—"

"It always has been. From the beginning."

He smiled. "And my touch will always give you peace."

"It already does."

Leo hauled Kyra into his lap and hugged her tightly. "You belong to me." It wasn't spoken in pride but in awe.

She smiled against his chest. "I would like that."

"And I belong to you." He tilted her chin up and kissed her. "You know that's part of it, don't you?"

"What can I do for you?" she asked. "If I am your *reshon*, what does that mean for you?"

"Your touch will heal me," Leo said. "When I am wounded, your touch will make me stronger. Your song…"

His expression went blank, and Kyra's heart sank.

She asked, "It won't be the same, will it? It won't be the same as it would be if your *reshon* were Irina. Because I don't know the same magic."

"It doesn't matter."

"It does."

"Ava was able—"

"Ava was human. Or at least she was to the Irina. She has no ties to the Grigori world. No one would ever question her loyalty, Leo." She rested her ear over his chest and listened to his heart beat. "They taught her magic, but it's not the same for me."

He said nothing, because he knew she was right. It didn't matter how much Leo loved her; he could not teach her the magic she needed to be what she wanted to be for him. She also knew he wouldn't let her go. Their connection was unique. She believed that.

"I love you, Kyra."

Would it be enough?

Leo set her on her pillow and put the tray on the low table beside them. They took turns feeding each other until they had eaten everything. Kyra couldn't finish what Leo had brought her, but she smiled and fed him the rest.

"You are what they call a bottomless pit."

He stretched out next to her. "There is a lot of me to fuel."

189

"Most Irin I've met aren't as tall as you. Most Grigori are taller, but they're not as strong."

"It's probably simple genetics. Everyone in my family was tall. But my cousin and I…" He winked. "We may have written a few spells to give us an edge. I don't know if they worked or if it's just in our blood."

"So your parents were tall as well?"

"I believe so. I didn't know my mother, just a few things about her. She was a healer. Sometimes I think I have memories of her, but I don't know if I'm really remembering or whether they're memories others have told me. Both of Max's parents were killed in the Rending. Our mothers were twin sisters. I think that's why we look so much alike."

"Your father?"

"I did meet him when I was seven. He was a mystery. Everyone assumed he was dead for many years. And we were never close. I don't think he was ever the same man after he lost my mother. Our grandfather is the one who raised us. He wrote our first spells." Leo turned over to show the line of spells that ran down his back. "Until we went to the academy, he cared for us. And he was very tall. He was our mother's father, so Max and I were all he had left."

So the Rending had taken Leo's family from him too. Though it happened before her birth, Kyra still felt a pang of guilt anytime one of the Irin mentioned it.

"It had nothing to do with you," Leo said.

"Are you sure it's not carried in the blood?" Kyra asked lightly. "Like genes for being tall?"

"I'm sure."

"There will always be some who don't see it that way."

"Probably yes." He rolled over and laid his head in her lap. "But there will be more who understand."

"I hope so." She ran her fingers through his hair and felt his chest rise and fall in a steady, relaxed breath.

She could do this for him. She might not have magic, but

she could do this. She could love him so well he wouldn't feel the loss. She would shove back her anger and swallow it whole to make room for loving Leo, who brought her flowers and fed her from his own hand.

I love you so much. I will make myself deserving of it.

After dinner, Leo ran a bath and put frangipani in the water, which filled the air with its heady scent. Then he lifted her and brought her to the bathroom.

"One step at a time," he said. "Tonight we try for no clothes."

Her face heated immediately. "No clothes at all?"

"Only if you want to, but I am curious why you are reluctant to let me see you." He teased her, trying to keep it light. "Do you have an embarrassing birthmark you don't want me to see? A tail you've been hiding?"

"No," she said. "My body is perfect."

Leo made a sound low in his throat. It was a hungry, raw sound that both thrilled and frightened her.

"Kyra—"

"Right now you see *me*. All of me. My face, but my mind and heart too." Her voice grew softer. "When men look at me… It's as if I don't exist anymore. They don't see me. Only my body."

"Hmm." Leo didn't say anything. He took her by the hand and walked to the bed, sitting down and putting his hands on her hips.

For the longest time he only looked at her, as if he was trying to see beneath her skin.

"I can't promise I won't lose my head a little," he said quietly. "Because, Kyra, I know you will be beautiful. When I see your bare skin, it will be overwhelming. But I will always see *you* first."

She nodded.

"When you see me without my clothes—"

"I've only seen you without your shirt," she said. "Not the whole of you."

He smiled. "Fine. Then imagine me right now. The whole of me, without a stitch of clothing on my body."

Kyra closed her eyes and imagined it, surprised when the same hungry sound left her own throat. Her eyes flew open.

Leo was smiling. "Good."

"You're saying that when I see you naked, I'll forget who you are too?"

"Hunger doesn't mean we forget who we're with. It only means that our bodies recognize each other like our hearts do. Do you think I've ever wanted a woman the way I want you? I haven't. Other women do not interest me." He brought his mouth to her belly, lifted her shirt, and nipped at the sensitive flesh. "This need is only for you."

She let out a low breath. "Okay."

He lifted her shirt again, running his fingers along her waistband. "May I?"

She nodded. As he peeled down her leggings, she felt the tiny hairs on her legs stand up. He lifted her feet and tossed the leggings away before he stood and brought her shirt over her head.

Kyra stood before him in her bra and panties, wishing she'd thought to put on the nice pair. She hadn't been expecting this that morning when she dressed.

Leo sat again, letting her become accustomed to the air on her bare skin. He put his hands on her hips and toyed with her panties, kissing along her belly. His hands moved back and cupped her bottom, his warm fingers sliding under the fabric that covered it.

"Yes?" he whispered.

"Yes." Feeling bold and impatient, she reached back and unclipped her bra.

Leo heard the fabric slide off and raised his eyes, devouring her breasts without a sound. With his gold hair and sharp gaze, he reminded her of a lion eying his prey. She dropped the bra to the floor and rested her hand on his broad shoulders.

Beautiful. He formed the word with his mouth, though no sound came. *Beautiful.*

He didn't touch her, but his gaze made her skin warm. Her heart pounded, and the liquid breeze caressed her skin.

Leo tugged at her panties. "May I?"

She nodded, and he slid them down her legs. He lifted one long leg and set it on the bed beside him, baring every part of her to his eyes. Leo ran the tips of his fingers over her legs, her knees, her bottom, her hips.

He bent and kissed the inside of her thigh, sliding his tongue up and making her gasp.

"May I?" he whispered, eyes closed as he breathed her in.

"Please."

CHAPTER

SIXTEEN

Leo tried to banish the sensual feast from his mind as he watched Kyra meditate in Sura's cottage the next morning. They were all gathered in the small room except for Niran's two soldiers who stood watch outside. Niran and Alyah stood by the door. Leo sat behind Kyra. They'd decided to experiment with his touch to see if contact increased her range or focus. Sura sat opposite her, legs folded in a meditative pose.

With his hands on her hips, Leo slid his fingers under her loose shirt, letting her feel his touch against her skin.

There?

No, lower. There.

Tell me.

I feel… everything. Everything.

Good?

So good.

Their hours of sensual exploration sat in the front of his mind, and Leo found it difficult to concentrate. Part of him had wanted to rush her. He'd felt desire before, but nothing like what he felt with Kyra. Part of him was intimidated by her. She was so beautiful, and he loved her so much. When the time finally came, would he embarrass himself?

"Focus," Sura said quietly.

Leo looked up. Sura wasn't talking to Kyra.

"Focus," he said again with a pointed look at Leo.

He nodded and shifted his attention, not to the pleasure of Kyra's skin but to the energy he felt coming from her. Her power, should she ever truly control it, was immense. He could feel her magic like an electrical current beneath her skin. He put his palms against her sides and imagined grounding her. He touched his *talesm prim* and felt his own magic come alive.

He could feel it. Leo sat behind her, sitting at the edge of her power and tasting the vast scope of it. He could feel when her mind opened and her consciousness flew upward.

He opened his eyes and met Sura's gaze. "She's having an out-of-body experience, isn't she?"

"I believe it's something like that."

Leo glanced at Alyah, but he could see the singer was as fascinated as he was. He could feel Kyra's consciousness leave her body, her soul resting like a banked fire in the center of her being. But her mind and power flew up and outward. He gripped her waist, and she leaned back into his chest, using his body as a cradle for her own. He felt her chest rise and fall. She was present and away, all at the same time.

Within minutes, her breath was slow and even. Leo looked down and her expression was restful except for a thin line between her eyebrows. He reached around and slid his palms under her own.

Their hands met and their fingers knit together; Leo was unprepared for the jolt of power that hit his chest.

His eyes rolled back and his body went limp.

He tasted the wind. Heard the rustling of trees.

Voices came from the distance.

He heard Kyra's breath in time with his own.

"*…more than the others…*"

"*She was dangerous.*"

"*—had to be moved.*"

195

"Arindam will not be pleased when he hears—"

"He must not hear."

"...protect the others. The children..."

A cacophony of thoughts entered his mind, a jumble of the Old Language and a dialect he'd never heard before. The rush overwhelmed him and his head swam. Thoughts beat at his mind. Voices came too fast. Too loud.

Slemaa.

He sucked in a breath at the sharp command.

Domem.

It was Kyra's voice in his mind. Her thoughts layered over the cacophony, untangling the threads like a weaver sorting her loom.

Domem.

He matched his breath to hers and found his thoughts again.

Four male voices. No, five.

Three women.

He couldn't count the children.

Muffled laughter.

"Leo."

Kyra.

"Leo, let me go."

Can't.

"You can. Let me go. I need to return without you in my mind."

Safe.

"I am safe. I've done this before. Imagine taking a step back."

He pictured her as she'd been in the cottage before him, her body resting against his, their hands knit together.

"Let go of my hands."

In his mind's eye, he let go of his white-knuckle grip on her hands and—

—blinked awake with Sura, Niran, and Alyah crouched around them, staring at Leo.

"Where is she?" Sura asked.

"At the compound," Leo said, flexing his hands to return circulation. "She's listening."

Niran asked, "Prija—"

"Moved." He focused on her breathing, which did not change. He traced a spell for clarity on Kyra's shoulders. Another for peace. "She will be able to tell you more. I was too overwhelmed by the number of thoughts, but she didn't seem to have trouble sorting them out."

Alyah asked, "So you were with her? You heard what she heard?"

"Yes." He bent and pressed a kiss to her neck, rubbing his hands up and down her arms. "She's like Ava. Kyra can let me hear what she hears like Ava can share what she sees. The only problem is I don't have the tools to sort through all the thoughts."

Alyah nodded. "It takes time."

Leo tucked a strand of hair behind Kyra's ear. "She's a long way from here."

Sura's gaze sharpened. "Could you see—"

"I couldn't see anything. I only heard."

Niran stood and leaned against the door. "So we wait."

It was only a few minutes later that Leo felt Kyra return to her body. Her breathing changed and her body lay more heavily against his.

"Leo?" she murmured.

"I'm here."

"Too bright."

He gathered her up and put her on his lap, tucking her face into his chest to shield her eyes while Niran and Alyah closed the shades in the cottage. He ran a hand over her arm and felt goose bumps.

"She's cold."

Sura stood and retrieved a blanket from the end of his bed. He put it around Kyra's shoulders while Leo rubbed her arms.

"I'm fine," she said.

"You sound tired."

She took a deep breath. "I went a long way. Leo helped me get farther."

"Where are they?" Niran asked.

"Around seventy-five miles north of here, but Prija is already gone."

"Are you sure?"

Kyra nodded. "I couldn't understand their thoughts exactly —I don't speak the Old Language—but I heard her name. I didn't hear her voice. I think they were afraid of her."

"They were," Leo said. "I heard them mention protecting the children."

"They have other women and children there?" Alyah asked sharply.

Kyra nodded.

Sura asked, "How many?"

"I'm not sure," Leo said. "Kyra?"

"I heard two children's voices. I think three women. I'd estimate there were perhaps ten Grigori with them."

"How sure are you?" Niran asked.

Leo looked at him sharply. "It's not an exact science."

"I'm ninety percent sure," Kyra said, putting a hand on Leo's shoulder. "It's fine, Leo. I was trained to be precise."

He stood, still carrying her. "You need to rest."

"I'm fine."

"I can feel how tired you are," he said, walking to the door without a glance at the others in the room. "You're taking a nap to get your strength up. Don't argue. If I know these three, they'll want to go running over the border as soon as you're well enough. Nap, then fight."

Kyra was already falling asleep on his shoulder.

A<small>FTER HE'D PUT HER TO BED, HE WALKED OUT TO THE PORCH</small> and looked at the others. They were gathered on the porch of Alyah's cottage, a short way down the path from theirs. Leo walked over to join them.

Sura asked, "Sleeping?"

"Out before her head hit the pillow."

Niran nodded. "Over one hundred twenty kilometers."

Alyah shook her head. "I can't imagine that range. We need to teach her the Old Language. She'll be far more useful when she understands their thoughts."

"It will also let her perform magic," Leo said. "Are you prepared for her to do that?"

It gave Alyah pause.

Sura said, "We'll need to cross the border before dark if we want to make it to an inn where I know the hosts. Do you think Kyra will be ready?"

Leo shrugged. "I have no way of knowing, but if she's anything like Ava after a vision, she'll sleep hard but it won't be for very long. A few hours maybe."

Niran was brooding in the corner.

Leo turned his eyes to him. "You're thinking very loudly."

The corner of Niran's mouth turned up. "You sound like my sisters now."

"I've had a glimpse of their minds," Leo said. "I'll take that as a compliment."

Sura said, "He's debating what to do about the women."

Niran nodded.

"What debate?" Alyah nodded. "We take out the Grigori and rescue the women."

Sura cocked his head. "Is it so black-and-white for you, singer?"

Niran said, "Their sire is not dead. It's not so simple."

"Why not?"

"Because," Leo said, "if their sire is living, they will do whatever he wants. Almost without question. They are virtual slaves. Do you want the slaves of the Fallen in your house?"

Alyah didn't appear to like that idea.

"If we'd already killed Arindam, it would be one thing," Niran said. "But those women are compromised. Their children belong to the Fallen. Their Grigori protectors are loyal. If we take them into our camp, we have no way of knowing if they would betray us. Neither would you. Geography might provide some protection, but that depends on how powerful Arindam has grown."

"But we can't just leave them there," Alyah said. "They're human. They will die if we leave them among the Fallen."

Leo asked, "How deep are you willing to dive in here?"

Alyah said, "We have our mandate from the council. The protection of the *kareshta*—"

"Is not your job," Niran said.

"I don't agree." Alyah's chin jutted out. "If you're not willing to do anything about it, then the scribe house will."

Sura raised a hand. "It's not a question of being willing, Alyah. It's a question of putting our own sisters in danger. Humans under thrall to a Fallen only think of the angel. They would betray us without hesitation."

"So you'll let my house take them," Alyah said. "I'm not asking you to shelter them, but those children are vulnerable. Those women are victims. If Arindam wants to take on the scribes and singers of Bangkok, then let him. Our watcher wields a black blade of heaven. We are not afraid of the Fallen."

Leo raised an eyebrow. "You speak for your house on this matter?"

"My house understands duty."

Niran nodded. "Very well. Call your brothers and sisters then. Tell them to follow us north. We will free those under Arindam's control and put them under the protection of the Irin house before we go after our sister. You can do with them what you will."

Sura spoke sharply to Niran, but Niran only raised a hand. "I'm not going to argue, brother. If the Irin want the responsibility, they can take it. I have no love for Arindam's sons. They had a chance to gain their freedom, and they chose safety instead."

Leo said, "So we have a plan then? We'll follow Kyra's direction to the first compound and take out the Grigori there, free the women and children before we move to the next compound?"

Sura nodded. "I know where he's likely to take her next, especially if they were afraid of her. There is another compound, even more isolated than the first. With Kyra's range, she should be able to listen for it once we get past the first."

THEY DIDN'T WAIT FOR KYRA TO WAKE. WITH THE PROSPECT OF a Grigori skirmish on the horizon, none of them wanted to sit idle. Leo packed up their things and loaded them into the van before he put Kyra in the back seat. They rode north over the border with little trouble. The guards were too excited about the prospect of meeting famous fighters from the US and Hong Kong to give them much scrutiny. Leo took a number of pictures with them before they drove deeper into the mysterious countryside of Myanmar.

They rode for hours, winding their way through river valleys and over mountains to a country inn where Sura was greeted by familiar hosts. Kyra was just waking as the van stopped, and Leo, Niran, and Alyah jumped out to unload their luggage.

Leo saw her blinking in the back seat.

"We're over the border?" she asked.

He nodded.

Kyra took a deep breath, closed her eyes. "We're close."

"Sura knew where he was going."

"Are they going after the women and children?" she asked in Greek, knowing they could speak anonymously in her native language.

Leo nodded.

Kyra frowned. "Are Niran and Sura—"

"Alyah has called the Bangkok house. The Irin are going to take responsibility for them."

"It's a risk. We don't know where their minds are. Their father is still living."

"Niran and I explained the danger, but Alyah wouldn't change her mind. Ginny is already on her way north with a few scribes."

"Singers would be better. The women would be more likely to trust other women. Unknown males will intimidate them."

"There's not enough," Leo said. "Ginny and Alyah will have to do."

She held out her hand, and Leo helped her from the van.

"What can I do?"

"How are you feeling?"

"Fine," she said, the corner of her mouth turning up. "I wasn't expecting company."

"Malachi can do that with Ava," he said. "See what she sees when she's having a vision."

Kyra said, "Did you think it would happen with us?"

He shook his head. "I wasn't even thinking of it, to be honest. I just remember feeling concerned because you were somewhere I couldn't protect you. Then I put my hands against yours and... boom."

"I felt you," she said. "When you arrived, I felt you. I was surprised. But you heard what I heard?"

"Probably not as clearly as you did. It was confusing."

"Human thoughts always are. You speak the Old Language," she said with a smile. "That means you can translate."

"I'll have to practice."

"So we'll practice." She took his hand. "Where are we?"

"An inn that Sura knows. He says the owners are discreet."

"And when will you go to the compound?"

Leo dropped his voice. "We'll do some reconnaissance tonight. We might even go first thing in the morning if it looks like a straightforward raid."

"The Grigori thoughts were unguarded," she said. "They'll be no match for Irin and free Grigori warriors."

"Let's hope not." Leo put an arm around her shoulders. "If we can scatter them and take their charges, that will be enough for me."

CHAPTER

SEVENTEEN

They didn't want to leave her at the inn alone, but they weren't expecting her to fight.

Their loss, Kyra decided. She could fight, especially against the scared boys who populated the compound in the hills. She'd seen the pictures Niran and Leo had brought back. She'd seen the small houses and the women, two with small children and one heavily pregnant.

"I can help with the women," she said. "I've fought before. I'm not helpless."

"Do you speak Shan or Burmese?" Alyah asked.

"No."

"Then you won't be much help," the Irina said, strapping on various knives and a small pistol. "Stay with the van and keep your head down. Don't attract attention if you can help it. Leo will be distracted enough as it is."

Kyra suppressed the urge to hit something. Unlike Leo, who could learn languages with a few looks, Kyra didn't have that gift. Though she was fluent in English, Greek, Bulgarian, Serbian, Turkish, and French, she had no knowledge of Asian languages. She'd never had any reason to think she would need them.

She sat in the rear of the van, watching Niran and Leo draw in the dirt as Sura looked on.

He'd come back to her the night before, fresh with excitement for the coming skirmish, even though he thought it would be a small challenge. It didn't matter. He was a warrior at heart, like her brothers. They were never happier than when they could battle an enemy. In this case, Niran and Sura were hoping Arindam's Grigori would flee before they confronted them. They had no desire to hurt boys unless the boys were dangerous to the humans in the valley, and according to Sura, there were no rumors of human deaths. Like his own brothers, the Grigori in this compound seemed to be living peacefully.

Kyra had her doubts.

She'd heard the thoughts of the Grigori in the compound. Though they might have been controlling themselves, it wasn't out of any great love for humanity. They were simply wary of attracting attention. She'd heard their hunger and greed. She had no illusions that they were the same kind of disciplined band that Sura and Niran led.

"I don't like this," Kyra told Leo when he approached her.

He put his hands on her shoulders and squeezed. "I'll be fine."

"I think you're all underestimating them."

"Why?"

"They're ruled by fear," she said. "Didn't you hear them too?"

Leo shook his head. "I only heard a fraction of what you did."

"But you heard their fear?"

"Of Arindam? Yes."

"Frightened creatures pushed into a corner can be the most vicious," she said. "They strike out unpredictably."

Leo nodded.

"Just be careful."

Leo narrowed his eyes. "Maybe I should take you with me. Not to fight, but to be where I can keep an eye on you."

"I'd be a distraction. Alyah is right in that. I'd like to help with the women."

"Help with the van," he said. "It's early, but if anyone comes along, you can play the helpless tourist."

They'd propped up the hood of the van. That way, if anyone looked, it would appear that Kyra was waiting on the rest of her party to return with help for the busted vehicle. There were more donkey carts than cars on the road, but Sura speculated that no one would question a tourist van with an engine problem too closely.

"You have your knives?" Leo asked.

"Yes."

"Good." He kissed the top of her head. "We're ready to go. Keep safe, and we'll be back shortly. I have my phone in my vest if you need me. If anything happens, call."

Without a backward glance, Niran, Sura, Alyah, and Leo jogged off into the forest, leaving Kyra behind.

LEO HATED LEAVING KYRA WITH THE VAN, BUT THERE WAS little she could do against trained warriors. She was proficient against humans, and she'd be fine with the women, but she didn't speak the language. Any assistance she could give would be more of a distraction than anything else. Niran wanted to go in quick and get out quicker.

They jogged down a rabbit trail through the forest, Sura leading the way. When he held up a fist, they all stopped on top of a small ridge. Switching to hand signals, he indicated he and Alyah would go right, toward the women's cottages, while Leo and Niran took on the main house where the Grigori lived. Leo brushed a hand over his *talesm prim*, noticing that Niran was chanting a mantra under his breath. Like Leo's *talesm*, Niran's *Sak Yant* lit with a low silver glow.

Though he'd never fought with Niran before, the Grigori moved much like Malachi, swift and silent. Following him, Leo ducked under vines and low-hanging tree limbs. He could see the steep roof of the building under the ridge.

They came upon the first guard at the end of the trail. His eyes went wide a second before Niran fell on him, covering his mouth and pressing his thumb into a point under the man's armpit. The man went limp at his knees, then with a swift blow to the head, Niran rendered him unconscious.

Tucking the guard under a bush, Niran nodded to Leo to continue down the path.

Leo found the second guard at the top of a stone staircase. He didn't use any fancy pressure points; he just punched the Grigori in the jaw, his massive fist snapping the man's head back. He put the fallen guard under a tree and followed Niran down the stairs.

The Thai Grigori moved with unearthly speed. Even Leo, who was known for his quick feet, had trouble keeping up. It was a blitz attack. Another guard met, another crumpled in a heap at Niran's feet.

They met their first real resistance when they entered the temple. Instead of the Buddha typical at the head of the altar, there was a great gold male figure with wings, his arms spread upward with two snakes wrapped around his wrists. Two Grigori knelt before him. Before Niran could reach them, the men spun and rushed Leo and Niran, gold knives in their hands.

"Behind you!" Leo shouted, catching movement from the corner of his eye.

Niran tossed his opponent in Leo's direction, spun, and met the two Grigori who had been standing behind the great doors of the temple.

All four Grigori bore knives and looked ready to use them.

Leo drew his silver knife, no longer reluctant to meet his

attackers. Sticking out his foot, he hooked his ankle behind the knee of one Grigori, bringing the man to his knees. With a quick stab, he drove his blade into the neck of the Grigori soldier, shoving him to the side as he dissolved into dust at Leo's feet. The other man jabbed Leo in the ribs with his blade, but Leo's *talesm* did not allow the blade to bite. Deflected by Leo's magic, the Grigori came again, quicker than Leo had expected. These soldiers were young but not untested.

A flurry of blows met his knee and his kidney, nearly taking Leo down. He brought his elbow around, smashing the face of the Grigori with one quick blow. The man reeled back, stunned by the sudden strike, then Leo darted behind him and brought his blade down quickly and cleanly into the spine of the second Grigori.

Dust in the air.

Leo turned and saw Niran still fighting one of the Grigori guards. The other lay on the ground, clutching his stomach while blood pooled beneath him. Leo started toward him, determined to put the Grigori out of his misery.

"Wait!" Niran said, striking his opponent to the ground with an open hand and a hooked ankle. "I want to question that one." He struck the Grigori again, snapping the man's neck with a sickening punch. The Grigori fell in a heap, his neck at an unnatural angle.

Niran walked over and flipped the bleeding Grigori to his back.

"Arindam," he asked. "Where is he?"

"Not here," the Grigori said, blood bubbling from his lips. "Not for months."

"Who took our sister?"

"Irin."

"You lie."

"Irin"—he coughed up blood—"and two of our Chin brothers from the west."

"Where is Prija now?" Niran asked.

"Too… dangerous. Chao-Tzang sent her away. He said she could not stay here. Our brother screamed and grabbed his head. She burned his mind."

"Yes," Niran said. "She does that. Tell me where they took her."

"West."

"I need more information than that." Niran pressed the heel of his hand into the man's belly, ignoring the screams. "Tell me where."

"Mong Kung," he said. "The hills west of the city. There is another temple to our father there."

Niran flipped the Grigori over and drew a blade from a sheath on his thigh. He stabbed the Grigori cleanly and stood as the soldier dissolved beneath him, then wiped the blood from his blade on the coat of the man he'd killed.

"Mong Kung," he muttered. "We need to find Sura. He'll know if it sounds true."

Leo and Niran left the temple, jogging down the stairs and toward the women's quarters where Sura and Alyah had gone. Leo saw a young soldier fleeing into the forest. He glanced at Niran.

"Let him go," Niran said. "He's no threat to us."

"We get the women and we go."

Niran nodded.

Leo was worried about Kyra at the side of the road. The Grigori who fled was running in that direction. Who knew if he was the only one.

"On second thought," Leo said. "You head to Alyah and Sura. I'll go back to the van."

"Very well," Niran said. "Though she's not as helpless as you think."

"It's not that she's helpless," Leo said. "It's that I'd be useless without her."

KYRA WATCHED THE FOREST FROM BEHIND SHADED LENSES AND waited. Every now and then, she'd hear something stir, but she thought it was only birds or small animals. She tried to look like a bored tourist, all the time keeping her senses open and aware of the humans and others around her. She didn't want to listen too closely and threaten her own consciousness. She knew if she reached too far with her hearing, she was deaf to anything else, and the last thing she wanted was to be vulnerable.

She heard an unknown Grigori coming and her hand went to her knife… but the voice veered away before it reached the road, heading back into the hills above her. There were humans up the road, but they were going about their daily life and didn't appear to be moving either toward or away from her.

Twenty minutes after they'd left, she heard Leo coming through the trees. He sounded easy and happy, and she knew nothing was wrong. She turned toward him before he broke through the bushes.

"There you are," he said with a smile.

"Everything went fine."

He nodded and embraced her. "We had to kill four soldiers who came at us with weapons, but the rest fled or we were able to knock them out. Have you heard anything from Sura?"

She shook her head.

Leo said, "Niran was going to look for them."

"Convincing the women might be difficult."

"It probably will be, but you never know. Most of it depends on how many women they've seen die. Do you remember Prague?"

Kyra nodded. How could she forget Prague?

The Fallen they'd killed outside Prague the year before had abused his human lovers horribly. He'd killed so many that the survivors were plotting to find a way out with their children even before Leo and his previous watcher, Damien, had led a team to extricate them and kill the Fallen. Most of the children they'd rescued were still in Damien's castle, learning how to control their sometimes fearsome power.

"We'll give them ten more minutes," he said. "Then we'll go in."

They emerged in eight. Niran carried a little girl, no more than three years of age, while Alyah carried a baby and three women walked behind them, Sura following. One of the women was visibly pregnant, though Kyra suspected another might be from the softness around her face. The other woman looked nearly dead. She followed Alyah closely, and Kyra suspected the baby the Irina singer was carrying was a Grigori son who had nearly drained his mother of life.

We're all murderers. We kill our own mothers when they give us life.

Her brother's bitter words never left her. Kyra's own mother was dead, of course. All the human mothers were. Looking at Niran and Sura, Kyra wondered if they carried the same guilt that Kostas carried like a yoke around his neck.

"Can I help?" she asked Alyah.

Alyah nodded to the nearly dead woman. "Do you speak any French?"

"I do." Kyra approached the woman, who began to cry and reach for her baby.

"Please," she said in broken French. "Please, my son."

"What is your name?" Kyra asked, bringing a blanket and a bottle of water to the woman. "Look, my friend is being so gentle with him. I promise—"

"He's my son," the woman said.

"She's from a hill tribe," Alyah said. "I tried to explain to the others, but I don't think she understood me."

Kyra put the blanket around the woman's thin shoulders and helped her into the back of the van while Leo and the others helped the other women into the middle seats.

"Sit next to us with the baby," she told Alyah. "She's not

going to listen unless you bring him close enough for her to see him."

Through rudimentary French, Kyra tried to explain to the human woman why her own child could be making her ill, but Kyra didn't know how much the woman understood. Eventually, as the van bumped back to the country inn, the human woman fell asleep, her bronze skin sallow and her cheeks hollow with sickness.

"I'm hoping Ginny brought Kenneth," Alyah said.

"Kenneth?"

Alyah smiled. "In another life, he's a linguistics professor at the university. Kenneth is originally from Hong Kong. He speaks and writes almost every language in Southeast Asia fluently. Preserving local languages is his passion. I think this girl might be from the Wa people. Part of her tribe lives in Yunnan Province, and Kenneth has probably studied them."

"How likely is Ginny to have brought him?" Kyra reached for the baby wrapped in a colorful pink cloth. "She's clearly attached, but she can't continue to care for him as she has been or she'll die. I don't think she really understood what I was trying to tell her."

Alyah happily handed the baby over to Kyra. "I'm hopeful," she said. "Kenneth is incurably curious. If Ginny told him she was going into Burma to get some women out, he might have volunteered."

Kyra wrapped the swaddling more tightly around the sleeping baby. Despite his mother's sickness, he was round-cheeked and blooming with health, sleeping peacefully with two fingers stuck in his mouth.

Perfect. All the babies were so perfect.

Her heart twisted.

What would it be like to have a child of her own? Was it possible if she and Leo mated? Her mind supplied the dream of a round-cheeked, blond baby with vivid blue eyes and milk-pale skin. She glanced up to see Leo watching her with an expression she couldn't read.

Longing. It might have been longing. Or that might have been her own.

She kissed the silky black hair of the boy in her arms and held him as they bumped over the country roads.

For now, the little boy was the son of a Fallen angel.

For now, his fate was balanced on the edge of a knife.

PRIJA IV

S he could hear the traffic in Mandalay and knew that, were it not for her damaged mind, she would have gone insane. Perhaps the city was a punishment for killing their Irin friend. The Grigori who took her had not been pleased.

They knew what had happened as soon as they opened the door. Prija expected them to search her, but they didn't. In fact, not a single one touched her from then on. They did drive through more populated areas though. They must have thought of it as a punishment.

So Prija killed the scribe, kept his knife, and nothing happened to her. She was not unpleased with that outcome.

She was unpleased with the conditions in Mandalay.

The human women there were kept in filthy quarters and near starving. Prija was thrown in a large room with a dozen of them. She did not have her *saw sam sai*. She didn't have any privacy. She was given a tin bowl, and twice a day, a large basket of rice was brought to the room. The women fell on it, starving. There was a shower in the corner and a pit toilet, but that was all. Most of them were thin and wan from the Grigori who were slowly draining their lives, but when the guards opened the gate and called their names, the women went to the door smiling.

They came back unconscious or nearly so. The other women laid the girls on their pallets and went back to gossiping or sewing or braiding each other's hair.

It disgusted Prija even though she understood the women were drunk on Grigori power. They couldn't help themselves.

It still disgusted her. The black shadow had become thicker and stronger. A fog hung around her mind.

The second night, one of the Grigori called her name. She sat in the corner, staring at the wall, and pretended not to hear.

"Prija."

Fools.

She stood and walked to the door. The smirking guard led her down a hallway and took her to another shower. This one had a door and was equipped with warm water. It was nearly luxurious. A clean set of clothes was laid on the bench by the shower, and fresh-scented soaps were by the sink.

Prija washed. She closed her eyes and let the warm water fall over her, filling her mouth and covering her face. She soaked her hair and wiggled her toes. Whatever else the night brought, at least she would be clean. It had been days since she'd had a proper bath, and she could hardly bear her own scent. She washed away the grime but was relieved when she turned off the water to find that the black fog that had wrapped around her was still there. It settled against her skin as she pulled on the cotton shirt and wrapped the skirt around her.

After she dressed, she knocked on the door and the guard opened it.

He led her down a hall and into a bedroom.

So much for being untouchable.

She didn't have much time. The Grigori—he must have been someone important because the room was spacious and had beautiful furniture—was already there. Before he could turn, Prija struck out with her mind.

"Tell them I want the woman to—" He broke off with a strangled cry.

Prija didn't wait. She struck again, as she had with the scribe in the van. The Grigori fell to the ground and bled from his ears as the guards rushed into the room.

"What have you done?"

A second guard walked in. "I told you!"

Prija hung back for a moment, watching the Grigori flail. Something kept her there. Kept her watching. Blood continued to trickle from his ears. His eyes were rolled back and his mouth was slack.

"She's a demon!"

You should go.

For the first time in years, the voice in her mind wasn't her own.

Prija walked out and wandered down the hall. She kept walking and got as far as the courtyard before someone stopped her. They threw a hood over her head and lifted her from her feet. She kicked out and struck in all directions with her mind, but she couldn't see anyone, and she could no longer hear voices, so none of her jabs hit a target. She was tossed over a shoulder and someone jogged. It was very uncomfortable.

"Here!" Whoever was holding her put her on her feet and started yelling. "Take her! Get her away from here. We don't want her."

Rough hands grabbed her upper arms. "We told you. She's a gift for Arindam. He will hear of your disrespect."

"You're nothing here," the other Grigori said. "And you'll be nothing in Bagan. You take her there and Arindam will kill you."

"We'll see."

Without another word, Prija was tossed in the back of the van and the doors slammed behind her. She tore off the hood and breathed a sigh of relief when she saw her *saw sam sai* safe in a corner under a bench. She looked around. Nothing about the van had changed. In a few minutes, she and her captors were traveling along the highway again.

CHAPTER
EIGHTEEN

L eo, Kyra, and their motley army returned to the small inn and quickly hid the women in their various bungalows. Leo had searched for the Wa language online and found a few passages of the Bible translated. Through that, he'd been able to speak enough to calm the panicked mother. She was safely stowed in Sura's bungalow with the other women, and Niran's Grigori guarded them.

He was unpacking the van when Alyah approached.

"Where is she?" he asked.

"Ginny takes her time, and she may have had trouble at the border."

"Is she going to be able to get all these women back into Thailand? They don't have papers. They have nothing but the clothes they're wearing."

"The scribe house will have taken care of that," Alyah said. "Once they arrive, we should be able to hand them off and keep going."

It didn't sit well with Leo that Prija had been moved so quickly. If she was that dangerous, the Fallen wouldn't be able to ignore her for long. And the quicker she caught Arindam's attention, the more difficult it would be to extract her.

"Rith is among the warriors Ginny is bringing," Alyah said. "He will be staying with us. He has a black blade with him."

"Dara's brother?"

"Yes."

Damien nodded. All Irin warriors knew what a black blade was. Leo had been struck with one, and it was only coals from the sacred fire that had healed him. Black blades were heaven-forged and brought to earth at the beginning of time. They had no equal and were the only way to kill one of the Fallen.

Only Irin scribes could wield a black blade, because the magic it took for mortal hands to control one had to be written on the skin. It was complicated and deep magic. Usually only elders or very senior watchers could control one. Warriors of Mikael's line took to the magic more readily, and considering both Rith and his sister were warriors, it was likely Mikael's blood ran in their veins.

Leo said, "It's unusual for someone less senior than a watcher to wield a blade like that."

Alyah nodded. "Our house is... different. In any other place, Rith would already be a watcher. In any other place, Anurak wouldn't be allowed to continue on as the watcher while serving as an elder in Vienna. It is only because female watchers are not technically allowed to exist that they have these... interesting loopholes, I think you would say in English."

"Because if Irina could be watchers," Leo said, "then Dara would be the watcher and Rith could have his own house."

"Exactly. But he believes in her leadership, so he stays to bolster her. It gives the rest of the scribes confidence to know a strong scribe *and* singer head the house, even if our watcher is far away."

Leo thought about his former watcher, Damien, and his mate, Sari, who were such a powerful couple. "Ideally, watchers and their mates would fill those roles. Long ago that was typical, was it not?"

Alyah said, "I'm as young as you are, Leo. I don't know how things were. Just how they are now."

"We're both operating at a disadvantage, aren't we?"

"I don't know." Alyah smiled. "Maybe being young means that we're not bound to the past like the others. The future will be what we make of it." Alyah nodded at Kyra and the little *kareshta* girl. They were walking through the forest, Kyra pointing out the birds flying overhead. "Maybe our world needs young ones like us because we see possibilities where our elders do not."

THREE HOURS LATER, GINNY DROVE UP IN A VAN WITH SUNSHINE TOURS! emblazoned on the side. A tall, dignified Asian man walked with her as three other Irin shifted things in the van and another walked to the office at the front of the inn.

Alyah met Ginny and bowed to both her friend and the tall man who accompanied her. Then she led them to where Leo and Niran were waiting.

"Leo, this is Kenneth, the scribe I was telling you about. He came along in case some of the women needed a translator."

"He anticipated us," Leo said. "Kenneth, we thank you."

Kenneth held out a hand. "It's very nice to meet you." His English accent revealed a crisp, British intonation. "Ginny tells me you're from Istanbul. I've heard so much about the library in Cappadocia; it's rumored to be the most complete in the eastern Mediterranean."

"I don't know about that as much as my watcher would," Leo said. "But I'd be happy to offer an introduction if you ever want to visit. Alyah speaks very highly of you."

"That would be wonderful," Kenneth said before he turned to Niran. "And you are the Grigori watcher from Chiang Mai?"

Niran started at the "watcher" label, but Alyah was quick to jump in.

"He is," she said. "Niran, this is Kenneth, a professor in Bangkok."

"And a scribe," Niran said.

"I am." Kenneth smiled. "Sadly, more swift with my references than my blades. But I do think I can be of assistance to the young women we're helping, if you'd be kind enough to introduce me."

Niran relaxed at Kenneth's warm, disarming introduction. He nodded and led Kenneth toward the bungalows, telling the professor what he knew about the human women, particularly the young woman from the Wa hill tribe.

Leo watched them walk toward Sura's bungalow where the women and children were staying. He wondered what Kyra would make of Kenneth, and if she'd trust the women and children with him. She was cautious, and he could already see her becoming attached to both the baby and the little girl.

She has a mother's heart.

The thought of Kyra carrying his child leapt into Leo's mind. He wanted that. In time. He wanted her to have the joy of motherhood and family. He wanted it for himself too. Leo didn't know how to be a father, but he had observed Malachi caring for his two small children. Leo knew he would have the same love that Malachi did with Geron and Matti.

"What are you thinking about?" Ginny asked him.

He sat on the porch. "Family."

Ginny sat next to him. "Is she your *reshon?*"

"Yes."

"Are you certain? Or is it wishful thinking?" Ginny's normally bright mood had shifted, and she sounded deadly serious. "Be sure, Leo."

"I'm sure." He turned his eyes from staring at the bungalows. "I think we both knew from the beginning. My voice was always the clearest to her. My heart always rested with her. And her touch... It was only the world interfering. First the battle in Vienna. Her brother's protectiveness. My reluctance to pursue her when I didn't know her heart."

"And now it's her health."

Leo said nothing. Alyah had performed a song to give Kyra strength, but he knew Ginny's magic was stronger. Kyra didn't appear weak after the excitement that morning, but Leo lived in a constant state of worry.

He couldn't perform the mating ritual and extend his magic to her without weakening himself for the coming fight. Yet he lived in fear that Kyra's life would blink out without warning.

But if he performed the ritual and linked her longevity to his, it *would* weaken him. Then if he died in battle, she probably would too.

"I'm going mad," he said quietly. "What should I do? If I give her my magic——"

"You'll be weak."

"But she would live."

"And if you died?" Ginny asked. "What then? If your lives are linked and you died in a fight, she'd likely die anyway. You know that, Leo. The sacrifice isn't worth it."

"Her life is worth *everything* to me."

Ginny sighed and rubbed both hands over her eyes. "Her life will always be tied to yours unless she has her own magic."

"I know. But I can't teach her, and Ava's not here. I think if I could get her back to Istanbul——"

"I'm sorry I yelled at you the other night."

Leo spoke cautiously. "Ginny, I have no intention of asking you for any favors. That's not why Alyah called you."

"I know." Ginny nodded. "But you love her. She's your *reshon*. You have every right to ask questions."

"But not every right to cause pain," Leo said. "I am sorry for that."

Ginny nodded, looking across the yard at the scribes unloading the tourist van.

"It was a long time ago," she said quietly. "I need to get over it."

"Scars remain, even after a wound heals. I can show you a few of my own, if you like."

"Why would I want to see that?" She smiled. "Everyone has their own stories. Their own wounds. Mine don't make me special."

"No, you're special for many more reasons than your scars, Ginny."

She grabbed his chin. "You have to stop being so sweet. Otherwise I'll be tempted to get rid of your girl and keep you for myself."

"You're not going to do that." He smiled. "Your heart is too good."

"You're killing me," she groaned. "Okay, let's go find Kyra."

Leo halted. "Why?"

"I can't fight with you in this one," she said, rising from the porch. "But I can give you an edge that will make you more focused. If you're not worried about Kyra, you'll be able to focus on fighting this Fallen. And I guarantee my crazy energy will be enough to keep her going for a good long while."

Leo's heart pounded. "Are you sure?"

"Positive. Besides, it'll give me an outlet. It's been a dry spell for me, and the energy I have built up is starting to get to me. I need to expend some big magic, and I'm more than happy to give it to your girl."

Leo grabbed her hand and rose. "Ginny, thank you."

"Thank me later," she said. "If she's anything like me, she'll be revved up afterward, so I'm guessing you'll want privacy."

Leo felt his face heat. "Are you talking about—?"

"Yep." Ginny waved a hand. "Come on. I don't have all day."

Leo walked toward the bungalow where Kyra was helping with the women. "Niran wants to leave tonight."

"I'll tell him you need to wait until morning. You'll want to stay with her and give her privacy until the first wave passes."

"Wave?"

"Energy, man." Ginny smiled. "This is as close to high or drunk that Kyra will probably get until you guys do your mating ritual. Nothing beats that, but this spell comes pretty close." Ginny stopped and put a hand on his chest. "Do you understand what I'm saying, Mr. Wholesome?"

His face must have been flaming, but he nodded.

"Good. Now let's find your girl, because you're not going to want to be in mixed company after we do this."

He swallowed hard. "She's in the bungalow with the women and children."

"Go get her and bring her to wherever you two are staying. I'll wait. You two need to discuss a few things before we start. No euphemisms. Don't be shy. Set clear boundaries for both of you. That's all the advice I'll give you. Other than that, have fun."

KYRA NARROWED HER EYES. "SO, THIS MAGIC SHE'S GOING TO perform…?"

"It will bolster your life energy with a huge punch of Ginny's magic. But the side effect of that will be… Well, I'm sure it's linked to life and the continuation of life and… the mating cycle and—"

"Oh!" Her eyes went wide. "You mean…"

"Sex," he blurted out. "You'll want to have sex. A lot."

"I see."

He nodded. "But you'll be in a somewhat… altered state. So before we… According to Ginny, the excitement and enthusiasm can be overwhelming. Your inhibitions will be lowered, so I need to know—"

"My inhibitions will be lowered?" Kyra's eyes lit up. "You mean I won't be so nervous?"

Leo frowned. "Why are you nervous? Am I pressuring you? Am I—?

"It's not *you*. Like I said, it's just the unknown. I start thinking about what will happen when we finally... consummate our relationship." Her cheeks turned red. "And I want to. But then I worry I'll do something wrong. Or that something will go wrong and you'll be disappointed."

"I would never be disappointed in you," Leo said. "Not ever, Kyra. I'm as unfamiliar with this as you are. We can learn together."

"But this magic will make me less nervous," she whispered. "It sounds like the perfect time to... experiment. Experiment more, I mean."

Leo's heart took off at a gallop. "I'm very willing to try that. But I want you to be sure."

"Am I going to be myself still? I'm going to remember everything, won't I?"

"Yes. According to Ginny, you'll just have much more energy. You might be light-headed, but—"

"Then I want to have sex afterward." Kyra nodded firmly. "This sounds like the perfect opportunity. I won't be nervous. And you're never nervous about anything."

Leo wasn't sure that was true. Just the thought of finally being with Kyra was enough to make him feel like a foolish and uncontrolled schoolboy. He'd barely become accustomed to seeing her skin bare. But he wasn't going to deny her either. She was correct. Most of their hesitance had to do with her nerves. If this ritual would diminish her anxiety, it was the perfect time.

"Okay," he said.

"Okay." She smiled. "Now you look like the nervous one."

"You have no idea."

GINNY SAT ACROSS FROM KYRA, BOTH RESTING CROSS-LEGGED IN the lotus position. Leo watched them from the side, surprised when a low, droning song came from Ginny's throat. Her song sounded like the wind through trees. Her palm thumped on the wooden floor in a steady rhythm as her power began to fill the air. It was unlike any singing Leo had heard, completely unlike Irina singing he'd heard from Sari and Ava.

Of course.

Though the Old Language was the same, Ginny was American, not European. The Irina of North America had been singing long before any European influence came to their shores. Even though Ginny had European blood, her teachers would likely have been indigenous North American Irina.

The song rose and fell in rhythm. He could see Kyra's face glowing with Ginny's power, but the song droned on, filling Leo's chest with an intense longing. Something in his heart listened and understood what his mind did not.

This is how it will be.

Her song will give you life.

Her voice will lift you from darkness.

Find her voice.

Leo was a scribe of tradition and duty, but his mandate was no longer to obey his watcher first. His mission was to help his mate find her voice. She was a daughter of heaven, redolent with power. One day he would hear her sing as Ginny did. As Alyah did. As Sari did. In her own voice—in the voice heaven had given her—Kyra's song would rise, and Leo would hear it.

"Vash shanda vet.
Vash vet Urielda. Vash vet Rafaelta.
Kulme shanda vet e livah.
Kulme vet. Oh Kulva vet.

Oh vet Urielda vashama."

Leo felt tears roll down his cheeks, his heart pounding with the beauty and power of Ginny's song. She called on Uriel, who gave the gift of life to all Irin sons and daughters. She called on Rafael's healing.

Ginny was Rafaene. Like his mother.

That was why her life-giving songs were so potent. She was a healer of Rafael's line. It was probably also why she didn't want to work within the scribe house power structure. Healers had a tendency to be the independent sort. Even among scribes, they were given special dispensation from combat for long periods of time.

Ginny was a healer, and she was healing Kyra before his eyes.

Kyra's face was luminous. Her eyes were closed, and he could see her pale skin glow with a golden light, as if Ginny's power was radiating from the sun. It wasn't unheard of. Leo had heard that Rafael's line thrived in sunlight and avoided areas of the world with long periods of darkness.

He didn't know how long she sang, only that as time passed, he could feel the power leaving Ginny—the manic energy she so often radiated—and feel it enter Kyra. He felt Kyra's energy reaching out toward his like gold threads that entangled him. He didn't realize he'd moved closer to her until their knees were touching. He stared at her. Her eyes were closed. Her face was lifted.

A hand patted his shoulder.

He blinked and looked up. Ginny was standing over him.

"Give her a little time to wake," she whispered. "She'll be fine. Her *livah* is very strong, but her mind is binding with her body right now. When she wakes, she'll be *very* awake, if you know what I mean."

Leo felt drunk by proximity. "What?"

Ginny patted his shoulder. "You'll be fine. Have fun."

"Okay."

"I'll see you back in Chiang Mai."

"Okay."

"Lock the door behind me. You won't want to be disturbed."

In a daze, Leo did as she told him, sliding the large wooden block across the door of the bungalow. Ginny had already closed the shades and lit candles before the ritual. The room was bathed in a gold glow, shadows softening the edges of Leo's vision until everything he saw felt like a dream. He turned back to Kyra and realized her eyes were open.

Her eyes were more than open. They were on fire.

CHAPTER
NINETEEN

Come to me, reshon.

Kyra said the words in her mind, but Leo obeyed them as if she'd spoken. He walked over and picked her up off the ground, lifting her as she thrilled in his strength. Most days, when she looked at Leo, she saw his smile first. His gentle eyes. The kindness in his expression.

That night, she saw the corded muscles in his arms and shoulders, the firm set of his jaw, his narrow hips and strong thighs.

She was ravenous with desire. She wanted to consume him. She had no thought of herself or her own body. No self-consciousness. No nerves. She only knew her body hungered and it was for him.

As soon as he set her down on the bed and knelt beside her, she sat up, grasping the end of his white linen shirt and pulling up. He raised his arms and helped her as she undressed him. Her mouth found its way to his shoulder and she licked out, tracing the lines of his *talesm* with her tongue. His skin was hot and alive with magic. His marks were glowing, and she knew it was because of the power suffusing the air. It surrounded them like the scent of flowers and incense. Smoke from a fire that burned inside.

"Kyra, slow down. Breathe."

"No. Off." She tugged at his waistband. "Skin. I want your skin. I need it."

Leo nodded and stripped down without another word. She tugged her dress over her head and pulled him over her, hugging his chest to hers as her legs tangled with his, and he held himself carefully over her so he didn't crush her under the weight of his body.

Kyra wanted to be crushed. She ached with it. She wanted the pressure of his body over her. Wanted his weight and the solid mass of him pushing her down. She felt like she might fly out of her own skin if he didn't anchor her.

Leo rolled to the side and wrapped her up, legs twisted around hers, arms binding her body to his. His hands were in her hair, and he guided her mouth to his. They were pressed together, every inch of her to every inch of him.

Kyra let out a breath she felt she'd been holding her whole life.

There.

There you are.

You are me and I am you.

We are home.

Leo released her lips and kissed all over her face, tasting every inch of her while Kyra's hands explored his arms, back, and shoulders. Her foot slid up and down the back of his leg, and he shivered when her toes passed over the soft skin behind his knee. She lifted her leg and wrapped it around the back of his thigh, opening to him.

Leo groaned and closed his eyes. "Kyra."

"Whatever you're going to ask for, the answer is yes."

"I want everything."

"Yes. And yes again. And yes to more."

He let out a breathless laugh. "Wait."

"I'm ready." She took his hand and placed it where his erection met her heat. She was more than ready. She burned for him.

Leo made a hungry sound in his throat and rubbed over the sensitive spot he'd teased so mercilessly a few nights before. Kyra's arms tightened around his neck a second before she came violently against his hand.

"Please, Leo."

"I love you." He waited until she met his eyes. "You are my *reshon*."

"I am your *reshon*," she whispered.

He took himself in hand and guided his rock-hard erection into her, inching in even as she urged him to go faster. The pressure was intense, but the ache was driving her to madness. She felt a void where none had been before.

And then she was full.

Kyra cried out and wrapped both legs fully around his hips, drawing him in closer and deeper until he cried out and bucked his hips against hers.

"Coming," he said, his voice hoarse. "Kyra, I'm—"

"I feel you." She sank her teeth into his shoulder. It felt so good. Everything about him amazed her. He surrounded her and filled her.

He was still hard. Leo pushed up and rocked deeper into her. "Does it hurt?"

She couldn't speak, but she shook her head. Nothing hurt. A small voice in the back of her mind told her it might hurt in the morning, but in that moment, she felt no pain. Her skin was exquisitely sensitive. She felt every inch of him. Felt the fine hairs on his legs and the quiver of his abdominal muscles as he moved carefully in her. She ran her hands up his arms and slipped her fingers over the corded muscles, tracing the dark lines that glowed brighter than the candles. She closed her eyes and let herself drift in sensation, shutting off her mind because she knew she was safe.

With Leo, she was always safe.

He came again after a few moments, lowering his chest to hers and capturing her mouth in a long kiss that made her toes curl. He remained snug in her, gathering her up as he rolled to the side.

"A few minutes," he said. "Then again."

"Yes."

"I love you."

"I love you too."

"How do you feel?"

"Amazing." She kissed his collarbone. "I feel amazing."

SHE MUST HAVE FALLEN ASLEEP, BECAUSE SHE WOKE UP AS HE WAS lowering her into a warm bath. The air smelled of frangipani and incense, and steam filled the small room.

"Come in with me," she said. "I don't want to be alone."

"I will." He took off the linen wrapped around his waist and slipped in behind her. As always, she was surprised and delighted by the way he moved. It would be natural for a large man to walk heavily, to move with purpose. But Leo moved with purpose and grace. He slid behind her and lifted her onto his lap. She could feel his arousal pressed against her back, but he didn't seem to notice it, pouring warm water over her from the pitcher he filled from the tub.

"Are you sore?" he asked.

She shook her head. Her energy had smoothed out, but she still felt euphoric.

Leo poured the water over her head and smoothed her hair back, brushing it to the side and kissing her spine.

"When we have time," he whispered, "when we are safe, I'm going to find the softest sable brush and mark your back with my vows. Pour my magic onto your skin and bind you to me forever."

She smiled. "Greedy."

"So greedy." He drew over her shoulders with his fingers, and she could feel the brush of his magic even without the ritual. "And when you are ready, when you've found your voice, you'll sing to me. And I'll carve your vow over my heart and keep it with me forever."

She shook her head. "Leo, I don't know if that will ever be possible. I don't know if anyone will ever trust me enough—"

"I know it is possible," he said. "I've seen it. I know you'll find your voice, Kyra. I'm going to help you find it."

She was silent for a long time, thinking of what he asked. "And if I don't?"

"If you don't find your magic?"

"What then? Will you go through life half as strong? If I can't give you your half of the mating ritual, will it make you weak?"

He squeezed his arms around her. "You make me strong."

"You're not answering the question."

"Because I cannot imagine a future without you finding your magic. The Creator wouldn't have put all this power in you with no way of your using it for good."

Kyra closed her eyes and leaned back, laying her head on Leo's shoulder as he pressed his cheek to her temple.

She loved Leo so much, but she also knew he could be naive. Kyra knew the world was far from fair. Not everything happened for a reason. Some fates were unavoidable. Evil *did* win. Not always, but often. Children died. Women suffered. The powerful ruled, and the powerless tried to survive.

But she loved him too much to say it. She loved him too much to darken his optimism. So she'd try. She'd pretend. Maybe if she loved him enough, it wouldn't matter. He had powerful friends. She had powerful family. If they lived quietly, maybe they could find peace.

Kyra wanted to try, even if ultimately they failed. She needed to try. She didn't have much hope, but she clung to what she had because the thought of losing a future with Leo hurt too much.

SHE FELL ASLEEP IN THE TUB AND WOKE ON THE BED WITH HIS kiss between her legs.

"Softly," she whispered.

"Yes." He'd shaved after their bath, and his smooth cheeks were warm on her inner thighs. He stretched across the bed, taking his time, luxuriating in her taste, and Kyra lay back and let the lingering ecstasy from the magic drift in her head. She closed her eyes and saw stars, but not the stars in the sky. These were a rising and falling pattern that grew brighter as Leo loved her.

Creation and destruction. In the heady moment of release, she saw the stars burst in her mind, raining around her without fading. They scattered and reorganized, chasing each other across her mind's eye.

"Kyra," he whispered.

Leo held her on the edge again; he didn't push her over. When she came, it was because she reached for it, reached for the scattered, pulsing light. She grabbed it and tugged it to her lips.

She climaxed on a sigh.

Do you see it yet?

WHEN LEO MADE LOVE TO HER BEFORE DAWN, IT WAS IN THE glow of a single candle. Every other light had sputtered out.

Kyra pressed her palms to his hips and felt the steady rhythm as he moved in her. She looked up, watching his eyes devour her face, her breasts, her belly. Watched him as he watched himself move in her, awe and hunger parting his lips. He wet his bottom lip and clenched it between his teeth. She felt his muscles harden beneath her fingers as the tension built. Sweat dripped down his chest and abdomen. Kyra felt it drop on her belly as he moved faster and faster.

He was so beautiful.

At the last minute, he looked up and met her eyes.

Awe. Pleasure. Pain.

"I love you," she whispered.

He gasped out her name and came, his marks lighting the dark room as the candle flickered out. In the darkness, he kissed her mouth, running his hands up and down her body as he stole her breath.

She slept with his arm and leg draped over her, his palm a pillow for her head. Kyra slept more deeply than she ever remembered before. In his touch was complete and utter silence except for a single voice.

His voice.

And it was whispering *reshon*.

CHAPTER
TWENTY

L eo slammed the Grigori's head into the wall and watched him crumple unconscious to the ground as Niran held another up by his neck.

"Tell us where our sister is," he said calmly, "or I'll let him do that to you too."

The young man was dressed as a monk, but Sura said it was only an insidious cover for the Grigori in this village. They dressed as monks to gain the trust of pilgrims, then took advantage of them. Many young women had disappeared in this secluded river valley. And though Niran, Sura, and Leo had searched the temple complex, they'd found no survivors.

"We haven't seen your sister," the Grigori said.

Niran tightened his hold on the man's neck.

"But we've heard rumors!" he choked out.

Niran relaxed his hand.

"There was a woman. One of the untouchables. Two of our kind brought her to our brothers in the north. She was to be a gift for our father. They were only there for two days when they moved on. The brothers there said she killed one of them. He was bleeding from his ears. They said his mind exploded."

"Where did they take her?" Leo asked.

"I don't know."

Niran's hand clenched again.

"I don't! She... she's dangerous. We don't want her here. We have a good relationship with the village."

"Your 'relationship' is nothing more than a front," Niran spat out. "You fool them into trusting you, then take their energy without their knowledge. You disgust me. You are a demon and an offense to heaven."

"Most of them come willingly," the Grigori said. "The girls like our attentions."

A movement from the corner made Leo turn. It was Sura. He wore an expression that Leo had never seen before. It was utterly cold and looked alien on the gentle man's face. They'd left Sura, Rith, and Alyah to explore the temple complex, searching for any women or children found there. As far as Leo knew, they'd found nothing.

"Sura?" Leo asked. "Did you find something?"

Silently, Sura walked to the Grigori Niran held, yanked his head forward, and pierced his spine with the silver knife he carried. Then he bent and plunged his knife into the back of the Grigori at Leo's feet.

The Grigori began to dissolve, but Sura turned without a word, shaking the gold dust from the edges of his trousers as he left them.

Leo watched silently, his eyes wide. Sura was usually the last to resort to violence, but he'd executed Arindam's sons without a flinch.

Niran dusted off his hands and stepped back. "We weren't going to get anything more from him anyway."

"What was that?" Leo said.

"Sura?" Niran sheathed his silver knives. "They were using the appearance of holiness to seduce the vulnerable. Women. Children. The elderly. Sura will not tolerate it."

"I've never seen him..."

"What? Violent?" Niran shook his head. "He's the most

dangerous of all of us precisely because he is the last one who will ever lose control."

Leaving the topic of Sura alone, Leo asked about the fractured information they'd gathered. "Brothers in the north, he said. Do you think he means Mandalay?"

"Possibly."

They'd been slowly working their way west, following the voices Kyra heard to the hidden outposts and enclaves of Grigori in Arindam's territory.

"Grigori are everywhere in Mandalay," Niran said. "It's a stronghold for Arindam's people, but it's too crowded for the angel."

"Most don't like that much company."

"No. Arindam himself will likely be somewhere more secluded, if he's at all the way Sura remembers him."

"So do we go to Mandalay or not?"

Niran paused. "How far is Kyra's range now?"

"With the infusion she received from Ginny and my help, nearly two hundred kilometers if she's rested and focused."

"We don't have to push her. We're two hundred fifty kilometers from Mandalay now?"

"Yes, but the Grigori here said she was only at this place 'in the north' for two days."

"Then we keep going west," Niran said. "West and north for now."

"Fine." Leo felt like they were on a wild-goose chase, but he didn't know what other options they had. There was little to no Irin presence in Myanmar, and the Irin scribes in northern India had no interest in the place. They didn't have intelligence on the region other than what they could glean from the Grigori they encountered.

When Leo and Niran walked out of the temple and into the courtyard, Leo saw Sura sitting in a lotus position, eyes closed, his back to the stone Buddha who greeted worshippers upon entry. The tall statue appeared to watch the silent man at his feet, observing with a raised palm and a serene expression.

"We found bones," Sura said after several minutes of silence.

"What?"

"You asked if I'd found something when I walked into the temple," Sura said, his eyes still closed. "We found bones. Bodies buried behind the vegetable garden on the edge of the forest. Adult bones. Children too."

No wonder the quiet man had executed the Grigori without a word.

"What did you do with the others?" Leo knew Kyra had sensed at least a dozen Grigori in the temple posing as priests.

Sura unfolded himself and rose. "They don't exist anymore." He walked down the steps and toward the van where the others waited.

Turning to the newly empty temple, Leo walked back inside, closing the shutters and latching them. He blew out the candles and smothered the incense. Then he walked out the front doors and propped a stone planter in front of them to keep the weather out.

It was a holy place that had been perverted by predators. Leo hoped true monks or nuns might find it someday.

Perhaps they might pray for the lost.

LEO KNOCKED QUIETLY ON THE DOOR TO THE COTTAGE HE AND Kyra were sharing in the villa high in the mountains. They'd spent the previous two nights in small country inns that were little more than campsites. But that night Niran had demanded plumbing. Rith and Alyah had searched online and found the luxury villa with cottages high on a ridge overlooking a river valley. It was an unexpected treat that also played into their cover as traveling exhibition fighters.

"Come in," Kyra called.

Leo poked his head in, and Kyra smiled.

"Why are you knocking?"

"I wasn't sure if you wanted privacy."

She put the book she'd been reading to the side. "Not from you."

Leo slid off his shoes and climbed next to her on the bed. He put his arms around her waist and his head on her breast, lowering them to the pillows as he let out a deep sigh.

"Long day?" Kyra asked.

"We didn't find anything. Nothing detailed, anyway. Niran thinks she was in Mandalay, but she'd be gone by now."

"We'll keep looking. I can do a reading in the morning and see what I hear. I'll focus to the north."

"Only if you're rested enough."

"The one this morning took hardly anything out of me. I'm fine."

Leo closed his eyes and inhaled her scent. She was soft touch and tenderness. She was rest.

"Sura found bones." It slipped out without his thinking. He hadn't meant to tell her.

Kyra tensed. "Children?"

"Yes. They didn't have any women there. I think they were human bones, not *kareshta*."

"We don't leave bones," Kyra said. "We're like the Irina. We turn to dust."

He clutched her tighter. "I'm sorry. I shouldn't have brought it up."

"Even the babies turn to dust," she said under her breath. "Not very much. Just a dance in the air and they're gone."

Leo's heart broke every time she talked about her past. "I thought Barak didn't kill his children."

"He didn't, but others did. He had a rival who once raided the compound where Kostas and I were kept. His men killed most of the women and children there. Kostas and I stayed under the floorboards where one of our older brothers hid us. We were valuable."

"But the others weren't?"

"Not like us. There were children killed that day. Then I'm sure my older brothers retaliated. I'm sure some of them killed that Fallen's children." She stroked a hand through Leo's hair. "It's a very violent world. There is no softness in it."

"You were in it." He knit his fingers with hers.

"I had a brother who protected me," Kyra said. "Kostas… he took the brunt of everything for me."

Leo spoke past the tightness in his throat. "Then I owe him a debt I can never repay."

"He won't let you pay him back. He'll tell you it was his duty to protect me."

Leo paused. "Should we call him? Just to let him know you're well?"

"I called Sirius on Sura's phone. I don't want Kostas to know where I am yet. He'd worry too much." She laughed a little. "He treats me with kid gloves, but he'll be happy for me. For us."

"I hope so."

"He will be," Kyra said. "He always talked about my having a normal life. Especially after I met Ava and learned how to make the voices stop. He wanted that for me. To have a family. A home. A real home."

"Is that what he wants for himself?"

"He doesn't think he'll live that long," Kyra said. "And he doesn't think he deserves it."

"Love doesn't work that way," Leo said. "It's a gift I hope he finds someday."

Kyra leaned over and kissed his head a moment before Leo's eyes shut. "I hope so too."

"No." She shook her head, her eyes closed. "I'm not getting any sign of Prija, but I can't be certain. There are so many people. So many Grigori. *Kareshta*. It's a huge compound, but I don't feel anyone familiar." A tear slipped from her eye.

"Kyra?" Leo put a hand on her shoulder. "Pull back."

"There's so much pain," she whispered.

"Pull back!"

"They need to take them away from there. The children..."

She started to sob quietly, and Leo put both arms around her from behind. He embraced her hard and felt blood on his cheek. It was leaking from her right ear.

"Kyra, pull back."

Her cries turned to moans and she began to shake. Leo raised his eyes to Sura in panic. He'd been able to pull Kyra out of her visions in the past, but she'd stretched so far, fallen so deeply, he could barely feel her. Her *livah* was stretched thin, nearly snapped away from her body.

Alyah strode over and put a hand on Kyra's temple.

"*Ya kazas!*"

Kyra's head fell to the side and she went limp.

"What did you do?" Leo yelled.

"She'll be fine," Alyah said. "I diverted her mind. The mental version of a hard, fast punch. She might feel sick when she wakes up, but she'll be fine."

Kyra began to retch, and Sura rushed over with a bucket. Her eyes were still closed and her body limp, but Leo held her hair back while she emptied her stomach of everything she'd eaten that morning. She didn't wake through the episode, but when Leo laid her on their bed, her eyes flickered open.

"Leo?"

"Alyah pulled you back from the vision."

"I felt trapped. There's someone there... Grigori maybe. He

sensed me. He knows I'm looking for someone. He tried to... hold me."

"Was it the Fallen?"

"Maybe. I don't know. It didn't feel like..." She slipped away again.

Leo brought a chair over and sat by the bed, bucket and washcloth ready if she felt sick again. When he looked up, Vasu was sitting at the foot of the bed.

"Why are you here?" Leo asked.

Vasu was watching Kyra. "She was very... *Dear* isn't the right word. Her father held her in high esteem, which was rare for him. He was very cynical."

"Barak cared for her?"

"In his way." Vasu shrugged. "As much as he cared for anything."

"She's not a thing."

"She was to him." Vasu looked at Leo. "He was not human, scribe. Don't try to explain his reasoning as if he was."

"You're not human either."

Vasu cocked his head. "They accused me of it sometimes."

"Of being human? Who?" Leo had a hard time imagining anything less human than Vasu.

"Barak and Jaron. They didn't understand why I wanted to stay."

"Why did you?"

Vasu rolled his eyes. "Heaven is boring. We are created to serve Him. I don't want to serve."

"I don't think you're a very good angel, are you?"

"No, I'm a terrible angel." He leaned over Kyra. "I wouldn't find them so interesting if I were a good angel."

"Angels love women."

"Angels don't love anything," Vasu said. "Or hate anything. At least good angels don't. We have no commitments. No attachments." He turned his eyes toward Leo. "We hold nothing dear because nothing is worth more than serving the one who made us."

"The Fallen don't think so. They're greedy for power."

"Yes." Vasu grinned. "But then we were all Fallen. Your precious Forgiven fathers too. They were only rewarded because they abandoned their children. That is your inheritance, scribe. You have your power, your knowledge, because your fathers valued you so little."

"If they valued me that little, I prefer to have the knowledge."

"Ha!" Vasu grinned. "You are wiser than you appear."

His eyes turned back to Kyra. "Do not mistake my optimism for naïveté."

"She does."

"I know." Leo knew Kyra thought he was ignorant of the realities of their world. He wasn't. He knew they had a hard road ahead of them. He simply chose to view it with optimism instead of resignation. "It takes far more courage to hope than it does to despair."

"And that is why I could not return," Vasu murmured. "Humans. Irin. *Kareshta*. Grigori. You are all so very…"

"Curious?"

"Odd," Vasu said. "You're odd. But the best of you are unexpected. And that is what keeps me from returning."

"I'm glad we can entertain you."

"Good." Vasu stretched out next to Kyra and played with a piece of her hair.

Leo had the urge to shove the Fallen off the bed, but he wasn't hurting Kyra. The affection he was showing her almost seemed… brotherly. Fond.

"I like her," Vasu said.

"I love her."

"That's very nice, but do you like her too?" Vasu's tone was curious, not confrontational.

Talking with Vasu was like conversing with an alien. "Is liking more important than love?"

"I don't know. Is it?"

Leo watched Vasu playing with Kyra's hair. There was something intensely childlike about the angel.

"I like to talk with her and spend time with her," Leo said. "She's funny and tells good stories. She's loyal to those she cares about and guards those who are weak. She understands sacrifice and strength. Maybe better than anyone I've ever met. So yes, I like her *and* I love her."

"She's not going to die, you know."

"I know. Ginny gave her power and as soon as we're able, I will perform the mating—"

"I kissed her," Vasu said.

Leo pushed back the flare of anger. "*What?*"

"In her dream. She probably doesn't remember it. I kissed her though. She'll be fine. I gave her some of my power."

"Why?"

"Why not?" Vasu said. "She's Barak's blood."

And that, Leo began to understand, was a little like Barak himself. Vasu, the mighty Fallen, was lonely for his old friends. Their children were as close as he could get to having them in his realm of existence.

"Vasu," Leo asked carefully, "what do you want?"

"I told you I like her."

Leo didn't know how to respond. On one hand, he was relieved. Kyra would be strong and healthy for years with an infusion of angelic power. It was how she'd survived so long without magic. On the other hand, he didn't believe that Vasu wanted nothing from her. The Fallen weren't altruistic. Of course, it was possible to manipulate them too.

"If you really care for Kyra, then you should give her brother some power."

"Which one?" Vasu twisted Kyra's hair around his finger. "She has many brothers."

"Her twin. Kostas. If he was hurt, she would feel it."

Vasu's eyes narrowed on Leo. "Would *you* give him power?"

"If I could. But my magic doesn't work that way."

"Rules, rules, rules," Vasu muttered. "That is another reason. Too many rules."

"What about rules?"

"Nothing." Vasu sat up. "So you want me to give her twin brother some more life?"

"Jaron was giving it to him, but Jaron is gone."

Vasu pursed his full lips. "Interesting."

"Will you do it?"

"I will... think about it." Vasu grinned.

It was likely the best answer he'd get out of the troublemaker.

"I'll let Kyra know you're thinking about helping her brother," Leo said. "I'm sure she'll be grateful."

Vasu disappeared and reappeared as a cat that jumped in Leo's lap.

"You try to create obligation in me. It's an interesting theory. I told them you were smarter than you appeared," the cat said, curling up on Leo's lap. "Now pet me."

"Are you serious?"

Narrow claws dug into Leo's leg.

"Ow! Fine." He put his hand on the back of the cat's neck and stroked down over and over again. Eventually the cat started to purr. Then it seemed to fall asleep. Leo sat that way for hours, watching Kyra sleep and petting a black cat who wasn't a cat as it slept and purred. A server came in and set up a small table for tea, but Leo didn't move. The sun hung heavy in the afternoon sky, creeping across the floor and warming the cat, who only purred louder.

Someone tapped on the door.

"Come in," Leo said quietly.

Sura walked in with Alyah at his side. "We were curious

how…" His eyes drifted down to the black, furry lump on Leo's lap. "That is not a cat."

Alyah said, "What do you mean it's not a… Oh." She frowned. "Why are you petting it?"

Leo rested his chin in his hand and leaned on the side of the chair. "Because he asked me to."

Sura sat at the low table. "I suppose that's as good a reason as any."

Alyah glared at the cat as if willing it to wake. Leo kept petting it. Any time he slowed, the claws dug in. He didn't know what would happen if you angered a Fallen angel who was sleeping in the form of a cat, but he decided he really didn't want to find out.

Minutes later, the cat must have felt Alyah's glare, because it rose, arched its back and yawned, then deftly jumped out the window and into the waning afternoon.

Kyra sat up in bed, her hair tangled around her face and her cheeks flushed. "Leo?"

"Are you feeling better?"

"There was a black cat in my dream," she said, rubbing her eyes. "He told me Prija was in a place called Bagan. Does that make sense to anyone, or am I finally going crazy?"

Leo grinned and turned to Alyah and Sura. "And that is why when the cat asks you to pet him, you do."

PRIJA V

I t was hot and dry in the place they called Bagan. At night it cooled off, but only a little bit. The cell—because it couldn't be called a room—had a single window that only let in a faint puff of air. But Prija had privacy.

Except for the Fallen.

He whispered to her mind—seductive, powerful whispers that made her head buzz. His voice was everywhere on the mountain. She dreamed of gold and silk. She dreamed of cool water and fresh fruit. When she woke, she was in her cell and the black shadow had become a dense fog that surrounded her.

Her captors finally presented her to the angel. They dragged her to the temple where the creature was lying on a low bed, surrounded by his sycophants and lovers. Prija had never seen anything like it.

He didn't look like her own father, who had appeared as a beautiful and powerful king. This creature was a monster. His skin was red and his eyes were bulging. Two horns adorned his head, and his muscled arms had wings growing from them. Snakes wrapped around his wrists, and human women curled over and around his naked body, massaging and pleasuring him as he spoke to Prija's captors. He was like one of the deities the humans worshipped, but all the goodness had been stripped away and perverted. There was only power and greed in Arindam's bearing.

"We have a gift for you, our father."

The Fallen looked her up and down. "What is it?"

"A powerful daughter of Tenasserim. She is a weapon for you, my lord."

"How?"

Her other captor, who was usually the quiet one, spoke. "She killed her own father."

A Grigori on Arindam's right side said, "What kind of female can kill one of the Fallen?"

"She killed one of our brothers in Mandalay."

A troubled murmur around her.

Prija forced herself to look at the horrible eyes of the Fallen.

He was measuring her with calculation. "Why does she live?"

"We told you, she is a weapon."

"A weapon turned against me."

Her captor didn't like that, but Prija forced herself to keep looking at Arindam. She had the creeping suspicion that the minute she looked away, she'd be lost forever.

Little one, you are more powerful than they.

His whisper was seductive.

Show me your power, and I shall make you my queen.

It was a lie. She could hear it in his voice. But she showed him anyway.

The black fog helped her. It was malleable in her mind, and she narrowed her power to a pointed stick. She jabbed at the talkative Grigori, imagining his temple pierced by a black spear. She heard him cry out and crumple beside her. She jabbed at him over and over. By the time her first captor was silent, the whole temple had grown still.

Arindam was smiling. "Now the other."

Prija didn't once look away from the Fallen. She kept her

eyes on him when she heard the other Grigori go running. There was a scuffle, and he didn't get far. Arindam's attendants brought him back to Prija, who slowly wrapped the black fog around her second captor's neck. She squeezed and wrung it out in her mind, keeping her eyes on Arindam while he watched gleefully as his child twisted before him.

When the second captor was dead, he asked her, "How do you feel?"

Prija said nothing.

How do you feel? he asked in her mind.

Empty.

Hollow.

Nothing. I feel nothing.

But Prija didn't tell the angel those things. She wiped her thoughts, concealing them from the Fallen. Instead of words, she sank into the black fog. She sank into it and let it fill her mind.

"Take her away," the Fallen said. "I'll decide what do to with her tomorrow."

Arindam's sons took her away and locked her in a different room, away from the others. When the fog reached out, it felt nothing.

The Grigori had learned to keep their distance.

The next day, no one came for her.

Or the next day.

Or the next.

Prija was silent.

TWENTY-ONE

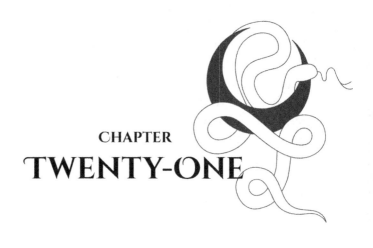

The city of Old Bagan was a hot, dry plain dotted with sparse trees and a thousand ancient temples and pagodas. It sat in a curve of the Irrawaddy River, the slow-moving tributary that ferried passengers, cargo, and small fishing boats north and south in the central plains of Myanmar. Kyra watched from the comfort of a shaded horse carriage as wooden boats moved on the river. According to Sura, they were passing time and distracting themselves while Niran, Alyah, Rith, and Leo surveyed the compound in the hills where Arindam was keeping Prija.

Kyra's own temples throbbed.

"Is it the heat?" Niran asked.

"A little bit. Mostly it's the noise."

From the time they'd descended from the Shan Hills and onto the central plain, a low, discordant resonance had begun in Kyra's mind. There were no spells that erased it. Even Alyah's skills had done nothing to block the noise. It was a constant, low hum that scraped against her mind and wouldn't let her rest unless she maintained skin contact with Leo.

It was one of the Fallen.

"Arindam," Sura said. "It is said he was a messenger in heaven."

"Which means he uses spoken power," Kyra said.

"Which means you will have little way of blocking his voice should he choose to turn it against you," Sura said. "You must be careful."

"I'm no one to him." She closed her eyes and put a hand over them to block the vivid sunlight. "He won't know I exist."

"If his sons have reported hearing you—"

"They can't hear me."

"But they can feel your presence. They tried to hold your mind in Mandalay."

"Maybe." She was short-tempered. "Perhaps. I doubt they consider me a threat. I'm a radar, Sura. Nothing more. Nothing less."

"You sell yourself short."

"I'm a well-bred antenna. That's hardly something for an angel to worry about."

"Why not?"

"Because," she snapped, "even if I can hear him, what can I do? *Nothing.* I don't have any useful magic. Not for combat. Not that would frighten a Fallen."

"Hmm." Sura closed his eyes and leaned back against the padded seat.

Kyra sat and stewed in the growing heat.

"Are you liking the pagodas?"

She took a deep breath. "If I wasn't very hot and very irritated, I'm sure I'd appreciate them more."

"We'll go back." He whistled at the driver and spoke to him. The cart began to turn and Kyra felt churlish.

"Don't," she said. "It's beautiful here. I'm just being cross."

"It's fine." Sura was predictably pleasant. "You're hot and you've had a headache for two days. I should have given you a dark room and music, not tried to show you the sights."

They rode in silence back to the hotel where they'd taken

rooms. There were far more tourists in Bagan than anywhere they'd been in Myanmar. Kyra was still getting used to seeing European faces again. It was one of the reasons, Sura explained, that Arindam had such a big compound near Old Bagan. Not only did the nearness of Western tourists give his sons good cover, but the hotels and tourist industry attracted young women from surrounding villages who came to work at the many hotels and restaurants near the temple complex. They came. They disappeared just as easily. There were always more young women from villages who needed work. Who was going to look for one who'd run off, even if her family came searching?

It was a typical pattern in the Grigori world. Kyra had been sheltered by her brothers, but no *kareshta* could hide from the truth unless they completely gave in to the madness. Wealthy tourists equaled Grigori presence because the poor would always come to work and serve where there was money to be spent. It wasn't the tourists who usually suffered; it was the most vulnerable who lived on the edges.

Despite the growing shadows of Grigori presence, Kyra was grateful for one thing about the busier tourist site. Very few people looked at her, other than those who were drawn to her angelic blood and typically sent her admiring glances. And more than half of those looks were diverted when Leo was with her. Some because they were more drawn to his golden beauty than her darker features. Some because Leo was more than a little intimidating.

It had shocked her to see the reaction when they arrived at the hotel and he was mingling with other guests. To her, Leo had always been the most gentle of men. She was surprised to realize human men were frightened of him. Women, of course, were drawn to him.

But unlike most Grigori, who were incapable of ignoring female attention, Leo hardly seemed to notice the admiring or wary glances. He moved through the world utterly self-contained, cheerfully curious, and wholly focused on her and her needs.

She'd had to shove him out the door that morning. He knew his touch helped to keep the Fallen's voice at bay.

"Let's have lunch," Sura said. "Leo will be cross with me if I don't feed you."

"Can we eat in our suite?"

"Of course." Sura hopped out of the carriage, which had taken them to the steps of their hotel. "Why don't you go to the room, and I'll order something light for us to share?"

"Thank you." She put up an umbrella and hated the fragility of her steps. Without Leo, everything in her body felt hypersensitive. Even her skin felt like it was picking up sound from the humans around her. The background noise grew louder the longer she stayed. She could hear the angel most of all, but she also was picking up disturbing thoughts from Prija. She'd homed in on the woman the moment they drew near the temples.

What she'd heard wasn't promising.

SHE WAS HIDING IN DARKNESS WHEN LEO RETURNED. WITHOUT waiting a beat, he slid his shoes off at the door, unhooked his knife holsters, and joined her on the bed, sliding a hand under the loose shirt she wore and pressing one palm to the small of her back while the other slid to cradle her head.

Kyra took a deep breath and let the silence envelope her.

"Better?" he said.

She nodded.

"How bad today?"

"It's the same. It hasn't changed since we arrived in the city."

"He's in the compound. We got visual confirmation today."

"How did you escape his notice?"

"I kept back with Rith. Alyah and Niran are the ones who saw him."

Though Irina had long ago developed magic to hide themselves from the Fallen, Irin still had a difficult time evading detection. Niran, a Grigori, and Alyah had the best chance of remaining under Arindam's radar and escaping detection.

"How many sons?" Kyra asked.

"I'd estimate nearly fifty in the compound, though only two-thirds are what I'd consider fighting age."

"That doesn't mean anything." A Fallen would send little children to fight if it suited his purposes. Children were disposable to them. They could always breed more. "Women?" Kyra asked.

"A dozen or so. Around half of them pregnant, according to Alyah."

"Children?"

"Kyra, why are you doing this?"

"I want to help."

Leo fell silent. It had been an ongoing argument from the time they'd descended the hills and Kyra had begun to hear the Fallen.

"I can help," she said. "I want to, and I promised the girls back in Chiang Mai I'd get Prija back."

"We have her brothers with us."

"They don't know," Kyra hissed. "Have they heard her mind? No. They have no idea what they're dealing with."

Prija had retreated so far into her mind that even Kyra was having trouble hearing her. She'd surrendered to the darkness around her. Every day, the wall grew a little harder. A little more dense.

Part of Kyra was grateful. Despite Prija's fractured psyche, her ability to block meant she could protect herself. Part of Kyra was worried. Too long in the darkness wasn't a good indicator of Prija's mental health. It would only take a certain amount of pressure from Arindam to crack her open if he wanted to. If the darkness Prija had gathered around her cracked open, Kyra didn't know what would happen. She could lash out at the Fallen. She could lash out at her brothers.

Kyra had seen both things happen.

"What is that?" Leo pointed to the corner.

Kyra had taken the cloth Intira had woven and draped it along the sofa in the sitting area. "Intira made it."

Leo stared at the weaving. "Is that a traditional Thai pattern?"

"I don't know. She gave it to me to give to Prija. Told me that Prija would know what it is. I was hoping it would give me some kind of insight into what she's feeling or how her mind works, but so far…" Kyra turned toward him. "Why do you ask?"

"Because it looks like Hurrian," he murmured. "But there's no way a child in rural Thailand would have seen anything like that."

"What's Hurrian?"

"It's the earliest known human musical notation," Leo said. "There are rumors that some very early scribes tried to record Irina song in a similar way, but scholars believe they're wholly human. Nothing supernatural about it."

"Strange. Why would Intira weave something like that?"

"She wouldn't." Leo sat up, sliding his hand into Kyra's to maintain contact. "Unless… Do you think Vasu—"

"Maybe."

Leo raised an eyebrow. "Her mind is brilliant."

"He'd be drawn to her," Kyra said.

Do you see it yet?

Kyra blinked. "Vasu visited me."

"I know," Leo said. "He kissed you too."

"What?" She shook her head. "Don't distract me. There was something about *seeing* the music. I bet he did show Intira something. Did you ever visit her cottage?"

Leo shook his head. "I wouldn't."

"She had... numbers. Equations? I don't know much about math, but can music be written with numbers? Is that possible?"

Leo frowned. "Music is pitch. Frequency. Tempo and rhythm. Harmonies are all based on mathematical ratios. I wouldn't know how to write it, but if you assigned numbers to certain notes, I imagine it would be possible."

"Intira's room was covered in equations. Maybe it's something she invented for herself. Maybe it's something Vasu showed her. Or a combination of the two. But is it possible that Intira is hearing something and Vasu showed her a way of writing it down?"

"What would she be hearing?" Leo said.

"I don't know." Kyra looked at Leo's hand holding her own.

Do you see it yet?

Kyra whispered, "Let my hand go."

"The noise—"

"It's not noise." She dropped his hand, put her fingers to her temples, and closed her eyes. "Vasu told me." She closed her eyes, and instead of focusing on her walls, Kyra threw her mind open. She ignored the ambient voices and focused on the low, humming background frequency. The "scratch" in her mind.

She focused on it and really listened.

The low, grinding notes moved slowly, but they pulsed with an aching, slow rhythm punctuated by screeching higher tones.

"It's not noise," she said again. "It's music."

It wasn't beautiful music. It was more akin to wind or waves than anything else. But there were notes. There were rhythms. Was this what Intira was seeing in her mind? Why would she want to show it to Prija?

Kyra kept her eyes closed and reached her hand out. Leo immediately took it, and the creaking sound ceased. "I think the Fallen have their own music," she said. "I think they... resonate somehow, and I think Intira has seen it. That's what she was weaving." Kyra looked at the blanket woven with mottled stars. "She was weaving the music of the Fallen."

Niran stared at Sura. "You taught her math. What do you think? Is it possible?"

Sura shook his head. "I taught her the basics of algebra since she seemed so interested in it, but she surpassed my knowledge long ago. I just try to find her books now. I have no idea if what she's writing in all those notebooks amounts to music." Sura looked at Leo. "You say this looks like some kind of ancient musical notation?"

Leo nodded. "I doubt she's seen it. But if she can hear the notes somehow and see the ratios of the harmonies—understand the music on a mathematical level—would it be that big a leap for her to write it down if someone showed her a code to do so? Kyra has been hearing the Fallen her whole life; she didn't realize it was music."

Kyra said, "What I've been hearing sounded like noise. No pattern. But when I listen closer—especially being so close to Arindam for days now—it *does* have a pattern. It's music. Just… really horrible music."

Leo said, "So if Intira has heard this angel and understands the music and the harmonies on a mathematical level, she could write it down given the proper language." He held up the weaving. "Which this appears to be."

Alyah said, "But who would…" She grimaced. "Vasu. Of course."

"Vasu was around when Hurrian notation came into being," Leo said. "It's possible there was even angelic origin. Maybe it was something they weren't supposed to share but did anyway."

"The Fallen have lots of knowledge they could share and don't," Niran said bitterly.

"Part of the bargain," Leo said. "The Forgiven were allowed to share because they left the earth alone."

"And the Fallen stay and wreak havoc," Niran said. "What does that have to do with me? I'm damned to ignorance by your people simply by virtue of my birth."

"Stop," Kyra said. "This isn't the time for arguments like this."

"It's never the time," Niran said. "Not according to the Irin."

Rith, the silent scribe who wore the black blade, spoke from the corner. "I've fought Fallen before. I have killed an angel. The music this little one sees is… interesting, but how does it help us kill Arindam? Because from what I've seen so far, this isn't a lone angel. He has children around him. Defenses. This is someone encroaching on Vasu's territory. Killing him will be nearly impossible with seven warriors." He glanced at Kyra. "And we don't even have seven if we're being honest."

Kyra ignored the insult because Rith was correct. She wasn't a true warrior. She was good for finding the Fallen. Good for pinpointing locations. But she wasn't a warrior.

Sura said, "There is such a thing as natural frequency. Can we assume it has a magical component? Do each of the Fallen have some kind of natural frequency? Is that what you're saying?"

"Yes," Kyra said. "I believe what I'm hearing comes from Arindam."

More looks between Niran and Sura.

They know something.

Leo said, "Would Vasu have given Intira this knowledge if he didn't have a purpose? He hates Arindam. This must be a clue we can use to defeat him."

"It's Vasu," Kyra said. "It might mean nothing."

"Intira told you to show this to Prija?" Sura asked.

"Yes," Kyra said. "She said Prija would know what it meant."

Niran spoke quietly. "If this is music that Prija can read, then it's useful."

"How?" Kyra asked.

"We need to get you to her," Sura said. "We'll attack the compound, but Kyra will need to get to Prija. That will be her priority."

"No," Leo said. "Someone else can—"

"No," Rith said. "We don't have warriors to spare. This started out as a simple rescue mission for one *kareshta* and has grown into a massive incursion into the heart of a Fallen stronghold. We have seven warriors. We can't spare one to get a coded message to a single woman who may not even be rational at this point."

"A single woman who was instrumental in killing Tenasserim," Niran said. "She's not a babbling idiot. Any injuries to her mind were gained in battle, and Arindam took her for a reason. Prija is still a formidable weapon."

Leo tried to jump in. "Kyra is not a warrior. She can't—"

"A formidable weapon?" Rith argued. "That may be true, but your sister is *his* weapon unless we kill the Fallen. And we can't spare a warrior to find her. Not if we're going to go kill Arindam."

"Kyra can't go by herself!" Leo shouted.

"She'll have to," Rith said, glancing at Kyra. "I've spoken to Alyah. She'll be fine. You can clear a path for her, scribe, but don't lose focus. Lose focus, and we all die."

Leo was seething. "I did not come to Thailand to lose my mate in your battle."

"No, you came to Thailand in order to facilitate communication and relations between the free Grigori, the *kareshta*, and the Irin scribes of Bangkok," Rith said. "Congratulations, we're working together now, trying to kill a Fallen who is abusing women and preying on humans in Myanmar. You're going to abandon the mission now because you're worried about your mate?"

"I'll do it," Kyra said, squeezing Leo's hand. "Leo, I have to."

"No, you don't," he said. "This is madness. The Grigori in there—"

"It has to be Kyra," Sura said. "Prija will listen to her."

"Sometimes," Kyra said. "Not always."

"Then you'll have to *make* her listen," Sura said. "There's a reason you were given this message." Sura lifted the weaving. "A reason the angel showed this to Intira. There is a reason for everything."

Kyra shook her head. "She won't listen to me. Not always. I have a fifty-fifty chance at best."

"No." Sura smiled. "You have a mission that must succeed for us to live. That means whatever must be done to make my sister listen, you will do."

L eo was in a rage. Kyra kept trying to hold him back, and he kept pulling away, pacing their room while turning over the mission in his head.

Six warriors and Kyra. Six. There had to be a way to get more. They had to. Kyra couldn't go into this battle. Granted, Niran and his men were far more effective than most Grigori because of their *Sak Yant* and discipline, but they weren't scribes. The only trained Irin warriors they had were him, Rith, and Alyah. He didn't know what battle magic Alyah had, but it couldn't be enough to make up for the numbers.

Why was Rith so determined to rush into this? Why couldn't they wait for more scribes from Bangkok? It was a short flight to the city. Why—

"Leo." Kyra was sitting hunched in the chair, rubbing her temple. "Please can you stop?"

"I'm thinking."

"And I'm in pain."

"Damn." He rushed to take her hand. She hadn't been trying to hold him back, she'd been trying to hold him. "I'm an idiot. I forgot."

She sighed, but her forehead relaxed when he took both her hands in his.

"I'm not usually this helpless."

"You're not helpless. You're operating at full capacity right now. That's the problem."

"Ha!" Her laugh was bitter. "Operating at full capacity. That's a new one."

"As long as I'm with you…" His face darkened. "I'm staying with you."

"But Rith said—"

"Rith is not my watcher. He may be leading this mission because he has the right magic, but he's not my watcher, and he can't make me abandon my mate in the middle of a battle. I agree with Sura. There's something on that weaving that Prija needs to see, and I think it has to do with why Arindam's men took her in the first place."

"Okay." She nodded. "Honestly, I think I'd be useless closer to the Fallen without you keeping me clear."

"Exactly. And if Prija is the weapon her brothers think she is, then she could be the one to turn the fight."

"She's…"

"What?"

Kyra shook her head. "She's angry. I can hear her. She's angry and dark. That's the only way to describe it. Imagine a black hedge around someone. That's what Prija feels like right now."

"Why so angry?"

"I don't know. She doesn't sound afraid in the least. Just… angry."

"Does she think… Could she be thinking that her brothers abandoned her?"

"Possibly? I can't talk to her from a distance, and there's no guarantee she's felt my presence or knows I can hear her. She might think she's been abandoned."

"Then when she see us, this anger should fly, shouldn't it?

She'll realize we didn't leave her."

Kyra offered him a sad smile. "It doesn't always work that way. By the time we find her, she may no longer trust her senses. She might not be rational at all. It's easy to get lost in the darkness."

"Have you?"

She nodded.

"What pulled you out?"

"Kostas," she said.

Leo looked at his phone. "Do you want to call him?"

She shook her head. "When we're safe. When it's happy news. Not worrying."

He wasn't sure it was the right decision, but it was *her* decision. "If you're sure."

"I'm sure."

He stood and lifted her in his arms, carrying her to the bed where he laid her down and slid behind her. He took his usual position. One hand under her shirt and flat against her skin. His arm cradling her head. "We need to sleep," he said, already drifting in the warm afternoon. "It's less than twelve hours before we attack the compound."

To Kyra's credit, she didn't seem nervous at all. "I'll stay with you. I'm not foolish."

"I know."

She grabbed his hand and put it on her breast. "Love me before we sleep."

"It won't be too much?" He'd been careful with her since arriving in Bagan.

"You are never too much."

Leo crouched in the forest, his dark clothes blending with the deep shadows surrounding him. He listened for the telltale footsteps of the night guard who had already passed by four times now. He was waiting for Rith's signal.

Arindam's compound in the hills was comprised of a dozen smaller buildings surrounding a temple with a familiar winged idol at the door. The Fallen lived inside the temple. His men lived and worked in the smaller buildings around it. During the day, much of the activity seemed to revolve around the angel. Women were brought to him. Food was prepared and offered. His sons came and went. Leo and the others had seen them stalking in the city below, but they had done nothing to confront them. They wanted the element of surprise. It was their best weapon against an angel and a superior force.

At night, a dozen guards patrolled the grounds, but none of them seemed particularly alarmed or watchful. Irin presence had not been detected.

A low birdcall sounded in the still air.

Leo nodded and Kyra tucked herself behind him, drawing her knives. The next time the guard passed by, Leo leapt on him, muffling any cry with his hand and stabbing a quick silver dagger into the spine of the Grigori. There would be no survivors here. There were no innocents among these men. They would spare the children and young men if they could, but the grown Grigori could not be allowed to live.

"On the right," Kyra whispered. "Coming down the path."

Leo ducked back. The first Grigori was already dissolving.

Kyra whispered, "Leo, there's another—"

"I know."

Within moments, the second guard passed by the steps of his friend. Just as he was bending down to examine the dust, Leo leapt again. This time the guard let out one sharp cry before Leo took his life.

"Damn." He dropped the body and let it dissolve.

"How did you know?" Kyra hissed.

"What?"

"About the second man." She closed her eyes. "The guards

are all gone. I don't hear any minds but our people along the perimeter."

"Good." He wiped off his knife. "I heard you the first time. About the second man."

She frowned. "I only spoke once."

"No, I'm sure I heard you twice." He took her hand and jogged down the path. "Unless I'm reading your mind now."

"I wasn't trying to push my thoughts to you," Kyra said. "I've never done that on purpose. Only when I'm searching."

Something about the accidental intrusion pleased him. "Perhaps it's because we're *reshon*," he said. Then he thought, *Perhaps you'll be able to hear this.*

Her eyes lit, and Leo grinned.

"This is going to be fun," he said. "And today it will be useful."

Can you hear this?

"Yes!" he whispered. "More later. For now we need to move."

They walked quickly down the path, aiming for the reinforced grey building where Sura reported that he'd seen Prija being held. In Kyra's backpack was the weaving Intira had done. Their job, according to Rith, was to find Prija, kill her guards, then evacuate the women and children from the compound. Kyra had the most experience with Grigori children, and the others were hopeful the women and children would follow her with Leo translating. If nothing else, she knew the spells that would knock them unconscious. She'd used them before and was more than willing to use them again.

Leo heard a few sounds of struggle in the distance and knew the others were making progress.

"They've taken out… maybe fifteen so far," Kyra said. "No, sixteen." She sucked in a breath and gripped his hand. After a long pause, she said, "They must have found the sleeping quarters."

Leo held her hand carefully and tried to imagine what it

would be like to hear lives being snuffed out. He'd seen them. He'd killed them. But to hear multiple lives ended, multiple souls released to heaven at once... That, he couldn't imagine. They were evil lives—the Grigori here showed no signs of tempering their soul hunger—but they were lives.

"The children," he said quietly. "The women."

Kyra nodded and began to jog.

They crouched behind a clump of bushes and watched the cinder block building. It was clear that the two guards knew something was going on. They chatted back and forth, one pointing toward the temple while the other shook his head. Some argument took place, but the one pointing toward the temple did not relent. After a few minutes, he walked off in that direction.

"Leo!"

"Wait here!"

She nodded, and Leo forced himself to leave her. He ran after the guard and intercepted him before he reached the temple. He pulled him behind another clump of trees in the garden, muffling the Grigori as he tried to shout. As soon as he had a clear shot, he plunged his knife into the man's spine and waited for the body to dissolve.

He crept back to the edge of the compound, knowing that the rustling and struggle must have been heard. Within seconds, more Grigori were coming out of doors.

The element of surprise was gone.

He ran toward Kyra, grabbed her hand, and dragged her behind as he rushed the last guard at the women's quarters. The man dodged Leo's blow and ducked under his arm, punching Leo in the kidney with quick jabs. This Grigori was not a helpless opponent. The man's elbow snapped back and caught Kyra in the nose. She cried out and blood poured from her nose. She fell to the ground and rolled away from his quick feet.

Leo roared at the sight of her blood and swung around, hooking the man around the neck with his massive arm. He snapped the Grigori's neck to the side with one sharp jerk, then watched the man fall under his own weight. Leo looked down.

Kyra was reaching toward the Grigori, her knife out and slicing the man's Achilles tendon at both ankles.

Leo grinned. "My woman."

"Is he dead? He's not dissolving."

The Grigori was spitting up blood and jerking in Leo's arms. He spun the Grigori around and plunged the knife in, tossing the body to the side as he helped Kyra up and wiped her face.

"Can you see?"

She nodded. "It might be broken." She stuffed a rag under her nose and pointed to the door. "But I'm fine. Let's go."

Without another word, Leo yanked at the doorknob, but the solid metal door didn't budge.

"Wait," Kyra said. She went to the dust of the last Grigori and scattered it with her foot. "Here." She bent down, grabbed the keys, and tossed them to Leo.

He tried three keys before he found the one that worked. Then he shoved them in his pocket and opened the door. Kyra kept behind him.

Leo kept his knife out. You never knew if *kareshta* would be hostile or not.

No males, Kyra whispered in his mind.

That is very handy.

A hallway stretched before them, four doors on each side. Leo tried one. Locked.

He tried the keys. No luck.

"Stand back," he said quietly. "These open in. I can work with that."

"How—"

Leo spoke to the first door in a loud firm voice. "Stand away from the door," he said in Burmese.

He heard scuttling and waited for it to stop before he drew on his magic and kicked in the first door. It swung in with a crash, but there was no sound on the other side. Peering inside, he saw two young women and a small girl huddling in the corner. The room smelled like human waste and urine.

"Kyra?"

She ducked under his arm. "Hello," she said quietly. "I'm Kyra. My husband and I are going to take you out of here and make you safe. Will you come with us?" Leo translated her words in Burmese as she spoke, hoping the women spoke the majority language of the region. By their relieved looks and quick nods, they did. They both scrambled to their feet, and one of the women picked up the little girl, who began to cry.

A quick burst of power filled the room with the little girl's cry.

Kareshta.

Leo looked at Kyra and knew his mate had felt it too.

The woman holding the girl soothed her as they moved to the room across the hall.

That room held a heavily pregnant woman who was nearly skeletal.

Grigori baby.

Leo and Kyra moved up the hall, gathering the women and children from Arindam's harem, but they did not find Prija.

"I don't hear her," Kyra said. "I thought I did, but now there are too many voices and I can't tell."

Leo knew she must be getting overwhelmed. He grabbed her hand.

She shook her head. "It's not helping. Not anymore."

"Let's get them out of here," Leo said.

He looked in the last room on the right side. It was empty, but there was a long stringed instrument in the corner. "Kyra?"

"Yes?" Kyra was trying to pick up two children who were tugging on her legs.

"Did Prija play an instrument?"

"Yes. It was stringed. Kind of... a teardrop shape. It had a blue jewel on the face."

He turned to the human woman next to him, the one from

the room across the hall. This woman also looked half-dead and was nursing a baby. A boy from the looks of her pallor.

"The woman they kept in here," he asked the mother. "Was she like you?"

"No." The woman pointed to the Grigori children. "She was like them. But darker. Evil like the men."

"What happened to her?"

"They took her away," the woman said. "I don't know where."

Leo nodded and ushered the women and children down the hall, jumping ahead to scout the area outside.

The fight had turned from silent to muffled struggle. He could hear scrambling in the forest around him and quick feet in the night, but he could see little. Even with his vision turned up to its most acute with magic, the night was moonless and pitch-black.

"Leo, we need to get them away."

He nodded. "Will they stay in the van, do you think?"

"They might panic if we leave them."

Leo heard someone crashing through the bushes. He braced himself to fight, but at the last minute, Sura broke through the trees.

He scanned the group quickly. "No Prija?"

"They moved her."

"Find her!" Sura said. "I'll take care of them." He switched to Burmese and a soothing voice. "My sisters, I will guide you and your little ones away from here." Leo could see the women and children drawn to Sura and his calm, centered spirit. "Pick up the little ones if you can. It will make the walk easier. Stay together." He looked back at Leo. "Find Prija. Find her. Rith and Niran are in the temple, but they're going to need Prija."

"I'll find her," Kyra said. "You take care of the children." She grabbed Leo's hand. "Let's go."

He followed her without a word.

CHAPTER

TWENTY-THREE

K yra could hear Prija. At first the *kareshta's* voice was a
low murmur. But as the violence erupted around them,
Prija's voice became clearer and clearer. It was a hiss-
ing, angry tone that pressed at Kyra's temples, but instead of
running away, Kyra ran toward the pain, clutching Leo's hand
the whole time. As long as she maintained contact, she could
sort through the voices. The heavy, violent hum of the Fallen.
The panicked souls of the Grigori.

And Prija.

"She's this way," Kyra said. "They moved her farther away
from the temple."

A whooshing sound came overhead, like the beat of a giant
bird's wings.

"What is that?" Leo said.

The dark music grew stronger. Fell back. Pulsed and beat
like... wings.

"Arindam can fly."

"Angels don't actually have wings!" Leo said. "That's human
mythology."

"This one does." Kyra ran toward the trees. "Don't let him
see us."

Leo was looking up instead of looking forward.

"Leo!"

"Cover." He snapped his attention back to her. "Got it. Where is she?"

"This way."

Keeping to the edge of the forest, they ran past skirmishes of one against six or seven. Some of the young men were fighting, but not very well. Kyra's heart broke to see their fresh round faces snuffed out over and over again. They were hardly more than babies. Her anger fueled her, and she kept running.

Prija felt her coming. The *kareshta* began to jab at Kyra's mind, sending sharp, painful spikes into it the closer they got.

We came for you, Prija.

Nothing but angry scratching at her mind.

Your brothers came for you. I came for you. Leo came for you.

More anger. This time it pierced her temple and Kyra nearly doubled over in pain.

"Damn her!" Leo shouted, still watching the sky. "Doesn't she know—"

"She doesn't know anything at this point," Kyra said. "Nothing makes sense. Everything is darkness."

She stood up, swallowed the bile in the back of her throat, and kept running toward Prija. There was a building at the edge of the forest, the farthest building from the temple. Two guards stood in front of it, both carrying guns, both bent over, clutching their temples in pain. Without slowing her run, Kyra drew out her knives and spread her arms, jabbing both Grigori in the back of the neck as she ran past.

Thank you, sister.

Kyra's burst of violence fed something in Prija, and the mental jabs softened.

Leo tried kicking in the door, but not even his massive strength could move it.

"It opens out," he said. "We need to find another way."

"Keys?" Kyra bent down and felt through the dissolving

bodies of the Grigori she'd stabbed, trying not to gag on the dust and gore. "I can't find any—"

"Window!" Leo wrapped an arm with the shirt of one of the dead Grigori and punched through a window. It was security glass and took several punches before it began to shatter.

He broke through the window just as Kyra smelled the first hint of smoke. Looking over her shoulder, she saw a dark form sweeping over the compound, fire dropping on the dry bushes and trees.

"Kyra!" Leo was in the building, waving at her. "Come."

She ran over, and he lifted her carefully through the shattered window. They were in a small kitchen, and the smells of rice and fish filled the room.

"The stove is still on." She turned it off and looked around. "The guards must have been interrupted at dinner." She walked past the table—a rice-filled bowl sat in the middle of it—and down a narrow hallway lit by a single bulb. She could feel Prija now.

The *kareshta* was in a room on the far end of the hall.

Let me in, Kyra thought at her.

No words, just a strangled, angry cry.

Let me in, sister.

Less anger. More pain.

Kyra paused. *I am your sister. I want to help you. Let me in.*

Nothing. No anger. No pain. The mental jabs stopped.

"Leo, open the door at the end of the hall."

"Are you sure?"

She nodded. The door was padlocked, but Leo broke a metal leg off a chair, slid it behind the lock, and popped if off with one quick snap. The door swung open, and there was only darkness inside.

PRIJA VI

T he moonfaced one was here. She was followed by the sunshine male, but the male was wiser than the others thought. He stayed back. The black fog thinned around Prija, but she didn't open her eyes.

Prija, I'm here.

The moonfaced girl was clever. She didn't try to speak to Prija's body; she spoke to her mind. She spoke in English, but Prija could understand that language even if she didn't like to speak it. Prija didn't speak anything.

I have a gift for you.

That was what Arindam's sons had said before she killed them. Prija snarled.

It's a gift from Intira.

A trick. Why would they carry a gift from a little girl so many miles from her home? She was so far from home. Prija's heart cried. She wanted the peace of her forest. The soothing rush of the water over her head. The simple laughter of the village children. Why had they taken those from her?

A weapon…

…killed her own father.

What kind of female can kill one of the Fallen?

Mind crushed from the inside.

This is why they are killed.

This is why they are feared.

"You should fear me," Prija whispered in her mother's tongue.

The sunshine male walked in. "Why should we fear you?"

Prija opened her eyes. She opened her mouth, but no sound came out. It had been too long.

The sunshine man intrigued her. His eyes were like water they were so blue. Who had water eyes? If she touched them, would her finger go through them like liquid? The mental picture nearly made her laugh.

"Why should we fear you?" he asked again, crouching down.

She wanted to speak, but the pounding wings of the Fallen exhausted her. He didn't have wings. Not really. But enough of his sycophants thought him a god that he'd created them with his mind. Her own father had been the same. Tenasserim could manifest things with his mind.

Just like Prija could twist the shadow.

But she didn't have a voice anymore. Using it was too exhausting. Killing her father had locked it inside. Because while she'd hated him with every part of her, she'd loved him in the same way. Killing him had been killing part of herself. That was what Sura and Niran never understood.

She'd also died that day. She'd died with Kanok.

A small gasp from the moonfaced girl.

"He was your twin," she said. "The brother who died. Kanok was your twin."

Prija closed her eyes again, but this time she couldn't block out the woman.

I know you understand me, she said. *I have a brother too.*

Prija's eyes flew open.

I have a twin. He is the other part of me. The woman's eyes were full of tears. *If he died, I might not want to live either.*

Prija looked at the sunshine man.

Maybe for him, the woman said. *Maybe I would live for him. Can you live for those who love you, Prija?* The woman reached back and brought a backpack out. She opened the zippered case and drew out a black-and-red-striped fabric.

Prija cocked her head. It was Intira's weaving.

"Intira made this for you," the scribe said. "She wanted Kyra to bring it to you. She said you'd understand."

"She said"—Kyra spread out the weaving—"you'd understand what it meant. And that you had to come back for Intira to finish. That she wouldn't finish unless you came back."

Stubborn, brilliant girl. Prija still didn't see it. She tried, but…

"Leo thinks it's some kind of music," Kyra said.

Music?

One of Prija's old visions came to life. Stars across the sky. Scattered. Rising and falling voices and notes.

Of course. Intira had taken her own stars and turned them into mathematics. Into geometry. It was how she saw everything.

Did she know?

How could she have known?

She couldn't hear anymore, but if Prija could *read* the music, she could kill Arindam the same way she'd killed her father.

This time when she opened her mouth, she couldn't stop the words.

"Who showed her this song?"

CHAPTER
TWENTY-FOUR

K yra couldn't speak Lao, but Leo could.

"Vasu," he said. "At least that's who we think showed her."

"I don't know… Vasu." Prija's voice sounded like rusted nails.

"He's one of the Fallen."

Prija's lip curled.

"But he's not… predatory. Or not always. He has helped us in the past. And he wants to kill Arindam."

"Wings," Prija choked out. "Not… real."

"They look real to me."

Prija shook her head. "Created. Mind."

"He can create wings with his mind?"

Prija nodded.

"So Prija"—Leo leaned forward—"if he can create things in his mind, what can you do?"

Prija's eyes dropped to the weaving. Then she looked at Kyra. "She hears him?"

"Yes. But she doesn't know how to write music this way."

"I don't." Prija shook her head. "Intira… not understand. Not all minds like hers."

Leo's heart sank. "So this means nothing to you?"

"I know what it means," Prija said. Her voice was growing stronger the longer she spoke.

Leo handed her water and watched while she drank.

"I know," Prija said, her voice a little smoother. "But I don't hear anymore. She thought she could write the music so I could play, but her mind sees things that others don't."

Leo didn't know how to wrap his mind around that, but he tried to make sense of what Prija was saying. "So you're saying that if you could hear what the angel sounds like, you can do… what?"

"Is my instrument still in the complex?"

"Yes."

"Then I can do what I do."

"Is that how you killed your father?"

Prija offered him a narrow smile.

Leo turned to Kyra, who'd been waiting patiently while Prija and Leo spoke in words she had no way of understanding. "Can you sing Arindam's song to Prija?"

She blinked. "Can I what?"

"Can you sing—"

"I can't sing. Leo, you know I can't—"

"Not magical singing. Just… singing. Let her hear what the Fallen sounds like. To your ears, sing that."

Kyra shook her head. "I can't."

"Why not?"

"There are harmonics. There are multiple notes. There are—"

"Tell her to show me," Prija said.

Leo looked between the two women. "She said you could show her."

"*Show* her the music?" Kyra threw up her hands. "I can't do that either!"

Leo smiled. "Speak to her mind, Kyra. Just like you have

been. Listen to Arindam's song and let her hear it too. You've done it with me!"

Kyra shook her head. "You don't understand. I don't know how I do that with you. I've never done it before. I don't—"

"Try." Prija spoke in broken English. She forced her lips and tongue around the words. "*You try.*"

Leo rose to his feet when he heard footsteps outside.

"It's Niran," Kyra said before he could turn. "The fight against Arindam isn't going well."

"I'll go," Leo said. "You stay with Prija and find a way, Kyra. Find a way to let her hear Arindam's song." He grabbed her chin and planted a hard kiss on her mouth. "I know you can do it. Just because it's not the same as the Irina doesn't mean you don't have a song."

K yra was left with Prija, still having no idea how she was supposed to "show" Arindam's strange music to the other woman.

"You can understand English?"

Prija nodded.

"More than a little?"

Prija shrugged.

Kyra sighed. "I wish I spoke more Thai."

"Lao," Prija croaked. "I speak Lao."

"Sorry. Lao." She rose. "You need your instrument from the other building to do this?"

Prija nodded.

"Then that's what I'm going to do." She took the gun Leo had given her from the holster at her waist. Silence was no longer an issue. The compound around them rang with sound. Crashing and screaming for the most part. The smell of smoke filled the air. "Can you use this?"

Prija took the gun and nodded again.

"Good. Keep your back to the wall and shoot anyone not friendly." Kyra just hoped that Rith didn't come in. He was the only one of the party that Prija had never met. "Unless he's carrying a black knife about this long." She held her hands a foot apart. "That one is ours. He's a scribe."

Prija curled her lip, but she nodded anyway.

A thought occurred to Kyra. "The men who took you. One of them was a scribe. Is he still here?"

She shook her head. "Dead."

All in all, it was probably for the best. They didn't need a seasoned warrior working with their enemy. "Okay, keep your head down and I'll be back."

"Not hurt." Prija sat up. "Only thirsty. Go with you."

"I'll bring water to you. Trust me, this place smells a lot better than the last one." She tucked her stray hair under the watch cap she'd tugged on earlier and ducked out the doorway, following the red glow outside.

The forest was in flames.

Luckily, the compound itself was clear of most brush or anything flammable. Kyra only hoped that Sura had gotten the women away before the fire started. She ran along the path toward the women's block where they'd rescued the others earlier, keeping to the shadows in the red glow of the forest fire. Overhead, she heard him and her eyes rose.

Arindam the Fallen was thick in the battle.

She didn't care what Prija said, those wings were real. She'd seen angels grow into monsters. She'd seen them appear and disappear at will. She'd never seen one fly. But when she finally saw the Fallen in the red glow of the fire, she knew what Prija meant. Whatever his original form, he had taken on the body of the idol she'd seen at some of the temples. He had the head of a man with a curved beak like a vulture. His muscled arms stretched out, and wings sprouted from the bottom of them. His body was that of a man, but instead of feet, he had massive claws that clutched a flaming branch.

He perched on the top of the temple and roared over the clearing as the scribes and free Grigori shot at him. One of Niran's men was using arrows, which seemed to be the only thing not bouncing off the monster's skin. When he roared, Kyra felt it like a pressure in her mind. She nearly went to her knees, but she remembered Prija waiting for her and moved on. As she ran, she didn't try to block the monster's song out. It was the same static, pulsing with an unearthly low rhythm. She focused on it and tried to think of it like the wind through trees —low and repetitive—and not a monster's siren call.

She entered the building where the women had been kept and was immediately hit in the face by the sour smell of urine again. Arindam truly was a monster if he could keep his own women in this filth. Kyra had seen a lot, but she'd never been subjected to conditions like this.

She ran to the back room and grabbed the long neck of the instrument she'd seen Prija playing, returning at the last minute to grab the thin bow that went with it. She rushed out and ran straight into Leo.

"What are you doing?" he shouted.

"Getting her instrument!" She looked over his shoulder. "What are you doing?"

"Getting nowhere in this fight. This angel is impenetrable to bullets, and we only have one archer."

"Not something you foresee taking into battle anymore."

"Niran anticipated." Leo grimaced. "We've killed all the Grigori or they've run. It's just the angel, but nothing we do is working. We can't even reach him. I think he's laughing at us."

On cue, a booming laugh echoed over the hilltop.

"I think you're right," Kyra said. "Let me take this back to Prija and see if we can get anywhere with it."

"Have you figured out how to—"

"No. Don't ask. I'm working on it."

Kyra ran back to Prija, and Leo turned toward the fire.

"**A**re they getting anywhere?" Niran asked him. The two men were crouched behind a low wall that had been shattered by the angel's fist. He was playing with them and enjoying it.

"Of course they are," Leo said. "They just need time."

"You're lying."

"You know as well as I do."

"Prija is fine?"

"She's healthy and angry as hell."

Niran smiled. "A promising combination."

"She's talking to Kyra."

His eyebrows went up. "I haven't heard her speak in years."

"Well, now she's talking to Kyra."

The news seemed to invigorate Niran. He rose and hurled a chunk of stone at the angel's perch on the temple. It fell short, but Leo had to admire the effort. He ducked down when a fireball hit the back of the wall.

Rith jumped over it a few seconds later. "We need to find a way to get him down or get us up."

Leo popped his head up and looked at the sharply sloped roof. "Getting us up would only result in us falling down."

"So we need to take him out of the air," Rith said. "Unless I can get close enough to him, I can't use this blade. I'm not going to risk throwing it at him. If he takes if from us, we have nothing."

"Can you make a spear of it?" Niran asked.

Rith shook his head. "It has to be held by my hand to make a killing blow."

Damn the rules of magic, Leo thought. The Fallen obviously hadn't heard of them, otherwise he wouldn't have wings.

"How do we make an angel fall?" Leo asked.

Alyah seemed to be having the most luck annoying the creature. Leo could tell by the amount of fire being thrown in her direction. He'd heard the Irina's battle song rise above the fire. It was the first sound of it that had wiped out the Grigori. They'd stumbled and fallen to their knees, only to be taken out by Niran, Rith, and the others. Since then, Alyah had aimed her voice at Arindam, making the angel waver but not quite fall. Every now and then, he'd lift and rise from the temple, trying to locate the source of her magic, but Alyah remained hidden, guarded by Niran's men.

Niran's eyes shone when he looked her direction. "I wish my sisters could do that."

"They'd be untouchable if they could."

"Is it possible?" Niran said. "If they learned the right magic?"

"I think so," Leo said. "My sister Ava has Grigori blood. She's mated to a scribe and learned magic from older Irina."

"So it's possible." Something relaxed behind Niran's eyes. "There is hope."

"Not if we don't kill this angel," Leo said. "Because if he loses interest in us and goes after the women Sura took, they're lost."

"I AM READY," PRIJA SAID, SITUATING HERSELF ON A LOW cushion Kyra had found in another room. She'd draped Intira's blanket over her shoulders and washed her face. She looked serene and powerful.

If only Kyra knew what she needed to do.

I can think words to you, she thought. *But I don't know how to copy his song. I can hardly make sense of it.*

"Do not copy. See it."

She huffed out a breath. "That means nothing to me!"

"Then think." Prija closed her eyes. "I will try to hurt him."

Kyra felt it when Prija struck. It was a wild jab, her energy shooting out in all directions, just like when Prija tried to hurt her during meditation. She felt the blood drip from her already swollen nose.

A red bloom rose in Prija's eye as a blood vessel burst. "Think!"

"WHAT WAS THAT?" LEO YELLED AS THE MONSTER FELL FROM his perch.

"Prija!" Niran rushed the creature, joined by Alyah and Niran's men. They leapt on the angel, but he twisted away, backhanding one of the free Grigori and grabbing Alyah by the throat.

"No!" Leo roared, rushing to the aid of his sister. He flung a knife at Arindam's eye. The creature screamed when it found its mark, and Leo's ears started to bleed.

Arindam dropped Alyah, who rolled into a ball and ducked her head down, protecting her throat while her Grigori protector stood over her, punching and kicking the Fallen, trying to beat him back. The angel reached out with one arm and grabbed the Grigori by the throat, twisting his neck to the side.

Niran's brother fell silently to the ground, and Arindam took to the air. The body dissolved, gold dust rising in the red glow of the fiery hilltop.

The angel perched at the top of the temple and screamed.

Leo felt Niran's rage and held him back. "Wait! Sacrificing yourself with a rash attack will do nothing!"

"Let me go!"

"Wait," Leo said again, wrapping his massive arms around Niran. "Take a breath. And wait."

Reshon, *you need to do something. We are dying.*

KYRA SAT UP AND PUSHED THE RED VEIL FROM HER MIND. THE Fallen's scream had taken her to the ground. She had hit so hard she was seeing stars.

She was seeing stars.

Kyra struggled through the pain and focused on the beating pulse of Arindam's song. It was a grinding noise. A pulse and a wave. She focused on isolating everything else from the noise of the angel until the pulse turned into light. The light glowed brighter against the night. Every beat shot like a star across the blackness.

A star. Another star. They moved and danced. Crossing each other. Rising and falling.

Rising and falling.

Waves.

Intervals.

She saw them and she heard them. They chased each other across the night of her vision. Stars scattering. Waves rising and falling.

Do you see it yet?

Look.

Her vision wasn't black anymore. It was filled with stars, glowing in the night sky. She isolated those of the angel, reached for Prija's quiet presence, and threw her mind wide-open to the other woman. She knocked down a century's worth of walls, threw open every door, and stripped her mind naked.

Look.

Kyra kept her eyes closed and watched the rising and falling stars. She watched a few spike like glowing plumes, rising above the waves, and they pierced her mind like needles. But as she watched, Kyra saw more stars. More waves.

They began in a low thrum that ran beneath the waves. At first they pushed up, barely a ripple beneath the glittering sea. But then the thrum rose higher. And higher.

Kyra heard the drone of Prija's instrument.

She didn't ask what the *kareshta* was doing because she saw it. When the angel's song went high, Prija's song went low. In time, the thrumming notes from Prija's instrument matched the waves from the Fallen. Then another note joined the first, waiting for the rhythm of the spiked plumes and matching them with a plucked note, canceling out the noise.

The painful spikes went silent.

"What's happening?" Leo asked.

At first it was subtle. The flames around them grew dimmer. The fire started to burn out. But then, as the sun began to rise above the Bagan plain, Leo noticed something else.

"He's... he's losing his form," Leo said.

"Prija," Niran whispered. "My warrior sister. You did it again."

The red veil around the Fallen wavered. The gold-tipped beak went first. Then the burning snakes around his wrists.

"What is she doing?"

"I don't know what it is," Niran said. "But he'll be weaker now."

In the distance, Leo heard the faint strains of something like a violin as Arindam tumbled and fell to the ground.

TWENTY-SEVEN

The music was everything now. When Arindam's song rose, Prija's fell. Kyra kept the connection between their minds, worried that if Prija couldn't see the waves of Arindam's song, she wouldn't be able to play whatever it was she was playing. Because whatever she was playing canceled out the painful waves of music emanating from the Fallen.

The music grew louder. It filled the room. No longer a scraping hum but a resonant hymn of unearthly beauty. Prija was playing opposite the Fallen, matching his frequency and tempo with her own. No music came from her throat, but Prija was singing. Not old magic, but new. Not Irina song, but *kareshta*. Wholly new, yet ancient at its core.

Kyra opened her eyes and saw her sister's face glowing.

"Do you see it?" Vasu appeared, kneeling beside her. "The little one saw it immediately."

"The stars we see in visions," Kyra said. "They aren't stars after all."

"They are. But we are the morning stars, and every star has a song."

"Intira can see it."

"Prija's brother saw it too. That was how they killed their

father, though they did not understand how. Their minds were tied together. The effort killed her twin. And his death nearly drove her mad."

"Do we need to be concerned about Intira?" Kyra asked.

"No." Vasu smiled. "I saw her dreams and recognized her genius. Her mind is a work of heaven, and it is beautiful. It is the young who are most interesting to me."

"Because you're young too, aren't you?"

That was what Kyra recognized now. The truth that had eluded her about this odd Fallen angel. Though Vasu was ancient to the earth, as an angel, he was a mere child. Of course he had an affinity toward children. He was one.

Vasu put his head on Kyra's shoulder. "Do you see it now?"

"I see it now." She turned and kissed Vasu's forehead. "Thank you for showing me."

"You're welcome."

He disappeared.

Kyra continued to watch Prija play, her face glowing with peace, her eyes closed, rocking in time with her instrument. She wasn't playing music. She *was* music.

"...when you've found your voice, you'll sing to me."

This was what Leo was talking about. Prija had found her voice. Not an Irina voice, but a *kareshta* one.

Wholly and beautifully unique.

LEO AND NIRAN RUSHED TOWARD THE FALLEN, THROWING themselves on the creature's back as he struggled to rise. Whatever magic Prija was working had caused the angel to stumble. Alyah stood on the edge of the courtyard, guarded by Niran's brother, singing over the chaos of battle. Her song lifted Leo, and his magic grew stronger. His *talesm* glowed. His hand was firm on his knife.

"On his back," he shouted at Niran. "Take him down!"

Leo ran around to face the angel, who was snarling. He didn't appear in his bird form anymore, but in the still frightening and beautiful form of an angel. He was seven feet tall and broadly built. His hair was black as a raven's wing and tied in a knot at the back of his head.

"Away from me, Forgiven get!" he shouted in the Old Language. "You have no power over me."

Ava's teasing voice rang in the back of his mind. *Remember, big guy. The bigger they are, the harder they fall.*

Leo ran toward the Fallen, knowing that if the creature got him in his grip, he was likely done for. But at the last minute, Leo curled and bent down, rolling into a ball and ignoring the slice of rock against his shoulders. He hit Arindam's shins, knocking the angel forward as Niran and Rith jumped on his back.

Leo quickly uncurled and flung himself on the angel's legs, pinning him down with his weight as Niran lay over the monster's shoulders.

"Do it!" he screamed at Rith.

The black blade rose. The angel roared. Rith plunged the blade into Arindam's spine, and the roaring monster fell silent.

KYRA CLUTCHED HER STOMACH, NAUSEA MAKING HER BODY shake. Prija dropped her instrument to the ground and clutched her temples, crying out as she fell to the side. The earth beneath them rolled and shook; then everything was silent.

L eo and Kyra walked off the mountain with their friends, one warrior lost but a sister found. Prija walked behind them, draped in Intira's blanket and clutching Niran's hand. Her other brother was at her side, carefully holding the instrument she'd used to sing against the angel. Rith and Alyah walked behind them, bloody and black with smoke. Everyone was exhausted, and tears ran down their faces from the heat and the sting of the fire.

They found Sura pulled over on the side of the road that ran along the east side of the temple hill. Seven human women were with him, and seven children. Four were girls. Three were boys with wide eyes who hadn't yet reached puberty. Their cheeks were soft, and they sat next to the van, listening to Sura.

Kyra held Leo's hand out of desire, not necessity. The minute Arindam died, the painful noise that covered the plain ceased. The land was silent now, except for the soul voices of the humans who lived and the Grigori who'd fled.

"We'll have to coordinate with the scribe houses in Dhaka and Dimapur," Rith said. "There hasn't been a scribe house in Myanmar since the Rending."

"We can help," Niran said, nodding to the Grigori boys.

"I'm sure Sura will want to keep the boys with us. They will have challenges we are more suited to dealing with. Since we know their father is dead, we don't have to worry about mental manipulation or their free will being compromised."

"Will it be the same with the girls?" Rith asked. "What should we do with them?"

Kyra's stomach sank. Despite the pretty words of the Irin council, she should have expected this. *Kareshta* were never wanted. The discarded mothers were never wanted. She could see the defeat in the women's eyes. The ones who had stayed with Sura likely had no other place to go. They were pregnant or had children from the angel. They were dirty and abused. Cast off from the powerful and unwanted by the world.

She tasted the bitterness on her tongue.

"What are we going to do with them?" Alyah asked Rith. "Find homes for them, of course. Where do you think they're going to go?"

"We've already taken responsibility for the others," Rith said. "The Bangkok scribe house—"

"I should have known," Kyra said bitterly. "I should have known."

Leo squeezed her hand. "*Reshon*, we will not abandon them."

"I know you won't, but this one?" She nodded at Rith. "I don't know you, and I don't trust you. Why would these women trust you? They mean nothing to you. *Kareshta* are not your problem. We never were."

Anger flared in Rith's eyes, but Kyra turned away from him. She thought about the temple in Chiang Mai. Could they take four more girls? What about the women who were pregnant? Would they agree to go to Thailand? At least four of them were carrying boys and would suffer through their pregnancies. There were ways to combat that, but only with Irina magic.

"Stop." Sura walked over and spoke quietly. "This is not the place to discuss these things. We need to get all of them to a safe place. Can your people help with that?" he asked Rith.

Rith gave a sharp nod and pulled out his phone. Kyra leaned on Leo's shoulder. She wanted a bath. She wanted a bed. She wanted the silence and peace of Leo's touch.

The angry scribe walked back a few moments later. "Dara has secured a house thirty kilometers from here. If we all get in the van, we can make it before the roads are busy. She wants us to wait for instructions from there."

Leo glanced at Niran and saw the man nod.

"Fine," Niran said. "Let's get everyone away from here and cleaned up. We'll all feel better once we're out of the open."

Kyra and Leo squeezed into the van. A twelve-person van carrying twenty-two people was hardly comfortable, but they managed. A short ride later, they rolled into a walled compound with mango trees covering a courtyard, and a large house in the center. With practiced efficiency, Sura and Alyah sorted everyone into groups and arranged baths for the little ones.

Leo picked her up and carried her to the room at the top of the house. It was stuffy, but opening the windows helped, and the room had an attached bath. There was no hot water, but Kyra and Leo didn't need it. They bathed each other, then fell into bed exhausted.

KYRA WOKE TO LEO COMBING OUT HER LONG HAIR WITH HIS fingers.

"Good morning," he whispered.

She stretched and nuzzled her face into his neck. "Is it morning?"

Leo pointed her head at the window. Grey light was giving way to a gold bloom in the east. She buried her face back in his chest. She wasn't sure she was ready to face the day.

"We slept all day and all night?" she murmured.

"You did. Prija did too. Whatever magic you two were working, it took the energy right out of you. I woke up a little last night." He smiled. "I was hungry."

"You're always hungry."

He bent over and kissed her lips. "And you always feed me. What a lucky scribe I am."

Heat marked her face. "I wonder if I will ever get used to your attention."

"I hope not. I love the color of your cheeks when I scandalize you."

"Leo," she whispered.

"Kyra."

She smiled against his skin. *Are you really mine?*

I am. I am forever yours.

She smiled harder. "It's easier now."

"You heard me?"

She nodded.

"When can we go away?" he asked. "I want to make you mine. I want the mating ceremony with you. I want to mark your skin. Make my vow." He kissed the top of her head. "Say yes, Kyra."

Kyra wanted it so badly, but there was still a hesitation in the back of her mind. "What if I never learn to sing? It will be an uneven mating. You told me yourself. Only my song can complete the ritual, and there is no guarantee I will ever sing. Not like a real Irina."

"Kyra—"

"I know... I know you think I'll find my voice," she said. "But that's wishful thinking, Leo. I do believe I'll find a voice, but it might not be what you're imagining."

"Then I will be content with your song, whatever it might be. But *ana sepora*, Ava will teach you. I know she will."

"Are you sure of that?"

"Should I call her right now?"

"I don't know…" Kyra gathered her courage and spoke her secret fear. "What if it's not good for me to learn, Leo? My blood is of the Fallen. What if learning Irina magic unlocks something dark in me?"

Leo pulled her away from his chest and tilted her chin up. He was frowning. "Do you really believe that?"

"I don't know." *I fear it.*

I see no darkness in you.

"There is darkness," she whispered. "Leo, there is anger. There is… rage. And bitterness. And everything—"

"Everything that makes us real," he said. "Everything that gives us humanity. We are not angels, and I thank the heavens for it. We love. And we suffer when we lose. We are jealous and generous. We are—none of us—wholly light or wholly dark. I have darkness too, Kyra."

She shook her head. "You are too good."

"I am not perfect. Far from it." He smiled. "Though I'll take your admiration for as long as I have it. No doubt, our years together will lend reality to your dreams."

"They're not dreams," she said. "I have seen evil. And I have seen good." She kissed him gently. "You are so good."

"I'm glad," he said. "Because that means I am deserving of you."

"Leo—"

"Say yes."

She closed her eyes and gave in to her heart. *Yes.*

"Say it aloud," he whispered. "Please."

"Yes."

He captured her mouth in a fervent kiss. A worshipful kiss. They made love in the gold light of morning, and he whispered to her how much he loved her. Kyra soaked in the sunlight and let Leo's love chase the last of her shadows away.

There was no darkness there. No shadows between them.

"We'll go to a house by the ocean," he whispered when their bodies were joined. "We'll run away and hide by the sea."

"I love you, Leo."

I love you, reshon.

BUT HAPPINESS WAS THE LAST THING ON KYRA'S MIND LATER that day when they met with the scribes from Bangkok. Dara joined them by video conference in the dining room of the house. Sura and Niran sat on one side of the table with Leo and Kyra. Rith and Alyah sat on the other.

"The women and children you evacuated last week," Dara said. "They are settled in homes. The girl is being fostered by an Irin family who speaks her language. The woman with the boy is staying in the scribe house for now. She won't leave the baby."

"Would you leave your baby?" Kyra asked.

"I have no children," Dara said. "But I hardly think a woman who'd been raped by an angel—"

"It's not your decision to make." Niran cut her off. "If she wants the baby, send her back to Chiang Mai. The child is male. We'll know how to help him."

"And the woman?" Rith asked.

"There are ways for human women to get well. To stay with their children," Kyra said. "Leo and I have both seen it."

Leo nodded. "But she needs Irina magic. And knowledge. You have to tell her the truth."

Dara scoffed. "She's human."

"She's been brought into the angelic world whether you like it or not," Kyra said. "She deserves to know the truth."

It was clear Dara didn't agree, but Kyra decided to ask about the others. "The ones we rescued from Bagan. What will happen to them?"

"We'll take the four girls of course," Dara said. "We have foster homes for them too. The boys must be trained by your Grigori brothers. We don't know what to do with them."

Dara's dismissive tone raised Kyra's hackles, but Sura put a hand on her knee and shook his head.

"We will care for the boys," Sura said. "We are better equipped for their challenges. But I worry about our young sisters. When you say they will be fostered, what does that mean?"

"It means they'll be raised by Irin families," Rith said. "As my sister said."

"And will they be trained as Irina?" Sura asked. "Will you teach them the magic they need to become full members of your world?"

Both Rith and Dara were silent. Alyah's face was painfully blank.

Kyra nearly choked on her anger. Only Leo's touch kept her steady.

"You have to decide," she said quietly. "Decide and *commit*. We cannot be your second-class citizens. We have lived in the shadows too long. Scribes want *kareshta* wives—some of these women are bearing Irin *children*—but the Irina won't teach them anything more than the most basic magic. We know *kareshta* can sing if they are taught."

"My own watcher's mate has Fallen blood," Leo said. "And Ava has been trained by ancients. Her song is powerful. She is an asset to our world."

"You want our blood and our wombs, but you don't want our voices," Kyra said bitterly. "I refuse to let these girls grow up feeling as if they are less."

"You ask us to give magic to those whose blood killed our mothers and our sisters and our children," Dara said. "You weren't there—"

"And neither were they!" Kyra shouted. "*Neither were they*. You are the children of the Forgiven." She gestured across the table. "Congratulations on winning the blood lottery. Because that is the *only* difference between us." Kyra glared. "Anything else you believe is self-delusion. I'm not asking you to train grown men or women in magic. I'm asking you to treat children as if they're not marked by evil. That's all I'm asking. If you're going to take those girls, don't foster them. *Adopt* them. Your people want for children, and we are offering you our own. Is that not what your precious council mandated?"

"It is," Alyah said. "I agree with Kyra. The girls should be given the full education of an Irina. If you do not agree, Dara, I ask for an audience with my watcher."

"As would I," Leo said. "I was assigned by the council to facilitate relations between the free Grigori here and the scribe house. I believe part of my assignment is to see to the well-being of innocent children caught in the conflict. If you do not agree that the *kareshta* rescued from Arindam's control deserve the full care, compassion, and education of Irina children, then I will need to speak to the watcher of the house."

Dara eyes didn't change, but a grimace around her mouth told Kyra she didn't like being reminded that she wasn't the true watcher. Perhaps it was an injustice, but it was the reality.

"Fine," Dara said. "We will leave the education of the children to the families who have volunteered to take them. *Just* as we do with Irin children. They will be treated no differently, Leo of Istanbul. Your assignment to my house is complete. Farewell." With that, the screen of the computer went blank. Rith rose, closed the laptop, and left the room without a backward look.

Alyah was the only one who stayed.

"They are rigid," she said. "But they are not bad people."

Sura said, "No one is saying they are. It is a difficult situation. We know."

"But those girls deserve to live a full life," Niran said. "A life where they are accepted and loved."

"I've already spoken to the Irin families who volunteered to take the girls," Alyah said with a smile. "All four are very, very eager for children. Any children. They are more than excited about welcoming them."

Kyra asked, "Are you sure?"

"Very sure. As long as Dara leaves their education up to their adoptive mothers and fathers, there will be no problems. I'll make sure of it. I promise you. I'll be sure to check in with all of them."

Sura said, "Alyah, you have become a true friend to us. If there is any help we can offer, please do not hesitate to ask."

"I may take you up on that." She looked at Niran. "The pregnant women here. Take them back to Chiang Mai. Do you need money?"

Niran and Sura exchanged glances. "Our father was… quite wealthy," Niran said. "Money is not an issue."

"Then take the women back. Care for them with your brothers. I trust your compassion, and I know Ginny will be happy to work with you to keep the mothers as healthy as possible."

Kyra said, "That's an excellent idea. I can share with her what I know and put her in touch with others who have more experience."

"We don't need to involve any scribe houses," Alyah said. "It's probably better that we don't."

Leo asked, "And Kyra?"

She frowned. "What about me?"

"You have fulfilled your own mission," Leo said. "Weren't you promised something in return?"

Sura smiled. "The *Sak Yant*. Your brothers are welcome to our hospitality and teaching, should they desire it, Kyra. I will make sure to inform your brother."

Kyra let out a long breath and turned to Leo. "It looks like both our jobs are finished. You know what that means, don't you?"

"A long-overdue holiday?"

"Not yet." She took her phone from her pocket. "First we have a long-overdue conversation with my brothers."

"Where will you live?"

Kyra looked helplessly at Leo. She'd put the phone on speaker so they could speak to Kostas together.

"We'll live in Istanbul," Leo said. "My home and assignment is there, and that is where Kyra can receive further training to utilize her gifts. Also, there is no place safer than a scribe house."

"Scribe houses have been attacked," Kostas said. "The house in Istanbul was attacked only a few years ago."

"And they have been defended," Leo growled. "There are seven highly trained scribes and singers in the Istanbul house and—"

"Has Kyra agreed to this?" Kostas asked. "Or did you assume her wishes, scribe? Does she *want* to live in a hot, busy city like Istanbul?"

Leo shut his mouth and breathed deeply while Kyra reassured her brother that Leo was not taking over her life. Reassured him that she was happy. Reassured him that she'd been fed that morning, she had clean clothes, and no one was coercing her into the present phone call.

He wondered if dealing with Kostas was going to become his new least-favorite pastime. The idea of requesting some kind of permission to take Kyra as his mate grated on him, but Leo recognized how close Kyra and her brother were. They had literally been tied since birth.

"Of course you'll be welcome," Kyra said. "You're my family, Kostas. That does not change."

So there'd be regular visits from his interrogator. Wonderful.

"And when will you be home?" Kostas said. "What will happen to our sisters here? You would abandon them?"

Leo's lip curled when he saw Kyra's face fall. He reached over and squeezed her hand.

"Kostas, Kyra has told me everything she's done for her sisters." Leo didn't try to keep the sharpness from his voice. "She's also told me that she's trained them as much as she's capable of. She is not her sisters' keeper. She's allowed to have her own life and find her own happiness. As a brother who clearly loves her, I would think you'd want that for her."

There was a long pause on the other end of the line.

"Take me off speakerphone," Kostas said.

Kyra pushed a button and put the phone to her ear before Leo could object. The conversation that followed was in a language Leo didn't speak, but he immediately made a mental note to learn it. Kyra's voice was soft but not pleading. After a few moments, she hung up the phone.

She didn't speak for a long time.

Leo rubbed her back and prayed to heaven that she wasn't second-guessing her decision to take him as a mate. It would be a transition for both of them, but Leo was convinced that leaving her brother's house was best for Kyra. He was equally convinced, especially after this trip to Thailand and Myanmar, that she needed her independence.

"Tell me what you're thinking," he said.

"I don't like making him angry."

"He's angry with you?"

"I don't know." She closed her eyes and leaned back. The way she curled into Leo's side reassured him. "He's angry... at life, I think. At the fact that I can't learn more without leaving home. At his inability to give me everything I need."

"He's protected you for two hundred years. With your power maturing and the knowledge you've gained both here and at home—the knowledge Ava can teach you—you can be more independent. Maybe this is what Kostas needs too."

"He won't see it that way. Not for a while."

Kyra's phone rang again, but this time when she picked it up, she smiled. "It's Sirius." She pressed the button to answer and put the phone on speaker. "That didn't take long."

"Is it true?"

Leo smiled at the clear pleasure in Sirius's voice.

Kyra smiled at Leo. "Leo is here. You're on speaker. And is what true?"

"'That damn scribe' was in Thailand?" he asked with a laugh. "I can't believe it!"

"Kostas was quick to spread the news," Leo said. "Hello, Sirius."

"Leo, do you love my sister?" Sirius asked.

He pulled her closer. "With everything in me."

"Good," the Grigori said. "She deserves the moon."

"And all the stars too," Leo said.

Sirius laughed, and Kyra hid her face. "I like him, Kyra. I always have. And I know you have too. I'm pleased for you, sister."

"Thank you, *bata*."

"Don't worry about Kostas. He'll get used to the change. He doesn't like anything he can't control. He's like an old man shaking his walking stick; you know that."

"The Grigori in Chiang Mai might help with that," Kyra said. "They've agreed to share the *Sak Yant* with you."

"That's excellent news."

"I'm going to warn you though. Only send mature brothers. The tattoos do help with control, but they also increase power."

Leo said, "Some of Niran's men could stand nearly equal with Irin scribes well versed in battle magic."

"Truly?" Sirius's voice had shifted from happy brother to wary commander. "That's good to know."

"It's a practice," Kyra said. "Not just a tool. That's why I'm telling you: Be careful. Choose wisely. Sura and his brothers take their vows seriously, and they do not stand for Grigori who only want power without discipline. If you send anyone who doesn't fall in line with their teaching, there will be consequences."

"I'll remember. Thank you for doing this, Kyra."

"You're welcome." She pressed her cheek to Leo's chest. "I needed this push, Sirius. Thank you for giving it to me."

"Her power is formidable," Leo said. "We couldn't have accomplished this mission without her."

"Kostas said you took out one of the Fallen?"

"And freed many women and children," Kyra said. "The Irin and free Grigori here will be sorting things out for a while."

"Will you stay to help?" Sirius asked.

"For a time," Leo said, stroking Kyra's hair. "But we have our own lives to begin. The scribes and singers in Bangkok are more than capable."

"And the *kareshta* in Chiang Mai have learned everything I am able to teach them." Kyra took a deep breath. "Our work here is done."

"Then come home after you take your holiday," Sirius said. "Leo should meet your family."

"I will," Leo said. "And you are always welcome in Istanbul, Sirius." With Sirius, Leo had no reservations.

"It's only four hours away. Don't worry." Sirius laughed. "You won't be able to get rid of us."

The air in Phuket wrapped around Leo's legs like a warm caress. It rolled off the Andaman Sea and rustled the fronds of the coconut palms overhead, teasing Kyra's hair from the knot where she'd tied it. The ocean waves lapped at the shore before them, lulling them with their constancy.

Kyra lay draped over Leo's chest, napping in the shade. It was warm on the island, but the breeze cooled them, and the small house they'd taken was only steps from the beach. If it became too warm, they could always retreat to the air-conditioned interior.

He ran his hand up and down her back, thinking about the ritual he'd perform that night.

He had the ink. He had the brushes. He had a piece of the sacred fire from Bangkok with which to pray and light incense. He'd been practicing his vows for days. He didn't want to get a stroke wrong. The words he wrote would become part of his beloved's skin, fusing his magic to her and binding them together. Though it was only a few lines that were the formal vows, he wanted every word he wrote to be perfect.

Leo was giddy as a bride the night before her wedding.

"Leo," she murmured.

"Hmm?"

"Should we go in?"

"Are you getting warm?"

Kyra tilted her head up, and her full lips spread in a warm smile. *I can hear you, reshon.*

He adored it when she called him *reshon*.

"There's no rush," he said. "We have the house all week."

"We both slept for two days." She sat up and stretched her arms over her head. "We've swum. We've eaten on the most beautiful beach in the world. I heard you this morning. Your vows are finished."

There's no reason to rush, he thought.

And there's no reason to wait. Her voice sounded like a chime in his mind. "I'm ready."

Kyra had made her peace with the ritual, even knowing she didn't yet have the magic to sing her part. Leo was convinced that Kyra would have her own magic someday. Whether it would be Irina magic or something unique to the *kareshta* was the mystery. If Leo had to guess, he imagined a combination of the two. Kyra's unique listening and projecting skills—that had only grown stronger over the days since she'd thrown her mind open to Prija—and the Irina magic she'd already begun to master.

She rose and offered her hand. "Come. Make me yours, Leo."

He didn't have to be told twice.

THE SHADES WERE CLOSED AND AFTERNOON SUN FILTERED through them, lighting the room with a golden illumination enhanced by candles lit by the sacred fire. Kyra sat on a pillow, meditating in the lotus position with her hair twisted on top of her head. She was bared to the skin, a perfect canvas for him to write his magic. They'd bathed together, and Leo had anointed her with almond and olive oil, massaging every inch of her body as he worked to prepare them both for the ritual.

"Will I feel it?" she asked.

"You'll feel the brush on your skin." He kissed her shoulder as he settled behind her. He was also bare, his ceremonial wrap the only clothing he wore. His *talesm* already burned with anticipation. "You'll feel the magic when I start. When I'm working."

"How long does it take?"

He smiled. "It takes a while."

"An hour?"

He laughed. "More than an hour."

"I'm glad I picked a comfortable cushion," she said. "And where do you paint?"

Leo smiled and lifted her arm, holding her delicate wrist in his fingers. He ran his tongue from her shoulder to the crease of her elbow, peppering kisses up to her wrist. "Everywhere."

"Everywhere?"

"Mmm." He released her arm and put his hands at her waist, kissing her neck and enjoying the scent of frangipani in her hair. "Everywhere. Every inch. I'm going to cover you in magic."

Goose bumps rose on her skin.

Are you ready? he thought.

I'm ready.

Leo began at the top of her spine, and the very first spells he performed were for longevity. All he had was the word of a Fallen angel that Kyra was protected. But from that night on, her life would be linked to his. As long as he lived, she would too, even if it was for a thousand years.

He traced the spells down her back. Long life. Protection. Wisdom. Strength. Every line was a promise. Every inch of ink was a mark of his love. He poured his heart into his magic. He poured his heart into Kyra's hands, knowing she would hold it gently.

His mate was still as a statue, but when he turned her to begin the spells over the front of her body, he saw her tears.

"Kyra?"

"I hear you," she whispered. "Your voice inside. When you're writing your magic, Leo. I hear you, and it's the most beautiful thing I've ever heard."

She broke him. Leo leaned forward and kissed her gently, careful not to smudge the words he'd so carefully drawn.

"*Ana sepora,*" he whispered. "I will see you fly, Kyra."

"As long as you're flying with me."

"Always." He put his forehead to hers and drew in a breath, warmed by the magic in the air. It filled the room like the fire of a setting sun. It highlighted the ebony strands of her hair and made her skin glow. She was luminous, and her skin reflected the mingled gold and silver of the magic that tied them together.

Leo continued, carefully placing each spell. Strength in her arms. Speed in her legs. Health spells tracing from her collarbones to her belly. He marked her with every protection he could think of. He gave part of his armor to her.

The ink was nearly dry over her skin when he curled his personal vow over Kyra's heart:

Daughter of heaven
I will love you.
Though the night is dark
Our love is light.
Though the world is grim
Our union gives hope.
Father of Light
We are one in you.
When our path is hidden
We will fly.
We walk in faith.
We walk in hope.
We walk in love.

Leo pressed a kiss to the center of his vow and set down his brush. When he looked up at Kyra's face, her eyes were a fierce gold.

I hear us.

He pressed his forehead to hers. *And I hear you.*

"It's not just the voice of your soul I'm hearing," Kyra whispered. "There's another music. We make it when we're together. A harmony between us."

"Can you sing it?"

Tears came from her eyes. "No."

"You mean not yet."

"I'll find a way to sing it to you someday, Leo. I promise. It's the most beautiful thing I've ever heard."

307

"The only promise I need from you is to be my mate. To love me when I'm unlovable—"

"You're always lovable."

"—and to challenge me when I'm thickheaded."

Kyra laughed. "I have more than a little experience with thickheaded men."

Leo kissed the tears from her cheeks. "Then we're perfect for each other."

"We are."

He smiled. "Say it again."

"We're perfect for each other."

"Exactly as we are."

They shared delicate kisses as the ink dried on her skin. Leo's breath came in pants. He was thick with tension, trying to control his hunger for her, but every moment their magic lingered in the air, it seemed to grow more intense. It didn't dissipate in the air like smoke but grew stronger. Heavier. More overwhelming.

"Leo?" Kyra's pulse was pounding in her throat.

"Soon." He scraped his teeth along her chin and reached for her shoulder, feeling the smudge of ink that wasn't quite dry. "I'll fix it later."

"What?"

He tugged the pins from her hair and watched it tumble down her shoulders, thick waves of dark silk he fisted as he brought her mouth to his over and over. Her lips were swollen from his kisses.

"Now?"

He glanced down at her heart and saw the ink dry on her skin. "Yes."

Without another word, he took her to the floor. Kyra wrapped ink-stained arms around his shoulders and long legs around his waist. They rolled across the wooden floor with their mouths fused together as dark red henna began to light with a gold fire. Kyra's magic came alive before his eyes.

"Leo!" She let go of him, her back arching on the floor as her body lifted in a wave of power.

"Kyra?"

Her eyes flew open, and they were no longer gold. There was fire behind them, sparking and glowing in the dim room. Brighter than candle flames, they met Leo's cool blue eyes.

"What's happening?" she asked.

"I don't know!"

Leo picked her up and put her on the bed, but the shocks to her body seemed to keep coming. She curled into herself. Every brushstroke illuminated with a vivid fiery light, as if it were burning itself into Kyra's skin. The light raced over her body, and Leo heard the light bulb in the bedside lamp pop before it went dark.

The power rose. The spells burned. And then they went out.

Reshon, are you hurt?

No. I feel… more alive than I ever have.

Kyra sat up, and Leo realized the spells hadn't stopped glowing, but they were no longer burning. They shone like a banked flame beneath her skin, streaking across her body in swirls and lines, following the curves and sinews as he'd drawn them.

"You are so beautiful," he whispered.

She rose and pressed him back on the bed, removing the linen wrap around his waist. "*Ana reshon.*" Come to me.

There were no more words as she slid over him. Leo rose and kissed her breasts, hugging her to his chest. He arched his back so Kyra could reach down and guide him into her body. When they were joined, he lifted his hips, thrusting deep as Kyra arched back, her hair falling so long that it brushed the tops of his thighs as he sat beneath her. His vows glimmered on her skin, a visible reminder of his promise to her.

Daughter of heaven
Daughter of heaven
Reshon

"I have waited so long for you," Leo whispered.

Kyra put her arms around his neck, holding him so tightly he nearly lost his breath.

"I have crossed continents," he continued. "I have fought battles. I have seen wonders, my love. But nothing that could ever compare to this moment."

She couldn't speak, but he heard her in his mind. He more than heard her, he *knew* her.

I love you.

You are my mate.

You are my reshon.

You are my home.

Leo felt his magic rise and meet hers in a kiss. Kyra rocked over him as her body tightened around him. He felt the latent power of his climax starting at his toes, growing and building as their bodies and souls became one.

Kyra's lips met Leo's, and he saw stars when he closed his eyes, rising and chasing each other across the sky. He heard the chorus of the heavens and the harmony of their union. He heard it as they came together, falling as they flew.

EPILOGUE

They stayed in Phuket for two weeks, experimenting with magic, touring the islands by boat, and resting. They slept late. They made love in the middle of the day. They went to night markets and swam under the stars.

And then they went home.

The plane to Istanbul landed in midafternoon; they heard the afternoon call of the muezzin as they crossed the Haliç Bridge.

Kyra had been in Istanbul many times, but this time she was returning as a member of a large family, not as a visitor. She'd spoken to Ava on the phone, and her friend had been ecstatic that Kyra and Leo would be living at the house. She was eager for company beyond Malachi's brothers and Mala, who split time between Cappadocia and the city. She was full of plans and news for her new sister, eager to introduce Kyra to more magical practice as well as having another female in the house full-time.

Kyra was still unsure how well she would manage in a large communal environment. She realized she was tapping her toes and pulling at the seam of the dress she'd bought in Thailand.

Leo squeezed her hand. "Nervous?"

She smiled. "A little."

"If it gets to be too much, you have to tell me."

"I will."

"My brothers can be annoying."

"I'll tell you."

"Especially my cousin. He means well, but—"

"Leo, I promise." She leaned over and kissed his cheek. "I'll tell you if I need some time alone."

Their cab wound through the old streets of Beyoğlu, dodging pedestrians and pushcarts. When they pulled up to the familiar wooden house, she saw Malachi and Ava standing outside, two small children held in their arms.

"The babies?" Kyra asked, her mouth agape.

"Not so small anymore."

"No, they're not." Kyra's heart leapt at the sight.

The little girl and boy bounced in their parents' arms, excited and waving at the bright yellow cab. Ava and Malachi scrambled to hold them, picking up a toy that went flying and laughing at their children's antics.

"Can we have one?" she asked without thinking.

"Please."

She turned to see Leo grinning.

Kyra's nerves fled. This was no trial. She would not have to prove herself. This was family. True family. As Leo grabbed their suitcases from the back of the cab and paid the driver, Kyra walked to Ava, who had tears in her eyes.

"I knew it," Ava said, grabbing Kyra in a one-armed hug. "I knew it. I've waited so many years for you two to figure it out." She sniffed. "And look at me. I'm a mess, but I knew it."

Malachi looked just as pleased, though he wasn't crying. "Can I help?" he called.

"I've got it." Leo joined them on the sidewalk, setting their suitcases down.

Malachi reached out for Leo and embraced his brother with

a hard pat on the back as the little girl he carried shouted questions at Leo in Turkish.

"Ask me," Malachi said. "I've waited a long time to answer this question for another."

Leo cleared his throat and stepped back, taking Kyra's hand in his. "Watcher, does the fire still burn in this house?"

"It does," Malachi said. "And you are welcome to its light. You and your own."

Ava grinned. "I totally know what that means now!"

Kyra was still a little confused. "What does it mean?"

"It means you're home." Ava grabbed her hand. "You're totally, one hundred percent, *home*."

"I can't believe they did all this," Kyra said, staring at the stars from the roof of the new cottage behind the main house. Someone had put a low wooden bed on the roof, covered in blankets and pillows. It was the perfect place to enjoy the night breeze and listen to the sounds of the city.

"They've been planning to buy the house next door as soon as the owners were ready to sell. There was an elderly couple who lived there for fifty years. They passed last year, but their children were trying to decide if they wanted the money more than the house."

"I guess they voted for the money."

"Which is good for us. Tearing down the wall between the houses was easy and it doubled the garden and courtyard space, which will be nice for the children. Plus"—he tugged a lock of her hair—"I think everyone was getting a little crowded in the main house."

The cottage was a single story with a roof garden that sat at the back of the new house. It was hidden by trees, and a small fountain bubbled outside the bedroom. It wasn't a spacious home, but it was private and far more than the single room Leo had lived in before. Kyra, who had never lived in a grand house, thought it was perfect.

She asked, "Was all this planned when you left?"

"No, but apparently the Creator must have known that I'd be bringing a mate home."

"Any mate?" Kyra teased.

"My perfect mate." He smiled and kissed her forehead. *"Reshon."*

"It feels good here," she said. "It feels like a home."

"The voices aren't too much?"

She shook her head. Ever since they'd mated, it had been easier to control the firewalls in her mind. The magic obeyed her more readily. The spells lasted longer. Irin magic or more confidence? Perhaps a little of both.

"I've traveled over so much of the world," he said. "But I love it here." He rolled to the side. "I love the breeze at night. I love the call to prayer. I'm going to love waking up to you every morning. I love—"

"The sound of your tinkling laugh!" came a falsetto voice from the courtyard. "And the batting of your buttercup eyes!"

"Lips like rose petals!" Another voice called from the direction of the house. "Hair like... seaweed."

Kyra stifled a laugh while Leo frowned.

"Seaweed is a terrible comparison, Max."

"Say something about her toes. He probably loves her toes too."

"I don't want her to think he has a foot fetish."

"He might have a foot fetish. We've never asked."

"OW!"

"What did you do?"

"I stepped on a Lego. Matti is vicious. I know she hides them on purpose."

"Like little Scandinavian land mines."

Kyra burst into laughter.

"Buttercup eyes makes no sense, Rhys!" Leo shouted. "And Max, you're just jealous. Get your own woman. I know you have one."

"I have plenty of them because I'm the better-looking cousin," Max yelled. "Kyra is already rethinking her decision."

A window slid open with a long creak. "What are you two doing? Leave them alone. Do you think I want you frat boys running off another woman? Don't I put up with enough from my kids?"

A few quiet moments.

"Sorry, Ava."

"We'll be quiet."

"We love you, Kyra."

"Please tell Ava not to beat us."

With an exaggerated huff, the window slid closed again, and after a few minutes, the courtyard was silent.

Leo said, "So my family—"

"Is wonderful." She kissed him. "They're wonderful."

"I'm very relieved you think so." Leo smiled. "Have I complimented you lately on your buttercup eyes?"

All Kyra could do was laugh.

CONTINUE YOUR JOURNEY IN THE IRIN WORLD WITH A PREVIEW OF THE STORM, MAX AND RENATA'S STORY, now available in ebook, paperback, and audiobook.

PREVIEW: THE STORM

Now available!

Also included: Bonus short story "Song for the Dying"

There was no road to the old house that sat on the edge of a mountain. An old and overgrown trail was the only path. It would take over an hour to hike in the heavy winter snow of the Dolomite Mountains. Even with the superior strength and stamina granted by his angelic blood, Maxim knew he'd be exhausted by the time he found her.

He'd parked his four-wheel drive in the closest town, cautiously following the directions of an old librarian a few villages farther south. Chasing rabbit trails to dead ends was commonplace at this point in his search, but Max knew he only needed one more piece of the puzzle.

He'd finally found a name for her hiding place. *Ciasa Fatima.*

It had taken him eighteen years to find that name. Eighteen years of lies and misdirection. Eighteen years of frustration. At this point, he didn't know if he wanted to find her from longing or sheer spite.

The librarian who gave him the name of the house was an ancient Ladin man who'd lived his entire life in Southern Tyrol and claimed to know the house Max was looking for. Once it had been the house of a great family, he claimed. They had a library to rival the duke's! Strange people would come and go. Soldiers and noblemen. Beautiful women and visitors from foreign lands. There were stories and legends galore.

Then two hundred years ago, everything went quiet. There were no more visitors. No caravans or dignitaries. One hundred years passed before signs of life emerged.

These days, the house was rented out to discreet and very private travelers in the summer. No one knew how it was listed, and it couldn't be an easy place to stay. There was no electricity running up the mountain and probably no running water. But the meadows that surrounded it were worth the hike. The view, the old man remembered, was breathtaking.

In the winter, of course, it was vacant. No one wanted to brave the snow and ice of the cold Tyrolean winter on their own, especially not on a mountain slope like the one around Ciasa Fatima.

Except during the winter solstice.

For a few weeks in the middle of winter, villagers claimed that smoke came from the chimneys and lights glittered on the mountain. Whoever stayed at Ciasa Fatima didn't come down into the village.

This did not surprise Max.

There was no one better at hiding than Renata.

Max crested the last hill and stopped to breathe, making a note that high-altitude training was an area of his fitness that could be improved. He'd become accustomed to the lazy heat and balmy sea air of Istanbul.

Perhaps there was a spell he could conjure for increased lung capacity. Maxim of Riga was an Irin scribe, and though most of his duties consisted of gathering strategic information for his watcher and other allies across the globe, he was still an accomplished practitioner of magic. All scribes had to be in order to wield the power granted to them by their angelic forefathers. Male Irin harnessed their magic by writing. Female Irina used their voices.

For scribes, the most permanent spells—those for increased strength, stamina, eyesight, speed, and long life—were tattooed on their skin in intricate *talesm* unique to each warrior. Max had tattooed more than most, caught for years in a friendly rivalry with his cousin Leo. Both of them were young for their race at a little over two hundred years old, but they were massive men with intense focus who had spent the majority of their lives surrounded only by warriors. With a single brush of his thumb, Max could activate a dense web of magic on his skin, giving him a coat of living armor.

But none of that armor helped when it came to tracking down one elusive Irina.

The hike had taken twice as long as he'd anticipated, and darkness had already descended on the mountain. It didn't interrupt the grandeur of the view.

The house beyond the snow-covered meadow was just as the old man had described. A typical Ladin house, almost a perfect square of solid architecture that could withstand the fiercest storm. It was backed up to the mountain slope, possibly built into it. The bottom story was stone and plaster, the top was weather-aged wood. It was in good repair from the steep-sloped roof to the large porch that wrapped around the second story. Two outbuildings stood to the side—a low stone cottage and a larger barn that looked like it had once been a dairy.

Max started toward the house, breaking a path through two feet of solid snow. He could see lights in the distance; it was dark, and he was freezing cold. The chimney smoked, promising warmth if he could just make the last frozen yards.

A storm was coming in, and Max couldn't stop his smile. He couldn't have timed it better if he'd tried.

He beat on the door, but no one answered. "Renata!"

Nothing but silence, though he could hear someone inside.

"I know you're in there, and it's freezing out here. If you want me to keep the ass you seem so fond of, then you'd better let me in."

Still nothing.

This isn't like her.

Renata *never* ran from confrontation. Instincts on alert, Max turned the heavy brass knob.

The door swung open on silent hinges, and Max walked into a kitchen out of a Tyrolean postcard. It was nothing like he'd expect of Renata. An old stove glowed in the corner, and a round cake dotted with fruit cooled next to it. Cinnamon and sugar drifted on air filled with the sounds of soft accordion music from an old record player. A kerosene lamp was centered on the rustic wooden table, and stacks of cut wood lay piled along the far wall. Dozens of pine boughs hung from dark wooden rafters, and intricately cut paper stars decorated them.

Someone had decorated for Midwinter.

Max stepped into the room, immediately removing his snow-covered boots and heavy backpack. "Renata?"

"Max."

He followed the sound of her voice through the kitchen and into the large open area dominated by a central hearth. More pine boughs hung from the rafters. More stars. Cut crystal lamps with glowing beeswax candles lit the room. Snow had started to fall beyond the frost-covered windows.

Renata was sitting on the floor in front of the crackling fire, hair long and loose around her, dressed in an old-fashioned nightgown. She looked surprisingly young and more than a little vulnerable.

Max was struck dumb at the sight. If there was anyone more jaded and cynical than him, it was Renata. But here she was, sitting in the middle of a snow-covered dream, her brown eyes locked on him as he slowly approached. She'd been crying. In her hands she clutched an old silver candelabra, the seven-branched kind the Irin people used to celebrate Midwinter, the longest night of the year, and the coming of new light and life.

What is this place?

Renata did not look happy to see him. Then again, he hadn't expected her to.

She asked, "How did you find this place?"

He knew she was angry, but he couldn't stop his smile. "It's only taken me eighteen years."

She stood, set the candelabra down, and reached for a robe on the chair beside her. She wrapped it around herself and stood tall. She was nearly as tall as Max. He loved that about her figure. Then again, he loved everything about her figure.

"I climbed the mountain to find you," Max said. "The snow—"

"You should go," she said. "You shouldn't have come here."

He caught her arm before she could walk away. "I'm not going anywhere."

With a whispered spell, she forced his hand away. Max backed up without thinking, his body obeying her magic even as his mind fought against it.

"We've already had this conversation," she said. "I'm not interested in repeating it."

"I wouldn't call that a conversation. You had your say. Now it's my turn."

"I didn't agree to that."

His temper spiked. "I tracked you down to the middle of nowhere. I hiked a mountain in two feet of fresh snow. I damn near froze my toes off to get here. You're going to hear me out."

Renata glanced out the window. "There's a storm coming."

"I know."

"Did you plan that?"

"Despite your obvious admiration for my magical prowess, I don't control the weather."

She refused to look at him. She walked to the kitchen and he followed her.

"Renata—"

"You can stay the night." She bent down to one of the cupboards in the kitchen and took out another lamp. "You'll leave in the morning."

"I don't agree to that."

She continued, "There's only one bedroom prepared, so—"

"That's fine. It certainly won't be the first time we've shared a bed."

"You can take the sofa in the living room." She lit the lamp and pulled her robe tighter. "I told you. No more. There is no electricity here. You can use the lamp on the table if you need light around the house. They put in pumps last year, so there is plumbing inside now. If you want hot water, you'll have to boil it yourself. The toilet is down the hall."

Max took a deep breath, forcing back the anger that wanted to take the reins. They did this to each other. They had been sporadic lovers, sparring partners, and wary allies for eighteen years. No one knew how to push his buttons like Renata.

"You made a decision," he said quietly, "that you decided was for *my* best interests—"

"You know I'm right."

"—but you never consulted me."

Max stepped closer until his lips were inches from hers. He could feel her energy, the pulsing, powerful magic that drew him. Max didn't need a fire when he had her. She'd thawed out the cold heart of him, and then she'd had the audacity to take that heat and life away.

"I'll sleep on the sofa," he said. "But I'll see you in the morning."

Sometime in the dead of night, she came to him. Part of him knew she would. Their attraction was a force of nature and always had been.

The couch was too small for his large frame, so he'd rolled out a pallet on the rug in front of the fire. With the thick wool rug, heavy blankets, and down pillows from the sofa, it was far from the most uncomfortable place he'd slept.

Renata slipped under the blankets and scooted her back to his chest. "Don't say anything."

He didn't. Max knew better than to question her need when he felt it just as keenly.

She laid her head on his bicep, using his arm as her pillow. Max combed his fingers through the length of her hair, bringing the weight of it to his lips so he could feel the satin against his skin. Then he laid his head on the down-filled pillow and tucked his arm around her waist, fitting her body to his.

This is how it should be. This is how it should always be.

"Rest with me tonight," he whispered. "Wake with me in the morning. I'm not going anywhere. Neither are you. It's time to finish this."

The Storm and "Song for the Dying" are now available in ebook and paperback. The audiobook edition contains only The Storm.

Now experience the entire Irin Chronicles series at your favorite ebook retailer. Download seven bestselling novels for hours of reading enjoyment and find out why reviewers are raving.

The Scribe (Ava and Malachi pt.1)
The Singer (Ava and Malachi pt.2)
The Secret (Ava and Malachi pt.3)
The Staff and the Blade (Damien and Sari)
The Silent (Leo and Kyra)
The Storm (Max and Renata)
The Seeker (Rhys and Meera)

A fascinating new series. Definitely recommended.

— NOCTURNAL BOOK REVIEWS

Loved this book!!! It had great intrigue and romance. It was sexy, well written and suspenseful. Just like with the *Elemental Mysteries* series, I was gripped from the very beginning.

— VILMA'S BOOK BLOG

Pure beauty. Pure bliss. Pure perfection.

— ANNA, GOODREADS REVIEW

ACKNOWLEDGMENTS

Finding the right words to say thank you is never easy. Finding the right words to acknowledge the contributions made by others to my work is darn near impossible most days.

First, I'd like to thank my newly expanded family. David and Colin, you hold my heart. Thank you for being so wonderful.

Second, to my assistants, the magnificent team of Jenn and Gen. Between the two of you, things get done. They don't always get done on time, but that's pretty much my fault. Thanks for being amazing and letting me focus on the words.

Third, to my writing friends. To Colleen Vanderlinden, Amy Cissell, and Cat Bowen, thank you for being awesome and smart and making me laugh daily. To Penny Reid and April White, thank you for holding me accountable and giving me a standard to aspire to, both personally and professionally. (Also, robot jokes are always appreciated.)

Fourth, to all the writers who inspire me regularly, there are too many of you to name or this book would be twice as long and readers would be ticked off because it would just be page after page of romance writers and fantasy writers and sci-fi writers who regularly astound me with their skill, professionalism, brilliance, and generosity. I love being part of this community.

Fifth, to the wonderful and welcoming country of Thailand who opened its arms to me and so many other travelers through its long and colorful history. Thank you, especially to Sak Yant Chiang Mai for your guidance and teaching about the practice of Sak Yant sacred tattooing. Thanks to my friend Ginny, who is the second person *ever* I've named a character after! Thanks for your hospitality, love, and amazing energy. We were so blessed by you and your family. We all hope to see you again soon.

And finally, to my wonderful publishing team who help me produce these books that readers seem to love. To my Irin first reader, Marketta Gray, who helps keep me in order. To my new and wonderful content editor, Heather Kinne. To my copy editing and proofreading superheroes, Anne and Linda at Victory Editing. And to the amazing professionals at Damonza for their work on this stunning cover and all the covers for the Irin Chronicles series.

Thank you all, and I'll see you next time.

About the Author

ELIZABETH HUNTER is a *USA Today* and international best-selling author of romance, contemporary fantasy, and paranormal mystery. Based in Central California and Addis Ababa, Ethiopia, she travels extensively to write fantasy fiction exploring world mythologies, history, and the universal bonds of love, friendship, and family. She has published over thirty works of fiction and sold over a million books worldwide. She is the author of the Glimmer Lake series, the Elemental Legacy series, the Irin Chronicles, the Cambio Springs Mysteries, and other works of fiction.

ElizabethHunterWrites.com

To sign up for her newsletter, please follow this link and receive free short fiction and news about sales, specials, and new releases.

Also by Elizabeth Hunter

The Irin Chronicles
The Scribe
The Singer
The Secret
The Staff and the Blade
The Silent
The Storm
The Seeker

The Seba Segel Series
The Thirteenth Month
Child of Ashes (Summer 2024)
The Gold Flower (Summer 2025)

The Elemental Mysteries
A Hidden Fire
This Same Earth
The Force of Wind
A Fall of Water
The Stars Afire

The Elemental World
Building From Ashes
Waterlocked
Blood and Sand

The Bronze Blade

The Scarlet Deep

A Very Proper Monster

A Stone-Kissed Sea

Valley of the Shadow

The Elemental Legacy

Shadows and Gold

Imitation and Alchemy

Omens and Artifacts

Midnight Labyrinth

Blood Apprentice

The Devil and the Dancer

Night's Reckoning

Dawn Caravan

The Bone Scroll

Pearl Sky

The Elemental Covenant

Saint's Passage

Martyr's Promise

Paladin's Kiss

Bishop's Flight

(Summer 2023)

Vista de Lirio

Double Vision

Mirror Obscure

Trouble Play